The American Thr

Crime Files Series

General Editor: **Clive Bloom**

Since its invention in the nineteenth century, detective fiction has never been more popular. In novels, short stories, films, radio, television and now in computer games, private detectives and psychopaths, prim poisoners and overworked cops, tommy gun gangsters and cocaine criminals are the very stuff of modern imagination, and their creators one mainstay of popular consciousness. Crime Files is a ground-breaking series offering scholars, students and discerning readers a comprehensive set of guides to the world of crime and detective fiction. Every aspect of crime writing, detective fiction, gangster movie, true-crime exposé, police procedural and post-colonial investigation is explored through clear and informative texts offering comprehensive coverage and theoretical sophistication.

Published titles include:

Ed Christian (*editor*)
THE POST-COLONIAL DETECTIVE

Paul Cobley
THE AMERICAN THRILLER
Generic Innovation and Social Change in the 1970s

Lee Horsley
THE NOIR THRILLER

Susan Rowland
FROM AGATHA CHRISTIE TO RUTH RENDELL
British Women Writers in Detective and Crime Fiction

Crime Files
Series Standing Order ISBN 0–333–71471–7
(*outside North America only*)

You can receive future titles in this series as they are published by placing a standing order. Please contact your bookseller or, in case of difficulty, write to us at the address below with your name and address, the title of the series and the ISBN quoted above.

Customer Services Department, Macmillan Distribution Ltd, Houndmills, Basingstoke, Hampshire RG21 6XS, England

The American Thriller

Generic Innovation and Social Change in the 1970s

Paul Cobley
Senior Lecturer in Communications
London Guildhall University

palgrave

First published 2000 by
PALGRAVE
Houndmills, Basingstoke, Hampshire RG21 6XS and
175 Fifth Avenue, New York, N. Y. 10010
Companies and representatives throughout the world

PALGRAVE is the new global academic imprint of
St. Martin's Press LLC Scholarly and Reference Division and
Palgrave Publishers Ltd (formerly Macmillan Press Ltd).

ISBN 0–333–77668–2 hardback
ISBN 0–333–77669–0 paperback

This book is printed on paper suitable for recycling and
made from fully managed and sustained forest sources.

A catalogue record for this book is available
from the British Library.

Library of Congress Cataloging-in-Publication Data
Cobley, Paul, 1963–
    The American thriller : generic innovation and social change in the
    1970s / Paul Cobley.
        p. cm.
    Includes bibliographical references and index.
    ISBN 0–333–77668–2 (cloth)
    1. Detective and mystery stories, American—History and criticism. 2.
    Literature and society—United States—History—20th century. 3.
    American fiction—20th century—History and criticism. 4. Suspense
    fiction—History and criticism. 5. Social change in literature. 6. Literary
    form. I. Title.

PS374.D4 C57 2000
813'.087209054

10   9   8   7
09   08   07   06

Printed and bound in
Antony Rowe Ltd, Chi

To a couple of avid readers of popular fiction:
my Mum and Dad

Contents

Acknowledgements

This book is part of a long-considered and ongoing project which began when I was a pre-teen in the early seventies: my Dad handed me a paperback thriller and said, 'Here, son, have a read of this.' My family – especially my brothers – kept the ball rolling, and it continues as I find in second-hand bookshops various 1970s thrillers which I didn't get to at the time. The project has been sustained in a way which is crucial to all acts of readership, through recommendations, counter-recommendations and conversations with individuals who are too numerous to mention here. You all know who you are and I'm grateful to you.

Other groups which I must thank include those who provided feedback in the research seminar held in the School of English and American Studies at the University of Sussex in November 1990, the communications research seminar at London Guildhall University in May 1998 and May 1999, the Socrates CDI-Project, Tübingen, in November 1998 and the 'No End to Thrills' conference, Lincoln, in June 1999.

There are, however, some people who deserve a specific thank-you. Clive Bloom is a crucial figure in the contemporary academic study of popular fiction, and I am grateful for his encouragement during the writing of this book for the Crime Files series. Both Clive and my editor, Charmian Hearne, have gone some way to abolishing the concept of stress which can sometimes be associated with academic book production. I owe thanks, also, to the Department of Art at London Guildhall University, who awarded me sufficient research monies in Spring 1999 to be able to put this book to bed. Roderick Kedward backed up my research ideas at an early stage; and during a brief arid period, John Whitley kindly gave me a number of leads which would have taken a while for me to procure on my own. Elaine Pennicott and Klaus Bruhn Jensen read part of the manuscript and provided criticism and – perhaps more importantly – encouragement.

It was Angus Ross who first introduced me to the possibility of academic work on the thriller quite a while ago, and he has always encouraged a historical approach. He has continued to give me support since this time, right up to the point of reading the manuscript of this book; I owe him a considerable debt of gratitude. Jerry Palmer has also been very close to this project for some years, once again reading and giving useful help with the manuscript. If this has been a burden to him it should be said that it serves him right for producing the seminal work, *Thrillers*, a book to which contemporary scholars are still in debt. While the book which follows might be able to demonstrate this academic debt quite clearly, it is less able to express the quality of Jerry's personal support over the years. Adam Briggs and Andrew Pepper also read the manuscript and gave indispensable help and advice to top off our many beer- fuelled, but most productive, debates during the 1990s. Friends can often make the best critics.

My most severe critic, however, is Alison Ronald, who is a living reminder to me that there are things that are somewhat more important than the quality of academic writing. Lastly, I must say, of course, that any errors or defects in this book are entirely my responsibility (although I reserve the right to later assert in court that this confession was obtained under duress by a group of embittered NYPD operatives who failed to 'mirandize' me).

Introduction

Revisiting the recent past

Since the early nineties it has become fashionable to make reference in a number of spheres, and in a way unthinkable in the 1980s, to the decade of the 1970s. A 'glam' revival – or a 'Glam Racket' as the Fall would have it – recruited, in some measure, the likes of Suede, Pulp and Morrissey in pop music. The Sex Pistols re-formed in 1996; disco returned with a vengeance; even prog. rock got another outing. Fashion reappropriated tight-fitting shirts and blouses as well as platform shoes; nylon and polyester made an unexpected comeback. Meanwhile, films like *The People vs. Larry Flint* (1996), *Boogie Nights* (1997) and *Velvet Goldmine* (1998) depicted 1970s America (and Britain in the latter film) as a playground of sexual and sartorial excess. Elsewhere in Hollywood, the egregious Quentin Tarantino rehabilitated 1970s icons such as John Travolta (*Pulp Fiction*, 1994) and blaxploitation goddess Pam Grier (*Jackie Brown*, 1997). Al Pacino, Burt Reynolds and Jon Voight, on the other hand, were rejuvenated without his help.

A plethora of other 1970s-related material is now part of the turn-of-the-century social and entertainment landscape. As Cornershop might say, it seems like the funky days are back again. Except there is always the nagging doubt about any 1970s item consumed in the present that it isn't like it was 20-odd years ago – and, moreover, it never was quite 'like it was' even at the time.

This is a book about thrillers, a very popular genre. It is also about the 1970s. And it is, above all, a book about gaining knowledge of what thrillers were like in the 1970s. Clearly, all of these are problematic enterprises. It is true, of course that, just as with clothes we can procure the old garment or just as with with music we can place the old record on the turntable, we can also get hold of the 1970s thriller and read it thoroughly. But how can we know that the novel, film or TV programme that we read over twenty years after it first appeared means the same as it always did? Even if we were around at the time, how can we know what it meant then?

Although artefacts like garments clearly do have 'meanings', it must be said that the questions that we have asked so far are compounded in their difficulty when we choose to focus on textual objects. Texts are so rich – sometimes merely by virtue of their length or how long they take to read – that the range and complexity of meanings which accrue to them can be extensive. This does not matter for most people, of course: films, novels and TV programmes are used for more immediate purposes such as entertainment, rather than for a meditation on the manifold significance of textuality. What they 'mean' can, we assume, be extrapolated from our understanding of the plot or structure of the text in question.

Such a 'shorthand' take on meaning is both very common and very necessary if human beings are to manage to get on with their everyday lives. However, it is worth noting that the same reductive tendency can become an escalating habit. Not only are the meanings and import of any text limited by consumptions of it which are not overly involved, but those limitations seem to be greater when the text in question comes from a specific *genre*. A genre text, it is easy to believe, does the same thing every time, no matter how much it professes to be different from all the others. Of course, if this was absolutely true nobody would have any enthusiasm for generic texts (and the strength of such a belief might account for some middle- to highbrow critics' consistent disdain of generic texts). But huge numbers of people do have enthusiasm for generic texts. Can it be the case that audiences are getting fooled all the time?

This book, therefore, is also about the concept of genre. We will need to ask at the outset how the concept can be understood in general, how it has frequently been (mis)understood and how it can be understood in relation to texts produced in the past. Furthermore, if we are to argue that audiences are not getting 'fooled' and are actually undergoing differentiated experiences in their interactions with generic texts, then we need to interrogate the notion of 'generic innovation'. Suggestions for dealing with these matters will run through the body of the book.

What is the thriller?

In the chapters that follow, we will be discussing generic texts in terms of their potential for different meanings and how specific meanings might – possibly – become 'fixed' at any one time. Immediately, then, there is a dilemma faced by our argument. If we suggest that meanings are shot through with the potentiality of transience – that is, they are subject to change over time – then it does not make sense to claim that there is a permanently stabilising entity called genre. If we claim that generic texts are very much geared towards firmly anchoring meaning, then it follows that the meanings of genres are not really subject to change. It is an intractable problem when stated so baldly. There is, of course, a means to steer a way through the straits which separate the somewhat artificial Scylla and Charybdis that we have just described. Moreover, this can be achieved not only for the genre presently under discussion but also for any broad popular genre, for example romance.

Two of the best analyses of the thriller, Palmer (1978) and Roth (1995), appeared almost two decades apart. Both embrace a wide array of texts and both provide a 'structural' analysis in which thrillers are found to have a basic set of 'structural' components – threats to the social order, heroes, villains, deduction, resolution and so forth – which are repeated in different guises by different texts. None of this, however, sounds at all promising for a study which wishes to address the core thesis of transiency and historically based meanings. In Palmer's analysis, for example, the 'root' meaning of thrillers is to be found in its 'genesis' and its 'structure'. Originating in the early- to mid-nineteenth century, the thriller is found by Palmer to institute a series of textual relations which remain crucial to it throughout ongoing decades. These relations comprise the role of the hero as a competitive individual professional, the threat of conspiracy, the role of the villain in this conspiracy and the restoration of 'social order'. Moreover, these textual relations are also found to be a refracting mirror of capitalist social relations. The thriller is thus a constant dramatisation of capitalism's logical desire to sustain itself and head off challenges to its hegemony. As such, the threat of conspiracy – a threat both to the relations of equilibrium in thriller narratives and to the veneer of capitalist success – is, reductively, the thriller's prime mover.

Now, structuralist theses of this kind can be read in terms of the way that they posit all thrillers as, essentially, the same entity. Each thriller will, thus, be a replay – albeit in fiction – of capitalist social relations. However, a little like Roth, I believe that exactly the opposite of reduction applies here, and this is where panoramic accounts of genres such as those cited come into their own. In the present study we will be operating from the premise that the notion of conspiracy is so wide and accommodating that it *enables* an expansive range of diverse texts. Except when flagrant rip-offs occur, all thrillers are actually totally different, even while still sharing the conspiracy theme. In addition, they will continue to be different for different audiences, in different places and different times. In this book we shall be considering a wide range of texts which all – either directly or sometimes in an exceedingly oblique way – bear connections to the vastly accommodating general theme of conspiracy.

For these reasons we will retain the designation 'thriller' in order – like Palmer and Roth, though for diametrically opposed purposes – to indicate our catholic embrace of narratives. Even so, there are numerous occasions when commentators on popular fiction have chosen more specific designations for the texts that they scrutinize; in the thriller genre these have included ratiocinative tales, Golden Age crime fiction, cosy, hard-boiled fiction, *noir*, and others. These groupings are often known as 'subgenres' and designate the specifics of an area of textual production within a larger genre. Occasionally, commentaries on subgenres are arranged around a narrowed focus because the analysis aims to demonstrate that the subgenre is, in fact, a discrete entity (see, for example, Hilfer 1990). More often, subgenres are explored simply because they exist. But, just as frequently, there is a need to consider subgroupings of a genre – in this case the thriller – in order to be able to present certain patterns as they appeared at a particular moment and to avoid getting bogged down in the discussion of a myriad of disparate connections across a huge genre.

Despite the fact that this book operates with quite a sweeping understanding of the thriller, then, it also divides into chapters on specific subgenres and themes. Indeed, because of the latitude of genre, it must also be said that such a division is doomed to failure. Firstly, subgenres, as will be evident in the forthcoming pages, are decidedly prone to overlaps: they are difficult to divide by themes and motifs and, almost always, this is the case for good reasons. We will return in the Conclusion to why this is especially so for investigations such as the present one which attempt to discover some grounds for historically specific readings. Secondly, the study of subgenres represents a narrowing of focus which does not fairly reflect the breadth of the generic corpus of texts. This is true, of course, of any consideration of popular forms: fiction is produced at such a rate that even an industry as lively as literary criticism cannot manage to keep up with it. There is no easy way out of this dilemma; but one measure I have taken is to provide lists of further reading at the end of Chapters 2–8 which can – again, problematically in taxonomic terms – provide an indication of the subgenre's reach.

These inevitable shortcomings are part and parcel of any endeavour concerned with the exigencies of analysis and the eschewal of reductionism. However, they should not stand in the way of providing pointers to the multiplicity, breadth and diversity of popular fiction as it is caught for a moment in an inquisitive gaze. This is doubly imperative when we stop to consider, as we indicated above, the way in which people's lives are so often dominated by the postponement of semiotic resources, by the short-circuiting of meaning which enables everyday existence to continue in a manageable fashion.

What is the American thriller in the 1970s?

So far we have said that the thriller genre is a broad entity but we have not mentioned the long-term factors which might be involved in shaping it as a textual phenomenon. As this is a question to do with the writing of literary history, the forging of generic canons and the neglect of historical audiences, the proper place for such a discussion is Chapter 1.

However, we can say something now about the body of texts which are the topic of this book. In order to deal with the questions of past generic output I have taken a case study from a given period. Furthermore, I have done this in an almost wholly arbitrary way. One reason for this is to avoid prejudging a period retrospectively and in a way which is overly instrumental. For example, one might make a judgement about the exact periodization of student activism in the United States, taking this sequence of years as the focus of study and subsequently force fictional texts to fit the identified themes.

Another reason is that general historical analyses of the kind carried out in this book are not equipped to deal with highly specific questions such as whether audiences read Victor Marchetti's *The Rope Dancer* (1974) differently if they read it without knowledge of his subsequent non-fiction espionage exposé written with John Marks, *The CIA and the Cult of Intelligence* (1975), or whether they read both, or either, after the events of Watergate were set in train. Bluntly, the ethnographic resources do not exist to make such an analysis possible.

A further, less academic reason for choosing this period in general is personal: as will I hope be clear from what follows, I am enthusiastic about a great many of the thrillers which are to be discussed.

Quite simply, then, the focus of this book consists of thriller texts from different media which arrived in the public sphere between 1970 and 1980. Some of these are discussed in some detail in the following chapters: non-fiction thrillers, hard-boiled texts, crime narratives, police stories, 'black' thrillers, paranoid narratives and revenge sagas. But once again, we should remember the number of texts which space restraints dictate that we cannot discuss. These include sub-genres such as espionage narratives, 'adventures', economic thrillers, disaster thrillers, serial killer sagas, soft-boiled private detective fiction, legal thrillers, capers, medical thrillers, texts featuring Bond-style secret agents/super spies, heist narratives and martial arts films, as well as various other miscellaneous texts that are even harder to categorise.

What stands out most about a case study of *American* thrillers in this period, however, is the existence of so many discourses in contemporary public life which attest to the genre's currency. If the ample phenomenon which Palmer identifies as pivotal to the thriller, the fear of conspiracy, is considered in relation to American social and political life, it is clear that there are rich pickings to be had. In classic studies, Bell (1964), Hofstadter (1964) and Davis (1971) have demonstrated that conspiracy fears have been at the hub of the American political landscape and that modernity has only served to heighten such fears (see also Chapter 7 below). In the 1970s, a set of historical circumstances transpired whereby articulations of such fears were hard to avoid.

Many important political events took place in the early 1970s. The Strategic Arms Limitation talks (SALT 1) were concluded in Moscow in 1972. In the same year Nixon made a presidential trip to China for a whole week, the longest such visit ever made by an American president. In 1973 the CIA destabilized the government of Allende in Chile, leading directly to an extreme right-wing coup, while in the same year Secretary of State Kissinger became inextricably entangled in the crisis in the Middle East. One epiphenomenon of this latter drama was the subsequent fuel crisis which exacerbated the already high levels of unemployment and inflation in the United States. It should also be mentioned that 1973 was the year that Vice-President Spiro Agnew resigned over tax indiscretions similar to the president's own. And woven intricately into the fabric of all these events were the circumstances of the last years of the Vietnam War and the scandal of Watergate.

The 1970s were a time when the material of thrillers – conspiracy, espionage, secrecy, crime and so forth – was a prominent part of other discourses in the social formation in America. Such material came little by little onto the political stage. Moreover, this was a time when public opinion – where it could be gauged – changed *gradually* in response to an accumulation of events, rather than suddenly in relation to a single event. The early 1970s in America was peculiar in that the mechanism of this accumulation became manifest. In a very specific way, the role of certain discourses came to be regarded by the public as crucial where previously they had been taken for granted. And, as history does not reach a conclusion with certain key events, there were constant sociopolitical problems that were seen to be unresolved.

Vietnam, conspiracy and deception in the making of Watergate as an event

On 18 June 1972, the *New York Times* carried the following report in one of its inside pages:

> Five men said to have been carrying cameras, electronic surveillance equipment and burglary tools, were arrested shortly after 2 A. M. today after a floor-by-floor search that led to the executive quarters of the National Democratic Committee here [the report came from Washington]. The suspects were charged with second-degree burglary.

The event under description was the burglary of the Watergate building, an event whose significance triggered a chain of circumstances which would eventually lead to impeachment proceedings in Congress, followed by the first resignation of an American president. Yet the small-scale misdemeanour described here was the tip of a colossal iceberg of deception and executive corruption.

As was to become clear over a period of years, the break-in at the Watergate was just a small part of a long-running government policy of secrecy which had accompanied the Vietnam War, a policy that was continued, and soon visibly extended, into domestic politics. When such policies became public knowledge it was inevitable that questions would be asked not just about the legitimacy but also about the reasons for such measures. Initial revelations of duplicity entailed that further revelations could be made and that recent political history would therefore need to be reassessed. This, at its lowest level, seems to be the logic of Watergate. Underpinning it was what Arthur Schlesinger (1968) called a 'crisis of confidence' associated with the rapidly growing public unease over the policies pursued in the war, compounded and exacerbated by the widespread secrecy and deception that accompanied them (see also Harward 1974).

A major condensation point for popular mistrust in the years before the Watergate affair was the crisis over the 'Pentagon Papers'. In June 1967, Secretary of Defense Robert McNamara set up the 'Vietnam History Task Force', a group of historians, political analysts and military officials in the Pentagon who were to produce a major study of the history of American involvement in Vietnam. Almost four years to the day, and about two and a half years after its completion, this history, known as 'The Pentagon Papers', was leaked to, and subsequently published in, the *New York Times*.

Although the Papers were an historical overview of past policy, they were considered by the Nixon administration to be secret documents. As a result, when they were passed on to the press by Daniel Ellsberg, a Pentagon employee, the White House had considerable misgivings.[1] The official reassessment of the war that the Pentagon Papers embodied went hand in hand with the government's high profile attempts to prevent the Papers' publication (following a legal battle over their initial publication in the *New York Times* they eventually appeared in the *Washington Post*: Ungar 1989, pp. 148ff. As McQuaid (1989, pp. 106–7) shows, Nixon's initial proposals for ending the war were a variation on established Democratic precedents; covertly, however, he not only authorized forays into, and the bombing of, Cambodia but also threatened Hanoi with the tactical use of nuclear weapons (cf. Ellsberg 1974, pp. 68–69).

The pattern of revelations which characterized the American domestic crisis wrought by Vietnam was to be reprised in the Watergate affair, although this time the narrativity of events was, if anything, more visible. The overwhelming characteristic of the affair is one that it shares with thrillers: an irruption into 'normality' which constitutes 'conspiracy' (Palmer 1978, p. 87). However, the kind of conspiracy that Watergate represents renders the theory of conspiracy as an immutable textual structure untenable. One victim of the Nixon policy on secrecy, the correspondent Daniel Schorr, asserts that what was unique to the conspiratorial ideology that informed actions in the period was 'the word *enemy* as used by the Nixon administration' (Schorr 1974, pp. 81–2). Here was a usage quite different from that which exists putatively in the public interest during times of war: in this era it was employed to describe large numbers of the domestic population.

Another factor in the public perception of conspiracy was the *accumulationi* of lies and deception. It can be convincingly argued that the continued lying by White House staff only increased public suspicion (see Barber 1977, p. 459; Ehrlichman 1982, p. 303) and, like a ready-made narrative, successive items of information promised more and more. When former presidential appointments secretary Alexander Butterfield revealed at the Senate Watergate hearings that Nixon had taped all his White House conversations, the press capitalized on all the issues that arose from it (see *Washington Post*, 17 July 1973, pp. A16–20; *Time*, 30 July and 20 August 1973). For Senator Robert Byrd the revelation was 'one more shovelful on the dungheap' (*Newsweek*, 30 July 1973, p. 13), a view reflected by the *Washington Post* editorial in its warning that witholding of the tapes indicated 'that the evidence does not in fact substantiate [President Nixon's] case', that is to say, it seemed to indicate Nixon's role in ordering the burglary and the covert campaign against the Democrats (17 July 1973, p. 17).

When the tape transcripts were finally released at the end of April 1974 and published in the major newspapers and in book form, there were general misgivings over the deletions that had been made during their preparation for the public. The crucial tape of a Nixon–Haldeman[2] conversation from 23 June 1972 was a notable absence from the released transcripts, and later became known by Watergate chroniclers as the 'smoking gun'. The tape, which proved Nixon had knowledge of the post-burglary cover-up from the outset, was eventually released on 5 August 1974, three days before his resignation and nine days after impeachment proceedings had officially started (see Kissinger 1982, p. 1198; Woodward and Bernstein, 1977, pp. 398ff.; Jaworski 1977, pp. 250ff.). If the release of the 23 June tape led to the reassessment of the previous release of the *edited* transcripts, like all the other revelations it also demanded a thorough reassessment of past policies publicly held by the administration.

As fate would have it, on the day that aide Butterfield's revelation of the routine taping of White House conversations was reported, it was also officially announced that Cambodia had been secretly bombed by the US on a massive scale since 1969. The *New York Times* actually broke the story a few days before the official announcement (having carried a story in May 1969 which intimated that heavy bombing of neutral Cambodia was indeed taking place).[3] Now the story was eclipsed in most newspapers by the revelations about the tapes. *Newsweek*, for example, in its first issue after Butterfield's revelations did not even address itself to the Cambodian bombing story. This was a busy time in the coverage of the conspiracy, not only with the news of the tapes but also with former Attorney-General Mitchell's testimony to the hearings throughout July. In spite of the fact that the bombing story was outweighed by the tapes and it concerned a war now thought to be over, it was of no small importance in the overall assessment of the Nixonian conspiracy. The tenor of such assessments was based on their conspiratorial character and their affront to the people (see, for example, Mankiewicz 1973, p. 139). More directly, of course, in his crime against the Cambodian people, Nixon was also fooling Congress, disdaining the American public and acting unconstitutionally.

It was easy to see how covert government acts escalated further secret measures. Daniel Ellsberg enunciated the links between foreign policy, secrecy, surveillance and personal liberties when he described the way in which Hersh's leaked 1969 story of the Cambodian invasion resulted directly in Henry Kissinger's request for 17 wiretaps (1974, p. 69), one more demonstration that a 'home front' was considered to exist by the administration.[4] The point to be made about the secret bombing in terms of the logic of conspiracy is that it was an issue that did not go away. In fact it returned to the grand arena of the debate through the statements of those Congressmen that called for impeachment in 1974, couched in forthright terms to do with law and professional ethics (see, especially, Drinan 1974, p. 73). Before too long, the secret bombing became part of a catalogue of 'crimes' committed by Richard Nixon (White 1975, pp. 394–7).

The fear of conspiracy, then, has its own specificities and points of investment for each period of history. In the 1970s the 'irruption' into an ordered world is more of a process of accumulated revelations over a number of years. In one sense, it is reasonably clear that public opinion, on the whole, regarded the corrupt shenanigans as part and parcel of the alien world of 'Politics' (see below). In another sense, the drama of government corruption was played out in a public sphere, through the media, and the theme of that drama was that many of those in power were no longer fit to govern. In addition, the new high profile for the tactics of deception emphasized their targeting of the individual. It was not necessarily the case that the bulk of the population felt that it was under threat of investigation nor that it immediately felt the effects of government policies in a direct way. But contemporary accounts of government activities – and thrillers – often stress the dimension of individual covert activities against individuals rather than political subversion in the abstract.

As early as 1970 *Newsweek* reported the discovery of a massive covert army surveillance operation focussed on 'political activists' (4 May 1970, p. 35); similarly, it became known in Washington at a later date that Nixon had compiled his own 'Enemies list' of 'leftist' organizations that he intended to move against under the guise of the IRS (Dobrovir et al. 1974, pp. 23–7). A significant proportion of the population were at risk from surveillance operators or could at least be perceived to be so (Westin 1967). Accounts of government-inspired conspiracies could also utilize the very facts of plots against individuals to inform their rhetoric. At a conference of anti-Nixon Watergate protagonists held in Delaware in 1973, many speakers assessed the whole period in terms of the rights of the individual and in terms of both American political tradition and the constitution (see Harward 1974). Unsurprisingly, one of the conference's main concerns was the First Amendment.

The thriller and discourses of duplicity in the 1970s

Discourses to do with conspiracy were remarkably prevalent in 1970s America, even if it is equally true that the vast majority of individual citizens were not necessarily embroiled in nefarious political plots. It is worth remembering, then, that our purposes in this account of some of the themes of the Watergate affair are certainly not part of an attempt to get at a 'final truth' about the relevant events, even if such a goal would be possible to attain. Nor do we intend to capture a particular kind of Zeitgeist, as is so often attempted by many kinds of history. More pointedly, we hope to demonstrate not so much 'what happened' during the period but to give a sense of 'what was commonly being said in public' in this time.

Almost uniquely, the Watergate affair represents a moment when the press played a central role and where the media can be said to have had an 'effect', if not in the direct shaping of public views at least in the provision of more and more evidence of duplicity for the public to utilize in its own construction of opinion. Probably more than at any other time in American politics, investigative reporting became crucial to the process of assessing the credentials of a president and his administration. In fact, one can go further and argue that, in this period, the press constituted a terrain where a struggle for hegemony over the rhetoric of American democracy was played out. Hentoff refers to the summing up by the judge in the Watergate trial:

> Justice Hugo Black emphasized that through the First Amendment, 'The press was protected so that it could bare the secrets of government and inform the people. Only a free and unrestrained press can effectively oppose deception in government.'
>
> (1973, p. 232)

Ungar (1989, pp. 306–7) concurs with this, and produces figures to suggest that it was precisely the First Amendment that was at issue in the Pentagon Papers case rather than matters of cash or circulation.

From the point of view of the media, the very notion of a free press and broadcasting system, enshrined in the Constitution, was under threat during Watergate and the Pentagon Papers affair. This is not to say that the importance of capital did not play a part in the media's *raison d'être*; however, at this time, the short-term ideological configuration which characterized American political events thrust the First Amendment into the foreground of hegemonic struggle. Clearly, the Nixon administration feared the media and targeted individual journalists such as Jack

Anderson and Daniel Schorr for persecution (see Anderson with Clifford 1974; Spear 1989, pp. 134, 148–50; Ungar 1989, p. 305; Hunt 1975, p. 183; Schorr 1974, p. 82). As a result, the 'press' and 'conspiracy' became almost synonymous, albeit in different ways, for both sides.

When the news of the burglary at the Watergate building broke, the media, in a characteristic fashion, seemed keen to emphasise the open-endedness of the item. *NBC Nightly News* finished their report on the break-in with the sound bite: 'I don't think that's the last we're going to hear of this story' (quoted in Lang and Lang 1983, p. 29). The same mode was adopted by other reporting of the incident. The *New York Times*, for whom, as we noted earlier, the events were not worthy of front-page coverage, tagged onto the end of their report the following: 'None of the suspects disclosed any objectives for entering the committee headquarters or affiliation with any political organization in the United States' (18 June 1972, p. 30). Although burglary is the only offence that can legitimately be mentioned in the article the reference in the copy to surveillance equipment carried by the burglars allows the reader to make a guess at the purpose of the break-in. This last sentence, though, is the crucial one. For those readers who may not immediately associate the incident with political sabotage by groups hostile to the Democratic Party, the use of 'objectives' and 'affiliation' acts as a guide for questions about further implications of the break-in. The same can be said of the article on the front page of the *Washington Post*; rather than choosing to leave unsaid anything that does not have a purely factual basis, the article creates the grounds for speculation by identifying this same aspect of the incident about which they cannot give any further information (18 June 1972, p. A1). Thus the Watergate affair was to thrive on the convergence of the media's apparently rediscovered centrality with regard to the Constitution, a government cover-up and the logic of a big 'story'.

Thrillers, the media and the public

Even in this summary history there is much that might find itself at home in a thriller text. More important than this, though, there is much that contemporary readers might recognize from the world of discourses outside the genre when reading narratives from inside the genre. But before we proceed to the next chapter, let us be clear about what we *do not* mean here.

We are not suggesting that all contemporary readers would share a unified perspective on Watergate and politics in 1970s America; nor are we saying that the political issues alone would coerce readers into specific readings of thrillers. Even though there was a recognizable surge of public opinion against the Nixon presidency,[5] the source of the swing in public opinion cannot be precisely located, because one single event did not bring about an immediate change. Moreover, there seems to have been a perception abroad that Watergate simply represented 'business as usual', or the kind of activity in which politicians always indulge, with the exception that, on this occasion, they were caught out and suffered the glare of publicity (see Brooks 1974, p. 21). Again and again Lang and Lang found that the polls of the period reflected a feeling that the ramifications of government deception did not immediately enter people's everyday lives (1983, p. 134); although corruption in the period was seen to be located in government, it did not mean that there was one general perception about Washington or a widespread perception that the system should go.

The link between a monolithic public opinion and thrillers, therefore, cannot really be posited. To be sure, the intense coverage of political events and the special role of the media in them remains, and without these, one could argue, it is difficult to understand many thrillers from the period as one reads them in the present. Certainly, to begin even to approach an understanding of how thrillers were read by contemporary audiences one has to have at least a base knowledge of some of the key political events of the decade, how they were presented in the media and the logic by which they became public property. Furthermore, in our discussions of thriller texts additional historical circumstances of a specific nature will become pertinent. Yet we must not rely solely on politics as it is covered in the mass media for an understanding of the determinants of popular reading in the period.

Assessing the possibilities of historical studies of reception, Jensen suggests: 'Studying the past, we may turn to other media-related discourses – for example, the representation of new media in old media, the temporal structures of content and the response of elite social actors to media' (1993, p. 26). This provides a useful agenda for the present study, and it is an agenda whose coordinates will be mapped in the next chapter. There we will be concerned with a number of theoretical issues to do with the concept of genre, reading and 'history'. The reader more concerned with developments in the American thriller than with theoretical questions is therefore advised to go straight to Chapter 2, and perhaps return to Chapter 1 after having read the rest of the book. The reader who is interested in following the argument in this book about the nature of genre is advised to start at Chapter 1.

Having sketched the importance for our investigation of history as it is presented in the period, we should add that the approach proceeding from Chapter 1 will involve us in a reconditioned genre theory along with a sense of genre texts as 'texts-in-history'. As a corollary of this we will be subsequently looking *closely* at thriller narratives: not because of any belief in the power of close readings to yield an 'ultimate' meaning, but rather because, as we shall see, there is a prevalent tendency to foreshorten, forget and diminish texts from the past even though they might be texts with which past readers might have engaged extensively. Part of our armoury for close scrutiny of texts will consist of tools from narratology which will enable the elucidation of the numerous tropes and narrative devices which complexly attempt to *re*present a world.

Following Jensen and according to principles outlined in the next chapter, we will also be looking at the way texts from one media are referred to in another. We shall be looking at what surrounds narratives (for clues about them). Chief among this kind of evidence will be reviews; but we shall also be considering relations between generic texts, especially if some texts, for some reasons, are found to be influential in some way.

And the purpose of our investigation will be, quite often, to root out instances of 'generic innovation'. By this we do not mean the appearance in a genre text of new elements in a manner which might be trivial (for example, a policeman with long hair wearing flared trousers). Nor do we mean wholesale transformations of generic plots (such as unresolved endings, anti-heroes and the like). We do not even mean those kinds of text which might be thrillers apparently without thrills, conspiracy, heroes and villains, and which supposedly fulfil the task of that well-known oxymoron, 'transcending genre'. Instead, we shall be unfolding a reader-oriented approach to generic innovation whose mechanisms should become clear towards the conclusion of the book.

1
Firing the Generic Canon

Texts in history: the truth is out there

A common-sense approach suggests that there can surely be no problem in interrogating a text from the past to find out what it 'means'. We simply need to procure access to that text and its 'meaning' will become apparent as we read it. The truth is 'in there', to invert the *X Files* strapline. The only difficulty, of course, is that we know that the status of texts changes in different time periods. *Gulliver's Travels* (1726) or *Robinson Crusoe* (1719) are nowadays presented as children's books, and take on an identity much different from the ones they assumed at their first appearance in the eighteenth century. Indeed, the common-sense approach needs to undergo immediate revision as soon as it is posited because few would assume now that the status or 'meaning' of a given text can be discovered through an isolated engagement with the work in question, even if such an engagement were possible.

In the last 20 years or so, academic work on the complexity of the reading process and audience/text relations has flourished in the study of TV, film, written fiction and so on (for example Morley 1980; Ang 1984; 1991; 1996; Radway 1984; Seiter et al. 1989; Gray 1992; Liebes and Katz 1993; Lull 1990; Gillespie 1995; Hermes 1996; Nightingale 1996). Much of this work has been concerned with the way in which determinants outside texts – including aspects of people's lives – have a central role to play in the way that texts are imbued with meaning. Some theorists have sought to investigate the twin roles of reader and literary text in interaction (Iser 1974; 1978; 1989); others have tentatively explored the 'horizon of expectations' (Jauss 1982) which exists beyond and before interaction with the literary text. Yet others have identified specific affiliations – say, political or occupational ones – which impinge fairly directly on the reading process (for example, Morley 1992).

Our task is to consider the webs of relations in which texts from the past were suspended at their moment of first appearance. If we were carrying out research into readings in the present, this would pose problems which might be overcome by judicious use of qualitative methodologies such as interviews or focus groups (see Denzin and Lincoln 1998). However, qualitative methodologies cannot put us in touch with readers from the past. Even where readers from the recent past are still alive, our interrogation of them will be beset by problems: 'are they remembering their interactions with texts as they happened?', 'are their remembrances shaped by water that has gone under the bridge since?' Thus, we must find an alternative means of understanding the place of texts in history, an understanding which is alert to the potentially huge range of knowledges which are brought by a reader to an interaction.

The work of Tony Bennett (1987; 1990) presents a useful approach to readers' knowledges in the concept of a 'reading formation'. He stresses the importance of a number of discursive practices that operate on readers before, and simultaneous with, a textual system, ordering the relations between texts in a definite way 'such that their reading is always-already cued in specific directions that are not given by those "texts themselves" as entities separable from such relations' (Bennett and Woollacott 1987, p. 64). The reader's knowledge of how texts are organized, and their relations with other texts, is largely a knowledge of how various institutions work – the film industry, publishing, broadcasting, advertising. A low level of understanding of relations between these is required for an audience to realize, for example, that an actor is giving an interview on a chat show at a given moment in time because his/her latest film is currently on general release. Such knowledge, in turn, might be built into a reading of the film.

At the same time, that which seems wholly *untouched* by institutional relations is often equally the result of similar determinations. For example, Bennett and Woollacott acknowledge Foucault's insight into the author as 'the principle of thrift in the proliferation of meaning' (Foucault 1986, p. 119), the way that a reader's understanding of authorship might be built into the reading of a text. In their study of the James Bond phenomenon they show that Ian Fleming – the original, but merely one of a number of Bond authors – exists not as a real person but as the nodal point of biographical accounts. They conclude that commentaries have 'Bondianised' Fleming's life and thus 'Flemingised' Bond as a figure for readers, providing one limit to the polysemous nature of Bond texts (pp. 89–90). Moreover, this is subject to change over time: as the output of the present Bond author, Raymond Benson, begins to exceed Fleming's there is even the possibility that some future readers will pay little heed to the biography of Fleming.

This attention to the probabilities of change in considering the longevity of Bond after Fleming suggests that the concept of 'reading formation' allows for a consideration of reading relations in different time periods. Strategies of reading the Bond texts in the 1950s, particularly national ones, are shown by Bennett and Woollacott to be important within the frameworks of other texts. One method of identifying these frameworks is through reviews: the review in the *New York Times* of the film version of *Dr. No*, according to Bennett and Woollacott, effectively sold Bond to the American public as a Mickey Spillane character (p. 83). In Britain, however, hard-boiled novels by Spillane and others, while popular in the late 1950s, did not become a point of reference for the reading of the Bond novels but were 'eclipsed by the earlier traditions of the "imperialist spy-thriller" which provide by far and away the most influential textual backdrop against which the novels were initially read' (p. 83).

As we can see, then, the concept of reading formation promotes an understanding of reading as an activity which can no longer be considered merely as the realization of textual meanings but is more suitably viewed, instead, as highly determined by ideological and commercial imperatives. Acknowledgment of the work of a reading formation also permits the analyst to consider texts as 'texts-in-history' and 'texts-in-use' – that is, as texts that are subject to particular readings rather than as entities with immanent qualities (Bennett 1987). We might tend to assume commonsensically that the 'meaning' of a text is 'in there'; but the interrogation of a reading formation consistently demonstrates that a text's meaning is constantly derived from factors outside of itself (in the past *and* the present).

This will be the case with any kind of text. Yet the tendency to assume an 'immanent' meaning is even more pronounced in the case of 'generic' texts. The reasons for such a tendency should become more apparent as we attempt a definition of genres in relation to audiences. Following this we will examine the ways in which we might overcome the distortions of short-hand takes on the place of generic texts in history.

Genre and audiences

There can be no term in the study of textuality which has been abused as frequently as 'genre'. As we have noted, recent study has left in its wake the imperative of factoring audiences into textual equations. Neverthe-less, genre is still being used to vindicate the notion of textual features as immutable. This state of affairs is the result of three things: the difficulty in thinking beyond common sense understandings of textuality, the problem of contemplating genres' breadth, and the contrary work of those who would formulate generic canons.

'Genre' *is* a concept that is in everyday use even if it is not named as such; but, to understand its implications and begin to consider the status of past generic output, there still needs to be a clarion call for the consideration of readers' work in effecting the concept. While every consumer of fictions has a rough idea of what 'genre' means – a short-hand textual classification, determining whether a particular fiction is expected to conform to previous experiences of texts on the part of the consumer – academic analysis of genre has taken matters one step further. The latter has been repeatedly organized around the belief that genre designates an entity which is unproblematically available, object-ively 'there' for study.

To be sure, approaches which define genre with reference to the explan-atory power of factors internal to texts – structure, plot, character, setting – have been with us since Aristotle.[1] And, unsurprisingly, apart from occasional nods in its general direction, what all genre theory left out was the audience. One possible reason for this is that when the worst varieties of genre theory leave the audience in, the consequences are often reductive and absurd. For example, Judith Hess Wright, writing originally in *Jump/Cut*, had this to say about the gangster film spectator: 'Viewers are encouraged to cease examining themselves and their sur-roundings, and to take refuge in fantasy from their only real alternative – to rise up against the injustices perpetrated by the present system upon its members' (1986, p. 49). Lest we gain comfort from the assertion that this view was offered in an article first published as long ago as 1978, consider the following, more recent, offering from George Lipsitz:

> Generic conventions encourage the repetition, reconfiguration and renewal of familiar forms in order to cultivate audience investment and engagement. Created mostly for the convenience of marketers anxious to predict exact sales figures by selling familiar products to identifiable audiences, genres also have ideological effects. Their con-ventions contribute to an ahistorical view of the world as always the same; the pleasures of predictability encourage an investment in the status quo.
>
> (1998, p. 209)

The tone is *marginally* more circumspect but the sentiment is the same: generic texts have a very limited range of meanings, the reader can discern only these, they are meanings which paper over 'reality' and, as a consequence, readers (apart from intrepid genre theorists, that is) either believe the unchanging version of the world that generic texts promulgate or are distracted from a 'proper' perspective on 'reality'.

Now, a genre text *may* be shown to possess the internal textual organization that genre theorists have discerned, displaying key elements such as a hero, problem- solving, and so on; but the manner in which these features are interpreted does not simply depend on the structure of the text as it has been identified by textual analysts. Repeatedly, reception theory has shown that textual meaning derives in large part from what the reader has imported him/herself. In addition to this, the reader's recognition of generic features such as problem-solving will rely on two things: a competence derived from reading previous texts within a given genre and 'extra-textual' cues within the reading formation which indicate the generic status of the text. As Neale explains with respect to movies, genres do not consist only of discernible textual features; they 'consist also, and equally, of specific systems of expectation and hypothesis which spectators bring with them to the cinema, and which interact with films themselves during the course of the viewing process' (1990, p. 46; cf. Austin and Gordon 1988). An investigation of readers' expectations may start, then, with an investigation of how generic texts might satisfy readers demands of *verisimilitude*.

Verisimilitude

Todorov (1977) identifies two kinds of norms by which a work or set of statements is said to have verisimilitude: the 'rules of the genre' and 'public opinion' or *doxa*. When somebody bursts into song during a musical, this is not, according to the rules of the genre, an indecorous act at odds with the statements in the text: the song is part of a specific regime of verisimilitude and falls within a range of expectations on the part of the audience that such acts are legitimate within the bounds of the genre. Where 'public opinion' is concerned, plainly this consists of a set of *expectations and understandings* of the world by readers rather than the world as a referent. In this way the *doxa* is a regime of verisimilitude in itself, constantly shifting according to a complex set of checks and balances which characterize the world of discourse in general.

As Todorov explains (1977, p. 87), it is more accurate, therefore, to consider verisimilitude as a principle of textual coherence rather than as an area in which there exists some relation between the fictional and the real world. What is fundamental to expectations about the thriller genre is the maintenance of a general level of 'credibility' which matches as closely as possible that which is held by the *doxa*. The thriller is characterized by its attempt to achieve harmony between the consistency of representation within the thriller narrative and what is believed to be credible – politically, socially, topically – at a given moment by public opinion. It is for this reason that commentators often make the mistake of believing that thrillers are more 'realistic' than other texts or that being 'true to life' is a specific and objective expectation harboured by thriller readers.

The specific regime of verisimilitude in thrillers cannot be stressed enough. As an expectation it runs through probably the entire corpus of thrillers and has encouraged certain asumptions about the relation of the thriller to history, as we will see. Even so, it is flexible in its tutelage and does not police other expectations in order to maintain them as strict rules (Cobley 1997). The 'rules' of detective fiction, for example, were spectacularly contravened in 1926 by Agatha Christie in *The Murder of Roger Ackroyd* (see Van Dine 1974 and Knox 1974; see also Tudor 1976, p. 22 on the Western). However, we must also say that while the parameters of generic expectation under the aegis of verisimilitude may be fluid, they frequently seem to be subject to two kinds of textual anchoring process.

Semantic/syntactic features and 'short-circuiting'

Altman considers two fundamental and inseparable constituents of genre: its 'building blocks' and the 'structure in which they are arranged'. He calls these, respectively, genre's *semantic* and *syntactic* aspects (1986, p. 30), a distinction which, if imperfect, at least allows for a consideration of print genres' equivalent of filmic iconography. This is to say, the semantic dimension does not just consist of the object depicted but includes the methods of realizing the object. In film this will comprise lighting, shots, set design and so on; in writing, this will incorporate all those narrative strategies, such as prose style, which are specific to a text. The syntactic dimension, on the other hand, refers to all those 'structural' features identified by previous genre theorists; for example, eventual revelation of the murderer in the 'whodunit'.

It is in the relation of the semantic and the syntactic dimensions that meaning is enacted; but as Altman insists, the semantic and syntactic should not be considered as discrete zones. Where genre theorists have defined genre in terms of the semantic realm or, as is more often the case, its syntactic realm (textual 'structure', etc.), Altman suggests that we could more profitably understand reader expectations in terms of an investment in the *combined* semantic/syntactic realm. As such, the role of the hero in the generic text – which is repeatedly considered a 'syntactic' element by theorists after Propp – should not be considered as separable from supposedly 'semantic' aspects such as his/her good looks, his/her 'goodness' or, if the text is a film, how the hero is shot or positioned in each scene.

Implicit in the theory of the semantic/syntactic as a territory where two aspects of textuality work in tandem is the notion that texts might have many meanings. The semantic/syntactic combination restricts potential meanings by making certain textual features seem naturally inseparable, a clichéd example being, once more, the idea that the 'hero' embodies 'goodness'. Most commentators accept that all texts carry a multiplicity of meaning (polysemy); yet, when a text operates within a generic system the potentially wide range of interpretations is, to use Altman's phrase (1987, p. 4) 'short-circuited'. The expectations which perform this task exist in a reading formation which includes discourses surrounding generic products, political discourses, journalistic discourses outside the domain of genres (e.g. documentaries), discourses about other parts of the fiction industry beyond that of a given genre, and so on.

As Altman is keen to point out in revisiting his semantic/syntactic model, there is a great deal outside the text which determines a genre, such that 'genres look different to different audiences' (1999, p. 207). He criticizes Neale and others for their excessive reliance on an understanding of genre expectations as largely created by the film producer's publicity machine, and through an examination of film publicity argues strongly that producers' discourse contributes surprisingly little to the generic character of films (1998; 1999). If anything, argues Altman, 'critics and not studios lie at the origin of most generic language' (1999, p. 127); as I will attempt to show in forthcoming chapters, contemporary critics' commentaries constitute an important piece of evidence on the trail of readers' meanings in history.

But Altman does not leave the issue there. He also criticizes the 'conservative' tendencies of theorists such as Hall and de Certeau who implicitly favour a producer-centred understanding of the generation of meaning in their models or 'encoding/decoding' and 'poacher/ nomad' respectively. Where they see the users of cultural artefacts as interacting with already produced material, Altman exhorts us to explore the use-orientation of readers. As such, there is a need to study the ways in which a cultural commodity such as genre is 'made' through the action of readers who harbour expectations. Such expectations are not just created by publicity; nor are they unproblematically the products of existing belief. Instead, they are the products 'also of knowledge, emotions and pleasure' (Jost 1998, p. 106). As we have noted, the reader's knowledge of other texts' semantic/syntactic functioning which s/he recognizes to belong in the same generic system as the text being read represents an important expectation, one which is bound up with questions of pleasures and knowledge.

If generic meaning is derived partly from knowledge of – or competence in reading – other texts in the genre, it follows that generic texts from the past assume a crucial status for the efficacy of genre in the present. How, then, can readers be sure that their knowledge of generic texts is not selective and tailored to the needs of the present moment? The short answer to this is that they *cannot*. Furthermore, the vast majority of readers are unconcerned that generic texts often become 'canonised' either by publicity discourses or by professional writers on the topic of the genre.

We could leave the subject here and simply build this recognition into our discussion of generic texts were it not for the fact that the present book seeks to reassemble the possible readings and determinants of readings of generic texts from a given period in the fairly recent past. To accept at face value the accounts given by canonisers would be to assume that contemporary readers' evaluations always coincide with those of future cultural historians – an assumption which is not borne out by the neglect of hundreds of works which have been popular and significant in their time. As we will see, 'canonisation' is an especially invidious version of the 'short-circuiting' process. It is for this reason that it will be worthwhile to unravel some of the means by which generic texts are constituted in specific corpuses of work and to consider alternative understandings of the relations between texts.

Generic canons and their alternatives

It is clear that any historian of fictional texts has such an unmanageable wealth of material to wade through that establishing the corpus for study involves, necessarily, *not* considering a huge number of texts. Hence, one of the most influential histories of the thriller, Julian Symons's *Bloody Murder* (1974), avoids discussing an 'enormous mass of more or less entertaining rubbish' (p. 10). This occurs time and time again in the literature of thriller criticism, with a succession of writers accepting a consensus on a central corpus of texts and their relevance to the history of the genre.[2] Symons' words (p. 141) on the subject of hard-boiled fiction, for example, are constantly echoed by a diversity of writers (see Panek 1987, p. 149; Binyon 1989, p. 38; Mandel 1984, pp. 66–80; cf. the comments of Crumley in Harvey 1997). Like so many commentaries on the hard-boiled, these hold up the examples of Hammett, Chandler and Macdonald. They also seem to owe a considerable amount to an essay of 1970 by George Grella which grounds the category of hard-boiled fiction in terms of American archetypes (see Grella 1980, pp. 103–20).[3]

The reason for this kind of canon construction is clear. Rather than admitting huge sellers who might have made an impact on public consciousness, historians of the thriller wish to preserve 'value'. As H.R.F. Keating puts it:

> I suppose if you look at the history of crime fiction in terms of what the public was reading year by year then obviously those writers [Bagley, Ludlum etc]...would have their tremendous weight. But because Julian [Symons] and other writers – me – are people who make judgments about books for better or worse; we tend to have a theory of what has happened based on what books we consider to be good. And on those terms Wheatley doesn't really come into the picture at all, or Ludlum or a good many others ...[4]

This is a widespread principle of exclusion and one which is often taken for granted. As such, Symons might be too obvious an example of the canonisation process. The 1992 edition of *Bloody Murder*, for instance, is even explicit in its desire to write out some of the *contemporary* exponents of the hard-boiled or noir school from the thriller canon.

Yet, if we take a more recent example of popular critical writing on the thriller we see exactly the same principle, almost in reverse. Haut (1999) attempts to provide a hip, up-to-date version of the Symons project of taste-making (Ellroy good, Grisham bad), in which the considered writers 'reflect the author's personal tastes' (p. 3) and the recent history of crime fiction is apprehended through the refracting prism of recently republished 'noir classics'.[5] In spite of the historical framework which Haut constructs – references to the politics of the Reagan regime, for example, and a whole chapter on the depiction of the city in noir fiction which never even countenances the notion that it may be as contrived as the depiction of the village in golden age, 'cosy' crime narratives – the texts he analyses are presented as the productions of auteurs or, at best, the reflections of a 'noir sensibility' (see also Pepper 1999). However necessary for a writing profession such a principle of critical exclusion might be, it tends towards the treatment of the text 'as if it were a hermetic and self-sufficient whole, one whose elements constitute a closed system presuming nothing beyond themselves, no other utterances' (Bakhtin 1981, p. 273). In short, the text is denied its place in history, its coexistence with other generic texts and its existence as the product of contemporary readings.

In any examination of genres in history which is grounded in principles of accuracy rather than evaluation there is a need to gain recognition of the *breadth* of a particular genre. O'Brien (1981), in his book on the cover art of 1950s thrillers, for example, shows that paperbacks – or 'pocket books' – were frequently consumed not so much in respect of any admirable generic characteristics but largely with reference to their (often garish) packaging. As such, the publicity discourses that made up the corporate identity of a distinct publishing venture constituted the genre as much – if not more – than intra-textual features of specific novels.

To take a very different example, Stewart (1980, p. 40) argues that the period in which little or no detective fiction appeared – known as the 'interregnum' and which most critics believe to exist between Wilkie Collins and Arthur Conan Doyle in nineteenth-century detective fiction – exists only because the precise syntactic structure of detective fiction that critics are looking for is not evident at this time. The impulse to canonise has the result, therefore, that a huge number of texts which have been popular and important on their own terms are written out of history. The texts that appear in the 'interregnum' are those that make up the popular literature of their age and, although bereft of the 'classic' syntax, they do not stand divorced and aloof from the development of detective fiction (see Greene 1970; Bleiler 1978). Detective fiction in this period, Stewart argues, was one part of sensation fiction (1980, p. 76). (We shall return to the role of sensation fiction in the formation of the thriller, below.)

More recently, several writers have almost abolished strict boundaries between genres by concentrating on popular reading as a broad phenomenon. Haut (1995), Bloom (1996) and McCracken (1998) all interrogate popular texts not so much in terms of specific genres but in terms of affiliations across genres. Haut sees postwar pulp culture as an aesthetic which covers texts as diverse as *If He Hollers Let Him Go* (1946), *In a Lonely Place* (1947) and *The Shrinking Man* (1956) in a way which is not dissimilar to the 'noir sensibility' referenced in his later book (1999). In the sophisticated analyses by Bloom and McCracken, on the other hand, there is a notable emphasis on the pulp mentality as more than a collection of texts. For them, the way that readers in pulp culture partake of diversity is virtually an emblem of the fragmenting effects of modernity. What their work shows is that we need to be aware of the way in which readers can operate with 'nomadic' tendencies (Radway 1988) rather than being confined to one preference or mentality.

Even more directly relevant to the thesis outlined in the present book is the work of John Sutherland (1978; 1981), whose writing – not so much concerned with thriller history, but overlapping with it – falls within the discipline known as the sociology of literature or the 'sociology of reading' (see Sauerberg 1983, pp. 93, 106).[6] Sutherland does two things: he puts texts within the framework of their popularity, the fact that they are bought/read for a number of institutionally determined reasons; and he places these texts among others of the same group in history. He is quite catholic in his embrace of 1970s texts: he therefore devotes chapters to *The Godfather*, Arthur Hailey, horror fiction featuring children as protagonists, *The Thorn Birds*, Erica Jong, bodice-rippers, *Star Wars*, Alistair MacLean and (briefly) James Clavell, *Jaws*, Harold Robbins, Washington novels, *Death Wish*, new Westerns, war stories of secret deals and Nazi resurgence, hijack and corporate crime novels, holocaust fiction, medical thrillers, documentary thrillers, disaster narratives, and tales of 'If Britain Had Fallen [to the Nazis]'. The role of bestsellerdom in histories of genre has invariably been glossed over by conventional generic criticism of texts, fixated as it is on 'good' syntax and style; Sutherland quite rightly indicates that bestsellerdom is an area that literary and genre historians cannot afford to ignore (1981, p. 247).

The commodification that bestsellers represent is just one way in which a body of texts' putative syntax is always already thoroughly mediated, dislocated and problematized. It is one demonstration of the way that genre texts owe their status to a complex set of relations which is constantly shifting in a far from uniform pattern. It is somewhat of an irony, however, that while bestsellers are usually the products of intense promotional strategies, their future neglect is the product of analogous strategies of critical *de*promotion. Texts which are hugely popular with readers and are both prevalent and influential in their day – Robert Ludlum's novels are just one example – are systematically written out of history if they do not appeal to the existing predilictions of institutionalised criticism.[7] The situation of genres in history, then, is by no means settled.

Thus, the question must be asked – how can we analyse the thriller in the face of all these formative processes? Is 'the thriller' simply a fixed entity, or is it just the product of short-lived contemporary determinations, buried in a mass of contextual factors and almost a figment of our imagination?

The thriller's breadth

As I indicated in the Introduction, the term 'thriller' has been chosen to indicate a whole array of genres and subgenres rather than one kind of syntax or trope such as 'detection'. The shortcoming of the term 'thriller' – that it is very occasionally used to describe specific generic entities (Harper 1969; Denning 1987; Merry 1977) – is obvious. However, the many benefits of its long reach – employed to good effect by others (Davis 1973; Palmer 1978) – should also now be apparent in reference to the foregoing comments on 'short-circuiting' in this chapter.

If investigations into textuality have discovered anything over the last 20 years, it is that texts are the sites of struggle. The numerous competing readings which might accompany an individual novel, film or TV programme is far more extensive than was hitherto realised. Judging what is the ultimate meaning of an individual thriller text, then, is no easy thing, let alone judging what the entire corpus of thrillers might be. Yet, the unmasking of those interested parties who have played a role in defining what constitutes the history of the thriller by no means implies that the question 'what is the thriller?' is undecidable. The history and status of the thriller is, instead, a site of struggle just as much as the history and status of the individual text. That is to say, the thriller cannot be left at the mercy of circumstance: it needs to be interrogated and re-interrogated, across its breadth, and from perspectives which move beyond and eschew the canonic impulse.

One of the most important works on the thriller, Knight (1980), explores the genre in a general way as the realisation and validation of a 'whole view of the world' (p. 2), but also, much more demonstrably, as deriving from multiple sources. Without entering into pointless debates as to whether detection takes place in narratives as remote in time as those that make up ancient Greek literature, Knight plots the advance of the detective figure and finds that a number of different kinds of text are responsible for such a character's emergence and progress. If one was forced for the purposes of analysis to define the 'thriller', in spite of what we have said about mutability above, then Knight's work provides a good starting-point.

Let us make the uncontroversial statement, then, that the contemporary thriller is not one genre but many. Put another way, it is 'heteroglossic' (Bakhtin 1981), or traversed by many 'voices'. Let us also add to this assertion that its origins can be found not just in one genre as is often argued (for example, Poe's Dupin stories) but in many genres, most of which – with one notable exception – became visible in the nineteenth or late eighteenth centuries. Each of these genres was itself multiply determined – by pre-literate genres as well as by closer literary relatives such as romance, gothic, the *Bildungsroman*, odysseys, ballads and chapbooks. Moreover, the lines leading all of these determinations towards the present day have become irrevocably tangled.

As a supplement to Knight's observations, we can offer the following list of the 'bases' of the thriller genre:

- Newgate confessionals (collected stories of criminal lives; Knight 1980, pp. 8–20)
- adventure stories (tales of travels and exploits, often in remote areas or strange lands; Cawelti 1976, pp. 39–41)
- ratiocinative tales (narratives of detection where deduction and intellectual questioning are paramount, as in Poe's Dupin stories; Cawelti 1976, pp. 80–105; Knight 1980, pp. 39–134; Moretti 1988, pp. 130–56)
- memoirs of police operatives (as in those of Vidocq; Knight 1980, pp. 26–37)
- sensation novels (narratives which revolve around a mysterious hidden secret, for example, Wilkie Collins's *The Woman in White* (1860); see Stewart 1980; Rance 1991; Pykett 1994)
- hard-boiled narratives (tales which are characterised by a particular 'trimmed-down' style and complementary world-view; Knight 1980, pp. 135–67; Ogdon 1992; Chapter 3 below)

Before we say much more about these, it should be clear that each of the 'bases' is traversed by the voices of previous genres. Chapbook tales of criminality pre-dated the *Newgate Calendar*; the *Odyssey* of Homer came before the adventure story; gothic narratives came before the sensation novel; and it was evident that there was a reading public for the romance, the epic, the tragedy and religious tracts (see Hunter 1990).

That we can identify partial antecedents for these 'bases' is significant, although not because it might enable literary historians to uncover the ultimate origins of a genre. Instead, it indicates that any genre in the present may include one or more features of previous genres and that the combination might be complex or such that it renders the old generic feature either unrecognizable or, at the least, different. This is the important point for the analysis of contemporary genres, and is the reason for promoting the term 'thriller' rather than trying to identify discrete subgenres with unilinear genealogies.

Without much difficulty, contemporary subgenres of the thriller can be shown to partake of the multiple 'bases' that we have mentioned (and which, we have suggested, possess their own bases). If we take an obvious example, the contemporary spy novel – especially as it has developed after John Le Carré – has frequently been analysed as, on one level, an offshoot of hard-boiled fiction (see, for example, Harper 1969, pp. 20–23; Barley 1986, p. 35). This is an observation, once more, of the dissolution of semantic/syntactic features in that the hard-boiled style (semantic *and* syntactic) is seen to be appropriate to the cynicism of superpower espionage both during and after the Cold War (semantic *and* syntactic) as it is depicted in spy stories. Moreover, in its focus on intricate deductions and on the exploits of characters in (potentially) hostile environments, the spy novel is semantically/syntactically related to the 'ratiocinative' and 'adventure', at least.

The same kind of thing can be said of all the 'sub-'genres under discussion in this book. The crime fiction I discuss in Chapter 4, with its focus on low life and street talk, is undoubtedly related to the Newgate confessional (as is the spate of gangster films produced in the early 1930s, to which the crime novel is also related). The stories of a black underworld discussed in Chapter 6 are linked semantically/syntactically with the fiction in Chapter 4, and also, in their own way, to the Newgate confessional. Not only this, because of a specific reading formation in which questions about 'blackness' are foregrounded, the black underworld texts are bound to genres of black detection (such as Fisher's *The Conjure Man Dies* (1932), itself carrying traces of the ratiocinative) and stories of black private investigators (like *Shaft* (1970), itself carrying traces of the hard-boiled).

In Chapter 3, the hard-boiled genre of the 1970s finds itself grappling with the heritage of the original hard-boiled school of the 1930s to 1950s, largely because elements in the reading formation in the period pose some serious semantic/syntactic problems.[8] The fiction about police operatives discussed in Chapter 5 evidently has generic relations with police memoirs, but some texts have links with the crime novel (because of their graphic and involved depiction of criminal activities) and some are traversed by the ratiocinative. Because of the particular reading formation of the early 1970s, one of the narratives examined in

Chapter 5 has strong ties with the paranoid texts which are featured in Chapter 7.

The revenge texts which are discussed in Chapter 8 can be seen as an outgrowth of the cynical voice instituted in the hard-boiled. As we will see, they are also linked closely to the paranoid narratives of Chapter 7 and, in their descent into the street, to the crime fiction of Chapter 4. (Questions of 'race' in the revenge texts especially, place them in an oblique relation to the black fiction of Chapter 6, and if the street is a hostile and remote environment in this reading formation, then revenge texts also relate to the adventure base.)

Finally, the paranoid thrillers have a rich generic heritage. They partake of the cynicism of the hard-boiled, the moral voice and buried secrets of the sensation novel, the strange environments of adventure and the intellectual challenge of the ratiocinative. Yet, as we will see, the paranoid thrillers are very much of their time and are strongly linked to contemporary subgenres, some of which we have already mentioned and another of which is the spy/espionage novel.

The thriller, then, is a complex hybrid, a huge body of texts from the industry of popular culture, each with tortile skeins of heritage to past texts and genres. As we have seen, the thriller is also partly the product of readers' expectations which are often encouraged by features of a 'reading formation'. In fact, if there is anything that lends organisation to the ravelled intra-generic strands of the thriller it is the expectation of a specific verisimilitude, the assumption of a close relation between the 'rules of the genre' and the *doxa*. We need to be careful, however, that after having demonstrated the multiple determinants of a genre, that we do not assume that these determinants count for nothing in the face of 'history'. Because thrillers fulfil the requirements of verisimilitude it would be easy to jump to the conclusion that they are straightforward 'reflections' of 'history' or the real world. Understanding thrillers from the past in this formulation would simply amount to a cross-referencing with the historical record in order to 'read off' and once again 'short-circuit' their meaning.[9]

In a powerful essay, Gallagher (1986) argues that, in addition to accounting for the breadth of a genre we need to be sensitive to – rather than patronising about – the historical period in which a generic text appeared. This is especially true if we wish to address questions of 'evolution' or 'generic innovation'. Against the critics who think that the Western film has grown progressively more widespread and sophisticated in its narrative structure, he shows that the genre has a much more complicated history. In the period 1907–1915 there were probably more Westerns released *each month* than during the entire decade of the 1930s, and as a result the Western, and numerous plots associated with it, were very much in the contemporary cinema-goer's consciousness (p. 205). Early cinema audiences were not only generically literate, they also inhabited a social formation which, it could be argued, was every bit as complex as our own.

A simplistic evolutionary theory of 'history', then, cannot be the ultimate guy-rope for fixing the meaning of generic texts from yesteryear (see Staiger 1997).

The abuse and use of history in understanding genres

For Gallagher, the problem with critics is that they ignore the evidence of reading practices, preferring a blanket assumption about the period in which genre texts are located.[10] Given that we are concerned in this book with the place of generic texts in past environments, and given that we have thus far stressed the discursive determinants of genre, we should say, then, precisely what we mean by 'history'. We are doubly bound to do this by the fact such commentators on the thriller as Haycraft (1979), Symons (1992), Panek (1987), Shadoian (1978), Clarens (1980) and Mandel (1984) share the assumption that history is the ultimate determinant, a last court of appeal whose character can be established with a minimum of difficulty.

Commenting on such tendencies, Bennett (1990, p. 53) notes that there are two senses in which writing on the literature/history couplet can conceive history. These are the sense of history as discourse and the sense of history as an extra-textual real. Anybody who has struggled over the ramifications of the concept of the frontier in American history or the manifold problems of the validity of the Fischer Thesis knows that history is a subject arranged around texts or, as Bennett says, 'what can be derived from the historical record or archive' (1990, p. 49). Although there are countless examples and discussions of the way in which history as it is written changes from period to period (see Jenkins 1997), it is only relatively recently that such debates have entered literary studies.

The theoretical movement towards the reconsideration of history within a formation of textuality – or, as Bennett puts it, where history proves to be an intradiscursive and mutable 'referent' (1990, pp. 50–1) – has become known as 'the New Historicism', a label which cuts across a number of disciplines but is mainly centred around literary theory (see Hamilton 1996; Veeser 1989). The New Historicism basically literarizes history and makes evident that the text of history is as full of lacunae as literary texts. One theoretical consequence of recognizing the textuality of history is that it no longer becomes that last court of appeal in which to settle arguments about readings of texts (Bennington 1987, p. 20). As a logical consequence, if history is no longer an explanatory principle outside the domain of textuality, then the next logical theoretical move is to consider history's effectivity as only part of the phenomenon of textuality as a whole (Porter 1990).

All this is not to say that the human inhabitants of the past experienced historical events only discursively. Such an assertion would be as absurd as to suggest that humans only suffer the effects of war, famine and wage slavery through discourse. However, there are a large number of events in the present that *are* only available to humans in a mediated way. While most inhabitants of 1970s America might have had direct experience of the Vietnam War through a loved one, acquaintance or themselves having done a tour of duty, details of the war in general would largely have been available through discourses such as 'news'. While the same inhabitants might have had direct experience of corrupt individuals leading to an opinion on the topic, political corruption on a larger scale could be viewed through televisations of events in the Watergate affair. Furthermore, the investigation from the standpoint of the present of how even unmediated events affected humans in the past *must* approach such events through discourse. History for our purposes, then, becomes one member of the discursive regime sustained by material means which is a reading formation.

'History' and generic innovation

The abuse of 'history' as an extra-textual referent has been particularly prevalent in histories of genres, and specifically with reference to questions of 'generic innovation' or 'evolution'. By relying on history or social change as a concrete, immutable backdrop, thriller histories have produced models of evolution based on either personal preference, literary worth, textual mechanisms abstracted from texts as isolated specimens, linear progression towards greater sophistication or disintegration, or often a combination of all of these. In some accounts, history has been seen as contributing to the 'semantic filling' of generic texts (for example, Symons 1992); other accounts see history in the 'syntax' of the thriller, those approaches suggesting that capitalist social relations of production are mirrored in the very structure of the thriller at its inception, and for all time, no matter what the 'semantic' content (for example, Palmer 1978). For the former, the movement of history and the demand for new semantic filling promotes generic innovation in the form of new subgenres, and stagnation in texts which retain aspects of the past (Symons 1992, for instance, plots the movement from detective fiction to the crime novel); for the latter, generic innovation effectively does not take place – no matter what semantic embodiment of social change exists – until the whole syntax of the thriller is superseded (Mandel 1984).

Although generic innovation *can* often revolve around some syntactic or semantic mutation, it is clear that neither of the above positions is satisfactory. Even when semantic or syntactic mutations do take place, in order for them to have any kind of effectiveness as innovation they will need to be subject to the appropriate ordering by a reading formation. That is to say, they will need to be the objects of specific investments and expectations by readers. What I am arguing is that reader investments in generic texts, which take place in a reading formation, are the crucial issue. If readers understand certain thriller 'content' to be new and innovative, then innovation takes place without a wholesale transformation of the genre's syntax. A film like *Scarface* (1981), for example, can still embody innovation as a result of its reception, even though its syntax is not far removed from *The Public Enemy* (1931). And while such generic innovation *is* to be thought of as a 'product of its time', it is expressly *not* to be considered as 'naive', 'primitive' or just one small step toward greater sophistication (see Welsch 1997). The *breadth* of determinants acting upon the reading of generic texts is as great in the 1970s as it is in the first decade of the twenty-first century. The role of social change in light of our recognition of breadth, then, is as one of a number of discursive processes which can affect the reading of the semantic/syntactic realm of thriller texts in terms of its 'topicality', 'relevance', 'freshness' – in short, in satisfying expectations of verisimilitude.

In summary, then, I have argued that the problem of understanding texts' reception in history is the result of failing to consider the extra-textual determinants in a reading formation. Moreover, I have argued that genre texts are doubly prone to this problem. This is because their potential multiplicity is subject to a plethora of institutionalised 'short-circuiting' devices: expectations of verisimilitude, processes of canonisation, foreshortened 'histories' of generic development and beliefs in the relation of genres to social change. While all of these might, in some measure, allow the consumer of generic texts to bracket out extraneous considerations and get on with the pleasurable business of reading the generic text, for the analyst they constitute a failure to acknowledge the breadth of determinants operating on genres, as well as a neglect of the reader. It will be our task in the forthcoming chapters not only to specu-late on the numerous determinants of contemporary readings but also, through close analysis of neglected features of generic texts, to restore to the latter their multiplicity, the very grounds upon which one reading rather than another might be chosen.

Two further comments should be added. As I have argued, the rela-tions between fictional texts within a reading formation can exert a commercial and 'artistic' determining force on texts within any genre under discussion. Thus, bestsellers, for example, can in some way 'define' a genre at a given moment. In the next chapter we will be examining how the 'blockbusters' of the 1970s contributed to and over-lapped with the 'thriller' in this period.

Secondly, if history is only one among a number of competing ele-ments in a reading formation it may be that relations between different textualities are overdetermined, so that features of fictional texts make their effects felt in the discursive practice of history. In the next chapter, therefore, we will also be examining the key role played by the over-lapping of history and fiction in the 1970s 'non-fiction thriller'.

2
Reading the Space of the Seventies

In this 1970s a number of thrillers an unprecedented prominence for readers: *Jaws, The Godfather,* and *All the President's Men* as well as such films as *The Exorcist* (1973) and disaster movies like *The Towering Inferno* (1974). While these texts can be read as thrillers without too much difficulty, they often have an ambiguous relationship to the corpus of thrillers as it is classified by either historians or the industries that produce the texts. We will argue that there are two general kinds of texts which play an especially important role in ordering readers' expectations in a reading formation. The 'blockbuster' refers to those texts (in film and/or print) which attract such an amount of revenue and publicity that it almost seems impossible for citizens participating in contemporary life to ignore them. The 'non-fiction thriller' refers to those texts which narrate, in a dramatic and often suspenseful way, events from current social and political affairs, such that those texts become a byword or shorthand reference for the events in question.

The non-fiction thriller

It is often assumed that the categories of writing designated by the terms 'non-fiction' and 'fiction' are fundamentally different. Fiction could be said to deal with imagined events, while non-fiction takes as its raw material facts about the real world. Yet even if this is correct, such a definition does not take into account the similarities involved in each mode's processing of its raw material. In America especially, in the period leading up to the 1970s, post-modernist writers challenged notions concerned with the status of the non-fictional. Novels by Norman Mailer, E.L. Doctorow, and William Styron among others dealt with documentary subjects in innovative ways. Similarly, less valorized texts such as

Irving Stone's books or Alex Haley's *Roots* (1976) demonstrated the narrowness of the line between biography and novel. At the level of the actual discourse employed by fictional and non-fictional texts, these examples seem to suggest, there is the capacity for considerable overlap. There may be a difference between the raw material of the fictional and the non-fictional but they share significant components in the act of representation.

In the last two decades Hayden White has questioned the very process of writing historical texts, insisting that history and fiction are related by virtue of the function of representation (for example, 1987, p. 121). Discourse, which includes fiction and history, is orientated towards the act of representation by means of invoking some kind of knowledge of the real world. As White points out, the conflation of fiction and history is not without precedent in historiography, particularly before the French revolution (1987, p. 123; see also White 1973), and this conflation obtained until the nineteenth century. White emphasises the fundamental similarity of the categories of signs utilized in fiction and in discourses about the world outside of fiction. Taking the fact of the distortion involved in ordering facts (which is well known by historians) White demonstrates that the fiction/history division is often posited simply on the basis of surface differences (1987, p. 125). By confronting the essential sameness of the principles involved in the process of narrativization White's project has seriously problematised the fictional/non-fictional division.

The recognition of difficulties in this division is by no means new. Countless analysts of textuality have devoted themselves to the question of what makes the fictional different from the non-fictional, many of whom wish to avoid positing a 'realism' which mutates from epoch to epoch. Branigan (1992), for instance, insists that the reader of a non-fiction begins with a notion of an historically 'real' situation and a mechanism of production from which the reader attempts 'to infer the direct, and relatively unmediated, consequences of the conjunction of that situation and the production'; the reader of a fiction does the opposite, beginning with the representation and then constructing a sense of the mediations involved (pp. 204–5). Valiantly, Branigan attempts to account for the impetus to read fictively (or non-fictively) by reference to cues *within* different texts; but even he must admit that there are such devices as marketing, *outside* of texts, which give cues for reading (p. 201).

More productively, Kress and van Leeuwen (1996) show how 'modality' can be understood across linguistic and visual texts. Certain sentences such as 'people think that the cat sat on the mat' have low modality because the marker 'people think that' serves to distance the reader from a direct statement regarding the cat's location of sitting. Similarly, in visual representation, low modality may be the result of a specific use of colour or a particular use of technology – Kress and van Leeuwen note that photo-realism is invariably highly valued and therefore has high modality (p. 164). Most importantly, however, they insist that the nature of fiction and low modality, or non-fiction and high modality, is produced by particular social groups. Those who are *already* convinced – owing to a range of social affiliations – that the cat *did* sit on the mat, will not, on reading the sentence, necessarily attribute low modality to the marker 'people think that'.

Readers of the non-fiction thriller are in a similar position. The narrative may 'objectively' contain all the devices that are associated with fiction of a particular kind – editing of the mundane, dialogue, narration of characters' thoughts, and so on: that is to say, potentially low modality. However, the reader may be able to overlook many of these 'fictional' devices if s/he is sufficiently confident during the process of interaction with the text, that what is being depicted bears a close relation to what was thought to have gone on in the real world. Such knowledge can be gleaned from publicity discourses about a narrative, news discourses, or any other means in the reading formation of imbuing a reading with the sense of non-fictional content. This, of course, is exacerbated by the very fact that the thriller's specific verisimilitude is constituted by the convergence of textual consistency and public opinion regarding the social and political world.

What follows is an attempt to identify how readings of non-fictional thrillers might have taken place in the 1970s and then become installed as a feature of readings of other thrillers. In spite of their status as 'non-fiction', the texts we will consider have crucial generic characteristics by virtue of expectations regarding their content. Among well-known non-fiction thrillers of the period there are narratives about private eyes (Armes and Nolan 1976; Pileggi 1976); about corrupt police operatives (Maas 1974 (filmed 1973): see below, Chapter 5); about professional thieves (Hohimer 1975 (filmed 1981); about 'super' cops (Whittlemore 1974; Greenberg 1977); about retaliatory commando raids against terrorism (Stevenson and Dan 1976); about Mafia families (see also below, this chapter); about Nazi resurgency (Erdstein and Bean 1979); and numerous narratives of rampant intelligence agencies (the most famous is Marchetti and Marks 1975).

Many of these texts (and the blockbusters) consist of more than one text in that they were soon made into films, and have a very close relation with the publicity which surrounds them. We will discuss a sample of these narratives in terms of how readings of them might be governed on the basis of their relationships with factors outside of themselves. As it is impossible to be exhaustive with regard to a given text's range of potential extra-textual cues, the following analyses can only ask preliminary questions about the constitution of a reading formation. Reviews, for instance, do not represent the ultimate authority on the contemporary reading of a text: to begin with, it is questionable what per centage of the cinema-going public reads *even one* review of a film, let alone reads it in a uniform way or accepts its premises. Nevertheless, as we mentioned in respect to Altman's (1999) arguments in Chapter 1, reviews provide one important set of provisional grounds for assessing contemporary opinion on a given narrative.

All the President's Men

All the President's Men is famous for being the book by the two reporters from the *Washington Post* who pursued the Watergate story from its beginning. Published in 1974, its appearance before the resignation of President Nixon guaranteed it an aura of topicality. *All the President's Men* is a narrative of events from a limited perspective, based around the two journalist protagonists acting, in the main, as one. On this point it is worth noting the first few pages where Woodward embarks on some work in the *Washington Post* offices:

As Woodward began making phone calls, he noticed that Bernstein, one of the paper's two Virginia political reporters, was working on the burglary story, too.

Oh God, not Bernstein, Woodward thought, recalling several office tales about Bernstein's ability to push his way into a good story and get his byline on it.

That morning, Bernstein had Xeroxed copies of notes from reporters at the scene and informed the city editor that he would make some more checks. The city editor had shrugged his acceptance, and Bernstein had begun a series of phone calls to everybody at the Watergate he could reach – desk clerks, bellmen, maids in the housekeeping department, waiters in the restaurant.

Bernstein looked across the newsroom. There was a pillar between his desk and Woodward's, about 25 feet away. He stepped back several paces. It appeared that Woodward was also working on the story. That figured, Bernstein thought. Bob Woodward was a prima donna who played heavily at office politics (1974 pp. 14–15).

The narrative in this passage shifts perspective from one character to another. Previously Woodward has been working on the story and the events narrated are ones in which he has been involved. It is therefore his impression of Bernstein which is offered first. Then, for the first time, the narrative's perspective shifts and we get Bernstein's impression of Woodward. It is significant that this is achieved by an almost cinematic device: the narrative's initiation of Bernstein's perspective begins with a look to Woodward's side of the office, the space from where Woodward's look and assessment of Bernstein's character has just been made.

For the reader, the point of all this at the level of narration is to satisfy any questions about who narrates rather than to set up the humour of their initial antagonism. Not only does the book give the 'truth' and the 'inside' account of Watergate but it promises knowledge which has hitherto been unavailable to the public. As the public presumably knows a certain amount about the affair, this book serves as a *fuller version*. At the same time, though, the narrative hints at a version that cannot yet be known. While its selling point is that it might tell the reader about all those details that the reader might not have acquired with regard to a story s/he already knows, *All the President's Men* preserves the logic of such revelations in its own way by leaving out some details about the affair for various reasons.

One of the most celebrated of these concerned Woodward and Bernstein's sources who had usually remained anonymous in the actual newspaper reports that had cited them. However, with regard to the main source, it was a non-revelation. Woodward's key contact – dubbed 'Deep Throat' by Howard Simons after a famous pornographic film of the period – remains unnamed, a fact that elicited various speculations (Haldeman with diMona 1978, pp. 135–7; 'Watergate on Film', *Time* 29 March 1976, p. 43; Gilliatt 1976). Clearly, the figure of Deep Throat provoked a lot of interest; not only does s/he lie at the heart of the narrative's logic of revelation and delay but s/he also embodies the story's paranoid motif (see also Chapter 7 below). Paranoid states are evident from the moment of Deep Throat's entry into the narrative; all those subsequent passages where the figure appears take on the paraphernalia of a spy story, utilising codes, secret rendezvous, the fear of surveillance, darkness and subterranean locations (p. 72). In order for Woodward and Bernstein's 'paranoid' interpretations about the Nixon administration to continue they require some kind of verification. Deep Throat provides confirmation of the suspicions resulting from prior research and encourages further research and conclusions (see especially pp. 132, 172, 316–17).

It is partly through the figure of Deep Throat that fear of the authorities is induced. Seemingly innocent situations suddenly become charged with meaning. For instance, when Deep Throat fails to show for an underground garage rendezvous Woodward is in a state of terror which manifests itself in multiple interpretations of what such an absence entails (p. 172). This spreads to Bernstein who, when he meets an FBI source in the innocent, clean and touristy atmosphere of the White House compound, constantly thinks he has been set up as the agent involves himself in everyday activities such as tying his shoelaces (p. 176). An ultimate answer to the riddle is not provided and, like other scenes of putative paranoia, their interpretation will depend partly on a knowledge of the Watergate affair for a reading of them as such.

One major 'external' determinant of readings of the narrative is the fact that, within two years of the publication of *All the President's Men* a high-profile film of the story had been released. In spite of this lag of time between the two texts, it could be argued that destinies of both the book and the film versions were intertwined from the outset and the enunciative imperatives of the latter shaped the narrative of the former, particularly as Robert Redford (who was eventually to play Woodward) effectively commissioned the original book and influenced the authors to play up their own participation and the human angle in the breaking of the Watergate story (see BFI n.d., p. 4).

Probably even more than the average Hollywood film, one cannot make judgements on the construction of the meaning of *All the President's Men* without taking into account the role of its stars. In addition to Redford's impetus in the generation of the Woodward/Bernstein project, Arnold (1976b) points to *Three Days of the Condor* (1975), Redford's previous film. Here, Redford plays a lowly copy-reader working for a branch of the intelligence services who finds himself on the run after his colleagues have been massacred by mysterious gunmen. As in many paranoid narratives of the period, the hero discovers that the gunmen work not for a foreign force but for a different branch of the American intelligence services, and he eventually takes this story to the press (the *New York Times* in this case). The suspense and paranoia that characterized the first narrative was carried over into the second: it was widely reported that 'Redford saw the film [*All the President's Men*] as a detective story not as a polemic against Nixon' ('Watergate on Film',

p. 42). Moreover, publications such as *Atlantic Monthly*, and the *Denver Post* had called the book 'a political thriller' and 'one of the greatest detective stories ever told' (BFI n.d., p. 5).

All the President's Men is clearly an important non-fiction thriller. It stands out in the 1970s as *the* text about Watergate, a text whose veracity is almost beyond question by virtue of the narrators' key role in the events depicted. As such, then, *All the President's Men* can be seen to be very close to the events. But if we look at this idea more closely, the events are only ever available insofar as they are mediated by signs and discourses. What is interesting about *All the President's Men* is that only if its modality was recognised as relatively low could the text be indisputably separated as a category from those other discourses that present social and political reality in the contemporary period. If one were to say that news discourses have primacy over a narrative published in book form one would have to take into account in this case the fact that the authors of this book were actually designated as the makers of the news by other texts, and certainly foregrounded in their own. The topicality of the book was so great as to separate the gap between the categories of news and non-fiction thriller (but for a more detailed consideration of the film's fidelity to the facts, see Leuchtenberg 1995).

Dog Day Afternoon

When leaving a Brooklyn branch bank in 1972, from which he and his companion, Sal Naturile, had conducted an armed snatch of $29,000, John Wojtowicz, a 27–year old Vietnam veteran, found that the bank was surrounded by police. The pair then held hostage nine members of the bank staff for 14 hours. As the media arrived on the scene to cover the siege it became clear that the robbery had been staged to finance a sex-change operation for Wojtowicz's transsexual 'wife', Ernest Aron. After negotiating a plane from JFK, Naturile was shot dead by an FBI agent at the airport and Wojtowicz was arrested. Although the attempted robbery took place and was covered on prime time television in New York, the texts of the event we will be concerned with consist of a famous *Life* magazine article, a 'fictional' book of the story, a popular and critically acclaimed film and some of the reviews and features that this spawned.

A few of the difficulties involved in negotiating these different texts can be mentioned now. In the *Life* article, the names of the protagonists are John Wojtowicz and Sal Naturile; this article and other sources reveal that, in the Greenwich Village gay community, Wojtowicz was known as Littlejohn Basso (Kluge and Moore 1972, p. 68; Bell quoted in Holm

1976, p. 3); the book, *Dog Day Afternoon* (1975) by Patrick Mann, refers to him as Joe Nowicki, known in the gay community as Littlejoe, while his partner in crime is called Sam; the film features Al Pacino in the main role, but this time the character is called Sonny. The film is called *Dog Day Afternoon* although its resemblance to the book of that name is superficial: as we have noted, the names of the protagonists are different, but the book focuses on the robbery as only part of its story. Despite its name, the film's credits attest that it is based on the *Life* magazine article by Kluge and Moore, and the original working title for the film was the same as that of the article, 'The Boys in the Bank' (see Holm 1976, p. 3). Finding the definitive text of the John Wojtowicz story, then, is a task fraught with difficulties, especially if one considers that news bulletins also covered it extensively.

At the head of the first page of Kluge and Moore's article there is a quote about Wojtowicz and Naturile from a teller in the siege – 'They'd have been hilarious – as guests on a Saturday night' – which appears beneath a photograph of the manager, Barrett, and one of the other tellers (p. 68). Clearly, this is like no other hostage situation that has previously been reported. The ruthlessness of the robbers and the antagonism between them and their captives is absent or, at the very least, muted. The article narrates such facts to stress the outstanding nature of its subject matter. Later, both Shirley Ball and Barrett have chances to leave the bank; the latter is to be driven to a hospital for a cardiogram but he declines the offer from the examining doctor while he alone is the only person to know that his diabetic condition is not serious (p. 72).

The most salient example of the moral ambiguity of the whole event is narrated in the form of a dialogue between Wojtowicz and Barrett. Most of the blurring of the lines amongst the captors and captives, and the lack of antagonism that has been mentioned has not constituted an explicit questioning of the society outside the bank. Then, the following passage occurs:

> Sometimes in the lengthening night, John Wojtowicz shares some of his puzzled thoughts with Barrett. He wonders aloud: 'Now, I can shoot *you* and they won't give me the gas chamber. But if I shoot a cop, I get it. Now I wonder: if I put a gun at your head and another gun in your hand and made *you* shoot the cop, would you get it?'
>
> (p. 70)

The presence of such statements indicates that the story of the siege is one which poses a set of profound moral difficulties. Chief amongst these is the question of whether John and Sal are necessarily bad people, although the final moralizing tone of the *Life* article starts to guide an interpretation.

The book (Mann 1975) attempts to go much further than the article and the film by presenting thoughts, events and motives in the life of its protagonist, Joe Nowicki/Littlejoe. This, of course, would be expected to exemplify a low modality, although, as Kress and van Leeuwen argue, for certain groups, supposedly low modality representations are, in a sense, more accurate. Diagrams, for example, may reveal a 'deeper reality' of a phenomenon for the scientific community than photographs (1996, p. 163). We cannot know that the novel version of Wojtowicz's story is the most accurate representation of the events for contemporary readers but it certainly has the ability to exemplify some aspects of the siege in a memorable way.

The character of Joe is one aspect of the narrative which might be more suitably illustrated in 'fictional' scenes. One of the reasons that Joe's character does not offer itself to easy explanation is because there is a more general blurring of morality which engulfs him. There are two ways of approaching this: one is through the organization of the generic elements of the text and another is through the almost flippant references to Vietnam in the narrative. If one considers the question of professionalism it is clear that, in one sense, the narrative presents Joe as an amateur. The accusation of amateurism is based, it seems, on the lack of a ruthless authoritarian streak in Joe. Moreover, this cannot be attributed either to a lack of expertise or a deficiency in Joe's character alone; instead it must be seen in relation to a general erosion in respect for authority. At one stage in the robbery one of the tellers accuses Joe of incompetence and bad language which provokes the following amusing response:

> 'Jesus H. Christ!' Joe burst out at the top of his lungs. 'This is a gun, Marge. One more word out of you and the slug gets you right in the left tit. What the fuck is the world coming to? I hold a gun on this broad and she badmouths me to my face? What is that?' (p. 114)

This is a blatant example of a world where the expected paraphernalia of authority – in this case, a gun – no longer elicits the required response unless it is accompanied by a certain poise and a lack of warm-heartedness.

Given that the amateurs are the protagonists of this story, Fredric Jameson suggests that the narrative requires a character version of the impersonality of post-industrial capitalism. Essentially, for Jameson, the social dissidence of the 'freaks' in the film is an embodiment of 1960s radicalism, protests against racism, sexism etc., which he insists is bourgeois in character because it is not class orientated (1979, p. 76). As a result, the film depicts Sonny and Sal as the amateur, idiosyncratic, human representatives of sixties protest while the FBI man in the film (Baker) is, in contrast, a professional yet uncharismatic (p. 86). Ironically, the character who is most 'inside' American society is totally flattened by it; the misfits – made especially so by their veteran status and the difficulties of assimilating the Vietnam experience into seventies America (see Chapter 8) – stick out like sore thumbs. Whether audiences would recognize the competition of human warmth versus cool impersonality, grass roots protest versus the untrustworthy establishment or bourgeois dissidence against the aloofness of post-industrial capitalism depends on the depth of analysis. However, it seems that extratextual cues about the film did not consider such general grounds for a reading of it.

Clearly, the story is merely about bungled crimes on one level. When Sonny attempts to lock the tellers into the safe one of them insists that she must go to the bathroom and he relents. This is amateurism; but more importantly, perhaps, it illustrates a lack of ruthlessness on Sonny's part. Similarly, the lengthy siege which ensues could be construed as a cack-handed attempt to circumvent a situation that should never have happened.[1] In the *New Yorker*, Penelope Gilliatt wrote of 'the first movie I know of about a bank robbery and an attempted hijacking to have been made as a farce' (1975). Holm (1976, p. 3) favourably compares *Dog Day Afternoon* to such films as *Bank Shot* (1974) and *Cops and Robbers* (1973). Other possible responses to *Dog Day Afternoon* centre around its gay theme (see Kay 1976; Babuscio 1976, p. 8; Wood 1976, p. 35). Such cues foster a reading of the text which highlights its complexity, diversity, and even the strangeness of truth over fiction at the expense of a possible reading of it as a suspenseful linear narrative.

Fredric Jameson has also argued that the story contains three novelties: the crowd's sympathy with Sal and Sonny (John Wojtowicz), particularly when the latter invokes the name of Attica; the fact that the bank robber is a homosexual who commits the robbery to finance a sex-change operation for his 'wife'; and that the siege turned into a media event which eclipsed the Nixon–Agnew nomination of the same day (Jameson 1979, p. 78). The means by which the film conveys these 'novelties' suggests a tension in the way that the narrative and the dialogue generate meaning. Early in the film, as the robbery turns into a siege, Sonny manically expresses his consternation about the police by mentioning the word 'Attica' to the bank manager; without any preamble, or any subsequent explanation of this word; the manager seems to understand exactly what Sonny means. A suitably informed contemporary audience would realize that 'Attica' refers to the prison where – only a short time before the events which are narrated in the film – armed police brutally suppressed a disturbance, leading to numerous prisoner fatalities.

Dog Day Afternoon, in this context, is almost the quintessential example of generic innovation in this period. Incorporating themes and material which, to reviewers, seemed extraneous to the thriller genre, the film actually generated extra-textual cues which problematized its reading as a genre text even though it could still be demonstrated to be a thriller. This was no doubt enhanced by its non-fictional status. In fact, some critics even acknowledged that the film was so thoroughly imbued with a sense of the import of social change in America that it expressed the commonplace nature rather than the 'weirdness' of the bank heist (Schickel 1975; Canby 1975).

The specific exigencies of magazine articles, fictional books, star cast films and raw material that is already a media event as it happens make *Dog Day Afternoon* a curious chimera. If genre is taken to be a limitation of the range of readings that can be generated by a text, while non-fictionality is to be characterized by its complexity and the strangeness of its truth over fiction, then the texts of the Wojtowicz bank siege constitute a clear example of overlap. Even when considering the text as a thriller, the extra-textual cues promote a reading of the film in terms of its complexity rather than as a pure gangster movie and the identification of such a tension in the text is one way of locating generic innovation.

The blockbuster

Further innovations during the period took place contiguous to the thriller. The 1970s saw the growth of a particular phenomenon with regard to the commercial production of narrative. This was not the bestseller, which had been around for some time, so much as the *massively popular* text which existed in a number of media and was subject to huge publicity. Such texts outsold their nearest rivals by some considerable distance, and, through advance publicity, subsequent circulation and marketing in areas outside the general remit of publishing became part of the cultural fabric of America and other countries, for short, or sometimes extended periods (Sutherland 1981, p. 9).

If we consider the first five titles from Sutherland's (1981) list of the top ten fiction bestsellers of the 1970s, it is notable that three of them can be considered to have a great deal in common with the thriller genre in general. The list is as follows: 1. *The Godfather* (1969) 2. *The Exorcist* (1971) 3. *Jonathan Livingston Seagull* (1970) 4. *Love Story* (1970), and, 5. *Jaws* (1974). *The Godfather, The Exorcist* and *Jaws* all resemble the thriller in a general sense, whether by virtue of the centrality of expectations of suspense to their narratives or by expectations of a concentration on the world of crime in *The Godfather*, for example. Not only did these texts exist in such massive- selling form as books, but they also gained a high profile in the 1970s as films, appearing very soon after the print version of their texts. If we look at the top grossing films of the 1970s in terms of rentals in North America we find in third place *Jaws* (1975) with $133.4m; fourth is *Grease* (1978), then come *The Exorcist* (1973) and *The Godfather* (1972).

All of these texts were also subject to new strategies of advance publicity designed to saturate the public with some kind of knowledge of the texts' contents. These strategies were often based on some aspect of the text which was not necessarily integral to the narrative, and occasionally involved marketing of products such as toys which had some reference to the narratives. Amongst other features which these texts hold in common, the important one for our purposes is that their extraordinarily high profile in American culture of the period entailed that they were perceived as the arenas for debate over the meaning of the contemporary social formation. In order to delineate the importance of these factors for the reading of American thrillers in the 1970s we will consider just two blockbusters.

The Godfather

The Godfather – whose first manifestation was in a novel by Mario Puzo (1970) – was one of a number of texts in the 1970s which took as their theme the merging of the old traditions of Sicilian or Italian families with the exigencies of the American way of life (cf. non-fiction such as Teresa 1973, Talese 1971 and Maas 1970; plus fiction, e.g. Quarry 1972 (filmed 1973)). The book spent 67 weeks on the bestseller lists after it was published in 1969, selling 1 million copies in hardback and 12 million in paperback before the film was released (Biskind 1990, p. 4). The film built upon publicity derived from the fame of the book and generated its own before it was even released (see, for example, Setlowe 1971). Part of the advance publicity for the film was centred around its main star who, by this time, was considered a legend in American cinema. Although he only worked on the film for six weeks (Biskind 1990, p. 6), Marlon Brando was the focus of much of the film's advance publicity in articles such as those describing how the living legend still had to take a screen test for the part of Don Corleone (see, for example, *Variety* 8 March 1972).

The recently appointed Paramount chief, Frank Yablans, was responsible for a 'Barnumesque' publicity strategy which involved, on the film's opening in New York, multiple staggered showings of the film in various cinemas and raised ticket prices (Biskind 1990, pp. 66–8). The press also reported various scams that were employed by queue-jumpers and ticket touts as well as a stick-up at a cinema showing *The Godfather* in New York which netted its perpetrators $13,000 (Cocks 1972b, p. 37). Biskind reports a plethora of spin-off products from the renaming of a recent Jean-Pierre Melville film to *The Godson*, to the creation of *Godfather* pizzas (p. 68). The publicity, it seems, paid off; the title of a *Variety* article of 9 May 1973 explains the situation: 'With All Else, "Godfather" into Perch as All-Time Rental No. 1, U.S.-Canada' (see also the figures in Green 1972a; 1972b). More important, though, is that the success of the film became part of the film's overall meaning as it was formulated by reviewers and critics (see, for example, Cocks 1972b, p. 37).

The narrative of *The Godfather* concerns Vito Corleone, an Italian immigrant to America who has built a business empire based on crime and who has trodden a path from penniless worker to exalted elder of the 1940s Italian-American community. Corleone has a number of sons, the youngest of whom is Michael, a college-educated war hero who wishes to build a life outside the family business. When his father is shot by a rival family, Michael is inexorably drawn into the family's concerns, eventually assuming his father's mantle after the latter's death. The possibility of a number of different readings within this framework means that the narrative is manifestly an arena of contest, especially to those intimately involved with its production. Puzo, for instance, claims contra those critics who gave a greater value to the social criticism contained within the film than the book, that 'the Vietnam and big business parallels were built into the novel' (Puzo 1972, p. 240). If he is correct about the general irony of the narration of the novel (ibid., p. 65), then there is every reason to suggest that readings might be arranged around a wry acceptance of the surface appearances and the acknowledgement of a deeper truth, a process of scepticism and cynicism that could be said to have been growing in the contemporary period with regard to Vietnam.

Reviewers were quick to highlight the very American theme of a movie which featured so much Italian in its narrative. So, *Time* among others christened the film 'an Italian-American *Gone with the Wind*' ('The Making of *The Godfather*', *Time* 13 March 1972; cf. William F. Buckley in Biskind 1990, p. 65, and Francis Ford Coppola quoted in 'The Making of *The Godfather*', *Time* 13 March 1972). Focusing on the portrayal of the essence of American life, such extra-textual cues often attributed complexity to *The Godfather* narrative in its cinematic version (usually to the detriment of the novel – see 'What Is *The Godfather* Saying?', *Time* 3 April 1972, p. 39). As Biskind shows, most reviews were divided along the lines of 'raves' or 'pans', and mostly the raves praised the film's diversity and richness while the pans classified it in generic terms or as a public relations exercise for organized crime or both (1990, p. 65).

Whether critics took the view that *The Godfather* was a subtle exploration of the American social system or a glorification of the Mafia they were all agreed on one thing. Moral ambiguity, and in this case the co-existence of traditional family values with organized crime, was now the order of the day. It was not so much that critics felt that moral ambiguity had not existed in previous decades but that, having become such a foregrounded issue amidst the carnage of Vietnam, it pervaded the very fabric of *The Godfather*. Any reading of the text in the period could only be made within the framework of an understanding that characters say one thing and mean another, make deliberately ambiguous statements or employ euphemisms such as 'I'm gonna make him an offer he can't refuse'.

Those critics that praised the text's subtlety and those who saw it as a PR job universally acknowledged in this way that crime in American society was a matter which could no longer be simplified except by refusing to accept its existence, an option that only the foolhardy would take. Whether by advocating banishment of the topic, emphasizing its complexity or by dismissing the text on formal grounds, the extra-textual cues encouraged a reading of organized crime as the central underpinning structure of American life. Yet, crucially, it was an *under-pinning* – not something that manifested itself in a tangible historical form, but below the surface. What remained on the surface was a view of the institution of the family as a benign structure and an oasis of stability amidst the peril of social change. While it was implied that crime was a central part of American life with visible manifestations, the *source* of *organized* crime remained intact in the extra-textual cues as a mysterious entity, hidden from view, and available only in the archetypal form of Marlon Brando.

Jaws

Jaws is the story of a great white shark which one summer terrorizes the seaside resort of Amity in the United States. It features three main characters: Brody, the concerned police chief; Hooper, a young marine biologist brought in from outside the community in order to investigate the shark; and Quint, a grizzled old sea-dog who offers his services as a kind of aquatic bounty hunter. A fourth character of subsidiary importance is the mayor of Amity, Larry Vaughan, whose main concern is the loss of business rather than the threat to lives that the shark's presence off the coast entails. Like *The Godfather, Jaws* was preceded by a barrage of hype which constituted the very fabric of it as a text.

The novel of *Jaws*, also like *The Godfather*, was generated by the film industry: negotiations to buy the film rights to *Jaws* were underway well before the book was ever published (Gottlieb 1975, pp. 11ff). However, if there is a difference between the hype that accompanied *Jaws* and that which accompanied its predecessors it is a difference of scale and specific strategy. *Jaws* became a marketable commodity not just as a film but as a whole range of other products (see Pye 1975). So, rather than being just a novel and film version of a text, *Jaws* was always already in the public domain, reshaped and remoulded even before it could establish an autonomous identity.

From the galley stages onwards, Richard Zanuck and David Brown, the famous Hollywood production partnership, used their names to publicize the book vigorously, gaining it 5,000,000 in sales in the first six months from its issue in paperback in January 1975 (Harwood 1975). Five and a half million books were still in print in the summer of 1975 ('Summer of the Shark', *Time* 23 June 1975, p. 32). Such hype continued; publications cashed in wherever possible on the *Jaws* phenomenon, thus generating more publicity for the film before it was released (see, for example, Cashin 1975), while the products associated with the film grew to include a vast array of toys, garments, ornaments, household goods and so on (see Day 1975). The emblem of the film – the jaws of a shark pointing up towards the surface of water – proved eminently reproducible (see 'A Nation Jawed', *Time* 28 July 1975).

It is ironic that such a capitalist enterprise concerns a text which can be read as containing a critique of certain capitalist imperatives: part of the narrative's plot involves the mayor's reluctance to close the resort even though Brody (Roy Scheider) virtually pleads with him to do so. Mayor Vaughan (Murray Hamilton) seems to want to turn a blind eye to the shark attacks as one more hindrance to the trade of the island during the impending holiday season. On the one hand, then, there is the virtually unstoppable, occult force of the shark and, on the other, there is the morally corrupt figure of the mayor. Put another way, Police Chief Brody feels morally bound to negotiate on behalf of the people between the immoral (Vaughan) and the amoral (the shark). Significantly, Vaughan's refusal to close the beaches leads to a shark attack on a young boy whose grief-stricken mother later physically assaults Brody for what she assumes is his negligence. It is notable that *Jaws* plays upon the familial loss for its illustration of the point: if the authorities represent selfish bureaucrats, then in this context they are a threat to the well-being of the family. Because of his duplicity in the service of self-gain, Biskind (predictably) suggests that 'Mayor Larry Vaughan is Amity's Nixon' (1975, p. 26). It can be argued that the shark must go in the name of capital – although the threat to innocent lives can be used as a cover for the real reason.

The employment of a bounty hunter, Quint (Robert Shaw), exposes the nature of the business relations upon which the island is built. Quint is 'nearly as dangerous to the social fabric of Amity as the shark itself' (Biskind 1975 p. 26); he spends most of his time on the ocean, like the beast he will pursue. He is overtly tough and grizzled – at one point, while on the boat, he crushes a can with one hand until it is a small piece of distorted metal; Hooper mimics this, crushing a paper cup. He is also unruly (a heavy drinker) but ruthless and amoral (like the shark) – accepting the task of killing the shark only because of the money he will be paid. Most outstanding amongst Quint's threatening features for the community, though, is that he is a bachelor who taunts the cosy domesticity of the island. Repeatedly, and especially directly at Hooper and Brody, he sings the refrain from an old sea shanty: 'Farewell and adieu to you fair Spanish ladies/Farewell and adieu to you ladies of Spain'. Clearly, Quint is transporting Hooper (Richard Dreyfuss) and Brody from the security of family life embodied in Amity to the Hemingwayesque machismo embodied in the domain of the sea. Quint is outside the social order that Amity represents and possibly an anachronism. He, like the shark, must be killed in order to maintain the social fabric of the island, and it is a death which, for Kael (1980, p. 196), represents the death of machismo.

The shark's subsequent demise – significantly at the hands of a family man, Brody, who has continually feared for the lives of his children – allows the police chief and Hooper to paddle back to the security of the island.[2] At this stage in the narrative of the film it is clear that the shark and Quint have embodied a threat to domestic well being; but if Quint's death represents the demise of machismo then the shark's death represents an end to the rampant sexuality that so threatens family life. This is not to say that audiences would necessarily follow the arguments of Kael, Biskind and others in attributing an allegorical status to the shark as an embodiment of new sexual attitudes, adultery, divorce and so forth. However, the fact that critics often guided interpretations of the text towards the threat that the shark poses to the security of family life embodied in Amity implies that there are at least grounds for the contemporary audience to recognize the import of that which is threatened among all the thrills.

Although there has been, for hundreds of years, sporadic speculation over the future of the family as an institution (see, for example, Lasch 1975a; 1975b; 1975c; Rapp 1982, p. 169), the 1970s ushered in a string of social changes which, taken together, commentators believed to be a serious threat to the future of the family. There were changes in the rates of and laws regarding divorce; an increasing number of women in waged work; an increase in the number of single-parent families; and, tied in with these, an increased emphasis, leading to a change in the law, on the right of women to control reproduction (see Degler 1980, pp. 445ff.; Friedan 1977, p. 413; Weitzman 1985; Fletcher 1988, pp. 98ff.). A number of commentators took note of statistics on family life and drew their conclusions in what Degler (1980, p. 450) calls 'a mass of lugubrious studies' on the decline or death of the family (see *inter alia* Farson 1969; Boyers 1973; Lasch 1977; Cooper 1971).

One of the most volatile debates centred on the control of reproduction. The regulation of pregnancy in general was the focus of heated argument in the wake of the introduction of new contraceptive methods such as 'the pill'. But abortion became the scene of an overtly *political* battle. The *Roe vs Wade* decision of 1973 – which effectively legalised abortion in America – led to a split among those activists who supported it and wanted it to go further, and those who wanted abortion to remain illegal. The debate and the struggle that resulted was soon to become organized around groups calling themselves 'pro-life' and 'pro-choice' (see Luker 1984, pp. 160ff.). For the New Right especially, those disturbing changes in the social formation, such as the feminist movement and pro-choice lobby, appeared to threaten to disrupt traditional ways of life, most specifically the family. If this was the case, then the traditional base of electoral power was also under threat (See Steinfels 1984, pp. 111ff.; Peele 1984, pp. 93ff.; Granberg 1978).

The potency of the family as an issue was precisely that it *appeared* apolitical and seemed to cut across political loyalties. The reading of *Jaws* that some critics hinted at, then, touched on what were actually very live political issues. For contemporary commentators, the vanquishing of the shark as an imaginary resolution of the crises in American domestic life that had dominated the previous few years constituted a very persuasive interpretation. And in the mid-1970s the shark emblem of *Jaws* that had been so ruthlessly marketed seemed to be everywhere.

The manifest thrust of the extra-textual cues in these blockbuster texts encourages readings of *The Godfather* and *Jaws* as narratives of extrinsic – yet problematically *intrinsic* – threats. Organized crime is clearly a part of American society but even the shark, a creature from the natural world, is allowed to kill because of the corrupt tendencies of Mayor Larry Vaughan. The problem of what is 'outside' and what is 'inside' American life, pursued with such vigour in these blockbusters, recurs throughout the 1970s American thriller.

Cues to reading

As we have noted on numerous occasions, the thriller has a special relationship with the non-fictional text which is a result of the thriller genre's specific verisimilitude. Also the non-fiction thriller cannot avoid having a very close relationship with a range of other thrillers because, as Jameson explains, the suspense and mystery element is often common to both (1979 p. 79). Given that this is the case, it is not surprising that the non-fictionality of certain thrillers might be influential in informing readings of other thrillers. Clearly, it is important that a major text like *All the President's Men* embodies themes of paranoia and mystery which help define fictional narratives of the period (see especially Chapter 7 below); likewise, the moral ambiguity about crime and the media prominence of the Wojtowicz texts contribute to other fiction concerned with these issues in the seventies (see especially Chapter 4 below).

In the case of blockbusters, of course, their non-fictionality is not an issue. Yet, the way in which these texts so redefined the public's relation to their textual material could not help but have repercussions for thrillers that trod the same ground. *The Godfather* entailed that all other narratives about the Mafia were for some time encoded with the blockbuster text's legacy of ambiguity, diversity and dissension in American life. Similarly, *Jaws* became the quintessential popular narrative of a seemingly unstoppable threat to modern America and its most valued domestic institutions. It must be stated, also, that such a schema, in which blockbusters and non-fiction thrillers define and determine readings of contemporary fiction is not to be interpreted as a mechanistic one; clearly, all texts within a given reading formation existed in complex relations with other discourses as well. However, in the realm of the discourses that make up such a formation, there are clearly areas which stand out at specific times for specific reasons.

One such area, as we have seen, concerns the location of 'inside' and 'outside'. Another important area is characterized by the logic of revelation. Many thrillers are, by virtue of the dynamic of suspense, fundamentally incremental in their narration and it might be thought that this is the dominant way in which the historical period is 'mirrored' in such texts. *All the President's Men*, especially, consists of accumulating riddles and loose ends which invite interpretations and are often solved by the narrative. In the next chapter we will consider hard-boiled fiction of the 1970s with a view to showing that the logic of its mode of revelation, while problematic, is one which, through different 'voices', 'visions' and 'realities', facilitates the social investments of readers.

Further Reading

In many ways the further reading that follows, and which continues at the end of subsequent chapters, represents a futile and fruitless task. Firstly, it omits some texts from the period. Secondly, it immediately raises the question of whether or not the 'correct' generic and subgeneric categories have been created and whether the texts placed in these categories should be there or not. In general, the placing of texts has been based on an understanding of the way they may have been presented to be read in the period. If such texts are found to be in the 'wrong' section, then it is a testimony to the difficulty of making strict taxonomies stick.

Printed texts – usually novels, but sometimes stories – I have listed reasonably conventionally by author surname. Because these thrillers can be found in a number of editions full bibliographical details have not been given. **Films** in this guide have been listed chronologically by month and year of their release in the United States. **Television thriller series** are limited to texts which received their first airing on network TV in the 1970s rather than long-running shows from other decades. These are also listed chronologically. For further details in this area the indispensable source is Martindale (1991).

For the record, we will begin by offering a recap on the blockbuster texts of the decade including non-thrillers. Non-fiction thrillers will follow.

Blockbusters

Print

1. Puzo, Mario. *The Godfather* (1969); **2**. Blatty, William Peter. *The Exorcist* (1971); **3**. Bach, Richard. *Jonathan Livingston Seagull* (1970); **4**. Segal, Erich. *Love Story* (1970); **5**. Benchley, Peter. *Jaws* (1974); **6**. McCullough, Colleen. *The Thorn Birds* (1977); **7**. Shaw, Irwin. *Rich Man, Poor Man* (1970); **8**. Sheldon, Sidney. *The Other Side of Midnight* (1973); **9**. Michener, James. *Centennial* (1974); **10**. Jong, Erica. *Fear of Flying* (1973) (see Sutherland 1981, p. 30).

Film

1. *Star Wars* (1977) ; **2**. *The Empire Strikes Back* (1980); **3**. *Jaws* (1975); **4**. *Grease* (1978); **5**. *The Exorcist* (1973); **6**. *The Godfather* (1972); **7**. *Superman – The Movie* (1978); **8**. *The Sting* (1973); **9**. *Close Encounters of the Third Kind* (1977); **10**. *Saturday Night Fever* (1977) (see Finler 1992, p. 479).

The Non-fiction thriller

Print

Armes, Jay J. and Nolan, Frederick 1976. *Jay J. Armes Investigator*
Ashman, Charles 1975. *The CIA–Mafia Link*
(*Serpico* style story of police graft)
Becker, Sidney 1975. *Law Enforcement Inc.*
Behn, Noel 1977. *The Big Stick-up at Brink's*
Bugliosi, Vincent with Gentry, Curt 1975. *Helter Skelter: The True Story of the Manson Murders*
Copeland, Miles 1978. *The Real Spy World*
Daley, Robert 1978. *Prince of the City*
David, Heather 1971. *Operation: Rescue*
David, Jay 1980. *The Scarsdale Murder*
Epstein, Edward J. 1978. *Legend: The Secret World of Lee Harvey Oswald*
Erdstein, Erich with Bean, Barbara 1977. *Inside the Fourth Reich*
Fawkes, Sandy 1977. *Killing Time: Journey into Nightmare*
Greenberg, Dave 1975. *The Super Cops Play It to a Bust*
Grogan, Emmett 1972. *Ringolevio: A Life Played for Keeps*
Hohimer, Frank 1975. *The Home Invaders* (a.k.a. *Violent Streets*, a.k.a. *Thief*)
Hunt, E. Howard 1974. *Undercover: Memoirs of an American Secret Agent*
Hynd, Alan 1970. *The Confidence Game: Kings of the Con*
Lindsay, Robert 1979. *The Falcon and the Snowman*
Maas, Peter 1970. *The Valachi Papers.*

Maas, Peter 1973. *Serpico*

Maas, Peter 1975. *King of the Gypsies*

Marchetti, Victor and Marks, John 1974. *The CIA and the Cult of Intelligence*

Moore, Robin et al. 1977. *The Washington Connection*

Pileggi, Nicholas 1976. *Blye, Private Eye*

Rather, Dan and Gates, Gary Paul 1975. *The Palace Guard* Rev. edn.

Roosevelt, Kermit 1979. *Countercoup: The Struggle for Control of Iran*

Siegel, Micki 1980. *Cops and Women*

Singer, Kurt 1980. *I Spied and Survived*

Steven, Stewart 1974. *Operation Splinter Factor*

Stevenson, William and Dan, Uri 1976. *90 Minutes at Entebbe*

Talese, Gay 1971. *Honor thy Father*

Teresa, Vincent with Rennen, Thomas C. 1973. *My Life in the Mafia*

Whittlemore, L.H. 1973. *The Super Cops: The True Story of the Cops Known as Batman and Robin*

Film

The Valachi Papers (October 1972)
(Based on the Peter Maas book, starring Charles Bronson)
Serpico (December 1973)
Attica (March 1974)
The Super Cops (March 1974)
Breakout (May 1975)
The Brink's Job (December 1978)
King of the Gypsies (December 1978)
(Based on Peter Maas' book)
The Hunter (July 1980)
(bio-pic about bounty hunter Ralph Thorson)

TV

Toma (1973)
('Factual' stories from the career of a New Jersey undercover cop)

3
'The Luxury to Worry about Justice': Hard-boiled Style and Heroism

Even though it covers a wide and varied scope of literary enterprise, the hard-boiled (sub)genre is frequently viewed as if it was the gift of its 'brand leaders', Hammett, Chandler and Macdonald. Its chief feature is usually said to be a special clipped and laconic prose style thought to be appropriate to depicting the hard realities of the modern world. Derived from journalism, American literary naturalism and the work of Hemingway, this style developed in America between the wars as a kind of 'pure' prose, an almost transparent vehicle for the reporting of 'objective' facts. Yet hard-boiled style has also been viewed as inextricably tied to a highly specific world-view. Willett (1992) and Marcus (1975) both see the hard-boiled genre in terms of its heroes' attempts to deconstruct and 'defictionalise' the 'reality' created by the personally interested voices of those they encounter. The version of 'reality' which the hero submits subsequent to this deconstruction, however, is 'no more definitive or scientific than the discourses presented to him' (Willett 1992, p. 10). Furthermore, the hard-boiled hero's role in reaching a moment of truth often explicitly 'renders universal principles of truth and justice subjective and presages moral inquiry as the detective's singular response to the atomised urban scenes of modernity' (Kennedy 1997, p. 44).

Rather than growing out of the sole efforts of its 'brand leaders', the hard-boiled genre emerged from the work of numerous practitioners who contributed to the magazine *Black Mask* in the 1920s. As is now well-known, *Black Mask* itself was far from being an ideology-free project: in 1923, for example, it published the notorious Ku Klux Klan issue (see Bailey 1991, pp. 41–3; Kennedy 1997, p. 44). Admittedly, the editors purported to be neutral and invited pro and con stories about the Klan (Bailey 1991, p. 41); but almost of all the resultant stories presented African-Americans as, at best, marginal or stereotypical. For Ogdon, this is part and parcel of the ideology to be found 'without fail at the *centre*' (1992, p. 71) of the hard-boiled genre. She sees the hard-boiled environment as one in which the hero is 'the sole "normal" person' (p. 77) and where emotional detachment – in the prose and in the hero – only serves to underline the abjection of criminals, the 'masses' and the marginalised of all stamps. For Ogdon, and especially for Haut (1995), the cynical awareness of the hard-boiled hints at paranoia, a component of the worldview of modernity which plays a pivotal role in our examination of 1970s thrillers (see Chapter 2 above and Chapter 7 below).

In the 1970s hard-boiled detectives appeared in long-running TV series – *Harry O* (1974), *The Rockford Files* (1974), *Vega$* (1978); in serious films – *Shamus* (1973), *Gator* (1976); in spoof comedies – *Peeper* (1975), *The Black Bird* (1975); and in print fiction series. One of the most commercially successful of these latter were the Spenser novels of Robert B. Parker, a series which consistently attempted to confront social changes while remaining within a recognisable hard-boiled tradition. In the first part of this chapter we will consider these novels by scrutinising the imbrication of their general style with the figure of Spenser, and speculating on the extent to which readers must take seriously the hard-boiled ideology 'at the centre'. For the purposes of comparison we will also consider a very different 1970s private eye, Dave Brandstetter, who appears in a series of novels by Joseph Hansen. Finally, we will briefly analyse what is often thought to be the archetypal 1970s movie – *Chinatown* (1974) – a private eye film whose cinematic narration might be understood as analogous to hard-boiled prose.

Hard-boiled style

The foremost characteristic of hard-boiled style lies in its short sentences, often devoid of adjectives and adverbs. The words that remain are generally those that are more commonly evident in everyday language rather than the 'flowery' terms used in literature. So 'said' will replace 'asserted', 'queried' or 'expostulated', for instance. In addition, the nouns used are usually concrete and recognisable while any adjectives that are employed will probably be inexact, such as, 'nice', 'bright' or 'big'. Verbs, too, will be stripped to a minimum with a heavy reliance on the verb 'to be'. This simplicity is carried over into the construction of hard-boiled sentences as well as the choice of words: the sentences will be mainly simple declarative ones, or a couple of these joined by a conjunction; subordinate clauses will be very infrequent thus lessening narratorial observation. When these sentences are used to describe events or actions the sequence is intact with the events being presented in the sequence in which they occurred, directly and unmixed with comment.

A passage from James M. Cain's *Double Indemnity* (1983) offers a sense of the no-nonsense approach of hard-boiled prose. When the murderous protagonists Phyllis and Huff are disposing of the body of Phyllis's husband, Nirdlinger, the gruesome nature of the deed is left entirely unmentioned in the narration:

> I ran over and grabbed his legs, to take some of the weight off her. We ran him a few steps. She started to throw him down. 'Not that track! The other one!'
>
> We got him over to the track the train went out on, and dropped him. I cut the harness and slipped it in my pocket. I put the lighted cigar within a foot or two of him. I threw one crutch over him and the other beside the track.
>
> 'Where's the car?'
>
> 'There. Couldn't you see it?'
>
> I looked, and there it was, right where it was supposed to be, on the dirt road.
>
> 'We're done, let's go.'
>
> We ran over and climbed in and she started the motor, threw in the gear. 'Oh my – his hat!'
>
> I took the hat and sailed it out the window, on the tracks. 'It's O.K., a hat can roll, – *get going*!'
>
> She started up. We passed the factories. We came to a street.
>
> On Sunset she went through a red light. 'Watch that stuff, can't you, Phyllis? If you're stopped now, with me in the car, we're sunk.'
>
> (pp. 60–1)

Disgust, repulsion, remorse and anxiety are not explicitly present. Such complete lack of histrionic emphasis is common in hard-boiled fiction. It is notable, too, that hard-boiled prose often attempts to emulate the casual style of spoken discourse, sometimes injecting argot or colloquialisms in order to deal with striking events in a seemingly disinterested fashion. As a result the depiction of violence in hard-boiled fiction (which is frequent) often gives an effect of irony, detachment and understatement.

Another salient characteristic of the hard-boiled style is that it accords almost equal attention to the description of inanimate objects (tables, guns, walls, antiques, etc.) and animate objects (people); there is an avoidance of speculation on the thoughts of characters in preference to describing their actions. Thus Hamilton (1987, pp. 141–2), in assessing Dashiell Hammett's style, notes that a crucial moment of emotion in *The Maltese Falcon* is objectified by the rolling of a cigarette. Raymond Chandler believed that the use of this technique produced a special pleasure for the reader, stating his contention that the reader is not interested in the fact that a man got killed in a story, for example, but that at the moment of his death he was trying unsuccessfully to pick up a paper clip (Chandler 1984, p. 214).

Such juxtaposition of tangentially related events or sentences is a marked facet of hard-boiled style and it serves to deflect direct discussion of emotions. A seemingly insignificant example from the end of Chapter 6 of Robert B. Parker's Spenser novel *The Judas Goat* (1983a) illustrates this. Spenser is in England, armed against a terrorist group he is pursuing and

> The shoulder holster under my coat felt awkward. I wished I had more fire power. The steak and kidney pie felt like a bowling ball in my stomach as I headed out onto Prince Albert Road and caught a red double-decker bus back to Mayfair.
>
> (p. 39)

The first two sentences are straightforward: Spenser feels awkward carrying firearms in a country where not even the police are armed and yet he feels, also, that he needs more fire power to protect himself. The final sentence appears to consist of description only; however, a closer scrutiny shows that it bears directly on the first two. Spenser apparently knows his way around this foreign city and tries to eat like the natives. But 'steak and kidney pie' , 'Prince Albert Road', 'red double-decker bus' and 'Mayfair' are all markers of what is, to him, an alien place and his awkwardness is reflected in the 'bowling ball' that weighs heavy on his stomach. The final sentence in this extract therefore acts as a metaphor to illustrate Spenser's present contradictory situation. Such description and juxtaposition of what are only tangentially related elements in a scene occurs throughout the Spenser novels, particularly in the 'climactic' fight scenes (see, for example, *God Save the Child* (1977a, p. 159); *Mortal Stakes* (1977b, p. 169)).

The hard-boiled hero: Spenser

Hard-boiled stories – especially those with a first-person narrator – can often seem to be a report of actions only. It is through the 'straightforward' depiction of 'objective realities', as in the extract analysed above, that the style apprehends the world of events and things. The hero thus performs but never reveals his/her thoughts or the thoughts of others, and this all seems to take place through a narratological device which Genette calls 'external focalization' (1982, especially pp. 189ff.). However, external focalization is not wholly applicable to the hard-boiled; Spenser will occasionally state facts of which he cannot objectively be sure, for example, of a character: 'He was hurt'. As such, narrator/characters like Spenser, and Chandler's Marlowe, can never be omniscient; yet as participants in the story relating it after the event they possess certain privileged knowledge which will allow them to tell of things that 'true objectivity' would have to omit.

The hard-boiled hero, then, is embodied in the style but at the same time attempts to control the access to the 'reality' of events which the style purports to facilitate. The 'supposedly realistic character of the genre', as Ogdon (1992, p. 75) asserts, 'implies that the hard-boiled writer (and his detective) are ideologically detached from those they describe'. In fact, this distance is significant; the hard-boiled detective is not to be thought merely in terms of psychological attributes; nor is s/he simply an 'actant' serving a role in the plot. The hard-boiled hero hero as detached observer is very much an ideological 'figure' (Denning 1998, pp. 46, 94, 139), a potential site of social investment for the reader. Accounting for the resurgence of hard-boiled fiction in the 1970s, Parker has said:

> Spenser is certainly a post-Vietnam figure. The '30s were a time of disillusionment as profound as this, when the Great War turned out not to have done much for anyone, and in both cases the question that's prominent is who is the justice and who is the thief.
>
> (quoted in Taylor 1987; cf. Greiner 1984, pp. 36, 41)

In concordance with this new meaning and as a result of social change the private detective has had to adjust to the new social forces that confront him/her in the fictional form of his/her adventures. Spenser is a 'figure' constituted simultaneously by and against those same social forces as depicted in the fiction, yet, more often, Spenser casts himself in the role of reporter.

In addition to being a 'figure' Spenser also partakes of 'seriality' (Kozloff 1989, pp. 68–9). Although Spenser's character might develop from novel to novel, or perhaps the reader will be offered more information about his past life (see, for example, *Pastime*, 1992), his existence in subsequent texts will continue in much the same way as previous ones. As such, investments by readers will be organized around an interest in how Spenser, with his established characteristics, will negotiate the events in the present narrative.

These ideological features of the hard-boiled hero do not negate roundness of character; far from it, in fact. As is customary in the hard-boiled tradition, the novels often begin with a client calling on Spenser or his office with a case and it is precisely this private status that allows Spenser his measure of distinctiveness. Unlike a policeman, Spenser is not caught in a potentially stifling hierarchic bureaucracy that demands such things as respect for official superiors and service to the public. Spenser's private life, therefore, merges imperceptibly with his business: hence the foregrounding of his disposition to humour, his (markedly 1970s) clothes, and his relatively innocuous pastimes (but significant markers of character): namely cooking, eating and reading. These serve to set Spenser apart as an educated modern bachelor.

Various indicators throughout the series of novels also assemble Spenser's macho credentials. His past as a heavyweight boxer and his war experience in Korea are characterised as trips through an existential proving ground which in turn gives him the power of judgement in his contemporary battles. The Korean experience, especially, distinguishes Spenser from his adversaries; in the novels Vietnam is implicitly a 'dirty' war. More importantly, his constant weightlifting and jogging are markers of masculinity: at the Harbor Health Club – Spenser's place of exercise – there is no mention (until the club is converted in the later novels) of females pumping iron. It is here that the private detective works out with Hawk, a black ex-boxer who makes a living as a hired killer and, in the later novels, becomes an independent sidekick for Spenser.

The Hawk/Spenser relationship frequently hints at a private macho code between hired heavy and private investigator, a code which dare not speak its name. However, the camaraderie is not explicitly homo-erotic, even though it falls into a broad American literary tradition of interracial masculine bonding which includes, among others, the Leather-stocking novels of James Fenimore Cooper, *Moby Dick* and *Huckleberry Finn* (see Lawrence 1971; Smith 1950; Fiedler 1984). This is a tradition with which Parker is certainly familiar,[1] and its point for these hard-boiled novels is that it involves the pitting of men against the threats of a forbidding landscape which can only be combatted through violence. As such, it provides an almost pre-constituted space for the working out of readers' investments; however, Parker's comments on the 'post-Vietnam' status of Spenser indicate that even he is aware that the framework of American myth in which Spenser operates does not have an eternal and immutable meaning. Machismo is employed to keep at bay the forces of 'evil' in this world of violence; the character of that evil will largely depend on the preferences of the contemporary audience.

Spenser and women

Another way Spenser's heroism is articulated concerns his encounter with women, especially Susan Silverman, his love interest from the second novel onwards. Susan has a suitably modern career, educational psychologist, which involves her not only working with families but situates her in the role of deciphering and elaborating Spenser's world-view. She is determined to make the most of her occupation and individuality and Spenser's encounter with her forces him to modify aspects of his character. He recognises some of his thoughts as 'sexist', making oblique references to the women's movement. In turn, he articulates this with the practicality of his cooking and food interests. Susan also elicits other responses, for example, a sense of chivalry following the final fight in *God Save the Child* and, more importantly, gradual commitment to one woman, as Brenda Loring, Spenser's fun-loving girlfriend in the first novels, gradually fades from the action. This, in itself, is a departure from the classic Chandleresque detective who refrains from any emotional involvement with women although Spenser insists on remaining independent and eschews family life (see, especially, the recent novel *Small Vices*, 1997).

In addition, Susan Silverman gains respect from the ruthless Hawk, who, we are told, is indifferent to anyone else; this emphasises her ability to carry out one of her functions in the novels – to establish a dialogue between the floodtide of feminism and Spenser's macho code. However, her powerful voice is often restricted to commentary. One explanation of this lies with the hard-boiled narration: because Spenser is tight-lipped about his efforts – except when indicating what he is against – Susan Silverman must, to an extent, act as a commentator. But this rationale for Susan's discourse is not entirely convincing; in fact, Susan's constant observations have led one critic to complain of Parker's clumsiness in instituting Spenser's 'cheering section' (Hoffman 1982, p. 138).[2]

The role of women in the novels is most clearly demonstrated in *Promised Land* (1978). The novel contains much talk of broadly feminist issues precipitated by one of the central characters, Pam, who has escaped from an obviously stifling marriage into the arms of a radical feminist group. However, it soon becomes apparent that the talk of the women has no material effect: 'They're theoreticians. They have nothing much to do with life,' Spenser declares (p. 113). As if to underline this there is a scene where one of the feminists attacks him physically, kicking him in the crotch. In theory, this should floor Spenser but, although hurt, he remains standing and goes on to subdue his assailant. As the terrain of the story switches to gun play and serious violence involving criminals, the feminist discourse becomes palpably redundant.

Nevertheless, in *Looking for Rachel Wallace* (1980) there is the possibility of a critique of Spenser's machismo. At a meeting of female insurance workers in their canteen, Spenser's ward, feminist writer Rachel Wallace, is manhandled by a security guard who wants to eject her from the building. She passively resists but Spenser reacts by punching the guard and his superior. Ms Wallace is furious and tries to explain that it would have been far more productive in dramatising the sexism of the company if they had been allowed to drag her out. She sacks Spenser, and for lack of a bodyguard is later kidnapped by an extreme right wing group. At this stage Spenser is aware that his macho act, far from protecting Rachel, has put her in danger. However, now that there is a situation of recognisably acute danger, violence is needed to resolve it and Spenser comes to the rescue. In the final scenes Rachel comments on and explains Spenser's actions:

> You couldn't remain passive when they wanted to eject me from the insurance company because it compromised your sense of maleness. I found that, and I do find that, unfortunate and limiting. But you couldn't let these people kidnap me. That, too, compromised your sense of maleness. So what I disapproved of, and do disapprove of, is responsible in this instance for my safety. Perhaps my life. (p. 216)

The novel closes on this note of competition between voices;[3] but Spenser's authoritative voice is also challenged in other spheres. Even in the act of making the narratorial voice heard, the novels allow for diverse readings.

Spenser, the police and the family

Spenser's relations with the police revolve around the dichotomy of public and private detection, the latter's ability to take place outside the law and a Spenserian rationale in which the freedom of the individual is concrete and the collective good is abstract. In *The Godwulf Manuscript* (1976) Spenser argues, 'I handle the problems I choose to; that's why I'm freelance. It gives me the luxury to worry about justice. The cops can't. All they're trying to do is keep that sixth ball in the air' (p. 70). In this formulation, the police discourse is secondary. But this situation is not without its contradictions: the Boston homicide cops, Quirk and Belson (with whom Spenser has most contact through the series of novels), are actually depicted as the elite professionals amongst police, manifested in the fact that they are rounded characters who partake of the same kind of seriality as the hero.

However, not all the police that Spenser meets are like the Boston homicide cops. When a corrupt policeman appears, for example Trask in *God Save the Child* (1977a), he is significantly a non-member of the elite police corps. In this way, Quirk and Belson do not play the 'amateur' (see Palmer 1978, pp. 11–12) to Spenser's professionalism. Instead, the elite police are professionals in their own field who have to administer social programmes, a fact which, if it was not evident from the world at large, was at least apparent in contemporary police genres (see Chapter 5 below). Moreover, on a number of occasions a fissure appears in Spenser's ideological insistence on self-sufficiency: like other private detectives he is forced to seek the assistance of the police in, for example, fingerprint verification (Parker 1977b, p. 55), and also requires them as official guards against mobsters who want him dead.

The credibility of the police in the Spenser novels therefore constitutes a significant generic innovation, not because it represents a minor change in the structure of the narrative but because it provides a place for specific contemporary investments in police work. The Spenserian alternative to police operations is chivalry and individual honour.[4] Thus, the incomprehensible enormity and diversity of the social with which the police have to deal is frequently treated by Spenser in terms of a mere casuistry whose core solution is a return to familiar units of social organization. Life outside sanctioned social units – the kind of work that the police deal with on a day-to-day basis – is depicted as abstract, threatening and pervaded by corruption, filth and crime. For example, the commune in *God Save the Child* is associated with drugs, sex and dirty movies, while its chief representative, Harroway, has supposedly corrupted a middle-class suburban boy. The fact that Charles Manson, convicted only a few years earlier, was the leader of the most notorious commune of the 1960s – an alternative 'Family' whose apotheosis resulted from misdirected violence – would not be lost on the novel's original audience (see Sanders 1989).

Similarly, the fictional student protest organization called SCACE in *The Godwulf Manuscript* is characterized by Spenser and others as a group of moaning hippies. It would be easy here to either describe this feature of the Spenser novels as 'right-wing nonsense' or, more sophisticatedly, suggest that the narratives 'interpellated' the contemporary readers to accept certain ideological perspectives. However, it is worth pausing for a moment to consider the complications involved in speculating on reader investments. In the period in which the early Spenser novels appeared there was an explosion of news and factual coverage of the Vietnam war in the American media, of which the effects on public opinion – particularly about protest – are a matter for dispute (see for example Carpini 1990, p. 38; McQuaid 1980, p. 10; Braestrup 1983; 1984). The inability of 'the Movement', the counterculture and 'radicals' in the period to win the hearts and minds of the bulk of the people has been noted by both historians and contemporary commentators (Gittlin 1980, p. 73; 1984; Hodgson quoted in McQuaid 1989, p. 125; Wolfe 1971, pp. 324–325; cf. Buhle 1991, pp. 251–252 and Schrade 1984, p. 80). But most historians agree that the killings of students at Kent State in 1970 represented a turning-point.

At the end of April 1970 President Nixon announced the invasion of Cambodia, an event which was pounced on by the press (e.g. *Newsweek*, 11 May 1970).[5] In an atmosphere of growing dissent in provincial universities,[6] National Guardsmen at Kent State University, Ohio opened fire on a student demonstration against the Cambodian invasion killing four students and wounding eleven. The traumatic nature of these events and the mass response seem to mark this as a crucial period in the history of protest. This is not to say that the coverage was entirely uniform in tone: on the night of the shootings ABC News put the Kent State events into a general story about campus unrest which was not the main news item on that evening (ABC News transcripts 4 May 1970). Moreover, it became known that there was a blue-collar anti-anti-war backlash over the next few days.[7] However, the protests against the Cambodian invasion, while not representing a consensus of grass roots opinion, were evidence for newspaper editorials and magazine features of a growing gulf between the President's decisions and the public's belief in them.

Politics and social life were not changed immediately; but ideological battles over Vietnam were now conducted on native soil and through the media as foreign policy issues were transformed into domestic ones. The Spenser novels represent part of that hegemonic struggle and it cannot be assumed that the audience for the narratives would, as one, read into them Nixon's famous view of campus radicals as 'bums' (*Washington Post* 2 May 1970, p. A1). It should be added, though, that the Spenser novels do seem to *invite* such an equation: the actual political purposes of radical groups in the narratives is never really made explicit – SCACE stands for Student Committee Against Capitalist Exploitation and, as with the feminists in *Promised Land* who attempt to purchase an absurd amount of guns for no discernible reason, it is apparent that they are an undifferentiated, indistinct and threatening 'other' (on this topic see especially Hoffman 1983, p. 137).

In order to protect naive and innocent individuals who would be corrupted in the name of abstract causes it is notable that Spenser's actions are often of a fatherly nature. In *The Godwulf Manuscript* Spenser is forced to beat up a young radical in order to gain vital information; like a father admonishing a child he tries to explain his actions:

> I said, 'Everyone gets scared when they are overmatched in the dark; it's not something to be ashamed of, kid.'
> He didn't stop crying and I couldn't think of anything else to say. So I left. I had a lot of information, but I had an unpleasant taste in my mouth. Maybe on the way home I could stop and rough up a Girl Scout.
> (p. 134)

In the same book Spenser observes an argument Terry Orchard has with her parents and comments 'If I told my father to get laid he would have knocked out six of my teeth' (p. 51). Spenser's activities in the public sphere, bringing criminals to justice by way of fatherly awareness, implies an isomorphism of social and familial relationships; it is as if the reassertion of patriarchy is a social panacea.

This argument in favour of patriarchy is set out through a series of family dramas which dominate most of the Spenser novels and are not just isolated in *The Godwulf Manuscript*. The theme runs through the novels in numerous guises – partly because it is a common expectation of the private eye genre anyway but also because of its contemporary topicality. Unsurprisingly, its articulation also overlaps with other ideological concerns. Terry's inadequate family background which makes her act rudely to her parents ultimately leads her to seek harmful surrogate families: SCACE, followed by the Ceremony of Moloch (a mystical cult of the kind which appears in such novels of the hard-boiled genre as *The Dain Curse*, 1929).

An inadequate family relationship is also integral to the plot of *God Save the Child*. Kevin Bartlett, the 'kidnapped' boy, has parents who are both too weak to make decisions, especially the father. Kevin therefore seeks the companionship of an alternative family – the commune – and Vic Harroway, whose bodybuilding activities are shown to be purely narcissistic and tied up with the 'perverted sexuality' embodied in the commune. It is notable that this novel also introduces Susan Silverman in her role of educational psychologist, partly to make visible the latent psychological undertones in the novel. Thus, Kevin's homosexuality is delineated in terms of the weak father/self-obsessed mother dyad. In the final fight Harroway loses – his excessive planning (with the weights) is no match for Spenser's compassion and the parents' love. Meanwhile, in the subplot of the story, it is important that the two arch-villains are the corrupt cop Trask (who was a family friend of the Bartletts) and Croft (a doctor wanted for performing an illegal abortion). Harroway, Trask and Croft all represent that corruption which feeds on the weakness of other individuals. The title, *God Save the Child*, is therefore ambiguous – from whom? Potential investments and possible answers to this for the contemporary audience might be expected to revolve around the erosion of traditional parental roles (see Chapter 2, above).

When a family does not function properly, in the reading that the novels seem to invite, members of the unit will (more often than not) flee to the world beyond that unit, which is itself depicted as a Hobbesian universe of predators. The pattern can be seen in *Mortal Stakes*: Linda Rabb is a problem child as a result of flimsily documented evidence on her family (p. 61). She flees from her parents to crime and vice and finally to her own new family. By fluke, though, all has ended well until the conspiracy of blackmail over her erstwhile career as a prostitute intervenes. Spenser confronts the blackmailers, Lester and Maynard, towards the end of the novel; by this time much of their bargaining power is lost as Spenser has persuaded Linda Rabb to make public, via a sympathetic journalist, her past life. It is therefore significant that this final showdown with the would-be disruptors of family life takes place in the Rabbs' apartment, with Spenser engaging in physical combat while the nuclear family of Marty, Linda and their son look on.

Although the instances of family dysfunction that Spenser encounters are ironed out by his benevolent masculinity, this does not preclude readings inspired by the multiplicity of the Spenser narratives. Nevertheless, as masculine – and patriarchal – violence can be seen to be a crucial site of investment in the Spenser novels, it is worth very briefly widening our discussion of the resurgence of the hard-boiled by considering a 1970s private eye for whom violence is of very little use.

The hard-boiled hero II: Dave Brandstetter

The character of Dave Brandstetter appears in a series of novels by Joseph Hansen.[8] In terms of the personal idiosyncrasy which seems to characterize the private eye character as s/he proliferated in the 1970s (Baker and Nietzel 1985), Brandstetter's can probably be said to be the fact that he is gay. In fact, homosexuality is integral to the novels as we will see. However, what probably stands out more than this about Brandstetter is that, although he is a private investigator, his occupation is by no means identical to that of the traditional private eye. In a host of writers' hard-boiled novels, the investigator is always self-employed. Unlike all of these, Brandstetter works for an insurance company called Medallion Life and his work involves him investigating claims which somehow seem suspicious. The protracted discourses on honour and the necessity of independence which are so much a feature of the Spenser novels are therefore absent from the Brandstetter narratives.

If anything, then, the kind of stifling hierarchy that Spenser avoids is responsible for employing Dave Brandstetter, and it is made worse by the fact that Medallion Life has his father as chairman.[9] Despite this, Brandstetter is allowed a measure of distinctiveness in that he only investigates 'death claims' – those cases where somebody connected with the insurance policy has died. Also, the reader learns more and more about Dave through the kind of extension of external focalization that we noted in the Spenser novels. While the difference between the two is that Brandstetter is not a narrator/character like Spenser, we will see that the hard-boiled style still allows restricted access to Brandstetter's thought.

In the first novel, *Fadeout*, Brandstetter is sent to investigate the circumstances which have caused country singer Fox Olson's car to have crashed into a creek without leaving any trace of a body. The rest of the plot of the novel is quite intricate and, like the novels of Ross Macdonald, involves complicated family configurations and webs of relationships from the past. However, the gist of the story is that Fox's wife, Thorne Olson, has been having a long-term affair with Hale McNeil, a man who believes that his son's homosexual proclivities are shameful. Fox, meanwhile, has recently been seeing a boyfriend, Doug Sawyer, whom he has not met since the Second World War and with whom he is still in love. Pornographic pictures of Fox and Doug which they took themselves as youths have been used by the mayor of the town, Lloyd Chalmers, to blackmail Fox when the latter threatened to stand against him in an election.

Brandstetter steps into this web and, as we can see, it is one in which homosexuality is central. But this does not stop Brandstetter performing the tasks of a conventional generic detective; at the end of Chapter 18 of *Fadeout*, after Doug has been arrested for the murder of Fox, Brandstetter immediately notices that a Mexican child at the place of Fox's death is putting something in her mouth. It is the rubber tip of the cane which belongs to Fox's rich father-in-law, Loomis, who is later incriminated by this evidence in the shotgun killing of Lloyd Chalmers (p. 150). This conventional clue-finding, of course, fulfils generic expectations.

Although the novels undoubtedly allow for readings informed by other texts within the hard-boiled genre, the narrator's tolerance towards different lifestyles allows for a much different revelation of 'reality'. The introduction of the theme of sexuality in *Fadeout* is very low-key: Brandstetter's lover of 20 years, Rod Sterling, has recently died before the narrated events to do with Fox Olson begin; as a result, the full range of their relationship is very much on Brandstetter's mind. Therefore, in the midst of events to do with his insurance investigations, Brandstetter's (plot) unrelated thoughts on the affair are narrated; as Thorne Olson demands to know why Brandstetter does not ask her about Fox's health, he goes into a dream:

> Bright and fierce, he pictured again Rod's face, clay-white, fear in the eyes as he'd seen it when he found him in the glaring bathroom that first night of the horrible months that had ended in his death from intestinal cancer (p. 10).

Again when he is questioning Loomis:

> '. . . Life plays funny tricks'.
> 'Sometimes not so funny', Dave said.
> Loomis' muddy eyes regarded him wisely. 'Them are the ones you got to laugh at hardest'.
> *I never will*, Dave thought, *not about Rod dying.*

(p. 67)

These two sequences cannot be said to be directly related to the logic of hard-boiled revelation except in the sense that they illustrate something about the character of Brandstetter. The depiction of Brandstetter's relationship with Rod begins some way into the narrative when he starts to think about his home; this is then followed by the narration of some of the events in their relationship beginning after the

Second World War, which consumes a whole chapter (pp. 45ff.). The hard-boiled style is here used to emphasise the commonplace 'reality' of gay sexuality.

That Brandstetter has been in a very stable relationship is important for the series of narratives. One reason for this is that his future sexual liaisons are shown to be meaningful; at the conclusion of *Fadeout*, for instance, he strikes up a relationship with the man he has saved from a murder charge, Fox Olson's boyfriend, Doug Sawyer (p. 176). Another reason that stable relationships might provide an area of investment is the publicity given to the contemporary proliferation of unstable relationships among both homosexuals and heterosexuals in the real world (see Weeks 1989, pp. 47–8). In contrast to this kind of promiscuity, Brandstetter's outlook is probably a more developed version of that set forth by the boy Anselmo, who, already tired of being used by sexual partners despite his tender age, says that sex should not be like a faucet that can be turned on and off (p. 107).

Rather than the semantic feature of homosexuality, though, the key innovation in the narratives would appear to be the way Brandstetter copes with the violence which is so often a feature of the American thriller. The macho credentials of the hero are wholly absent from the Brandstetter novels. One reason for this must be that Brandstetter is in an occupation which, outside fiction, is even less reknowned than private detection for its high levels of adventure. Brandstetter's operations in the narrative are never supported by an emphasis on either violence or the need to dominate the opposite sex, even though gayness would certainly not prevent him from using force (see the conversation in *Fadeout*, 1986a, pp. 161–62).

It is significant, therefore, that all of the Brandstetter novels of the 1970s, where the investigator meets the killer during the denouement, rely on a resolution which involves an absolute minimum of violent acts. This is demonstrated by the hard-boiled prose in the following extract from *Fadeout*:

> The intelligence went away. 'I didn't do it.' Then, very fast and very surprisingly, there was a hatchet in his hand. He squatted for it, came up with it and swung it at Dave's head in the same single motion. Dave ducked, rammed his head into the boy's belly, grabbed his knees, lifted. Phil's head slammed back against the mixer barrel. Dave felt him go limp. The little axe dropped. The boy slumped to the ground.
> (p. 172; cf. *Death Claims*, 1987, p. 188; *Troublemaker*, 1986b, p. 175;
> *The Man Everybody Was Afraid Of*, 1984a, p. 165)

The climax of the final Brandstetter narrative of the 1970s, *Skinflick*, features not a confrontation of investigator and killer as in the other texts, but the dramatic rescue by Brandstetter of the drowning transvestite Randy Van (1984b, p. 200). The contrast with the Spenser novels – especially *The Judas Goat*, where the narrative works resolutely to a monumental punch-up at the Montreal Olympics between the combined forces of Hawk/Spenser and a 305-pound weightlifting champion called Zachary – could not be clearer.

As we have seen, one of the most crucial of Spenser's interests is the state of the family, and the final fights often take place within range of a family in the narrative. In this light it is also interesting that Evans (1980, p. 170) notes that, in three out of six novels, Spenser beats up homosexuals. Does homosexuality necessarily have to occupy a subordinate place in detective fiction? Obviously not; but it is worth mentioning that, outside the text, it took three years for Hansen to get *Fadeout* published after he had written it (Geherin 1985, p. 183). Moreover, while *Fadeout* is quite clearly a hard-boiled detective novel there is arguably still a lingering question as to whether the Brandstetter novels are primarily detective fiction or primarily narratives of homosexual life (see Hansen quoted in Baker and Nietzel 1985, p. 222; Geherin 1985, pp. 180–1).

Doubtless, the depiction of the varied facets of homosexuality is rendered in such a way as to maintain the range of generic expectations and investments of potential thriller readers. Yet, in light of our analysis above, we can confidently say that the Brandstetter and Spenser narratives are differentiated on the grounds of violence as well as sexuality. Whether the homosexual theme in the narratives was read sympathetically in the 1970s is, of course, another matter.[10] Moreover, it is difficult to prove that this is the case one way or the other. However, there is evidence to suggest that many voices existed in the 1970s which insisted that the decade was a period of lost innocence and greater sophistication. This is precisely the theme which is associated – somewhat problematically – with one of the most famous hard-boiled texts since the inception of the genre.

Chinatown

Chinatown's plot is complicated and difficult to summarise. Jake Gittes (Jack Nicholson), an LA private eye in the 1940s, is hired by the 'wife' of Hollis Mulwray (Darrell Zwerling) to procure evidence which will prove the adultery of her husband; Gittes does this, whereupon the photographs of the 'woman' with Mulwray are published in a city news-paper. But Gittes notices that, beside the 'adultery', Mulwray has been acting strangely: he is the head of the water authority in Los Angeles but he has still been spending an inordinate amount of time checking the water disposal pipes to the sea. Jake returns to his office to find that Evelyn Mulwray (Faye Dunaway) is waiting there to see him. Not only is she totally different in appearance from the 'Mrs. Mulwray' who hired him, but she is also threatening legal action. Soon after this, Hollis Mulwray is found dead in a largely dried out reservoir. After investigating the scene and almost getting his nose cut off by henchmen (Roy Jenson and Roman Polanski) Jake goes to meet Noah Cross (John Huston), who hires him to find the woman that Hollis Mulwray was seeing. While doing this Jake also makes enquiries into the recent land deals in the area and finds that much of the fruit-growing parts of the valley near LA have been recently bought by people who he soon finds are either dead or in a specially run nursing home. The land has been sold very cheaply because there is no water; water is being temporarily diverted, as Hollis Mulwray suspected.

Jake is accompanied on his enquiries by Evelyn Mulwray and, after a fracas at the nursing home in which she rescues Jake, they sleep together. However, she is called away in the night and he follows, only to find that she is visiting the woman with whom he had photographed Hollis Mul-wray. Jake confronts Evelyn and she only tells him that it is her daughter. When he goes home he is awakened by a call which tells him to go and meet Ida Sessions (Diane Ladd), the woman who initially impersonated Mrs Mulwray. On entering the address that he was given, he finds the first 'Mrs. Mulwray' dead on the floor and the police – led by an ex-colleague of Jake's, Lieutenant Escobar (Perry Lopez) – jump out and ask him why Ida had his phone number. Escobar sets Jake loose and he goes to see Evelyn again and she finally admits that the woman she visits, Catherine, is her sister *and* her daughter, as a result of a union with her father, Noah Cross.

The climax of the film takes place in Chinatown where Jake, Evelyn, Catherine, Noah Cross – who evidently murdered Hollis Mulwray because the latter learned of his multi-million dollar extortion plan – plus Escobar and his subordinates, are involved in a multiple confronta-tion which results in Evelyn being shot through the head by the police.

As the film's director, Roman Polanski has pointed out (South Bank Show 1980), the film is shot almost exclusively from a position very close to Jake Gittes. This is equivalent to the way that the hard-boiled detec-tive in print fiction sets about the task of assembling 'reality' – from the limits of his own perspective. The device also signals a stress on the optical nature of Jake's work by constantly having him in the early part of the film looking through binoculars (at Hollis Mulwray on the beach), in a car wing mirror (at Hollis), at photographs developed in his office of Hollis and Noah Cross, through a camera on the boating lake (at Hollis and Catherine), through a camera from a villa roof (at Hollis and Catherine, incorporating a shot of the camera lens which reflects what Jake is shooting) and at photos of Hollis and Noah Cross in the office of Yelburton (John Hillerman) which establish a crucial link in the plot.[11]

Yet, as with print fiction, whether this necessarily entails that the film can only be read within the constraints of whose point of view is represented is very much open to question. The first shot in the whole of the film is of a series of still photographs of a woman having sex with a man outdoors; the camera zooms out from these to show that the photographs are being held by Curly (Burt Young) and that he is, with Jake, in the latter's office. Can we argue that the viewer is invited to take up the position of Jake in the viewing of the photographs, cynical and almost weary of the subject? Or is the viewer likely to be in a position similar to Curly's, outraged and humiliated? Or is it more likely that the viewer may be presented with a question by the photographs that s/he may desire to be answered? These are just three likely possibilities for a reading of the sequence.

Jake's view, it can be argued, is actually in jeopardy for much of the film.[12] The whole concept of Chinatown signifies the limit of his knowledge and experience. Noah Cross says to him, 'You may think you know what you're dealing with, but believe me you don't.' When Jake smiles, Cross asks 'Why're you smilin'?' Jake replies, 'That's what the District Attorney used to tell me in Chinatown'. Jake indicates to Evelyn some of the reasons for his leaving the police department and why Chinatown has such a resonance for him: 'You can't always tell what's going on...I was trying to keep someone from being hurt and I ended up making sure she *was* hurt.' This confession represents a stark contrast to the self-assured machismo of many of the Spenser narratives. In the final moment of the film when Evelyn has been shot by Loach (Dick Bakalyan) in Chinatown, Jake seems to be between catatonia and strangling Escobar. His colleague, Walsh (Joe Mantell), intervenes, saying, almost conclusively, 'Forget it, Jake: it's Chinatown.'

The impossibility of understanding is a crushing blow to Jake's hard-boiled – but fragile – cynicism. But it is also interesting in terms of understanding the hard-boiled purview. Ogdon argues: 'Those who populate and pollute the universe of the hard-boiled detective story are described in terms of excess: excess smell (stink), excess body fluids (sweat, urine, tears, vomit), and/or excess desire (sexual proclivity, sexual perversion, greed, cunning and so forth)' (1992, p. 76). Yet, while the world at large is threatening and abstract in the Spenser narratives, the eponymous Chinatown is beyond significations of this kind. Let us also be clear that the central taboo in the film (*pace* Cawelti 1985, p. 510 and others) which, like Chinatown, so threatens Jake's flimsy self-assurance, is not a 'disgusting' father–daughter rape; instead, it is the almost inconceivable consensual incest.

Critics writing well after the film was released have tried to show that *Chinatown* is somehow an updated, ironic and much less innocent version of the classic private eye story (for example, Wexman 1985, pp. 91ff.). Indeed, others have argued that it is 'postmodernist' (Cawelti 1985, p. 511). But is the inpenetrable nature of the social world in the hard-boiled a new theme? In light of arguments about the inscrutable nature of Chinatown what, then, are we to make of Sam Spade's (Humphrey Bogart) final enigmatic comment in the 1941 film version of *The Maltese Falcon* that the black bird is the stuff that dreams are made of? Or how Marlowe is apprised of the fruitlessness of his whole project of honour in *The Long Goodbye* (1954), when it turns out that Terry Lennox, whom he has protected throughout, has concealed the identity of the murderer – his first wife?

Even so, publicity for the film framed it as 'a traditional detective story with a new, modern shape' (CIC 1974, p. 1). Contemporary film reviewers also contributed to readings of *Chinatown* as a film about the demise of old certainties in the 1970s. Writing in *Esquire*, Simon suggests:

> What really brings the film into the 1970's is the loss of innocence that permeates its world: the boundaries between right and wrong have become hazy even in the good – or better – people, and the two genuine innocents of the film are both, in one way or another, victimized.
>
> (Simon 1974)

That these boundaries have *suddenly* become hazy is not true for everyone; earlier we saw that Robert B. Parker closely equates the morality of the 1930s with the 'post-Vietnam' climate of the 1970s. The point is that there is a *specific* haziness of the boundaries in the 1970s hard-boiled text caused by the action of historical circumstances and the reading formation upon a potential reading of the hard-boiled genre. Audiences were able to read into the haziness their knowledges of the conspiratorial nature of contemporary government activities in the Vietnam and Watergate era, the changes in sexual mores and attitudes toward the family in the 1970s, rising crime rates, the plethora of contemporary paranoid texts (see Chapter 7), the depiction of criminal activities in crime novels (see Chapter 4) and so on.

Although there were readings which resembled Simon's, the extra-textual cues to the film were not all of this sort. Penelope Gilliatt, for instance, in the *New Yorker*, located *Chinatown*'s specificity in its depiction of avarice: 'Because of its emphasis on greed, "*Chinatown*" is a thriller for grownups' (Gilliatt 1974a). For Cocks in *Time*, however, there is no doubt that the film is well within a certain thriller tradition: 'Towne's script makes a nod to another Los Angeles mystery writer, Ross MacDonald [*sic*], most markedly in its use of familial trauma in the plot solution' (Cocks 1974). Yet it is precisely the fact that it is a genre text which makes the film deficient for Cocks, raising 'moral questions and political implications that are never plumbed at greater than paper cup depth' (1974). The profundity (or not) of the film's statement on contemporary life is therefore mitigated in these assessments by the fact that the film is a thriller.

The reviewers' readings of the film are thus subject to a tension which is not unlike that of the oxymoronic but nevertheless overused phrase 'transcending genre'. There is an impulse to 'short-circuit' readings of the film as a genre text, but this is constrained by a desire to signal its contemporary relevance. Readings which took their cue from such formulations – as well as other features of the reading formation – would be simultaneously investing in the semantic dimension (the putative 'lost innocence') while also ('falsely', perhaps,) registering a 'syntactic' innovation – a new negative thriller of foiled expectations.

The same kind of process can be seen in the whole 'updating' of the hard-boiled genre in the 1970s. In *Chinatown* and the Spenser and Brandstetter narratives arguments about independence and hierarchies are played out at length, specifically in relation to the police in the former two examples. In all of the texts gender and machismo are central: at their *utmost* in the Spenser narratives, and *explicitly in terms of their absence* in the Brandstetter novels and in *Chinatown*, where Jake not only makes himself vulnerable in the face of love but is also bested by a 'midget' who calls him 'Kitty Cat' before administering symbolic emasculation through the mutilation of Jake's nose. The family, too, has its role to play across all the examples: Spenser defends patriarchy with violence, while Brandstetter, although loving his father, not only presents a stark contrast to him in being able to maintain a stable relationship but is also tolerant of other sexualities and other units of social organisation. *Chinatown*, too, is very concerned with the family, whether it is the bureaucratic violence meted out by the incestuous Cross family concerns or the fact that Curly's cheating wife is re-installed in the domestic sphere with a black eye as the insignia of her transgression.

Arguments about the perspectival nature of hard-boiled heroism and hard-boiled style that we mentioned at the beginning of this chapter are obviously quite powerful. Like Knight's observations on Chandler (1980, pp. 135–67) they force a critical rereading of the whole hard-boiled tradition, especially the way that it has been so beloved of 'intellectuals' from W. H. Auden onwards. Yet, as we have seen, the hard-boiled genre contains multiple voices which will not be restrained. In addition, as the case of *Chinatown* shows, the cynicism of the hard-boiled is forced into representing something new every time by the action of extra-textual cues in a reading formation. The problem of whose 'reality' is assembled in hard-boiled fiction is undoubtedly an ongoing concern, one to which the genre is not entirely oblivious. It is this dilemma of vision which is extended in the 1970s by street crime narratives.

Further Reading

Print

Bergman, Andrew 1974. *The Big Kiss-Off of 1944*
Bergman, Andrew 1975. *Hollywood & Levine*
Block, Lawrence 1974. *Five Little Rich Girls*
Block, Lawrence 1975. *The Topless Tulip Caper*
Block, Lawrence 1976. *Time to Murder and Create*
Block, Lawrence 1978. *The Burglar in the Closet*
Constantine, K.C. 1973. *The Man Who Liked to Look at Himself*
Coxe, George Harmon 1971. *Fenner*
Crumley, James 1978. *The Last Good Kiss*
Feiffer, Jules 1977. *Ackroyd*
Franklin, Eugene 1972. *The Money Murders*
Friedman, Bruce Jay 1970. *The Dick*
Gores, Joseph N. 1972. *Dead Skip*
Gores, Joseph N. 1974. *Interface*
Gores, Joseph N. 1975. *Hammett*
Halliday, Brett 1971. *Count Backwards to Zero*
Hjortsberg, William 1978. *Falling Angel*
Lewin, Michael Z. 1971. *Ask the Right Question*
Lewin, Michael Z. 1973. *The Way we Die Now*

Lewin, Michael Z. 1974. *The Enemies Within*
Lewin, Michael Z. 1978. *The Silent Salesman*
Lyons, Arthur 1976. *The Killing Floor*
MacDonald, John D. 1970. *The Long Lavender Look*
MacDonald, John D. 1971 *A Tan and Sandy Silence*
MacDonald, John D. 1974. *The Dreadful Lemon Sky*
Macdonald, Ross 1971. *The Underground Man*
Macdonald, Ross 1973. *Sleeping Beauty*
Macdonald, Ross 1976. *The Blue Hammer*
Rovin, Jeff 1975. *Garrison*
Rovin, Jeff 1975. *The Wolf*
Sharp, Alan 1975. *Night Moves*
Simon, Roger L. 1973. *The Big Fix*
Simon, Roger L. 1974. *Wild Turkey*

Film

Darker than Amber (August 1970)
(Travis McGee movie)
Chandler (December 1971)
Hickey and Boggs (August 1972)
(*I Spy* spin-off)
Shamus (January 1973)
The Long Goodbye (March 1973)
(Chandler remake)   *The Manchu Eagle Murder Caper Mystery* (March 1975)
(*spoof private eye*)
The Drowning Pool (June 1975)
(Featuring Lew Archer)
Farewell, My Lovely (August 1975)
(Chandler remake)
Peeper (October 1975)
(private eye spoof)
The Black Bird (December 1975)
(ditto)
Gator (May 1976)
(sequel to *White Lightning* – see 'Revenge')
The Big Fix (October 1978)
(Based on Roger Simon novel)

TV

Cannon (1971)
Longstreet (1971)

Banacek (1972)
Banyon (1972)
Cool Million (1972)
Barnaby Jones (1973)
Faraday and Company (1973)
Griff (1973)
Harry O (1974)
The Rockford Files (1974)
Archer (1975)
Bronk (1975)
Charlie's Angels (1976)
City of Angels (1976)
Richie Brockelman, Private Eye (1978)
Big Shamus, Little Shamus (1979)
The Duke (1979)
Vegas (1978)

4
What Do We 'Believe' When We 'See'? Views of Crime

Having raised the issues of different views, realities and voices in our discussion of the updated private detective genre, in this chapter we will concentrate on similar matters in the presentation of the crime story. In particular, we will consider at greater length the narrative strategy touched on in the last chapter: 'focalization', 'the angle of vision through which the story is filtered in the text' (Rimmon-Kenan 1983, p. 43; cf. Genette 1982 and Chatman, 1990).

'Vision' in narrative

The theme of 'vision' – who sees what – is very much germane to the question of generic innovation in thriller narratives of the 1970s. The way in which vision perhaps structures the reader's interaction with the text is a subject with a long lineage in film and literary criticism and is usually conceptualized by reference to the terms 'point of view' or 'focalization'. Focalization is specifically important as a topic for us in that it has often been discussed as a means to illustrate how a reader is necessarily 'inscribed' in the text or 'constituted' by it. Finding out about past readings according to this formulation, then, should once more depend on simply discovering how certain devices in fiction create just *one* view of the narrative for the reader. If such a procedure were tenable, of course, then our consideration of potential readings in the 1970s would become a much simpler task; predictably, however, it is not. Nevertheless, the consideration of different types of focalization still allows important insights into the general workings of fiction.

Numerous studies[1] have assessed developments in 'point of view' or 'focalization' in written and/or cinematic narrative; but by far the most troubling – and notorious – formulations were proposed by a body of film theory which appeared in the 1970s. The lack of specificity in these analyses of 'vision' in film, where the problematic dovetailing of an undifferentiated human subjectivity with an overall subjectivity of the text was integral, derived from a fusion of principles taken from the then translated works of Althusser and Lacan (see Browne 1979, p. 106). In these analyses narrative devices *inscribe* the human subject in the text's own 'subjectivity', or structuration, the latter of which was usually found to be complicit with that of 'the State'. The human reader is, crudely put, a subject of both the text and the existing order, or, if one prefers, the reader is coerced into accepting the 'vision of reality' offered by a particular kind of textuality.

Such arguments about textuality (for example, Heath 1981; MacCabe 1974; 1977; 1978; Mulvey 1975; for more informed analyses, see Browne 1996 and Mayne 1993), frame the text-reader exchange as an interaction that works to the text's benefit. But the two main criticisms of this body of theory are, firstly, that fictional texts are unlikely to inscribe readers into a view of the world which matches the text's 'subjectivity' if that text is recognized by the reader as being a fiction or simply writing (see Lodge 1981); secondly the subject (or reader) that is to be inscribed in the text according to 'inscription' theories is frequently conceived as having no conflicting preferences prior to the interaction with a text – that is, s/he is largely a blank sheet.

Yet one can see where inscription theories were going in their attempt to demonstrate that the reader is recruited to the project of the text if one considers the perspectives which they implicitly criticize. These latter often seem to elide the processes of textuality involved in the act of representation or, at best, sustain naïve belief in the possibility of a fully accurate depiction of the world. Interestingly for our purposes, the verisimilitude of contemporary crime fiction has frequently been the object of such perspectives. According to Haut, for example, crime fiction is a simulacrum which it is difficult to distinguish from the real world: 'Suddenly, creating an artifact indistinguishable from reality became the preferred way to depict society and the conditions by which people are driven to extremes' (1999, p. 128). Claims of this kind are invariably based on the idea that, in the crime novel, the reader is straightforwardly 'shown' rather than 'told' about 'reality'.

In the well-known literary historical debate on precisely this topic, 'showing' and 'telling' in narration, the discussion of focalization is crucial, and it is broached in terms of relations between the 'narrator' and the 'focalizer' of a narrative (Rimmon-Kenan 1983, pp. 106ff.). As we saw in the last chapter, the proximity of narrator to focalizer is itself central to the illusion of non-judgmentality which characterizes a tough style. The narrative events and people in hard-boiled fiction are filtered through the seemingly laconic, surface-observational narration of the likes of Spenser or Brandstetter. Apprehension of the same principle can also be extended to the discussion of crime fiction. A proponent of 'telling', Wayne Booth offers a flavour of the relevant arguments when he asserts: 'By giving the impression that judgment is withheld, an author can hide from himself that he is sentimentally involved with his characters, and that he is asking for his reader's sympathies without providing adequate reasons' (1961, p. 83). Booth's contentions should be borne in mind as we confront the notion that the crime novels of the 1970s represent an even greater realism – and a qualitatively greater freedom for readers – than that of the hard-boiled story.

As we shall see in the work of Leonard and Higgins, characters' use of obscene vocabulary, colloquialisms, idioms, etc., as well as techniques of effacing the role of the narrator, are thought to be bound up with the task of 'showing'. Yet, we need to be clear about what is happening in such instances of narration. As we have argued, verisimilitude – rather than being a free-standing 'accurate depiction or showing of reality' – depends very heavily on the expectations of readers. It would be an oversimplification, therefore, to suggest that the snappy dialogue that can be demonstrated to be *inside* the texts of some 1970s crime fiction was alone responsible for a belief in the verisimilitude of a narrative on the part of its readers. Let us consider, instead, how it allows reader engagements.

'Leave me out of it'

Elmore Leonard reached the peak of his fame in the 1980s and 1990s, but his first crime novels were bestsellers in the 1970s, following his career as a screenwriter and an author of Western novels (see Williams 1993, pp. 186ff. and Geherin 1989, pp. 1ff.).[2] Gradually, and then in an accelerated way in the 1980s, Leonard's crime novels gained the reputation for a certain kind of realism manifested particularly in the prose style in which they are written. What is instantly apparent on reading any Leonard novel of the 1970s is the proliferation of a number of different focalizations of the story events. The hard-boiled prose of the narrative discourse slips imperceptibly, even during close reading, into a discourse which is close to, and transmits some feelings of, a character. As such, it is often felt to represent a true, authentic street patois (Geherin 1989, p. 10). Leonard himself has said,

> I started to realize that the way to describe anywhere, *anywhere*, was to do it from someone's point of view... and *leave me out of it*. I'm not gonna get poetic about this street... That's not what I do.
>
> (quoted in Geherin 1989, p. 10)

This specific kind of verisimilitude which requires almost photographic, but nevertheless partial, accuracy demonstrates how focalization justifies a fallible viewpoint, where detail of a scene is left out because it is not in a character's perception (ibid., p. 44). Focalization therefore has more than one purpose in Leonard's novels and can sometimes even have contradictory purposes.

When Leonard's novels slip into a discourse that is 'close to' that of a protagonist, the prose is not exactly that of the character but nevertheless resembles the character's language in its choice of words, rhythms and so on. This phenomenon is often mentioned briefly in classic works on narratology but is not often covered in any depth (for example, Lubbock 1926, pp. 256–7; Friedman 1955, p. 1178). One place outside the anglophone world where this topic has been almost integral to an extensive intellectual project is the Bakhtin School (Bakhtin 1984; Vološinov 1973). For Bakhtin, an important component of novelistic discourse is the ability to exist in a double-voiced orientation; that is to say, the discourse of the novel is not just the unified prose commanded by the author or narrator but is, rather, the product of different, sometimes competing, voices. He identifies an 'orientation towards *someone else's speech*' (1984, p. 191) – a phenomenon he calls *skaz* – which is precisely the kind of orientation that dominates Leonard's narratives.

What might be said to be happening when a character's idiom is represented in Leonard's novels, yet the quotation marks are eradicated, is an irruption of the character's subjective world into the world of the narrative prose. In this way, the discourse of possible authority is now dominated by the voice of a character. Moreover, this seems to negate the postulation of a 'classic realist' style (MacCabe 1974) in which the prose outside quotation marks effaces its production and poses as the voice of authoritative realism in texts. The irruption of characters' thought processes into this space may therefore have far-reaching consequences (cf. Cohn 1966; Lodge 1981). Having suggested this, though, we should not immediately get carried away with an inflated idea of characters' emancipated state; instead, let us first look a little more closely at the phenomenon of of *skaz* in the novels.

Bobby Shy in 52 *Pick-up* is such a coke-head that the surface appearances narrated when the focalization is close to him are in a language unmistakably meant to resemble his:

> Bobby Shy was listening. He could blow coke and not miss a word; there wasn't any trick to that. He was dipping into the Baggy again: with his Little Orphan Annie spoon – little chick with no eyes or tits but she was good to hold onto and bring up to your nose, yeeeeeees, one then another, ten dollars worth of fine blow while Alan was talking out of his cut mouth, telling about the man coming to see him.
>
> (1986b, p. 118)

A paragraph later, it is very difficult to say whether a traditional external focalization takes place or a focalization close to Bobby is happening when a set of sentences as simple as the following is set out: 'They were in Doreen's apartment because when Alan called he said he wanted to meet there. Alan, Bobby and Leo. It was one thirty in the afternoon. Doreen was in the bedroom asleep' (p. 119). Here it is difficult to distinguish the narrator and character/focalizer. There are absolutely no phrases of the type 'it seemed to him' in Leonard's thrillers; and while the discourse is in a seemingly neutral idiom it is difficult to attribute it to any one character or narrator. All that we can immediately be sure of is that someone is involved in a monologue which is not perceived by the other characters, but it is narrated, nevertheless, in the third person.

In light of the explicit orientation to '*someone else's speech*' of Bakhtinian *skaz*, then, we can see why Rimmon-Kenan chooses to call this kind of narration 'indirect interior monologue' (1983, p. 115; cf. Cohn's reservations, 1966, p. 104). This serves to indicate that an 'interior monologue' is taking place and that it is narrated indirectly, in the third person – but it is the monologue of someone who cannot always be easily identified. Now there is no reason to assume that 'indirect interior monologue' in thrillers necessarily represents an instance of solely textually based generic innovation – it crops up in a plethora of thrillers and has been present as a key narrative device since Jane Austen at least. However, as Cohn points out, indirect interior monologue

> often sustains a more profound ambiguity than other modes of rendering consciousness; and the reader must rely on context, shades of

meaning, coloring, and other subtle stylistic indices in order to determine the overall meaning of a text.

(1966, p. 112)

Rather than the competition of voices per se, therefore, the kind of openness described here is the key point for us. In concordance with our previous arguments, we would certainly have to add to Cohn's 'stylistic indices' the paramount importance of key reader investments in the rendering of the events and the consciousnesses of the characters in these novels.

Focalization in *52 Pick-Up*

In 52 *Pick-up*, married man Harry Mitchell goes to his girlfriend's home one day and is held by three masked men who show him a film of himself and his girlfriend and announce their intention to blackmail him. Unfortunately for them, Harry does not have the money that they require; he first tries to tell them this and then, later, after revealing all to his wife, starts to fight back. The main characters in the narrative are Harry Mitchell; his wife, Barbara; the head of the extortionists, Alan Raimy; and his two accomplices, Bobby Shy and Leo Frank. Each seem to share in the bulk of the focalizations[3] and the immediate conclusion to draw from this is simply that the narrative is dense with different perspectives. However, it is also worth noting that there are a great number of instances where the focalizations close to characters are almost merged with those of the external focalizer. This is hardly surprising, as they often amount to brief descriptions of actions – 'he said' etc. – or dialogue. On other occasions, though, the external focalizer's appearance will be subtle, but on close reading, quite definite. In Chapter 6, for instance, the focalization is close to Mitchell in his meeting with his employee, John Koliba. Then Mitchell pours some drinks and walks round his desk; the point of the scene is that Koliba watches Mitchell intently all the time, throughout the interview. Presumably, Mitchell turns his back on Koliba at more than one stage and so, even if he 'feels' he is being watched, only what he 'feels' can be focalized from a position close to him. Yet, the narrative states that Koliba definitely *does* watch him. Leaving aside the unlikely possibility that there is a sudden switch of focalization to Koliba, we must conclude that this is an instance of subtle operation by the external focalizer or narrator.

As with the hard-boiled novels discussed in the last chapter, the crime novels of Leonard do not manifest extensive knowledge of a character's motivations. The narration may be executed by focalizations which we have called *skaz* or 'indirect interior monologue' but, paradoxically, the reader does not get a great sense of what goes on in the character's mind, only their surface actions and most pressing plans. In *52 Pick-up*, for example, during the moments when the focalization is close to Leo Frank, we do not know what is happening with the characters that are absent from the scene. This is true, of course, of many stories. Yet in Leonard's novels the reader has been offered a tiny amount of knowledge of each character with each switch of focalization which is possibly enough to tantalize but not to satiate.

These switches of focalization are what Barthes (1974, p. 75) characterizes as delays, fundamental narrative features which simply prevent the swift and successful conclusion of the narration. In addition, they are self-conscious delays, indicative of the *elements that are not narrated*, allowing space for readers to speculate on what happens between narrated scenes. The 'surface' narrative is therefore one possible narrative drawn from the almost unlimited number of arrangements of events and different focalizations that could have been narrated; it is a 'version' in the same way that Kubrick's movie *Barry Lyndon* (1975) is a version of the Thackeray novel, or a plot summary may be a 'version' intended to bring out, for instance, the sexual element in a story (Herrnstein Smith 1981).

The way that the shifting focalizations in Leonard's novels quite obviously represent only one possible version or enactment of a potentially infinite number of alternatives is worth pondering for a moment. One way to think through the problem of who is focalizing when Mitchell and Koliba have a drink (see above) is through the cliché of the 'objectivity' of the 'camera eye'. It is hardly surprising that this has been mentioned by critics so often when one considers that Leonard found fame first as a screenwriter. However, it must be remembered that Leonard's narratorial strategies are not geared to present multiple perspectives on one event as occurs classically in a film such as *Rashomon* (1950); instead they are utilized to create a sequence of scenes in a linear chronological sequence. The narrative, while presenting multiple focalizations, therefore, presents only one version of the event as a whole.

Similarly, any set of 'prior events' involving a group of characters in a 'criminal setting' involves a narrativization of criminality. In *52 Pick-up* there is a focus upon one particular attempt among many possible others (of perhaps a more petty, less fraught nature) to get easy money, in large amounts, outside the law. Here, the key elements are the actual focus on one particular scam but also the way that Mitchell – hard-working, respectable, law-abiding – is narrativized in relation to the idea of criminality. To be sure, he is implicated in events; but the reader is invited also to scrutinize him against the backdrop of criminal activities and their setting, the Nude Models establishment, for instance. The plurality of focalizations seem appropriate for depicting the criminal milieu: the pornographer, the embittered union rep, the coke user, hard-worker, thief, snitch, entrepreneur – all are given their say however distasteful it may seem.

This is the aspect of Leonard's work which most frequently receives attention (see Arena 1990). Along with the foregrounded multi-voiced nature of his narratives it is often assumed that Leonard's crime novels are the acme of disinterested depiction. For Taylor (1997), they are accounts of a post-Foucauldian dispersal of power; for Haut, Leonard's novels do contain an ideology but 'it would take the skills of a literary archaeologist to uncover the contents of that ideology' (1999, p. 136). It is, perhaps, significant that both of these conclusions are drawn from a text-based scrutiny of Leonard's post-1970s work, particularly that which features police.

The Switch

Leonard's novels present a startling picture of a seemingly amoral world: of urban Detroit: Dodge Main, Ford's Rouge Plant, Polish workers from Hamtramck, hustlers, dudes, DeHoCo, Wayne County and a host of other signs rendered potent in the narratives by the existence of corresponding signs in the real world. It is now well known that Leonard relies heavily on both his own research and that of his assistant, Gregg Sutter (see Geherin 1989, p. 79; *Arena* 1990) to achieve a level of verisimilitude specific to the thriller. In 1978, for instance, Leonard spent a great deal of time researching the homicide squad of the Detroit Police Department, resulting in a factual article for the *Detroit News Magazine*, plus the novel *City Primeval* (1982; *Arena* 1990). That Leonard divides his writing between fictional and non-fictional modes, both of which are tropologically more similar than we tend to register (see Chapter 2 above), gives further credence to the verisimilitude of his novels. His novels might be seen as a 'version' of an already narrativized criminality, that is to say it co-exists with other narratives of criminality, including non-fiction ones.

A key theme running through Elmore Leonard's thrillers in the 1970s is also the title of his 1978 novel, *The Switch*. In this novel, two petty criminals – Louis and Ordell – decide to kidnap a middle-class housewife – Mickey – and make their fortune by ransoming her to her husband, Frank. Unfortunately for them, Frank has become tired of Mickey and has been planning to divorce her so that he can live with his mistress, Melanie. He is therefore quite pleased that the kidnappers have taken Mickey off his hands and refuses to pay. The narrative is concerned with working out this plot until the final pages where Louis and Ordell, after having established a friendship of sorts with Mickey, decide that all three of them should kidnap Melanie and hold her to ransom. This last part of the narrative is the 'switch', but a switch of this kind takes place in all of Leonard's 1970s crime novels.

The ability to recognise that there is a lack of certainty in the criminal world and in the world at large is accompanied in Leonard's novels by a resolve on the part of the central character to 'turn it around'. In *The Hunted*, Rosen has been hiding out in Israel after having testified against some gangsters in Detroit. When his picture appears in a newspaper, the gangsters come to get him and he is aided by a U.S. Embassy marine guard, Davis. At what can be considered as the pivot of the narrative, Rosen and Davis are involved in the following exchange:

> 'You're thinking, I can't reason with Val but maybe I could make a deal with him.'
> 'Unh-unh.'
> 'Pay him off.'
> 'No, I was thinking you could kill him', Davis said. 'Turn it around, hit him before he hits you.' (1985a, p. 105)

Similarly, in *Unknown Man No. 89*, Jack Ryan has been offered some money by Francis Perez to convince a woman with whom Ryan has become romantically engaged to sign away the fortune of her dead husband. It is a proposition that comes, once more, at a pivotal point in the narrative and in Jack's life. An interior monologue and an indirect interior monologue follows the proposition:

> Do it and take the money.
>   Don't do it. Forget the whole thing.
>   Go to the police. Call Dick.
>   Tell Denise everything and leave.
>   Or-
>   Christ. He saw it coming. He had seen it in his mind before, glimpses of it, but not as clearly as he saw it now.
>   – tell Denise everything and don't leave. Turn the whole thing around. Ace Mr. Perez. (1986c, pp. 134–5)

A possible reading of the *Switch* theme is offered by the final pages of the novel which bears it's name. When Louis, Ordell and Mickey kidnap Melanie in the last paragraph of the novel they are all wearing Richard Nixon masks (p. 184).

The idea of the switch in this context is therefore quite specific: to double-cross someone is not necessarily the sole prerogative of 'traditional' criminals. The morality of double-crossing no longer comes into the equation. One of the reasons for this is the specificity of 'turning it around'. As Perez says in *Unknown Man No. 89*, 'Never shit a shitter' (p. 148). In *Swag*, when Stick has just robbed a supermarket he is assaulted by two men who try to rob him and, despite the apparent absurdity of being robbed of his ill-gotten gains – an attempt to 'shit a shitter' – he shoots the two men (1984, pp. 112–15). This serves in all the novels to fix the generically specific terrain of gunplay, violence, retribution and fatalities that make up the criminal world.

All of these are probably at work most clearly in *52 Pick-up*. Harry Mitchell is an ex-Dodge Main blue-collar worker who, by way of the American ethic and postwar credit consumerism in conjunction with clean living, has elevated himself to the level of modest business owner. His one lapse – with Cini, a girl the age of his own daughter – has brought him into contact with the lower depths. Bobby, Alan and Leo are young and corrupt; they are involved in a range of narcotics and pornography deals and think that they can pressurize Mitchell. The latter's resolve is narrated by his wife as she almost embarks on an affair with Mitchell's friend, Ross; she tells him that, during his service as a Second World War air force pilot Mitchell shot down seven German planes as well as two British Spitfires which mistakenly attacked him:

> 'There was a hearing,' Barbara went on, 'an official investigation. Mitchell explained the situation as he saw it and, because of his experience and record, he was exonerated, as they said, of any malicious intent or accidental blame. The general, or whoever it was, closed the hearing. Mitch stood up and said, "Sir, I have a question." The general said, "What is it?" And Mitch said, "Do I get a credit for the Spitfires?" He was held in contempt of court and sent home the next week, assigned to an air base in Texas.' (pp. 87–8)

What this anecdote signifies in terms of Mitchell's conflict with the blackmailers is not so much his bravery and efficiency in the air force but his potential ruthlessness, lack of compassion and a lack of respect for established rules.[4] In the novel, the switch metaphorically enacts all the sterling values that built a nation (thrift, hard work, family loyalty) and couples them with a sense of vengeance and retribution which, as Geherin (1989, p. 45), Williams (1993, p. 188) and others have pointed out, derives from other genres' heroes, those of the Western novels where Leonard began his novel-writing career (see *City Primeval*, especially, p. 156)

If one wanted to frame Mitchell as the hero of the narrative, then, in these terms it would be very easy to do so, and one might even posit that he represented a dominant discourse in the text. On the one hand, one could say that Mitchell, and characters in the other novels, have very strong motivations, involving a combination of circumstances and long-term convictions, for effecting the switch. In *Mr. Majestyk*, Vince's economically stated hatred of prison serves to validate his actions against mobster Frank Renda (p. 35). In the examples which we have already cited, Stick acts to save himself and his booty (in *Swag*), Mickey needs to escape the dreariness of her life imposed by husband Frank (*The Switch*) and Ryan needs to escape the life of alcoholism which has afflicted him (*Unknown Man No. 89*). These are all the deep-seated reasons which accompany a specific instance of criminality which forces the protagonists to act. However, the other feature of this which needs to be addressed is the necessary resolution of the plot within the space and codes of the criminal milieu. These characters may have cogent motivations, but they are all forced into the realm of criminality. If they are to be considered heroes in the traditional sense, it is clear that their need to work within the criminal world will lead to some adjustments in the status of their characters and/or those of the already established criminals.

If the reading formation for these texts was one where a sufficiently problematized view of criminality existed, then it is possible that the traditional boundaries separating heroes and criminal villains might not apply. As can be seen (see note 3 to this chapter), the focalizations in *52 Pick-up* are very biased towards Mitchell; in *The Switch*, they are also heavily concerned with the kidnap victim – Mickey – and the kidnappers – Louis, Ordell, and to a lesser extent, Richard Monk.[5] There is no reason to suggest that this distribution of focalizations will *necessarily* engender sympathy from readers; in the apparently amoral world of criminality in these narratives, new codes of social conduct apply. Yet George V. Higgins indicates the connection between criminality and narrative resolution: 'Good guys are people who believe in Due Process of Law. Bastards are people who care not a whit for Due Process of Law. Bastards get results' (1972, p. 348).

If this is to be subsumed under a general narrative dynamic – the strong movement towards resolution which is characteristic of many thrillers – then we must add that it is one which offers a range of different potential investment points according to distinct reading formations. If a historical reading of Leonard's novels is to be posited, then, the multiple focalizations and the switch must be assumed not simply to 'constitute' readers eternally in a certain political way, but to offer the possibility of an interaction with the text's generic specificity which is moulded by the reading formation. What might be the specific meanings for contemporary readers of shifting focalizations and uncertain locations of criminality?

'One more shovelful on the dungheap'[6]

The boundaries of the law in the 1970s had shifted in such a way as to allow the proliferation of previously marginal discourses which were now available for narrativization. Amidst the Vietnam War, government covert activities and the protest movements it can easily be forgotten that America in the late 1960s was suffering a great deal of domestic concern about a crime wave. The riots of the mid-1960s in Oakland and Watts could not be considered as purely political phenomena; instead, controversies raged over the socio-economic determinants involved in such criminal activity (see Chapter 5 below) . In addition, voices were now raised about how the 'Great Society' project of Lyndon Johnson announced in the 1964 presidential campaign (see Boller 1985, pp. 308–14; Farber 1994, pp. 105ff.; Divine 1987; Kaplan and Cuciti 1986; Zarefsky 1996; Luke 1986; O'Reilly 1995, pp. 273ff.) was terminally undercut by the billions of dollars poured into the war in south-east Asia.[7]

For the majority of the public, the criminal offences which were most disturbing involved serious crime rather than the minor misdemeanours of the peace activists. The rate of violent crime in the United States rose by 25 per cent between 1960 and 1965, and over the next five year violent crime jumped by 82 per cent; enough, as Thernstrom and Thernstrom suggest 'to produce real public worry' (1997, p. 173). Watts and Free preface their public opinion survey on the issue by saying:

> The 1960s were plagued by soaring crime rates which peaked in 1968 when serious crime rose 14 per cent above 1967. In 1969 the increase was 9 per cent. The year-to-year comparison advanced to 10 per cent in 1970, slowed to a 6 per cent increase the next year, and registered a welcome 4 per cent decline in 1972.
>
> (Watts and Free 1974, p. 95)

These figures alone do not guarantee that a belief in the erosion of law would inevitably ensue. Nevertheless, the soaring crime rate did contribute to the construction of an arena of debate concerned precisely with this matter. The primary reason for this probably resides in the Nixon administration's initial high profile stance on the subject of law and order in the 1968 campaign, and on which it was subsequently unable to deliver (O'Reilly 1995). Yet the debate was certainly accelerated when the government deceptions stemming from Vietnam and Watergate became known (see, among a plethora of others, Voorhis 1973 and Mankiewicz 1973).

As the revelations of government double standards increased the process of reassessment that we have noted already began to be applied to questions of law. Debates in Congress during the Watergate affair, as one would expect, paid particular attention to the principle of legality. Inevitably, the Constitution was invoked to provide a framework for addressing the question of law during Watergate. In urging the impeachment of Nixon, Thornton pointed out that the contravening of laws has implications for a much wider field than the immediate one of politics:

> We have before us a momentous and difficult decision. I have approached it as a matter of law because I have faith that the people of this country believe that a system of law to which all men are subject is a system that we want and must preserve.
>
> (1974, p. 65)

What such statements do is to broaden the remit of the figurative prosecutors of Watergate and take it beyond the vulgar, removed world of politics. In an obvious sense the rhetoric of law serves the purpose of bolstering the task of bringing the President to book.

Yet it appears that Watergate did not constitute a major national issue according to the polls, although the issues of law associated with it in general did. In the spring of 1974 Watts and Free found the following:

Poll of 'Degree of Public Concern About Major National Issues'

1. The rise in prices and the cost of living
2. The amount of violence in American life
3. Crime in this country
4. Corruption and lawbreaking on the part of government officials . . . .
19. The significance of the Watergate affair in terms of our political and governmental system.

(1974, p. 20)

The pollsters give their evaluation of the breakdown of the figures:

> The public was highly worried about corruption or lawbreaking on the part of government officials (composite score 90). Yet the Watergate scandal as a specific issue was relegated to the lower half of the priority list with a score of only 72, even though in its varied ramifications it clearly involved serious violations of the law by a good many government officials, a number of whom have already been convicted, and it eventually led to the first resignation from office of a President of the United States. (Watts and Free 1974, pp. 26–7)

The link between crime, the law and corruption in government is essentially the same here as in the Congressional discussions of such matters. Put quite simply, the public view of crime is that it is no longer a phenomenon that is extraneous to political life; but crime as it is experienced in everyday terms – especially violent crime – is, undoubtedly, far removed from the deceptions of the Nixon administration.[8] (We will return to this question in Chapter 8.)

Large-scale corruption, of course, is not an unfamiliar theme for the thriller; but in an age when the government employs burglars, gets caught and covers up so poorly, the question of who deserves the authority to speak is inevitably thrown into relief. 'Who is the justice and who is the thief?' to borrow the cliché from Robert B. Parker (see Chapter 3 above). It might seem plausible, therefore, that the multiple focalizations in Leonard's novels act to dramatize a crisis of authority, or a 'crisis of confidence' (Schlesinger 1968). However, such homologies of world and textual structure are difficult to prove, and largely useless in the information that they render about readers. What we can deduce, however, is that there were certainly grounds for contemporary readers to invest the seemingly non-ideological formulations of crime stories with understandings and investments derived from current discourses on criminality. This is a possibility that we will also play out in respect to the narratives of George V. Higgins.

'It's not my job to clean up their act; it's my job to tell you what they did'

It can be argued that in Higgins's narratives the narrator is concealed more often than in the indirect interior monologue of Leonard's novels. In a novel such as Higgins's second, *The Digger's Game* (1988), for example, we can estimate that only about 3 or 4 per cent of its length is taken up with narrative prose, including such phrases as 'he said'. As Friedman (1955) maintains, in this mode dialogue dominates and narrative prose seems to serve merely as a stage direction; or, as Higgins puts it himself, his novels dealing with crime in the 1970s,[9] are like news in that 'The quotes make the story' (South Bank Show 1987).

Clearly, Higgins's novels are often commented upon in terms of an advance in the accurate depiction of reality and this reality is the result of a putatively exact recording of actual speech with few, if any, modifications (for example Hughes et al. 1982, p. 178). In a sense, though, this can simply be understood as a new model of reflection in which the work of authorial, implied authorial and narratorial organizing principles is effaced. A motto which Higgins offers as an instruction to budding writers is

> First: Know thyself
> – Plutarch
> Then: Try to keep it to yourself
> – Higgins

(Higgins 1991, p. 31)

Implicit in this motto is the idea that the author should remain absent from the narrative. Elsewhere, Higgins has made this clearer; speaking of the sexism, racism and general unpleasantness of some of his characters he says, 'It's not my job to clean up their act; it's my job to tell you what they did' (*South Bank Show* 1987). The chief corollary of this eschewal of judgment for Higgins is that he 'require[s] participation' (ibid.).

The participation that Higgins requests is quite clearly a part of all readings of all fictional texts as a result of the inability of texts to make determinate, or fully realise, their object. As the work of Iser attempts to demonstrate, textuality – especially fiction – is shot through with gaps such that readers are constantly filling in details which a narrative has neither the time nor space to offer. These will include a character's hair colour (if not 'given'), the weather in a scene (if not 'given'), the wallpaper in an interior (if not 'given') and so on (see Iser 1974; 1978; 1981; 1989; Fish 1981). Yet Higgins uses an even more telling metaphor to characterize the reader's participation in the realization of his texts: 'I prefer to think that the reader going through them is marshalling the evidence himself and reaching his own conclusions about the morality and the courage and the behaviour of the people' (*South Bank Show* 1987).

It is well known that Higgins was once state prosecutor for Massachussetts, and had also been a journalist. In both professions, the presentation of quotes is a far from neutral activity. What is omitted, for example, might be as important as what is narrated. In this way, Higgins's understanding of textuality is closer to that of Fish (1981) than to that of Iser. Implicit in the notion of marshalling evidence is that 'reality' does not exist in an unproblematic way before the text but is actually constituted by the act of representation (Hall 1997). As with Leonard, the narratives of Higgins are 'versions' of events, compelling because they are known *through* those versions.

In Higgins's second novel, *The Digger's Game*, the gaps between focalizations allow for what Higgins calls 'participation'. Jerry 'Digger' Doherty is a family man who has a habit of getting into financial difficulties as a result of his weak character. He owns an inn which provides most of the income for his wife and family but it is there that he meets shady characters. At the opening of the narrative he has returned from Las Vegas after a gambling trip during which he lost $18,000, a sum he owes to 'the Greek'. The narrative concerns the Digger's growing consternation over the debt that he is unable to pay the Greek and the attempts he makes to procure the money. It also concerns the Greek's involvement with Torrey and Schwabb who are allied to an ageing Mafioso and who decide that the Greek is a liability and needs to be killed.

The narrative combines instances of 'local colour' or one-liners with plot progression; but, equally, there are numerous instances where plot progression seems absent.[10] In the following example from *The Digger's Game*, Jerry Doherty is questioned by a driver who wants him to do a 'breaking and entering' job:

'Speaking of which, I assume you're not a shitter or anything.'

'No,' the Digger said.

'You know you're not a shitter, too, don't you?' the driver said.

'Well, I'm pretty sure,' the Digger said. 'I never done much of this but when I been in some place, I never did, no.'

'Well, in case you get the urge,' the driver said, 'wait till you get home or something. I had a real good guy that I always used, and he was all right. He could get in any place. You could send him down the Cathedral and he'd steal the cups at High Mass. But Jesus, I used him probably six or seven years and I never have the slightest problem with him, and the next thing I know, he's into some museum or something they got out there to Salem, and he's after silver, you know? And he shits, he turned into a shitter. Left himself a big fuckin' pile of shit right on the goddamned Oriental rug. Well he wasn't working for me or anything, and hell, everybody in the world was gonna know the next day he was in there, because the silver was gone. But that was the end of him as far as I was concerned, I didn't have no more use for him. The thing is you don't want nobody to know you've been in there until you're ready, okay? So no shit on the desks or anything. Keep your pants on.'

(pp. 3–4)

The information on criminal procedure is negligible and the sequence is one of many that offer substantial diversions into potentially interesting sub-narratives. If any part of Higgins' narratives can be singled out as the location of 'realism' then it is probably here: characters seem to have an unbounded discourse of their own and speak of matters which are not apparently germane to the plot.[11]

The question that needs to be asked regards the extent to which a supervisory role is played by any textual or non-textual entity in Higgins' narratives. We can say that the role of the implied author in an epistolary novel such as *Les Liaisons Dangereuses* (1782) is to place the 'documents' of the narrative in a specific way. This sheds some light on the similar role that is enacted in Higgins' novels where an implied author is responsible for the specific instances of dialogue in the narrative that are allowed to be narrated. All those potential conversations in the narrative that are not narrated are rejected by the implied author; all those conversations that are incorporated into the narrative have been sanctioned by the implied author. The clearest example of this is towards the end of *The Digger's Game* when a very short chapter (pp. 162–3) narrates Harrington's call to the police after the narration has almost constantly been close to Jerry, Torrey, Schwabb and the Greek. What we are trying to suggest here is that there does seem to be a way of analysing the text in order to detect a measure of intentionality in the narrative prose. However, given the tiny amount of narrative prose that appears, it would be impossible – or at the least very difficult – to observe in detail the character of a guiding hand by reference to prose which is made up of the kind of bland constructions we have already noted (such as 'he said').

Another place where one might seek a textually located contribution to the production of meaning would be in the events narrated in the dialogue. Early in *The Digger's Game* Torrey and the Greek are having a conversation about Torrey's recent extensive sexual activity. This includes Torrey's claim that he has recently fellated a young woman whom he has picked up at a club; what he feels to be of note is that the young woman was an insurance clerk and that she had evidently applied a strawberry flavoured spray to her vagina immediately prior to meeting Torrey for the first time that evening (pp. 23–4). The only comments on this episode are the Greek's: 'I'm not gonna bring up kids in a world, people walking around with vanilla pussy, hot fudge cocks. This country's going to the dogs, you know that, Richie? Guys like you (p. 24).' The reader's reaction to the anecdote, of course, does not have to tally with the Greek's. However, soon after this, a paragraph featuring further assessment of Torrey by the Greek lends some perspective to Torrey's character which might enable a reader to assess him:

> 'I look good because I want to look good and I work at it,' the Greek said. 'Not because I want to go around like a goddamned pervert. You want to go around in those yellow things, shirts, pants, the white shoes, it's probably all right, you look like a nigger pimp. Don't matter to you. I got some self-respect'.

> (p. 24)

At this moment, the reader can see Torrey through the eyes of the Greek and the former's lurid style is hence revealed. Nevertheless, ultimately it does not matter whether Higgins or the Greek are expert witnesses; the reader can construct a picture of Torrey which does not necessarily correspond to that which might be intended by the narrative.

Crime and the verisimilar

That Higgins's texts may be arranged in the reading formation as a realistic narrative about criminals and/or as a thriller is of consequence – along with Higgins's claims of accuracy – in the establishment of a narrative's verisimilitude. For example, the *New Yorker* comments on *The Friends of Eddie Coyle*: 'A brilliant thriller...The No. 1 Fast Read of the Winter' (quoted in Higgins 1973, p. 2). Such comments frame a possible reading in terms of a heavy emphasis on narrative resolution coupled with a set of expectations about what the thriller genre at that moment implies. In addition, most bookshops file Higgins's novels in the crime/mystery section (see *South Bank Show* 1987). On the other hand, there is a heavy emphasis in textual cues on the studied realism, implicitly *de-emphasising* the generic nature of the Higgins novels. For example,

> 'Digger is so real that the next time you order a drink from a bartender, you'll look at him hard, wondering what he does on his days off.'
> *Los Angeles Times* (quoted on the back cover of Higgins 1988)

'Reeking of authenticity... chilling... the most penetrating glimpse yet into the real world of crime.'

New York Times Sunday Book Review

'A real find... tough, authentic, down to the last gritty detail of language used by the crooks and the police – this short novel reads like something ripped out of an actual case history of crime.'

American Publishers' Weekly (quoted in Higgins 1973, p. 2)

The last claim, of course, is somewhat absurd in that a police report – if that is what is referred to as a 'case history' – never contains as much dialogue as a Higgins novel, with the exception, perhaps, of an interview transcript. Nevertheless, it is clear that the realism of Higgins's narratives is part of the public knowledge embodied in the reviews. The specific mechanisms for rendering that air of realism may therefore be, in a sense, secondary, merely offering a way of working out certain investments with regard to the text rather than engendering a specific viewpoint.

Yet it is not just realism that is prefigured here, but a verisimilitude based on experience of the commonplace. After all, a fiction about something as uncommon as the American Presidency or rocket scientists can be more or less 'realistic'. What is important here, though, is everyday situations. Higgins's narratives feature a universe of crime in which individuals attempt to save their own livelihoods but do so by means of a conventionalized amorality that they do not recognize because it is bound up in domestic exigencies. The world in which Higgins's characters live allows no recourse to the strength that might derive from, say, a personal moral code. Family and other aspects of everyday life are integrated into criminal business despite attempts to keep both dimensions separate. In *The Friends of Eddie Coyle*, Eddie sends his wife upstairs while he calls Foley with a tip-off, but it is his worry over the fate of his children and his wife that makes him dread a possible sentence of two years' imprisonment that hangs over him.[12] Similarly, the Digger is lured into the robbery of a fur warehouse in order not just to get the Greek off his back but to curtail the worries and the nagging of his wife, Aggie. The Digger also has the added difficulty of appeasing his brother, Paul, whom he has taken money from, lied to and, as a result, brought FBI suspicion to rest on the priest. Once more, these concerns with the family are not just connected to the plots of the narratives; for example, in *The Digger's Game*, Jerry argues with Aggie over their adolescent son who is continually masturbating in the toilet, and they both blame each other for his behaviour (p. 43).

The seemingly pointless conversations of characters which we have mentioned above are thus writ large in Higgins' narratives. Verisimilitude – even the specific verisimilitude of the thriller – is firmly embedded in the dilemmas of mundane everyday existence and domestic life. The coexistence of traditional family values with crime had provided a potent motif and multiple points of investment for audiences of *The Godfather*. In Higgins's novels, similar investment points are offered, although the crime is distinctly disorganised and the glamour is conspicuous by its absence.

Reading into crime

Leonard, and particularly Higgins, could equally have been said to have been pre-empted in their use of focalization by numerous authors, especially Hemingway. In fact, if one wanted to take this further, one could suggest that the only textual innovation that the novels of Leonard and Higgins represent is a semantic one: their wholesale incorporation of obscene language (see *Arena* 1990 and *South Bank Show* 1987). If Hemingway's narratives from the 1920s onwards contained focalization techniques almost identical to Higgins's, then we must posit a specific and possibly transient interpretation of the meaning of focalization in the texts of the 1970s. That this mode of narration was focused on crime is significant: as we have noted, for public and administrators alike, crime was a problem with no easy solutions and no easily identifiable sources.

We cannot say that multiple focalizations in the crime novel of the 1970s prove that authors were seeing political reality in a different way; nor can we say that the presence of multiple focalizations in texts manoeuvred the reader into sharing this vision of political reality. As we suggested at the beginning of this chapter, by invoking the world outside individual texts the more problematic 'inscription' theories at least embody the insight that there are more factors at play beyond the determining force of fictions on a reader. Where considerations of readers and their environments have been absent or downplayed there has been a tendency to promote the idea that there are purely textual means of ensuring verisimilitude, that there are some devices which can apprehend 'reality' and that there are some which are not so good at the task. Here, if the devices are the right ones, the reader will be 'shown reality'. As such, good practice in depicting the real depends on the implementation of appropriate techniques.

However, we can now suggest, alternatively, that a conjunction of events filtered through other discourses might produce the grounds for the specific reading of the crime novels we have discussed in this chapter. It is on these grounds of reading that innovation is to be found: in so far as the seventies crime novel is 'syntactically different' from its counterparts in other decades – and, contemporaneously, within the larger thriller genre – it is because it is designated as such by surrounding discourses. Innovation can be seen to reside, therefore, in the reading of texts with seemingly new semantic elements as well as the reading of these texts within a formation that signals them as novel and innovative in some respects.

We have seen how the new coordinates of criminality in American social life might have contributed to the grounds for reading Leonard's multi-voiced narratives. By the same token, it is no coincidence that George V. Higgins not only wrote crime novels in the 1970s but also wrote two texts set in Washington. The first was a novel, *City on a Hill*, whose events took place in 1973 and which involved senators, aides and journalists in the nation's capital. The second was a non-fiction book about Watergate called *The Friends of Richard Nixon* (1975b), which involved the same. Like his crime novels, these books were peopled by mean-spirited and weak-willed characters who dominate the narratives with their dialogue. In one sense, one could say that the cut-throat world of Higgins's crime novels was displaced to a slightly different milieu; in another sense, the corruption of Washington was to be read into Higgins's crime novels.

Further Reading

Print

Cain, James M. 1975. *Rainbow's End*
Cain, James M. 1976. *The Institute*
Condon, Richard 1972. *Arigato*
Crawford, William 1973. *The Chinese Connection*
Ferris, Wally 1970. *Across 110th Street*
Hill, Lance 1975. *King of the White Lady*
Mann, Patrick 1975. *Dog Day Afternoon*
Murray, William 1977. *Mouth of the Wolf*
Nash, N. Richard 1975. *Cry Macho*
Pronzini, Bill 1974. *Snowbound*
Rostand, Robert 1976. *The D'Artagnan Signature*
Schrader, Leonard 1975. *The Yakuza*
Stark, Richard 1974. *Butcher's Moon*
Trevanian 1976. *The Main*

Wager, Walter 1970. *Sledgehammer*
Westheimer, David 1974. *Over the Edge*

Film

Satan's Sadists (January 1970)
Bloody Mama (March 1970)
The Moonshine War (July 1970)
Angel Unchained (August 1970)
The Grissom Gang (May 1971)
(Based on Faulkner/Hadley Chase)
The Last Run (July 1971)
Prime Cut (June 1972)
Across 110th St (December 1972)
Dillinger (June 1973)
The Friends of Eddie Coyle (June 1973)
This Is a Hyjack (June 1973)
Harry in Your Pocket (August 1973)
Mean Streets (October 1973)
Charley Varrick (October 1973)
That Man Bolt (December 1973)
Crazy Joe (February 1974)
Thieves Like Us (February 1974)
Macon County Line (May 1974)
The Nickel Ride (May 1974)
Mr Majestyk (May 1974)
99 And 44/100% Dead (June 1974)
Truck Turner (June 1974)
Big Bad Mama (September 1974)
The Yakuza (March 1975)
Capone (April 1975)
Lepke (May 1975)
Crazy Mama (July 1975)
Angelo (April 1976)
Street People (September 1976)
Death Collector (January 1977)
Feedback (March 1979)
The Lady In Red (August 1979)

5
'Keeping That Sixth Ball in the Air': The Police

The police genre or subgenre is by no means a new thing; in fact, police routine features as a major component in the very inception of the thriller genre (Knight 1980; Panek 1990). It can be argued, however, that the foregrounding of police professionalism in the procedural genre associated with the novels of Ed McBain and those of Sjöwall and Wahlöö is a specifically post-1945 phenomenon. In the last two decades of the twentieth century especially, organised police forces and individual police operatives appear to have come into their own in the broader genre. At the present there seems to be a critical consensus in commentary on thrillers – and especially on their verisimilitude – that the (American) police represent the 'real goods' (Messent 1997; Ellroy 1994). Such a consensus derives, frequently, from what appear to be strictly generic issues: namely, that the police story constitutes a significant advance over the private eye subgenre. Even here, though, the advance is couched in terms of the police genre's superior verisimilitude, the way that the sheer variety and danger of urban police work in the real world outweighs the straightforward mundanity of security operations and private detection. For Ellroy and others, the private eye genre is – by comparison with preferred narratives about the police – a complete confection and a thoroughgoing conceit.

Yet it is not only that the police genre is argued to possess a greater potential of verisimilitude. Implicitly, the *contemporary* police genre is seen to be more 'realistic' and more representative of a '*noir*' mentality, or the reality of 'the city' (Haut 1999; cf. Willett 1996). In James Ellroy's *LA Quartet* novels – and especially the film of *LA Confidential* (1997) – it is evident that the police series *Dragnet* is satirised in different parts of the narratives. This programme, which evolved from a radio show and ran on American television from 1952 to 1959 and then intermittently from 1966 to 1970, was a public-relations exercise engineered largely by the LAPD. Such a jaundiced outlook on the show was not unique in the 1980s: the attitudes and the style of the original series had already been mercilessly pilloried in the comedy film 'remake' of it (1987), a satire starring Dan Aykroyd which took the character of Joe Friday as an emblem of antiquated discourses about crime and social forces.

In the face of this contemporary 'knowing' perspective, though, it should also be mentioned that *Dragnet* is well remembered as the embodiment of veracity in its day (see, for example, Symons 1992, p. 193; Panek 1987, p. 172; Knight 1980, p. 168), as is *Z Cars* in a slightly later period in Britain. What seems to have changed in police genres – and the decade of the 1970s is pivotal in this respect – is not the standard of generic verisimilitude so much as the discourses which underpin it, the *doxa* that we discussed in Chapter 1. Although it would be all too simple to say that the criminal perspectives and complex moral imperatives which we have noted in previous chapters had become more widespread and prevalent in the 1970s, it *is* apparent that there *were* discourses abroad which did seem to contribute to such a case. Even before Watergate and the revelations of unlawful government actions in the Vietnam war, questions were being asked about the sterling character of domestic institutions.

Joseph Wambaugh and the new centurions

Let us consider an example of this; an example which, in fact, refers to the work of a writer who has been instrumental in maintaining the critical focus on the police genre since the 1970s. Joseph Wambaugh was a detective sergeant with the Los Angeles police department who turned to writing novels about the routine, diversity and psychology of police work. These include *The New Centurions* (1970), *The Blue Knight* (1973), *The Choirboys* (1975) and *The Black Marble* (1977), in addition to his non-fiction work such as *The Onion Field* (1973). He also created the highly influential – but not overly commercially popular – TV series *Police Story* (1973), in which he featured as both an actor and as a character. While his novels garnered favourable to ecstatic reviews, the films of them fared less well.[1] So much so that, following the debacle of the movie of *The Choirboys* (1976), Wambaugh pulled out all the stops to gain control and produce a script for the film of *The Onion Field* (1979); a script which would not be subject to studio interference. This discrepancy between the favour bestowed upon the novels and the critical opprobrium lodged against the film versions may be one reason that Richard Fleischer's movie of *The New Centurions* (1972) was given such critical short shrift. A closer look at the reviews, however, reveals more focused complaints.

The novel of *The New Centurions* is concerned with the experiences of three rookie cops, their five years in training and their graduation into the melee of the Watts riot. What is reasonably clear about the novel is that it attempts to depict the rich tapestry of experiences which makes up the average policeman's life. Especially when reading the book in the opening years of the twenty-first century, it is fairly evident that this is a novel which is sympathetic towards police operatives without being sentimental or politically extreme. Yet reviews of the film were almost unanimous about the behaviour of the policemen: '*The New Centurions* is a sort of Agnew production in praise of the police,' wrote Penelope Gilliatt (1972) in the *New Yorker*. 'Never a bribe passes and the rule of the gun is upheld.' For her, the movie is almost like a recruiting film for the LAPD. Zimmerman, in *Newsweek*, echoes this theme when he writes: 'The Los Angeles cops here are paragons, as though the great comrades of those old Notre Dame football movies had all decided to go into police work' (1972). Both he and Gilliatt worry that the police are just not dirty enough in this depiction:

> The film makes not a single mention of graft, never shows a cop 'cooping' (sleeping on the job) or shaking down pimps or prostitutes. For all its supposed realism, the film never mentions the heroin traffic, which could not continue without the complicity of thousands of cops.
>
> (Zimmerman 1972)

While Cocks, in *Time*, is more circumspect with regard to the kind of incendiary statements that Zimmerman makes in the last sentence, his feelings about the film are basically the same:

> None of these centurions are on the take, none corrupted or vicious or even cynical. To be sure, Roy's wife leaves him and he hits the bottle for a while, but he, like the other cops, is portrayed as a lonely battler against iniquity, mostly unloved and generally misunderstood.
>
> (1972c)

How could it be the case that the reviews of the film were so uniform in their condemnation of a vision of the police which does not foreground corruption and cynicism?

In attempting to answer this question we will shed some light not just on the police genre in the 1970s but also, perhaps, on its fortunes beyond this decade.

'To exemplify what society should be rather than reflect what it was'

One of the most prominent police narratives of the 1970s consisted of a non-fiction thriller, a major film, a TV series (1976) and the culmination of a city-wide investigation into police corruption which was made public with the findings of the Knapp Commission delivered in August 1973. Each of them took as its focus an individual policeman, Frank Serpico, a New York cop who was

> the first officer in the history of the Police Department who not only reported corruption in its ranks, but voluntarily, on his own, stepped forward to testify about it in court. He did so after a lonely four-year odyssey in which he was repeatedly rebuffed in his efforts to get action from high police and political officials, continually risking discovery at any moment by the crooked cops he rubbed shoulders with every day, and finally, out of desperation, after he went to a newspaper with his story.
>
> (Maas 1974, p. 11)

This is a fair synopsis of Maas's book *Serpico* (1974) and it occurs quite early in the book's narrative for the benefit of those who do not know the story already from the news. The book is organized as a telling of the 'truth' of Serpico's experiences and, like Sidney Lumet's 1973 film of the Serpico story, proceeds with a flashback: it begins with the shooting of Serpico which puts him in hospital for a prolonged stay and which ultimately results in his leaving the force; it then traces his story chronologically until that moment.

Rather than being totally restricted to one character's view of events, the narration of Serpico's story proceeds along the lines of the kind of semi-omniscience which we have witnessed in some hard-boiled narratives. Generally, the narrative does not present the thoughts of other characters in the story, nor does it narrate events involving them; instead, it sticks to narrating events in which Serpico was involved and it presents Serpico's own thoughts sparingly enough to suggest that they were volunteered by him during part of the research to aid in constructing the narrative. But there are times when one can claim that the narrative veers in the direction of omniscience. These are occasions when it reveals that it is based on research either about history – Chapter 8 is about graft in New York City during the century – or when it is about individuals significant to Serpico – for example, the feelings of an ex-girlfriend are narrated (p. 160). As a rule, however, this question of the narration does not arise because, like *All the President's Men*, the non-fictionality and credibility of the narration can be said to be guaranteed precisely because of its partial focus.

So this story of corruption in the police force is very much Serpico's own, and the details of his motivations and life are somehow symbolic of the times. A flavour of this is given in Chapter 3, which starts with the first of a continuing series of in-depth accounts of Serpico's youthful experiences. For readers who may not have gained the knowledge from extra-textual cues, the book has already made clear that the contemporary Serpico looks like a hippie and, although this is largely precipitated by the fact that he has worked undercover for some time, it is also made evident that he identifies with some countercultural attitudes. One story from childhood, however, is undoubtedly precious to him:

> [On one Sunday afternoon] when Frank was ten, he burst into the greenhouse crying because some kids had taunted him for wearing hand-me-down clothes. His father listened, and then told him a story about a prince who disguised himself in rags to see what the citizens of his kingdom were really like, only to be chased away by them. When the prince returned the next day dressed in full regalia, the townspeople who had hooted at him bowed and scraped, but he sent them packing, telling them they ought to be ashamed of themselves, that he was still the same person. 'So you see,' his father concluded, 'it's not how a man looks. It's what he is inside that counts.'
>
> (Maas 1974, pp. 25–6)

This brief passage and the parable that it recounts say a great deal about what will concern Serpico in his subsequent fight against corruption, dealing with the deceptiveness of appearances, the perils entailed by certain rules of respectability, the importance of class differences, the triumph of exposing duplicity, and so on.

The narration suggests how such disparate motivations became crystallised through certain notions about the role of the police force in society:

> what he remembered most from his boyhood was a concept of the cop as 'good' – and beyond this that a cop was the personification of

authority and prestige and respect. When a cop came down the sidewalk and said, 'Move along', one moved, and fast. (Maas 1974, p. 39)

Later, Serpico dismisses his own naivety in this matter (p. 39), but it is worth adding that this movement from naivety to analysis is strikingly similar to that of other idealists who later came to identify with counter-cultural values. Ron Kovic, in *Born on the Fourth of July*, which appeared a few years after *Serpico* in 1976, details how his extremely enthusiastic idealism with regard to America, the marines and the war in Vietnam were systematically eroded over a period of time. One could say that, initially, both Kovic and Serpico so believed the hype about the right-eousness of the war and the police respectively that their eventual loss of faith in them was total. As a result, their 'hippiedom' – symbolized most readily by long hair and moustaches/beard – represented the only poss-ible vehicle for their feelings about what the system *should* be. This kind of reorientation, the way that the 'outsider' is more of an 'insider' with respect to traditional American values and idealism, is rehearsed in such films as *The Graduate* (1967) and *Easy Rider* (1969), and also in narratives such as *Dog Day Afternoon* (see Chapter 2 above) and some of the texts discussed in Chapters 7 and 8 (below).

Probably the most emphatic commentary on 'how things are' and 'how things should be' in *Serpico*, though, results from the double narra-tion of one specific event (an event which is central in the film version and the pilot for the TV series). Shortly before Serpico is shot in the face he finds himself in court for the trial of one of the felons he has recently arrested:

> [The] white numbers operator that Serpico had arrested, Vincent Sausto, alias Mickey McGuire, turned to him in court and said, 'Hey, you know they're going to do a job on you,' and when Serpico asked him who he had in mind, Sausto said, 'Your own kind,' and Serpico asked, 'What do you mean my own kind, the Italians?' and Sausto replied, 'No, cops!'
>
> (Maas 1974, p. 197; cf. p. 13)

It is almost as if the criminal has a greater insight into the workings of the police than the seemingly naive Serpico. What is more important, though, is the double-cross motif that is articulated twice: those who should be Serpico's allies are not what they seem. In this way, the narrative of police operations shares an affinity with *All the President's Men* – the clandestine and serpentine nature of Serpico's attempts to stem the tide of corruption in the New York Police Department draw him into a world where one can never be sure who is listening or who one's allies are.

In a sense, Serpico is a Deep Throat figure: both continue their legitimate police or White House duties while feeling that information should be fed to somebody in order to expose rampant duplicity. This is a process which involves fear and apprehensiveness. Deep Throat disseminates his information to fortuitously like-minded people, while Serpico's information initially meets with a less enthusiastic response from those who receive it. Both also represent the part of the story's content which is to do with vindicating the comparative honesty of the media. By taking his story to the *New York Times*, Serpico is practically demonstrating that the only morality that can serve his cause is the muck-raking one that informs media exposés (Maas 1974, pp. 204ff; cf. the comments of Mayor Lindsay, pp. 250–1).[2]

Yet *Serpico*, while it seeks to expose the widespread corruption amongst the guardians of public life, also narrates more regular occupational details about police work. One key incident involves the young cop's reflection on the immediate, unquestioned backup he receives when alone and apprehending a number of suspects in a car (p. 70). In light of examples of community such as these, Serpico's statement before the Knapp Commission hearings which appears at the climax of the book attempts to set an agenda for the future:

> A policeman's first obligation is to be responsible to the needs of the community he serves.
>
> The department must realize that an effective, continuing relationship between the police and the public is more important than an impressive arrest record.
>
> (pp. 244–5)

The occupational and civic roles of the police, as well as the difficulties inherent in the task of policing and the support systems necessary for the administration of the law, were all issues which, arguably, underpinned the narratives of Serpico. When these narratives gained even more prominence with the release of the film, however, these pressing matters became lost in the publicity mix.

Reviewers of the film foregrounded the way in which it contained a narrative that inflected certain contemporary political currents without dealing directly with the world of federal politics. Pauline Kael's summary statement of such concerns is a very powerful one and can almost be taken as representative of the period:

We have no word, as yet, for justifiable paranoia – that is, for the sane person's perception of a world become crazily menacing – and in terms of behaviour there may not be much difference between living in terror of actual enemies and living in terror of imaginary enemies, particularly if the natural enemies represent the whole system of authority.

(Kael 1973 p. 107)

As Kael implies, the exposé of police corruption carries with it a social dimension which is very specific for contemporary readings.

Unsurprisingly, there were found to be grounds in the Serpico story for making observations about the American social formation, and one way reviewers were to address this was by identifying the film's 'attitude'. Andrew Sarris in the *Village Voice* asks, 'Is there a valid connection between honesty and non-conformism or is it merely a coincidence in Serpico's case?' (Sarris 1973b).[3] Sarris' complaint is that the issue of police corruption is lost in the general celebration of countercultural values in competition with the establishment. Comparing the 'facts' of the Serpico story with the products of the writer of the book, the two writers of the screenplay of the film and the film's director, he adds: 'It would seem that Serpico, Maas, Salt, Wexler and Lumet have taken the line of least resistance in transforming a saga of corruption and persecution into special pleading for an alternate life style' (Sarris 1973b). Any complexities that either the texts of the book or the film allow is reduced by this apparently feasible formulation (cf. Silber 1976, p. 80)

The problem of the Serpico narratives for the critics was that they failed to convey the complexity of occupational situations. Pauline Kael complains:

The people and issues are so simplified they seem exaggerated . . . We don't get a clear view of Serpico as a rookie, to see in what ways he was different from the other rookies, and we are never brought to identify with his year-in-year-out doggedness.

(1973 p. 107)

On one level one could argue that this is simply untrue; as we have seen, Maas's book gives considerable attention to Serpico's youth and rookie years in order to spell out his motivation. Similarly, a substantial part of the film narrates Serpico's early years on the force.[4] Moreover, it would be close to impossible to reflect with any great accuracy the diversity and drawn-out nature of police work. But Kael's view is of a piece with other criticisms of the narratives: 'the Maas book is a popularizing account of

Serpico which practically deifies him' (1973, p. 108); the depiction of Serpico in the film is as 'a doe-eyed Diogenes in a city on the take' (Sarris 1973b), or, as John Simon in *Esquire* suggests, as 'A sort of saint or hermit, who talks to his cockatoo as St. Francis did to the birds, and is followed by his sheep dog as St. Jerome was by his lion' (1974a).[5]

Editions of Maas's book carried quotes from *Newsweek*: 'Serpico did all that one man could do – and more', and the *New York Times*: 'No one can come away from *Serpico* without admiration for one man's lonely integrity'.[6] Notwithstanding such veneration there *were* counter-arguments to these positions. In statements accompanying below-the-line publicity for the film, Serpico himself was emphatic in the problematization of the 'hero': 'I graduated from Boy Scout to Saint. Baloney! In terms of conventional morals I don't even qualify for a Sunday School prize' (quoted in Gibbins 1974). What is lost, perhaps, in the reading formation in which the texts appear is the problems inherent and the resources needed when 'it is incumbent upon a cop to adhere to a stricter standard of conduct than the average citizen, to exemplify what society should be rather than reflect what it was' (Maas 1974, p. 76). The pronounced disdain of the police reflected in the comments of reviewers of the film of *The New Centurions* seems to suggest not simply a weary cynicism but an impassioned lament. The sentiments of the reviewers seem to reveal enough outrage and horror for us to infer that it is borne of a recently shattered idealism about morality in the public sphere.

That this period in the history of the thriller genre should be marked, initially, by critical scorn and skepticism with regard to police integrity is certainly remarkable. In fact, it is doubly remarkable in that the 1970s was to witness an unprecedented explosion of police narratives onto the entertainment scene. In print, old hands like Ed McBain continued to publish bestsellers, while newcomers such as Wambaugh and K. C. Constantine produced critically well-received books. In the cinema, the Dirty Harry series sustained a strong following (see Chapter 8), while the narratives of no less than three films focused on the exploits of real-life detective, Eddie Egan – the commercially successful *The French Connection* (1971) and *The French Connection II* (1975) as well as the less lucrative *Badge 273* (1973). Non-fiction narratives such as the books about the 'Super Cops' (Greenberg 1975 and Whittlemore 1973) and the film depicting their exploits (1974) presented details of police life which were viewed as 'strange but true'. And corruption remained on the agenda in films like *McQ* (1974) and *The Take* (1974). By far the strongest evidence of the burgeoning of the police genre was offered, however, by television.

Television police series seemed to harbour a greater range of possibilities to deal with the unlimited breadth of police work. Over the period of a season they might be able to touch on issues raised by different kinds of misdemeanour and the diverse determinants acting upon the interaction of police and public. This is not to say that all police series produced in the 1970s were characterised by narratives geared towards acute social investigation. One of the most popular, *Columbo* (1971), for example, traded exclusively in 'inverted whodunits' set in an upper middle-class milieu, leaving little or no possibility of social comment or investment. Moreover, the idea that the cop show had simply *replaced* the Western as the foremost TV genre was increasingly a topic for popular discussion.

However, it seems to be the case that the police genre was, in a quite specific way, especially ripe for investments by audiences at this time. There was a convergence of forces in the social formation during the period which not only fostered degrees of cynicism about police operatives in a fashion which had not been encountered before, but also a set of discourses which served to heighten the complexity of public understanding of police work. Before we proceed to look at a couple of examples of the police genre on television in the seventies, let us consider some of the evidence of contemporary discourses about police work.

Policing the crisis of confidence

In 1967, the President's Commission on Law Enforcement and the Administration of Justice identified 420,000 people working for approximately 40,000 separate law enforcement agencies spending $2.5 billion a year (pp. 91 ff). Since 1945, the police in America had become part of a large and unwieldy bureaucracy. In the face of mounting crime, departments repeatedly opted for specialization, transferring vice control, traffic regulation, crime prevention and a range of routine tasks from ordinary patrolmen to organised squads (Fogelson 1977, pp. 240 ff.). At the same time, legal precedents made law enforcement and administration more difficult for police operatives. A series of landmark Supreme Court decisions, designed to protect against unsafe convictions, followed in quick succession during the 1960s. *Mapp* (1961) restricted previous guidelines on search and seizure, *Escobedo* (1964) re-drew the grounds for gaining confessions from suspects, while the cases of *Wade*, *Gilbert* and *Stoval* (all 1967) introduced new edicts on eyewitness identification and line-ups. One of the most momentous decisions, however, concerned *Miranda* (1966), which required police officers to read suspects their rights before placing them under arrest (Fogelson

1977, p. 239). From the view of the police, as Jerry Wilson of the Washington, DC force argues, none of the purposes of the new laws could be disputed; yet the 'commensurate increases in police personnel and court facilities' necessary to make the laws effective in most cities were never provided (1975, p. 30).

The changes in policing structures and in the law on suspects engendered no small measure of conflict. As Fogelson puts it, police departments

> authorized uniformed officers to stop, question, and if they deemed it necessary, frisk anyone who aroused their suspicion. As a result of these changes, the big-city police now intervened in all sorts of situations which in the absence of a strong complaint they would have ignored a generation or two before. By so doing – by arresting a taxpayer for gambling, citing a motorist for speeding, and ordering a few teenagers to keep moving – they generated a great deal of resentment.
>
> (1977, p. 241)

In addition – and in contrast to Britain – the American police lacked the weight of custom or traditional respect of the public. The sociologist Albert Reiss suggests : 'The police in the United States have occupational prestige. They do not have status honor' (1971, p. 215). As Reiss and all other researchers into American police work have found, the most common complaint among rank-and-file police operatives regards the failure of citizens to show respect for authority.

In police work this perceived erosion in deference manifested a sociopolitical dimension as well as a grass roots one. In their work for the President's Commission, Reiss and his researchers found that the citizen was described as 'agitated' or 'excited' in 48 per cent of all citizen-police encounters when an officer was deemed 'hostile', 35 per cent when he was 'brusque' or 'authoritarian', 42 per cent in which he openly ridiculed a citizen, and 57 per cent when the officer 'subtly ridiculed' or belittled a citizen (1971, p. 51). Sociologists of the period repeatedly found that police–citizen encounters were potentially so fraught with communicative misunderstandings and the threat of hostility and violence that police counter-assertions of authority were frequently liable to escalation. Studies called for a renewal of citizens' understanding of the civic role of the police (Livermore 1980; Lundman 1980; Rubinstein 1980; Wiley and Hudik 1980; cf. Reiss 1971, pp. 179 ff.).

At the same time, however, flashpoints arising from routine police–citizen encounters were almost always at the root of disturbances with a

palpable political or socio-economic bearing, instances where resentment had built up over time. Thernstrom and Thernstrom (1997, p.
163) suggest that the police were crucial catalysts in the urban riots of
the 1960s not just because police actions were usually the precipitating
incidents in disorders but also because, for African Americans especially,
the police represented a visible instrument of 'white' authority (cf.
Wambaugh 1970 and Richardson 1974, p. 180). In a poll taken by the
National Opinion Research Center, alongside the work of the President's
Commission, it was found that 63 per cent of whites thought the police
to be 'almost all honest' while only 30 per cent of blacks believed this to
be the case (cited in Richardson 1974, p. 183). The much-vaunted explosion of crime rates in the 1960s – especially in respect to violent crime –
did include a tripling of rates of arrest of black men on homicide charges
(Thernstrom and Thernstrom 1997, p. 173). Yet whatever inference can
be drawn from this it is also well-known that over the next thirty years
black men were to become *murder victims* at twice the rate that they were
in 1960 (ibid., pp. 262 ff.).

The relation of 'race' and downgrading of authority was to solidify
among the police. Police complaints about the lack of respect for authority were all too easily inflected along lines of ethnicity (Coles 1971).
When compounded with feelings of low status, complaints on the one
side from the while middle class about the non-delivery of the law and
order that President Nixon had made his campaign platform in 1968,
and complaints of racism on the other side from African Americans and
Hispanics, it was hardly surprising that 'occupational paranoia' set in
among the police (Fogelson 1977, p. 238). The police force throughout
the 1960s was also staffed overwhelmingly by whites, although a black
recruitment drive during the early seventies met with some success in
some cities (ibid., p. 248); and this dominance of whites in the organization could lead to considerable difficulties for any young black people
who had the temerity to join the force (Alex 1969).

Worse than 'occupational paranoia' and the threads of institutional
racism in police departments, perhaps, was the setting up – partly in
response to the rise in deaths of officers on duty – of right-wing police
cadres within the force, among whom were the Law Enforcement Group
(New York) and the Fire and Police Research Association (Los Angeles)
(Fogelson 1977, p. 239). When the influence of these kinds of cadres
extended to the rank and file it led to illiberal attitudes to the public as
well as such measures as the suspension of community relations programmes (see Richardson 1974, p. 184). In addition to conflict with the
growing 'ethnic minority' communities, then, some of the police also

found that they wanted to oppose the liberal discourses which had given rise to the *Miranda* and *Escobedo* decisions and which so frequently seemed to hamper them in doing their jobs.

These broader liberal discourses were to have a profound effect on attitudes toward policing in the United States. Undoubtedly their mainspring had been the culmination of the civil rights protests and the inauguration of the Great Society programme. As many have observed, one effect of the battle for civil rights in the United States during the 1950s and 1960s was that American citizens in general became more acutely aware of *their* rights: as consumers, as citizens, as taxpayers and as police suspects (see, for example, Farber 1994, p. 109). At the same time, President Johnson launched the Great Society programme to fulfil his campaign promise in the 1964 election. Passing a huge number of domestic bills in a period comparable only to that of the New Deal, the administration also announced a widespread 'War on Poverty' (Zarefsky 1996). Central to the 'War on Poverty' was welfare provision in the form of AFDC (Aids to Families with Dependent Children) which was rapidly taken up by huge numbers. The reasons for this sudden uptake revolve around the phenomena of increased single parenthood, migration from the South, discrimination, an increase in drug addiction and high rates of youth unemployment (Piven and Cloward 1971).

However, welfare provision in the United States continued to provide an arena for heated public debate. The 'War on Poverty' remained a topic for social analysis in America well after its 'demise' in the early 1970s, with the left typically complaining that it was a reform measure which did not address fundamental inequality while the right has var iously attributed its 'failure' to the creation of a dependency culture or the improvidence of individuals (see Murray 1984 and Mead 1986). What all commentators would agree – even those who seek to explore a conservative/liberal consensus on welfare issues (Handler and Hasenfeld 1991) – is that the 'War on Poverty' was largely responsible for a new public perspective on contemporary events which was more alert to the manifold implications of social determinants. It is true that the limited media coverage of the 'War on Poverty' as a major programme tends to infer that it was an issue that lacked newsworthiness, although there is evidence to suggest that when coverage did occur, it was positive towards the programme (Menzies 1986; Green 1986). Nevertheless, it can be argued that the social determinants of poverty and, by association, crime became cemented in the American consciousness in a fashion which had not been previously experienced, perhaps, since the 1930s.

Because the vision and the rhetoric of the 'War on Poverty' was not met by concomitant results, it was not surprising that disillusionment set in among the American public (Zaresfsky 1996 p. 205; Gelfand 1987; cf. the comments of Robert B. Parker, Chapter 3 above). In fact, it has been suggested that welfare, along with the extension in civil rights during the period, encouraged some Americans to view the Great Society as a 'nigger' society (O'Reilly 1995, p. 245). Ethnicity, rights and poverty had become publicly foregrounded as a contemporary Gordian knot: where matters to do with one were raised, at least one of the others would invariably be entangled in it. Police genres, perhaps, would seem an apposite place for the playing through of these matters as, indeed, in some cases, they were. As a result of the strong demands of verisimilitude entailed in the genre they could not help but touch on contemporary social dilemmas, even when they were at their most obtuse. Although it is easily forgotten, the issues of racism, criminal rights, corruption, reform and the social determinants of poverty were to be central to the police series developed around the character of Lieutenant Theo Kojak.

'Who loves ya baby?'

Between 1973 and 1978, Universal's *Kojak* was one of the most popular TV police shows ever aired. It was a major ratings hit in the United States (see *Variety*, 31 October 1973) and it went on to spark a heated battle over which TV channels would buy it in the United Kingdom (see *Evening Standard*, 10 December 1973). Played by veteran actor Telly Savalas, Kojak became a huge mainstream figure with his trademark lollipops, his distinctive bald head and features, and his signature enquiry to cops and villains, 'Who loves ya, baby?' In spite of his lack of conventional musical talent Savalas went on to become a successful recording star, a cabaret artist and a transgenerational sex symbol. Audiences even began to conflate Savalas with Kojak, as 'Kojak' lollipops appeared in confectioners and 'Kojak' cuts were available at the barber's (Daly 1995). In short, Kojak was very much a character who embodied a site of social investment for the reader; as Denning (1998, pp. 46, 94, 139) would put it, Kojak was an ideological 'figure', like the hard-boiled hero (see Chapter 3 above), whose social significance lends him an existence outside a fixed set of texts.

The proliferation of various images of the police operative or private detective – the detective as disabled (*Ironside*), as urban cowboy (*McCloud*), as Medical Examiner (*Quincy*), as bra-less women (*Charlie's*

Angels), as black (*Tenafly, Shaft*) and even as ordinary and physically unattractive (*Cannon*) – is well known, especially on American TV in the 1970s. Yet, the social significance beyond the sometimes superficial exigencies of the image, is usually crucial in sustaining widespread audience investment. This is certainly so with Kojak. The character first appeared in a feature-length pilot which set the tenor for the series that followed and provided the foundations for readings of the protagonist. *The Marcus–Nelson Murders* (March 1973) was a dramatisation of a true-life drama, the case of the Wylie–Hoffert slayings which began to unfold in New York City in 1963. The story dealt with the brutal murders of two young white middle-class women (Jo Ann Marcus and Kathy Nelson), career girls who shared a flat into which the murderer had gained entry. It goes on to detail the way that, eight months later, with pressure mounting on the police, a young Brooklyn man with learning difficulties, Lewis Humes (Gene Woodbury), is arrested on suspicion of a couple of attempted rapes and subsequently charged with the murders of the white women. The Manhattan detective leading the Marcus–Nelson case, Lieutenant Theo Kojack,[7] is suspicious about the arrest and the confession from the very outset. Further investigation by him reveals that the evidence, the confession and the arrest procedure in the case are all highly suspect. In league with a seasoned defence lawyer, Jake Weinhaus (Jose Ferrer), to whom he riskily leaks information, Kojack attempts to clear Humes's name.

It is worth mentioning that the film, directed by Joseph Sargent, was scripted by Abby Mann, a writer who had become famous for his Oscar-winning screenplay for the film *Judgment at Nuremburg* (1961). As with the earlier film, quite a few scenes in *The Marcus–Nelson Murders* are set in the courtroom. Even more important, perhaps, is that the dogged champion of the defendant in real life was not a detective but a reporter called Selwyn Raab. His book eventually recounted the full details of the case and it was he who kept the defence lawyer in touch with relevant information. Given what we have observed about the role of the press in the 1970s thriller, this is notable. In a scenario which recalls both Serpico and Deep Throat, Kojack tells Weinhaus that he is taking a risk in leaking information because 'I was expecting somebody else to do it – but nobody is'.

The film opens with a caption and a voice-over which states that the film is a dramatisation of real events (with subsequent compressions, name changes, etc.) in a case which preceded the Supreme Court's *Miranda* decision of 1966. The opening shot shows a live televisation of Martin Luther King's speech from the steps of the Lincoln Memorial on

28 August 1963. The TV is being watched by Jo Ann Marcus (Elizabeth Berger), and so the event places the action in a specific year, before the *Miranda* decision. In addition, the momentous nature of the speech is of consequence to the plot, as it is later suggested in the case that most American black people would be likely to know where they were when the speech was made. Most crucially of all, though, the speech plays as the brutal killing takes place, with King's dream that 'my four little children will one day live in a nation where they will not be judged by the color of their skin but by the content of their character' echoing on the soundtrack as the prelude to a hideous miscarriage of justice.

As soon as the police are mobilised following the killings, it is Kojack's voice-over which is insistently heard. New York's biggest ever manhunt gets underway, with police squads from Manhattan, Queens and Brooklyn, and with Kojack wearily intoning his view that the collected detectives have promotion in mind. Much later, when Bobby Martin (Roger Robinson) is pulled in for murdering someone in a drug deal, he bargains for immunity by offering to name the Marcus–Nelson murderer. This is an important lead and an indispensable link in the plot, but Kojack's voice-over still reminds the viewer bitterly that the life of a Puerto Rican drug pusher is not worth that of two white, middle-class career girls.[8]

The way in which the suspect is arrested and then questioned is obviously central to the case and the narrative. Humes is pulled in by patrolman Stabile (Paul Jenkins) the night after an attempted rape on Mrs Alvarez (Antonia Rey). He has been trying to keep warm in a derelict house but when questioned about the crime says that he thinks he saw the attacker – a man physcally much different from himself, according to Rita Alvarez's description – and that he would be willing to help. That Humes becomes a suspect in this way in spite of the lack of 'clues' is not as removed from routine police work as it seems: as Reiss points out, most detective work depends on locating an individual who may be known in the community or a previous offender rather than following leads (1971, p. 108).[9] When taken to the station in Brooklyn he meets Detective Black (William Watson), who sets up an identification procedure involving Mrs Alvarez. The procedure involves her looking through a peephole at Lewis Humes alone as he says, at Black's instruction, 'Lady, I'm gonna rape, you; lady, I'm gonna kill you'. Hearing the words that were used by her attacker, Mrs Alvarez becomes agitated and pronounces Lewis the criminal.

As if this identification procedure without a line-up was not enough, another pre-*Miranda* scene is enacted when detectives Corrigan (Ned

Beatty) and Jaccarino (Val Bisoglio) arrive. Humes is not read his rights but he is put in a room for questioning about the contents of his pockets. One item that he was found to be carrying was a photograph of a blonde woman in a country setting, a photograph that the Brooklyn detectives believe to be of Jo Ann Marcus. Deprived of sleep and unaware of the crime that he is being interviewed about, Humes dictates a 61–page confession. Kojack is immediately suspicious when he drives down from Manhattan to read the document, but this is lost in the self-congratulation in the station. Later, as Kojak questions the suspect, flashbacks reveal the squeaky clean version of events offered by the detectives, preceded by Humes's version in which the confession was beaten out of him.

In the process of establishing that the photograph is not of Jo Ann Marcus and was dumped in New Jersey where Lewis found it, that the detailed map of the Marcus–Nelson flat offered in the confession is drawn with two pens and contains annotations in handwriting other than that of Humes, and that details in the confession indicate that Humes did not even know he was being questioned on a murder charge, Kojack invites Detective Corrigan to the Assistant DA's office for some informal questioning. Corrigan there tells Kojack and Assistant DA Goodman (Robert Fields) that he knew when the young suspect was not telling the truth: 'I know when they're lying, their stomachs move in and out.' In spite of the fact that the attacker in the Alvarez attempted rape case was described as black, it is made clear at this moment that Humes's implication in the Marcus–Nelson murders is very much tied up with common police racism. As Jake Weinhaus later adds in court 'Law and order is being used in this country as a catchphrase for "stop the nigger"'.

As we have mentioned, Bobby Martin, a minor drug dealer, is pulled in on a charge of suspected murder and does a deal with Kojack to entrap one of his clients, a young white burglar and heroin addict, Teddy Hopper (Marjoe Gortner), whom Kojack knows and whom Bobby insists has confessed to the murders. Initially, Kojack is as insistent that Teddy is innocent as he has been about Lewis Humes. However, after a somewhat suspect entrapment procedure in which Teddy has all but implicated himself, Kojack loses his temper the night before Humes's trial and starts to beat a confession out of Teddy as he is in withdrawal. Fellow detectives pull Kojack back saying, 'You're doing exactly what you said the young guys from Brooklyn did.' If this does not give a sense of the way in which the narrative is by no means a neat portrayal of right and wrong as easy opposites, the rest of the narrative does.

When Humes is acquitted, the camera does not pull back from the courthouse to provide an Olympian view of the triumphant American judiciary. Instead, Kojack is back in his office and somewhat reluctantly accepts a telephone invitation to visit Lewis Humes and his family in celebration at the acquittal. He is then shown parking near a tenement which is mercilessly dilapidated even by the standards of the iconography of this film. At the party, where one of Humes's male relatives shakes hands limply with Kojack, the only white man there, and treats him with contempt, Lewis presents Kojack with a painting of the detective holding back the legal wolves. Kojack accepts the picture but the film shows no signs of reaching a conclusion. As the family gather round the television with the detective to watch Lewis' release on the evening news, the bulletin concludes with the prosecutor in the case, Mario Portello (Allen Garfield), saying that this is not the end.

The following scenes show Humes being retried on the same tired evidence for the attempted rape of Mrs Alvarez. This time he is convicted, and although he is a first-time offender and it is clear that his conviction is a political measure, he receives a five- to ten-year sentence. As the film ends, Kojack's voice-over dominates:

> I saw for the first time what Jake Weinhaus meant when he said 'When there's no justice, there's violence.'
>
> I remember the first time I walked the beat. I felt that we were doing the most wonderful job in the world. I thought of us as 'watchers of the city', protecting what was best in it.
>
> Some people say the community gets the police force it deserves. I say the police force *is* the community.
>
> That was the end of the Humes case. Except that it changed my life – and yours.
>
> The Humes case was cited in the Miranda decision of the Supreme Court which demands that his constitutional rights be read to a man under arrest . . .

Kojack then goes on to list the fortunes of the players: Detective Black still on the force, Humes 'who never had a chance from the beginning' still in jail, Teddy 'who was convicted of murdering two girls because he was terrified of going back to prison', Portello elected as an assemblyman and Kojack, despite dreaming of handing in his badge, 'The truth is, I still go on'.

The final scenes accompanied by the voiceover show Kojack, driving his car onto the pavement, exiting it and chasing a petty criminal in a horribly run-down enclave in New York. This clearly sets up the series that is to follow; but even in the liberal reformist mood that the film can, perhaps, be accused of, it is quite a bleak ending. In fact, the chief part of the verisimilitude in the pilot and the series consisted of this bleakness. Universally, critics praised the unremitting ugliness of the city's slums as depicted in the film. This, of course, was helped by shooting entirely on location, especially in Spanish Harlem and the Brownsville section of Brooklyn.

However, audiences' attention was not just drawn merely to the authentic squalor of pre-urban renewal New York; the techniques of filming also helped. There is constant background noise on the soundtrack especially traffic sounds. In one scene where Humes is berated in the street by his brother for getting entangled with the police, the two characters move further and further away and their conversation diminishes over a long period, making it clear that just one microphone has been employed in the scene. Similarly, it appears that hand-held 16mm cameras were utilised on outdoor shots (and some indoor ones such as the courtroom) lending to the documentaristic feel. Even the television series which, for reasons of profit opposed by its star (see Daly 1975, p. 120) filmed many of its interior scenes at Universal's studios in Hollywood, was praised for 'an air of realism which permeates the show, giving it an almost "You Are There" aura' (*Variety*, 26 October 1973). For *Time* the series showed 'New York City in all its roach and racketeering misery' (26 October 1973).

In the pilot, the police stations had been as real as the outdoor locations and just as squalid. The series was to lose this a little but it compensated, perhaps, with realism elsewhere. When the series was first shown in the United States, in October 1973, there was controversy about the violence, particularly in the first episode, 'Siege of Terror', which starred Harvey Keitel as a mobster (see especially *Variety*, 26 October 1973 and *New York Times*, 25 October 1973). The characters' speech also was found to be candid: *The Daily News* commented: 'There's no phony wasted dialogue in "Kojak"', a 'gripping, realistic production'.[10] Arguably, this realism was the main cue for reading the film and the series even if the character of Kojak, the lollipops, the sharp suits and the catchphrases were soon to gain prominence. Yet the phenomenon of realism in the series was based on the generic verisimilitude meeting with 'doxalogical' verisimilitude, what audiences believed about the social formation. While the series was susceptible to the obvious criticism that it did not depict the out and out mundanity of police work (filing, report writing, etc.), it was found to be not dissimilar to other non-fictional discourses. In *The New Republic* Rosenblatt argued: 'The structure of *Kojak* takes its inspiration from the news... What are stories in the news are ideas and events on *Kojak*; rape, cops, citizen responsibility, vigilantes, guns, kids, ethnic groups' (quoted in Daly 1975, p. 122).

The chief feature of *Kojak* as a series and as a figure, then, is that the 'realism' or verisimilitude operated within the new tangled co-ordinates of public knowledge about racism, criminal rights, civic corruption, reform and the social determinants of poverty. What were thought to be 'old' styles of depicting the police were implicitly criticised in the praise heaped upon *Kojak*. It is tempting to conclude in the manner of Goldilocks, that *The New Centurions* had too little corruption for the critics and the public, that *Serpico* had too much at the expense of police work and that *Kojak* was just about right in its balance. What is more important, however, is that all of these texts undoubtedly strive to construct, through a specific verisimilitude, a vision of the police which is somewhat different to mainstream or prevailing views. American police work is shown as one activity interacting with a huge set of formidable social forces including many which have come to prominence in contemporary discourses: the problems of racism, rights and corruption.

Too often, police genres have been analysed in terms of the ways in which they present imaginary resolutions to complex social problems, fictional conclusions that, it is frequently implied, amount to ideological palliatives. Yet it is in the very nature of generic verisimilitude in the thriller that there is reference to the real world of social conditions. While this might be the case with private eye fiction as well as police genres, the quality of that reference will be different. There is an established theme of locating and uncovering the site of social problems with specific reference to dysfunctional families in the hard-boiled tradition. For hard-boiled narratives, concentrating on highly localised resolutions – the luxury to worry about justice – makes a lot of sense. Such localised resolutions may occur in police narratives but, as Kojak says, he still goes on. He tries to keep that sixth ball in the air. Far from being an ideological palliative, then, resolution in the police genre only reveals to an audience well apprised of the convoluted nature of social existence the infinite number of resolutions which must take place before there is absolute equilibrium.

Further Reading

Print

Ball, John 1976. *The Eyes of Buddha*
Brown, Carter 1972. *The Aseptic Murders*

Brown, Carter 1974. *Night Wheeler*
Constantine, K.C. 1972. *The Blank Page*
Constantine, K.C. 1975. *A Fix Like This*
Coughlin, William J. 1973. *The Grinding Mill*
Droge, Edward F. 1974. *In the Highest Tradition*   McBain, Ed 1972. *Sadie When She Died*
McBain, Ed 1973. *Hail to the Chief*
McBain, Ed 1973. *Let's Hear It for the Deaf Man*
McBain, Ed 1975. *Blood Relatives*
McBain, Ed 1976. *Goldilocks*
McBain, Ed. 1976. *Guns*
McBain, Ed 1979. *Calypso*
McDonald, Gregory 1977. *Flynn*
Mills, James 1972. *Report to the Commissioner*
Moore, Robin and Machlin, Milt 1975. *The French Connection II*
Nolan, Frederick 1974. *No Place to Be a Cop*
Stebel, S.L. 1975. *Narc*
Thorp, Roderick 1979. *Die Hard*
Uhnak, Dorothy 1970 *The Ledger*
Uhnak, Dorothy 1973. *Law and Order*
Uhnak, Dorothy 1973. *The Investigation*
Wambaugh, Joseph 1970. *The New Centurions*
Wambaugh, Joseph 1973. *The Blue Knight*
Wambaugh, Joseph 1973. *The Onion Field*
Wambaugh, Joseph 1975. *The Choirboys*
Wambaugh, Joseph 1977. *The Black Marble*

Film

The French Connection (October 1971)
Fuzz (May 1972)
(Based on an Ed McBain novel)
They Only Kill Their Masters (November 1972)
(Reasonably genteel whodunit)
Magnum Force (December 1973)
(Clint Eastwood as Dirty Harry for the second time)
The Seven Ups (December 1973)
Busting (January 1974)
Man on a Swing (February 1974)
Newman's Law (May 1974)
(Liberal dose of paranoia)
The Take (May 1974)

(Insider account of graft)
Report to the Commissioner (January 1975)
(Based on the James Mills novel)
The French Connection II (August 1975)
Mitchell (September 1975)
The Enforcer (December 1976)
(Third outing for Dirty Harry)

TV

Dan August (1970)
McCloud (1970)
(Dennis Weaver as the New Mexico sheriff in New York based on the
   1968 Don Siegel film *Coogan's Bluff,* starring Clint Eastwood)
Cade's County (1971)
Columbo (1971)
Madigan (1972)
(Based on the 1968 Don Siegel film)
The Rookies (1972)
The Streets of San Francisco (1972)
Chase (1973)
Police Story (1973)
(Series famed for its gritty realism and characterized by the lack of a
   regular cast; created by Joseph Wambaugh)
Amy Prentiss (1974)
Chopper One (1974)
Get Christie Love! (1974)
Kodiak (1974)
(Set in rural Alaska)
Nakia (1974)
(Native American cop in New Mexico)
Police Woman (1974)
(Most famous of 1970s series featuring a female detective)
Adams of Eagle Lake (1975)
Baretta (1975)
The Blue Knight (1975)
Caribe (1975)
Joe Forrester (1975)
Starsky and Hutch (1975)
Bert D'Angelo (1976)
Delvecchio (1976)
Jigsaw John (1976)

Most Wanted (1976)
Serpico (1976)
(Based on the 1973 film and book)
CHiPs (1977)
Dog and Cat (1977)
Nashville 99 (1977)
David Cassidy – Man Undercover (1978)
Dear Detective (1979)
Eischied (1979)
Paris (1979)

6
Sambos or Superspades?

There can be little doubt that the history of the thriller has been troubled by the spectres of both gender and 'race'. Indeed, if we are to be honest, we should also stress that it has also exhibited difficult relations with class. Where gender, 'race' and class may have been, in the past, conspicuous by their very absence, it should be clear that in the 1970s each were more apparent in the genre as telling – albeit frequently marginal – discourses. Although there has been little writing on the topic of class in relation to the thriller genre, in spite of the useful preliminaries provided by Knight (1980) and Worpole (1983), there has, since the 1980s, been a great deal of coverage of gender and ethnicity (see, for example, Cranny-Francis 1988; Heilbrun 1988; Munt 1994; Vanacker 1997; and Bailey 1991; Freese 1992; Kennedy 1997). This literature has largely been precipitated by new understandings of audiences and responses to newly produced generic texts.

In light of recent work, then, a statement such as Roth's, that 'gender is genre and genre is male' (1995, p. xiv) must therefore be deemed problematic on a number of grounds. It is a typical 'structuralist' conception of the topic in which genre is an omnipotent vessel: no matter what is poured into the vessel – narratives written by females, narratives of female heroes – the 'generic structure' remains omnipotent and the meaning of the text means the same (cf. Palmer 1978; Wright 1975). Moreover, Roth's pronouncement is essentialist: is action *essentially* male? Is ratiocination really an *exclusively* masculine quality? Even for the 'classic' texts which he discusses there seems to be a solid body of evidence to suggest that the thriller is far from being irrevocably male (see, for example, Slung 1988; Light 1991, pp. 61–112; Williams 1999).

The long reach of the police genres which extends into social issues and which we have discussed in the preceding chapter, was one place where one might expect issues to do with gender roles to be played out. As we have seen in the discussion of *Kojak* (Chapter 5 above), ethnicity was coming to play an increasingly troublesome role in the genre, binding with matters which resist easy solutions, one of which, of course, is class. It is interesting, then, that gender and 'race' are posed conjointly in a television series of the period rather than a film or a print fiction. In addition, they are even thrust centre stage in way which, especially in American thrillers, would be unlikely for the arena of class. Before we proceed to discuss this narrative, then, we should say something very general about gender and 'race' in the 1970s thriller and mention how the current chapter will proceed.

In spite of a number of television series in the genre featuring women protagonists – including *Charlie's Angels* (March 1976), *The Bionic Woman* (April 1977), *Nancy Drew Mysteries* (February 1977) and *Police Woman* (September 1974) – it can be argued that 'race', especially African-American ethnicity, was much more insistent in its encroaching on the thriller during the period. The variety of thriller narratives by or about women which seemed much more amenable to, or even 'utopian' (Keitel 1994), in terms of a feminist project only began to arrive in earnest with the 1980s. Further, it seems that such narratives were more usually found in print media. Romm (1986) notes that a number of female-led thriller series did appear on US TV in the mid-1970s but suggests that they did not succeed beyond the decade and that they differ greatly from contemporary TV narratives' representations of women. A similar situation to the one Romm describes obtained in respect to ethnicity although, tellingly perhaps, the emphasis was on cinema and print and in magnitude far exceeded the pull of gender on the genre.

The 1970s witnessed a highly visible explosion of black talent and a developing breadth in the variety of representations of black protagonists, especially in the thriller genre. These embraced the 'black movie boom' (Bogle 1994), generally believed to have been inaugurated by *Sweet Sweetback's Baadasssss Song* (1970), the writings of Iceberg Slim (Robert Beck), TV series such as *Tenafly* (October 1973), black novels of the street such as Vern E. Smith's *The Jones Men* (1974) and Gil Scott-Heron's *The Vulture* (1970), and the experimental novels of Ishmael Reed. Having noted the way that this period represents a certain kind of flowering of black talent and black representation, we will proceed by looking briefly at a television police series which evolved from a seemingly much different novel; then we will consider the narratives of a famous black private eye and, finally, we will discuss the novels of an auteur who appears to sit quite comfortably within the crime narrative genre.

'No female hero ever disagrees or is in conflict with her boss'[1]

Get Christie Love! was first aired on American television in January 1974. The series revolved around the work of an undercover police woman in Los Angeles and ran until April 1975. It was loosely based on the career of a New York cop, Olga Ford, who also penned some of the episodes; but the pilot was more firmly based on a 1971 novel, *The Ledger* by Dorothy Uhnak. Uhnak's stature as a writer in the police genre is comparable to that of Wambaugh and, like him, she has invariably presented her own experiences in her novels, either as a detective in the New York City Transit Police Department or observing other aspects of law enforcement. Although these experiences are, as she admits, themselves presented in condensed or dramatic form (Uhnak 1978, p. xvii), the differences between *The Ledger* and the subsequent adaptation of it as a vehicle for the Christie Love character are instructive.

The narrative of *The Ledger* concerns a young white female detective, Christie Opara, who is working for the Special Investigations Squad of New York City, under the command of Chief Supervising Assistant District Attorney, Casey Reardon. Having investigated a shooting at the home of known mobster Enzo Giardino, the police have hauled in Elena Vargas, a Puerto Rican prostitute who is close to the mafioso. Reardon believes that she knows the whereabouts of the organisation's ledger, a document which, in police possession would allow the breaking of numerous lucrative rackets. In order to crack Elena, Christie is assigned to find out as much as she can about the prostitute's background. Much of the narrative is then taken up with Christie's investigations, which offer a rounded picture of the social conditions which lead Elena into vice.

Woven through this narrative is Christie's relationship with Reardon, a part of the events upon which Elena seeks to make capital. In terms of the police hierarchy, Christie is already his subordinate, but she is also becoming an object of his sexual domination. It is revealed that her policeman husband has been killed while on duty and while Christie was pregnant; she is also shown in some scenes in the novel caring for her young son, engaging in banal tasks such as ironing. When she finds that Elena worked for an abortion clinic and also terminated a pregnancy there she says to her: 'I find it difficult to equate an abortion with an act of morality' (1988, p. 142). Elena's retort is fierce and invokes ethnicity and class:

'I was unwilling to bring into this world a fatherless child. My abortion was an act of morality for that child. Of course, we cannot be equated, you and I. It is a different world for your son than it would have been for mine. You saw my sister's children. There are *nine* of them. Yes, they are beautiful, now. But one by one, they will go out and become what other people will make of them. Just some more *little spics*.' Elena clenched her hands tightly in her lap. 'My act of morality, my act of protection, was for the child.'

(p. 143)

This speech can be seen as the emotional fulcrum of the novel. As we have noted (Chapter 2 above), questions about the status of the family often provided a seemingly apolitical arena for political battles during the period.[2] Here, the issue for Christie is whether to believe that Elena's tough morality is a veneer gained from her recent career in vice or whether she is truly being honest with herself.

At the climax of the novel, Christie has discovered that Elena *did not* have an abortion; rather she had a young son whom she does not wish Giardino to know about lest he uses the child as leverage against her. Giardino already knows the whereabouts of a child whom he believes is Elena's although he is not aware that she has sold him a red herring, feeding the mobster details of a child who was born to a cousin of hers. Reardon has the identity details of the real son, however, and threatens to mail them to Giardino unless Elena reveals the whereabouts of the ledger. It is significant that Christie physically tries to prevent her superior from mailing the details just as Elena relents and reveals that she, blessed with a photographic memory, *is* the ledger.

The novel of *The Ledger*, then, emphasizes the role of motherly protection and figures the tribulations of motherhood in the characters of Elena – who is quite prepared to sacrifice someone else's child to save her own – and Christie who cares for the sanctity of life in her own child but cares for others also. Christie is a compassionate character, sometimes naive and self-effacing, trying to make the best of a career and parenting. Even though she is independently-minded she defers to her boss. The adaptation of the novel as *Get Christie Love!* is a somewhat different proposition. To begin with, the main character, Christie (Teresa Graves) is black. The very first scene in which she appears has her posing as a hooker, evidently to ensnare a killer who has been murdering prostitutes. Approached by a white john who aggressively haggles over the price, she dismisses him and walks on. 'Nigger,' he shouts after her. 'Nigger lover,' she replies, pleasantly. Minutes later when she confronts the killer, she bests him without a gun also, but without too much trouble. This sets the tone for the rest of the narrative: unlike Christie Opara, Christie Love will not be physically or sexually overcome by men.

Christie's dominance in the TV version is the key transformation in the process of adaptation and it is not an issue separate from ethnicity or genre. Christie's relationship to Captain Reardon (Harry Guardino) emphasises the sexual current which is evident in the novel but other issues to do with hierarchies arise, too. Reardon pursues Christie, trying to gain an invite into her flat for coffee, once near the beginning of the film and again towards the end. On each occasion, Christie has the upper hand. Similarly, on issues of police work within the department she will not be pushed around. It is curious that the ethnic dimension in some police hierarchies in the genre serves to locate authority in the establishment figure. Starsky and Hutch, the two cops in the series launched in April 1975, for example, are maverick cops who get results, it is true; however, it is clear that they will never be able to fully circumvent the stone wall of authority embodied in their black boss, Captain Dobey (Bernie Hamilton). Yet, when the ethnic and gender dimensions are different, it seems that the opposite applies: Christie Love is simply more streetwise, devious and dominant than her superior, Reardon.

That Christie is as strong a figure as her boss is clear from the climax of the pilot. Where Christie Opara in the novel tries to prevent her boss from mailing to Giardino the details of Elena Varga's son, Christie Love stands back and, with Reardon, calls the bluff of Helena Varga (as she is here, played by Louise Sorel). Earlier, Christie Love has also refrained from commenting on the issue of abortion, which may or may not be significant, which may or may not relate to her view of Varga in the plot or the fact that she has no children, or may or may not relate to the fact that the pilot show appeared after the *Roe* v. *Wade* decision on abortion. A clearer indication of Christie Love's strength of purpose and singlemindedness is offered in a minor episode which appears in the novel and the adaptation. At one stage in the narrative Christie finds herself alone in a lift with a mob henchman. In the novel he is a ruthless Italian named Lomarco and not that far removed in character from Al Capone's right-hand man, Nitti. In *Get Christie Love!* His name is Loomis and he is an unattractive Anglo who, in his blond facial hair especially, resembles an ancient Greek giant. As Christie is menaced by the henchman who wields a stiletto provocatively she attacks him the first moment that she sees he is vulnerable. In the novel, she is terrified and runs off the instant he falls to the floor; in the pilot, however, Christie uses her skill in martial arts to incapacitate Loomis (Lee Paul) and place him under arrest.

Christie Love's combination of sassy street wisdom and foxy good looks is, without doubt, of a piece with her blackness. *Police Woman*, NBC's rival to ABC's *Get Christie Love!* and launched in the same year, was derived from the work of Uhnak but was also a spin-off from an episode of *Police Story*. As we have seen, *Get Christie Love!* used Uhnak as a source, but unlike NBC's series which starred Angie Dickinson as white cop, Pepper Anderson, it was also derived from certain films popular at the time, especially *Cleopatra Jones* (1973). This latter was one of a number of B-movies that would often share a bill with martial arts films such as *Enter the Dragon* (1973), and, as we will see, was to become part of a wider category of representation known as 'blaxploitation'. Tamara Dobson plays the eponymous government agent, an attractive black martial arts exponent whose narcotics work places her somewhere between the international escapades of a James Bond and the community policing of a Kojak. Although the narrative frequently plays for laughs it is still worth noting that Dobson is extraordinarily dominant as the main character and, like Christie Love, is not afraid to tell her emasculated boss, Crawford (Dan Frazer – the actor who also plays Kojak's boss), where to get off.

What is interesting about *Get Christie Love!* and its many sources is that it tends to throw into doubt the idea that genre is a vessel. Granted, the series was one of a number in the police genre which allowed for different aspects of social life to be explored and for different kinds of attributes in the body of a police operative to be centre stage. However, it provided a cocktail in which martial arts might be used to deconstruct female physical weakness and sexuality might be employed to undermine both institutional and racial hierarchies. To be sure, this is an uneasy cocktail for many to swallow.[3] However, before we confront these problems let us consider the narratives of a character who is similarly troublesome yet is probably the most well-known figure in the history of the black thriller: the private detective, John Shaft.

'He's a complicated man/And no-one understands him but his woman/ Shaft'

Shaft is probably most famous by virtue of the 1971 MGM film by the black director Gordon Parks. But he is actually the creation of Ernest Tidyman, a white reporter from Cleveland who, incidentally, was given an NAACP Image Award in 1971. Shaft appeared in five novels in the 1970s: *Shaft* (1970), *Shaft's Big Score* (1972), *Shaft Among the Jews* (1972), *Shaft Has a Ball* (1973) and *Good-Bye, Mr. Shaft* (1974). However, as with

Christie Love and Christie Opara, there are salient differences between the first novel in the series and the famous film version. These differences revolve around image. In the book, Shaft is still a streetwise black man; in addition, he has significantly contemporary characteristics: raised in Harlem, Vietnam veteran, post-1960s attitudes towards sex. But in other ways he is also an archetypal hard-boiled character.

In much of the film Shaft is promoted as a cool motherfucker who is at home on the streets. The opening titles sequence of the movie does a lot of the work here as Shaft (Richard Roundtree) is shown strolling down a bustling, socially mixed Manhattan street, jaywalking across junctions and giving drivers the finger. Shaft is dressed in a long brown leather coat, a check jacket and a beige polo-necked sweater. As he makes his way along confidently, the film's theme plays on the soundtrack, a theme which is synonymous with this and other 'black' films from the period, and which has connected its composer, Isaac Hayes, with the movie world sufficiently for him to become a black film hero himself in *Truck Turner* (1974).[4] Hayes sings, 'Who's the black private dick/That's a sex machine to all the chicks?'; but also asks 'Who is the man that would/Risk his neck for his brother man?' and 'Who's the cat that won't cop out/When there's danger all about?'

Reviewers of the film took a pretty uniform view of its racial politics. Penelope Gilliatt in *The New Yorker* called *Shaft* a 'bandwagon race picture' (1971, p. 19), while Oberbeck in *Newsweek* complained that the film largely concentrates on 'setting up Shaft as a super-cool dude' (1971, p. 80). Two black critics lamented at greater length: 'How come James Bond, sick, sick superman of Western chrome has to be put into blackface?' (1971, p. 21), asked Owano in the *Village Voice*, echoing Riley's contention in the *New York Times* that the film is 'an extended lie, a distortion that simply grows larger and more unbelievable with each frame' (1971, p. B15). There were dissenters from this view: Canby, for example, the resident critic at the *New York Times*, refused to get carried away with the 'race' angle and assessed *Shaft* as a good thriller (1971, p. B11). Yet, the parameters for reading set out by these critics was fairly clear.

The chief concern here – and it is a concern which freqeuntly muddies the water of analysis – is 'blaxploitation', the label given to the large number of texts in the early seventies, particularly crime and action films, which were thought in one way or another to embody 'black exploitation' (Leab 1975, pp. 237 ff.). Blaxploitation, although it was only ever loosely defined, involved a number of features. Critics white and black saw certain films as simply pouring black iconography into white vessels. Sometimes that iconography was deemed inherently racist, encouraging a feast on, and commoditization of, the image of blackness. For Leab, this cycle had gone on too long: 'whether Sambo or Superspade, the black image on screen has always lacked the dimension of humanity' (1975, p. 5). In the instance of *Shaft*, a certain kind of image was aggressively pushed by marketers who had been hired by MGM to reach the lucrative black cinema-going sector: Shaft was portrayed in the marketing as a 'lone, black Superspade' (*Variety*, 28 July 1971, p. 5; Leab 1975, p. 251; Reid 1993, p. 83). This raises another aspect of blaxploitation: the way that 'white' money is responsible for the manipulation and dissemination of images which purport to be 'black'.[5]

Undoubtedly, sensitive issues were at play; the image of the African-American as an active force in social life was the site of a political struggle. In the wake of the non-violent stance which had dominated the battle for civil rights in the 1950s and 1960s, a new version of active protest had evolved from student groups and other political movements such as those mobilised against the war in Vietnam (Jacobs and Landau 1967). Stokely Carmichael and others heralded not passivity but 'black power' (Carmichael and Hamilton 1968), inaugurating in the process a more public and dynamic sense of 'race pride' (Rhea 1997). The Black Muslims remained a force after Malcolm X's death but were also accompanied by other forthright separatist groups such as the Black Panther Party (Seale 1970). As more affluent American whites increasingly moved to the suburbs, the steady migration of blacks to northern cities which had been taking place since the beginning of the century accelerated with a 98 per cent growth of the urban black population in the period 1950 to 1966 (Boyer 1996, p. 8). The urban riots of the late 1960s emphasized not just black anger but also the redrawing of the lines of racial divide. The Kerner Commission Report predicted that the United States was 'moving toward two societies, one black, one white – separate and unequal', with black citizens making up the bulk of the population of cities (O'Reilly 1995, p. 264; Boyer 1996, p. 6; Thernstrom and Thernstrom 1997, p. 209). Meanwhile, rather than adhering to the old metaphor of the 'melting-pot', academics began to talk about America in terms of the 'rise of the unmeltable ethnics' (Novak 1971).

Much was at stake in the representation of powerful African-Americans. The movements of the 1960s had provided an affirmation of ethnic identity, perhaps solidifying a racialized outlook. Certainly part of this affirmation was an assertion of African-American 'strength', 'power' and 'action'. Similarly, slogans such as 'black is beautiful' could be very powerful in discourse even while life demonstrated that black was ugly, considerate, spiteful, generous, mean, brave, cowardly, proud, ashamed, and all the other myriad attributes of humanity. So when the blaxploitation films posited strong, attractive black heroes it was difficult to determine immediately whether these were 'affirmative', a dilution of 'affirmative' images to render them sterile, traditionally empowering black folk images, appropriations of traditional black folk images by white money for profit, an exacerbation of already existing white stereotypes of blackness (for example, rampant sexuality), simply 'negative' images, or what.

In the late 1960s, heroic black characters came into their own, invariably featuring in action movies with stars like Jim Brown, Calvin Lockhart and Ossie Davis (Leab 1975, p. 237). Yet, if mainstream films are customarily charged with trading in stereotypes and larger-than-life scenarios – in respect of both black *and* white protagonists – commoditization of the black image is, perhaps, easier to discern in print fiction. Consider, for example, the Superspade series of books by B. B. Johnson, which actually pre-date the film of *Shaft* but nevertheless seem to a exploit a certain kind of 'blackness'. The following passage comes from the second novel in the series, *Black Is Beautiful* (1970):

> I woke up with this feeling under my belt like champagne and chitterlings topped off with six cream puffs don't make it. But when Dean (mother) Rucker's daughters, Maggie and Jiggs, ages ten and twelve respectively, lay out the menu for the Friday evening faculty get-together, there is something for everybody. You eat, drink and hold the complaints. This gastronomic hazard is all part of Green College, where, I, Richard Spade, teach a black studies course, tutor future karate and judo experts and now, like today, help Bud Fountain put the football squad through its paces. (p. 5)

Here we can see some of the ingredients for the problematic cocktails we mentioned earlier, *Get Christie Love!* and *Cleopatra Jones*: spectacular black pride, martial arts in the service of aggressive heterosexuality, and an amused playing with stereotypes. As with the straplines for the film of *Shaft* – 'Shaft's his name, shaft's his game' (Leab 1975, p. 252) – it is simply far too tempting to read into the name 'Dick Spade'.

Blaxploitation is just one part of a much wider set of problems in the sphere of ethnicity and representation which we will return to shortly. It is, of course, important to take note of it in analysing *Shaft*; however, we can argue that the presentation of the film as a blaxploitation 'text-to-be-read' was conducted by a number of forces, none the least of which was the aforementioned marketing enterprise. The main transformation such blaxploitation has wrought in the narrative concerns some semantic features of the hard-boiled hero. While the cinematic Shaft is a leather-coated dude, in the book, he spends most of the story in an increasingly bedraggled grey flannel suit redolent of the more conventional hard-boiled protagonist. As Roth suggests, hard-boiled detectives are immune to the niceties of appearances and instead work doggedly 'in battered hats and suits that look as if they had been slept in' (1995, p. 244). Concomitantly, in the plot of the novel and the film, Shaft is the quintessential hard-boiled hero in being aloof from many of the ideological and institutional imperatives of the other protagonists. In fact, the plot is precisely concerned with the way in which Shaft is hired by a local black mobster to find his daughter and then how he plays the mobster off against Buford, a boyhood acquaintance and current black activist who may know the whereabouts of the missing child. The organisations that the mobster and the activist represent are both shown to be worthy of Shaft's contempt.

That Shaft is a hard-boiled hero is nowhere more clear, however, than in his orientation to the other, in this case a homosexual coffee shop cashier who has looked at him the 'wrong' way:

> 'Goodbye, there,' the cashier sang to him.
> Shaft leaned over the counter to whisper.
> 'You know where the boathouse is in Central Park?'
> The fag nodded eagerly. Shaft looked at his watch.
> 'I'll be there at twelve-forty-five. No, make that at one A.M. sharp. Okay?'
> 'Do we have to meet in the park?'
> 'Well, if you don't want to . . .'
> 'Oh, all right.'
> '*Ciao.*'
> '*Ciao.*'
> The muggers and that one deserved one another. He hoped the little fart was a karate champion; he would last ten minutes longer that way. Until somebody stuffed his brown belt in one ear and pulled it out the other. Knotted.

(pp. 34–5)

This is a fairly vivid demonstration of one feature of the hard-boiled 'ideology' which Ogdon (1992) identifies and which we met in Chapter 3 above.[6] Nevertheless, later in the narrative, there is some space for questioning relations with the other, although significantly the issue here is 'race', not sexuality:

> Shaft felt a little sorry for the driver. He was an inoffensive man in most ways except that he was a Jew. Shaft could reason about the Jews and he knew full conviction what his reason told him, but he still did not like them. They were in his Harlem childhood, in the candy store, in the clothes store, in the little grocery story in the little liquor store, and in the hock shop. The money store. He hadn't liked them at all in any of those places or the way they had treated him or the way they had treated anyone else. They were the merchants of misery and the feeling would not leave him, no matter how many Jews he now knew and liked. But the cab driver's offense of being Jewish was hardly enough to inspire Shaft's desire to torment him. He disliked Jews but he hated cab drivers.
>
> (p. 63)

In spite of the forthright espousal of racist attitudes, here, we should resist the temptation to prejudge and proffer a blanket condemnation of the character. Far from being simply a black hero created by a white writer within a white subgenre, it can be argued that Shaft's black status can be said to actually disrupt some of the more taken-for-granted aspects of the narrative.

Take, for example, the assessments of Shaft by the other two major protagonists in the novel. The first is from the black Harlem mobster, Knock Persons, who has hired Shaft to find his daughter and the second is a indirect interior monologue from Buford, the activist of questionable integrity:

> 'You're a black man. Somewhere inside of you you know what this girl's feeling and what she's thinking. But you're also part a white man because of what you do and where you been. And you smart enough to go back and forth between black and white man'. (p. 51)
>
> Shaft was...what? Shaft was one of the opportunists, the bastards who could hustle both sides of the street. Now *there* was a sonofabitch that couldn't be trusted. Shaft was a pimp for the whores of whiteness.
>
> (p. 61)

For Reid, these movements between identities amount to indisputable evidence that Shaft traduces his brothers and sisters in Harlem and 'upholds a middle-class, raceless value system' (1993, p. 86). If we were dealing here with a valorized form of fiction, rather than a thriller which has been debated for its racial coordinates, we would be able to pronounce Shaft's movements between identities as stunning elucidations of 'border crossing'. Either way, it is difficult to deny that, in foregrounding 'race', *Shaft* makes it a plural phenomenon: 'race' is not just what African-Americans experience; it is a construction which is subject to situation and circumstance and consequently the experience of all.

Shaft was an enormous box office hit, especially among black audiences (see *Variety*, 28 July 1971), and even if we assume that audiences were composed of cultural dupes who swallowed the marketing hook, line and sinker, this still does not really account for the qualities of the film that were found compelling. Perhaps the qualities of Shaft as a character and *Shaft* the film are more various than critics allowed. Rather than being a 'race'picture in the sense of presenting 'race' as a reductive, monolithic entity, *Shaft* necessarily invoked the manifold vicissitudes of a racialized persona in the social world. There seem to be substantial grounds for a reading of the Shaft narratives not just as new wine in old bottles, not just as stereotypical, but as challenging the preconceptions and the cultural paraphernalia which lend to the illusory fixity of identity. Shaft may be black, but this does not mean that this is the only way that he can identify with other humans. His evaluation of the crook and the amateurish and insincere activist – both his 'brothers' – is stated categorically in the narrative (p. 103). There can be little doubt that he couches his convictions in a fashion that is very much comparable to the way that phoney activism and outlawry are viewed by Ed and Digger, the detectives in the novels of a black writer from a slightly earlier era, Chester Himes. The figure of Shaft, then, while being the most famous in the blaxploitation pantheon, is a contradictory and conflicting one.

No signifying

Our preliminary remarks about blaxploitation have indicated that cultural critics had difficulties with some of its products. Rather than revisiting these texts as fans have done increasingly, until very recently it seems that there has been, instead, a general collective amnesia about these years in the history of black popular culture.[7] The most curious fact about Paula Woods's *Spooks, Spies and Private Eyes: An Anthology of Black Mystery, Crime and Suspense Fiction of the 20th Century* (1996), to take one example, is her almost complete elision of the 1970s. In her selection and in the editorial material which accompanies it there is no reference to the period. Even the useful chronology which she offers at the end of the volume jumps from 1969 to 1981, although there are entries for the birth-dates of John A. Williams, Ernest Tidyman and Ishmael Reed (pp. 394–5). For some reason the decade is seen as a watershed, separating Chester Himes from the likes of Gar Anthony Haywood and Walter Mosley.

The chief problem underlining any enterprise such as that of Woods is that of classifying a body of cultural production as 'black'. Does 'black' refer to the consumers, the producers, the content of the representations or their form? As we have seen, in the realm of production and consumption there have been numerous arguments to the effect that 'black popular culture' in the twentieth century is the creation of white business[8] and, in a vexed fashion, it has involved 'misrepresentation of black people.[9] As if these problems were not enough, a further predicament exists which Mercer (1994; cf. Tagg 1988) has usefully characterised as 'the burden of representation', that is the demand – made especially of 'black art' – to represent the 'whole' of black experience. Put another way it is the demand that depictions 'represent' the manifold effects of marginalisation of racial identities, a task which, even if it is desirable is, arguably, impossible. One way out of this impasse has consisted in the delineation of an 'authentic' African-American (or black, or, in a more sophisticated way, diasporic) culture. It has also proved profitable because there is such a rich vein of African-American culture which is still being mined having become buried by the white supremacist tendencies inherent in processes such as canonisation and the writing of histories (Baker 1984; Gates 1988).[10]

This perspective can be seen as achieving two things: a movement beyond the idea of putative 'positive' images of racial identity, a recognition that racism can reside not just in displays of 'aggressiveness' or 'contempt' but also in the acts, representations and thought processes of the 'well-intentioned' (see, especially, Gates 1986); and the establishment of a black tradition at a formal level – the vernacular, a major constituent of which is the African-American word juggling known as 'signifyin(g)' (see Gates 1988 and Levine 1974, pp. 244–58). One of the most influential recent works on black writing in the thriller genre has used exactly this perspective, and for good reason. Stephen Soitos's *The Blues Detective* (1996) covers the history of the black detection genre by suggesting that there are four tropes of black detection: the *black detective persona* (sense of family/community; application of African-American consciousness); *double-consciousness detection* (detective as trickster; masks and mistaken identities; amplification of plot by black themes; lots of digression); *vernaculars* (blues, jazz, language use, signifyin(g), food, dance); and *hoodoo* (voodoo). These tropes are found to be at work in what, for many years was considered the 'first' black detective novel: Rudolph Fisher's *The Conjure-Man Dies* (1932).

This digression upon black vernacular criticism, and especially Soitos's book will, hopefully, be to good purpose for understanding the critical neglect of black thriller genres in the seventies. One thing that comes out of Soitos's account is that there is a constant slippage between 'form' and 'content' in the fiction that he analyses and in his terms of reference. A subject-matter like 'double-consciousness' which is *in* the narrative events is not simply a formal issue. In Altman's sense, as we argued in Chapter 1, this is a matter of genre fiction's 'semantic/syntactic' status; another way to put it is that an issue like double-consciousness is a 'voice' (in the Bakhtinian sense; see, for example, Bakhtin 1981); it partakes of both the semantic and syntactic.

Clearly, Soitos has identified a strong tradition that exists in the corpus of work that makes up the 'black' thriller or detective fiction and it is one which is amply fitted to his analysis of the works of Pauline Hopkins, Rudolf Fisher and, later, Ishmael Reed. However, he also includes a chapter on the fiction of Chester Himes, especially the novels featuring detectives Gravedigger Jones and Coffin Ed Johnson, and it is here that the limits of his theory are evident. As is well-known, Jones and Johnson were two cops in a series of novels set in Harlem and written in the 1950s and 1960s. Frequently, they could be said to represent a 'black' sensibility, standing up for the embattled community; more often, though, they demonstrated that they were embittered about crime and its causes. That Himes was a black writer of detective fiction – one who also included a great deal of dialogue in the vernacular – does not necessarily guarantee that he will fit Soitos' frame. In fact, Himes' Harlem novels were explicitly hard-boiled potboilers written for the the French *Série Noir* imprint, and this is root of the problem: they embody not so much a style as a world-view or a 'voice' (see Pepper 1996, p. 73).

Undoubtedly, it is unsatisfactory to say that Himes is effectively a 'white' writer because he operates in the hard-boiled frame with the characters of Ed and Digger fitting the mould of the wearied observers of violence and absurdity in life. As Pepper writes

> Ed and Digger's language might be tough and unpretentious but it is also a 'black' one. Their aspirations might be noble but they are constantly undermined by frustration and bitterness that is itself the product of racism. Their belief that crime is crime whatever the skin

colour of the perpetrator might be honourable but it is increasingly untenable given the extent of racially-determined inequalities.

(1996, p. 102)

But suggesting that Himes's Harlem novels, composed to order in France, with a strong hard-boiled voice, are actually thoroughgoing African-American narratives, contributing to a black vernacular tradition, clearly will not do.

The black vernacular tradition stresses, as one of its constituents, the complex role of signifyin(g), the verbal jousting that we noted earlier. A major part of signifyin(g) consists of ritual insult, the playful but frequently obscene denigration of an opponents family, friends and his/her own person. But one might ask whether there are occasions when the word play of signifyin(g) is inappropriate and cannot take place. In a series of 'black experience' novels which came to prominence in the 1970s and whose depictions of crime and the underworld won them a ready audience of thriller readers, the narratives are dominated by such occasions. After a tense confrontation in the 1973 prison novel *White Man's Justice, Black Man's Grief* by the African-American writer Donald Goines, the following is offered: 'There was no signifying, because every man, including Sonny, knew that it was no idle threat. Death walked among them on that small ward, just as close as it walks wherever violent men are incarcerated' (1973, p. 98).

Donald Goines (1936–74) had a short-life and an even shorter writing career. The latter spanned just five years yet produced 16 novels, five of which were written under the pseudonym 'Al C. Clark'. Before he became a writer, Goines was a ghetto kid who had a career as a bootlegger, thief, pimp, heavy and drug pusher and suffered the ravages of heroin addiction (Stone 1977). He was gunned down by two white assassins in 1974 at the age of 39. Interestingly, Goines's work is still in print (published by the legendary Holloway House[11]) as are the works of Iceberg Slim and some of the fiction of Joseph Nazel. Each have also had a steady readership among aficionados of crime fiction. Yet it is clear that for all his popularity, Goines' novels have, in particular, been marginalised because they are so raw and because they do not fit nicely with current critical predilections.

His second novel, *Dopefiend* (1971), tells of a young lower middle-class couple who get drawn into a life of heroin addiction. Much of the action takes place around a 'shooting gallery', run by a hideously obese pusher called Porky who not only supplies dope but provides the squalid space for users to shoot up and then 'nod'. In return, Porky not only gets the clients' money but also the opportunity to watch female clients while masturbating from the comfort of an old armchair. Later, when the female customers are hooked and short of cash for heroin, he accepts live sex shows for payment or forces them to copulate with his Alsatian dog while he masturbates.

Terry, the protagonist of the story, gets hooked on heroin and becomes a thief, loses her job in a department store and then becomes a prostitute to finance her habit. Minnie, a slightly older prostitute and addict, takes Terry under her wing when the latter is thrown out by her parents. Minnie finds Terry a flat in the same block as herself, but also uses her to gain fixes. This is largely because Minnie is finding it difficult to turn tricks in the advanced stages of her pregnancy. At the end of the novel, Minnie is desperate for a fix but has no money. She goes to Porky who makes her copulate with his dog before sending her back to her flat. In a daze, and coming to terms with her utter degradation, Minnie hangs herself with a clothesline. She is discovered by Terry, who beholds Minnie's naked body hanging from the light fitting and also most of the semi-born dead baby that is hanging between Minnie's legs. Terry has a complete breakdown and is taken away for what will probably be a life in an institution.

All of Goines's material is uncompromising. It gives copious details of the underside of life and does so with a thirst for graphic depiction that goes beyond straightforward realism into a kind of narration that is closer to literary 'naturalism' and which demonstrates an almost pornographic 'frenzy of the visible' (Williams 1991). In our discussion of crime fiction (Chapter 4) we have noted how writers and critics alighted on one mode of 'realistically' portraying life on the street. This consisted of presenting character-level 'visions' or 'focalizations' of events. If there is anything which immediately stands out about Goines' fiction it is an (even more?) intense desire on the part of the narrator to present an explicitly detailed picture of some of the most troublesome aspects of people's lives. Consider the following from *White Man's Justice, Black Man's Grief* (1973). The main character, Chester Hines (pun intended), has become an inmate at a county gaol and has already developed a sense of contempt for an existing inmate, Tommy, who flagrantly rapes weaker white prisoners. Then further humiliation of a white prisoner takes place:

> As the young white boy went down on his knees, Chester shook his head at Tommy's stupidity. The man was in enough trouble already, now the fool was doing just what he shouldn't have been doing...

'Oh, God, white lady, that's it! Hold it right there,' Tommy said, still trying to impress the onlookers. 'Oh, Jesus, goddamn, this is the best head in the goddamn world. I'd give up my front seat in hell for this cap. Oh,' he moaned, really feeling it now, 'don't let a drop get away, motherfucker.' He held the white boy's head tightly with both hands.

Mike tried to pull back, but Tommy had too hard a hold on his head. Tears of frustration ran down Mike's cheeks as the black man held his head and began to come in his mouth. The boy choked on the long black penis in his mouth, but Tommy continued to hold his head tightly. Come ran from Mike's mouth and down the side of his chin. He choked and gagged, but it didn't do any good. Tommy held on for dear life.

Chester looked away. The rest of the men watched for different reasons. Chester caught the eye of one white boy, the boy was staring daggers at Tommy. If he'd had a gun, he'd have shot Tommy dead in his tracks. That's one more witness against you, Tommy my boy, Chester thought to himself.

When they finished, Tommy wiped his penis off on the white boy's shirt. 'There, bitch, if you get hungry tonight, there's some joy juice for you to lick on.' He laughed loudly at his own joke, then glanced at the old man, who wasn't smiling. 'What's wrong, Pops? You got a love for these funky ass white punks?' He asked harshly.

'No, boy, I ain't got no love for them, but I believe I can stomach them more than I can a nigger like you. And when I use the word *nigger* in your case, it means just what it implies.'

(pp. 72–3)

It isn't just the indisputably graphic nature of the depiction which is outstanding here but also the way in which conflict is accentuated, particularly in the use of the word 'nigger'.

In Goines's world, life is brutish and short, and certainly this is exacerbated by – or the wholesale result of – racism or its epiphenomena such as drugs and crime. Blacks and whites live in different worlds and are largely in conflict. Yet Goines – while he is keen to document in fiction the lives of ghetto blacks – does not feel 'the burden of representation'; the fiction has no fear about doing its 'dirty laundry' (Mercer 1994, p. 238) in public. Although 'race' as a collective identity is omnipresent in Goines' narratives, black characters are not joined by a vernacular tradition; nor do his novels allow for the exploration of the rich heritage of African-American culture. Instead, characters, rather than being unproblematically united by a common cultural heritage, are constantly in collision and are seen as part and parcel of conflicting social forces (for example, crime and law) and axes of identity beyond those of 'race' or 'ethnicity'.

One of the chief sources of conflict concerns activism in relation to crime. In the novel *Black Gangster* (1977), the ex-con and Detroit black mobster Prince suffers the greatest threat to his hegemony not from the police but from a posse of activists called the Black Cougars who have waged war on all the dope dealers in town. The twin banes of dope addiction and exploitation of the community which run through Goines's novels were, Stone (1977) argues, the defining experience of the author's life from the moment he returned as a teenager, hooked on heroin, from the Korean War. Probably the best examples of conflict, or of the heteroglot aspect of Goines fiction, though, are the conflicting voices in the Kenyatta novels written under the pseudonym 'Al C. Clark'. In *Crime Partners* (1978), the two main characters are Billy and Jackie, small-time hoodlums who, at the beginning of the novel, try to rip off a heroin addict who has money in his apartment. They end up killing the addict who, in a drug-fuelled rage, has savagely beaten to death his girlfriend's young daughter. In turn, Billy and Jackie regularly buy guns from Kenyatta, the charismatic head of a secret black organisation dedicated to the destruction of dope dealers and the execution of white police operatives. Billy and Jackie seek assistance from Kenyatta's organisation for individual heists. Meanwhile, on the trail of both of these is a detective duo, Benson and Ryan. Both are dedicated and professional policemen, but the novel explores the fact that Benson frequently suffers the indignities of institutionalised racism.

It is difficult to say which is the dominant voice in the narrative of *Crime Partners*. Kenyatta's crusade is like an underworld narrative and does indeed continue into three more novels. Yet the story of Billy and Jackie is a very human one involving dilemmas of love, relationships and gender, not unlike some of the narratives that occur in the novels of George V. Higgins and Elmore Leonard. And then there is the partnership of Ryan and Benson which, in its professional loyalty and friendship is not far removed the buddy genre (Alexander 1996), yet is riven by the issue of 'race'. In *Kenyatta's Escape* (1974), for instance, Benson experiences real turmoil in the aftermath of a police siege of black activists as a result of his conflicting axes of identity – racial and occupational:

> As he watched, Benson wondered about the sharp feeling of pride that went through him as he saw the dead bodies of his comrades … With eight policemen killed, the newspapers would play it up big. This was the first time to his memory that any black or white crooks had made

such a dent in the police forces at a single shootout. Instantly he felt ashamed in the feeling of pride at what the Black men and women had done. After all, he was an officer also, and these were his comrades, so there was nothing to be proud about.

(pp. 54–5)

Frequently, the interracial buddy genre – exemplified by the *48 Hours* and *Lethal Weapon* films, for example, or the American literary tradition of bonding which we discussed briefly in Chapter 3 – deflects explicit racial conflict by playing out other oppositions (domestic stability versus relatively benign mental instability in the *Lethal Weapon* series) or focussing on masculinity and violence. In the Kenyatta books, by contrast, the racial conflict between Benson and Ryan, or Benson and his occupational identity, is not papered over by playful differences which obliquely signify some measure of underlying harmony. Even though it is co-extensive with occupational identity, it is precisely what it is: racial conflict.

What is clear about the Kenyatta novels is that, perhaps more explicitly than the 'experience' novels of Goines, they demonstrate in their view of the world, some aspects of hard-boiled fiction and other thriller genres such as crime and police stories – conflict and the harsh exigencies of contemporary life; but not the hideousness of the other or the lure of honour and justice. In the wake of the riots of the 1960s, rising crime and the 'War on Poverty', African-American identity was under assault not just from social determinants but also by government-sanctioned ideology. The Moynihan Report of 1965, which was a government paper inquiring into urban disturbances, sparked a lasting controversy by concluding: 'At the heart of the deterioration of the fabric of Negro society is the deterioration of the Negro family' (in Rainwater and Yancey 1967, p. 5). There was therefore felt to be a strong onus among African-Americans in the ensuing period to combat negative images, heightened by NAACP condemnation of the 'negative' images in such films as *Foxy Brown* (1974) (Hill 1972; Leab 1975, p. 258). One major product of this impulse which, in a fairly direct way, was a response to the Moynihan Report was the book and the television epic by Alex Haley, *Roots* (1976 and 1977) (see Cobley 1986, Athey 1999 and 'Color Adjustment', 1992).

Such positive images as those disseminated by *Roots*, however, seemed to have held no interest for Goines. Characters such as Prince in *Black Gangster* make it clear that they believe whitey to be just as fucked up as African-Americans are said to be in white supremacist discourse. In Goines's novels there is no one unifying positivity, nor is there a stable sense of unity in being black. Identities might seem to offer a promise of autonomy or compartmentalization in the narratives; however, the social forces always already working upon them – and these forces include heroin addiction, of course – are simply so great, so pervasive and so omnipotent in their collective action that racialized identities appear fragmented and temporary. Moreover, this is a fact of identity which should be recognized by all who feel compelled to understand humans solely with recourse to the dimension of one experience. When questioned about the representations of African-Americans in *Shaft* Gordon Parks was compelled to complain about the requirement of positivity:

> Ideally, Parks is looking forward to the day when black actors can afford to be just as sloppy or villainous on screen as anybody else, but that day hasn't arrived, in his view. It's still necessary to counteract 'all the damage done by Hollywood films for years and years'.
>
> (Gold 1974, p. 27)

More recently, Hall has criticised not just the homogeneity of representation but also those formulations about identity which rely unproblematically on a putative homogeneity of experience:

> [I]t is to the diversity, not the homogeneity, of black experience that we must now give our undivided attention. This is not simply to appreciate the historical and experiential differences within and between communities, regions, country and city, across national cultures, between diasporas, but also to recognize the other kinds of difference that place, position and locate black people. The point is not simply that, since our racial differences do not constitute all of us, we are always different, negotiating different kinds of differences – of gender, of sexuality, of class. It is also that these antagonisms refuse to be neatly aligned; they are simply not reducible to one another; they refuse to coalesce around a single axis of differentiation. We are always in negotiation, not with a single set of oppositions that place us always in the same relation to others, but with a series of different personalities. Each has for us its point of profound subjectification. And that is the most difficult thing about this proliferation of the field of identities and antagonisms: they are often dislocating in relation to one another.
>
> (1992, p. 31)

This far-reaching conclusion also has benefits for the analysis of genre, too: readings alive to the possibility of issues about identity and readings which attempt to be alert to different points of investment for different identities offer a new way of seeing. Perhaps, as Daniels argues (1996, p. 15), blaxploitation took place *before* and *continued after* the 1970s, the difference with the early part of this decade being that black people started to get in on the act as producers and consumers. Certainly, 'whiteness' was at least momentarily decentred in the thriller: Goines's narratives, for instance, invariably tell the reader when characters are white. Elsewhere, we can begin to do the work for ourselves (see Chapter 8 below).

Goines's intense desire to depict urban existence cannot be separated from the impulses of the thriller as a whole, especially in this period. It is as if Goines's fiction strives for verisimilitude because there is a wish to reveal – or at least represent – realities which are not presented elsewhere. Indisputably, there are a set of issues to do with vision, here, which have been raised already in respect of the hard-boiled subgenre and, especially crime narratives. The conduit through which these subgenres confront verisimilitude comprises a thoughtful use of 'focalization'; Goines's fiction, on the other hand, does not trade in sophisticated narrative devices. Yet, while his novels might be judged to consist of conventional realist narration the fervour to reveal which characterises them is striking. The desire to depict a world which coexists with the one which is more frequently offered up for representation is not just a feature of Goines's fiction. The same impulse – broached, admittedly, in a much different way – is the *sine qua non* of the 1970s paranoid thriller.

Further Reading

Print

Goines, Donald 1974. *Cry Revenge*
Goines, Donald 1974. *Swamp Man*
Johnson, B.B. 1970. *That's Where the Cat's At, Baby*
Tidyman, Ernest 1971. *Shaft Has a Ball*
Tidyman, Ernest 1972. *Shaft Among the Jews*
Tidyman, Ernest 1972. *Shaft's Big Score*
Tidyman, Ernest 1973. *Good-bye, Mr. Shaft*

Film

Cotton Comes to Harlem (June 1970)
They Call Me Mister Tibbs (July 1970)
Sweet Sweetback's Baadasssss Song (April 1971)

Cool Breeze (March 1972)
The Final Comedown (May 1972)
The Legend of Nigger Charlie (May 1972)
Shaft's Big Score (June 1972)
Come Back Charleston Blue (July 1972)
Superfly (August 1972)
Melinda (August 1972)
Hammer (September 1972)
Trouble Man (November 1972)
Black Gunn (December 1972)
Hit Man (December 1972)
Trick Baby (January 1973)
Black Caesar (February 1973)
The Mack (March 1973)
Coffy (May 1973)
Sweet Jesus Preacher Man (May 1973)
Shaft in Africa (June 1973)
Super Fly T.N.T (June 1973)
Cleopatra Jones (July 1973)
(Martial arts)
Gordon's War (August 1973)
(Paul Winfield as Vietnam veteran waging war on drugs gangs)
The Slams (September 1973)
Hit (September 1973)
The Spook Who Sat by the Door (October 1973)
Willy Dynamite (December 1973)
Hell Up in Harlem (January 1974)
(Sequel to *Black Caesar*; dir. Larry Cohen)
The Black Six (March 1974)
(Revenge)
Three Tough Guys (March 1974)
Foxy Brown (April 1974)
(Revenge)
Black Eye (April 1974)
Three the Hard Way (June 1974)
Black Samson (August 1974)
Solomon King (October 1974)
(Ex-Green Beret leads commandos against Middle-Eastern revolution-
   aries)
The Black Godfather (December 1974)
TNT Jackson (February 1975)

(Martial Arts)
Lord Shango (February 1975)
Sheba Baby (April 1975)
(Pam Grier as tough female private eye)
The Black Gestapo (April 1975)
Cleopatra Jones and the Casino of Gold (June 1975)
(Martial arts sequel)
Bucktown (July 1975)
(Racial revenge)
Friday Foster (December 1975)
(Pam Grier again)
Hit Potato (April 1976)
(Martial arts)
No Way Back (June 1976)

TV

Shaft (1973)
(Based on the 1970 film and novels by Ernest Tidyman)
Tenafly (1973)
(Middle-class black private eye)

7

Just Because You're Paranoid It Doesn't Mean They're Not Out to Get You

Although paranoia is a complex psychological affliction, it is probable that most people could suggest a reasonably strict definition of the word.[1] But this is not to say that paranoia is a stable phenomenon with a fixed meaning; rather than being a highly personal character trait, paranoia can be seen to be applicable to organizations or to represent a general mindset. In one of the most famous essays in the field of American political science, Hofstadter describes paranoia in politics as an oratorial style which relies on the notion of a conspiracy against 'a nation, a culture, a way of life' (1964, p. 4). He illustrates his argument by means of examples from a 1951 speech of Senator Joseph McCarthy, an 1895 statement of the Populist Party, a Texas newspaper article on Catholicism from 1855 and a 1795 Massachusetts sermon on the threat to Christianity that resides in Europe (pp. 7–10). What is crucial to Hofstadter's analysis is that paranoia, although often politically right-wing, is a strategy which can be employed by a number of actors within the breadth of the political spectrum; the threat envisaged in the paranoid style is always one concerning the core of American life. If we are to consider the paranoid thrillers of the 1970s it is important to bear in mind this general flexible concept of paranoia which might inform contemporary readings as well as a number of more specific formulations of the phenomenon.

Clearly, the paranoid style could become fixated on diverse aspects of the contemporary social formation. However, there are a number of points of emphasis in the period which must be taken into account: these involve notions to do with McCarthyism, residual Nazism, the invasion of privacy entailed by the growth of surveillance, and the general undermining of individual freedom by agents of corporatism. For opponents of the Nixon Administration during the Watergate period, McCarthyism came to signify a general American tyranny in political life rather than the use of smear tactics in the press (for example, Hentoff 1973, p. 217). Writing on Watergate in 1973, Mankiewicz utilizes an imaginary paradoxical scenario to illustrate the McCarthyist logic of the Nixon administration: the government marshals all its forces against the Soviet Union – including gross infringements of civil liberties – in order to prevent the infringements of civil liberties which it believes communism to represent (1973, p. 123). For Americans in the contemporary period, the link between such a scenario and the logic of the situation in Vietnam would not go unnoticed; a famous military announcement illustrated the contradictory logic of annihilating a small town: 'It was necessary to destroy Ben Tre to save Ben Tre' (Herr 1978, p. 63; see also Knightley 1975, p. 106; Hellman 1986, p. 89).

A further aspect of paranoia in the 1970s may be considered, at first glance, to be built on less than sturdy foundations. This is the fear of the resurgence of Nazism and/or its unseen role in the unwritten political and economic history of post-war America. Although this theme was worked out in fiction more than anywhere else in the period (for example, Nolan 1976; Levin 1977 or British novels such as Forsyth 1973) there were also real precedents for linking Nazism with the corporate power structure in America. In the realm of non-fiction it became widely known that Nazis had fled to South America after the war (see Arendt 1983) and an international non-fiction bestseller told of a Nazi-hunter's penetration of 'the Fourth Reich' in South America (Erdstein with Bean 1979). But for America there was a far stronger link between Nazism and contemporary events.

Towards the end of the Second World War 'Project Paperclip' was launched by the US Army with the aim of transporting over 100 rocket specialists from the defeated Germany to America. Most of these were scientists who had worked for the Nazis on the V1 and V2 rockets (Goebbels' Vengeance Weapons), among them Werner von Braun and Walter Dornberger (see Logsdon 1970, p. 49; DeWaard and DeWaard 1984, p. 13). In the immediate postwar period, then, the development of rockets was a thoroughly military offensive operation. Von Braun worked for the army, which developed its own programme and administration in 1956 in the form of an Army Ballistics Missile Agency (ABMA) and which preceded the establishment of a National Aeronautics and Space Administration (NASA) in 1958 (DeWaard and DeWaard 1984, pp. 32 ff.). From this point onwards von Braun became a national figure (Murray and Cox 1989, pp. 51–2). Thus, the brave world of President Kennedy's 'New Frontier', clearly exemplified by the space programme, was underpinned by a scientist whose main claim to fame had been the development of a deadly weapon which wreaked havoc on civilian communities in the Second World War. Such knowledge may not necessarily lead to accusations of residual Nazism; however, von Braun's visible profile in what had become a highly invested feature of American public life in the late 1950s and through the 1960s[2] allowed for an interpretation of public institutions as built on a foundation of crime and corrupt opportunism.

As I noted in the Introduction and Chapter 4, above, discourses concerning a 'crisis of confidence' associated with unease about secrecy and government policies pursued in the Vietnam War, were undoubtedly abroad in the American social formation. The case of the 'Pentagon Papers' had shown previous Presidential policy in an appalling light.[3] Moreover, the pattern of revelations which had produced such public dismay about Vietnam was to be reprised in the Watergate affair. Crucial to this process was the constant prevarication over the release of recordings of White House conversations after the Watergate hearings had decreed that they be made public. As we have seen, the Nixon administration became more and more entrenched until it began to regularly see 'enemies' among 'leftist' organisations and, especially, the media. The 'press' and 'conspiracy' thus became almost synonymous, albeit in different ways, for both sides.

Amidst the growing perception of the news media as an almost genuine 'fourth estate' during the period there was a further, not entirely surprising adjunct: the creation of folk-hero status for investigative reporters. Many commentators (for example, Mankiewicz 1973, p. 190) conflated Woodward and Bernstein with the *Washington Post*; in addition, as Ungar notes, 'Enrolments in schools of journalism and communication skyrocketed' (1989, p. 309–10). However, as nearly all the accounts of Watergate testify, the affair required a massive number of dramatis personæ even in the area of investigation, a fact that it is often possible to forget. It is true that journalists were instrumental in bringing facts to public attention, both in Watergate and elsewhere, for example, the Karen Silkwood murder (see Hildyard 1983, pp. 1–23); it is also true that reporters of political events became recognisable figures: as well as the ones I have discussed I could also mention in this context the names of David Halberstam, Roger Hilsman, Neil Sheehan and Seymour Hersh.[4] Yet it is possible that the individual images and exploits of journalists stood in for the media as a whole.[5]

Committed journalism is manifestly crucial to the paranoid thriller, where the murky world of residual Nazism, surveillance and conspiracy has a stark contrast in the truly public arena of the press. In this way, more than any other, the paranoid style of the 1970s distinguishes itself from that of the 1950s, when McCarthyism kept many Americans looking over their shoulder through fear of accusations of 'un-American activity'. Rather than the public sphere being used in the service of the government to expose, smear and vilify innocent citizens, in the 1970s it is the device whereby innocent citizens are saved from the conspiracy hatched in the very seat of government. The role of journalism since the McCarthy hearings had therefore undergone an almost complete political turnaround.

If the changed conception of the press represents a transformation of the whole notion of paranoia as it can be applied to American political life, the same can be said for the contemporary thriller – only more so. Rather than merely incorporating aspects of paranoia into their narratives, thrillers develop some of paranoia's implications. A great many problems engendered by the events of the early 1970s were generally felt to have been left unresolved;[6] in the paranoid thriller the narrative either leaves the reader in no doubt about the source for a possible resolution or with an explicit rendering of a resolution of paranoid fears. This is not to suggest that such thrillers serve as an ideological palliative;[7] but it *is* to suggest that there are strong grounds for a contemporary *political* reading of such texts.

The paranoid thriller

In the following section we will discuss novels and films dealing with different aspects of a general sense of paranoia in the period. The first set of texts that we will discuss have been largely ignored by commentators despite their popularity. An actor/producer who retired from his profession to write novels, Robert Ludlum began his career with *The Scarlatti Inheritance* (1972a) in 1971.[8] The entire corpus of this work explores the manifold nature of paranoia in the 1970s, although the economic is the conspiratorial motive force of history in the novels. Coupled with this, the theme of a 'hidden history' takes centre stage (cf. Sutherland 1981, pp. 240–4). In *The Osterman Weekend* and *The Matlock Paper* the equivalent of the hidden history theme is the recurrent dual world metaphor: the precarious nature of surface existence and the turbulence of another world with which it coexists. Moreover, the revelation of a world underlying the recognized one is made all the more startling by the fact that it does not occur in an explicit war scenario. Like the Mafia in *The Godfather*, it is part and parcel of American life. As a result, in *The Osterman*

Weekend and *The Matlock Paper*, the threat of corruption reveals itself in preeminently domestic situations: at the heart of the family in the former and amidst the surrogate family that makes up a campus community in the latter.

The Holcroft Covenant

In what is probably Ludlum's most famous novel, the above-mentioned themes are significantly fused. *The Holcroft Covenant* deals with the coming to fruition of a Nazi plot hatched in the closing stages of the war and although the narrative does not deal with all the participants of this plot they are made omnipresent actors in the story both by the extra- textual cues and the opening pages of the text. The back cover of the first American paperback edition of the novel (Ludlum 1979a) is dominated by large red letters which proclaim:

> FOURTH REICH
> IS WAITING TO BE BORN.
> THE ONLY MAN
> WHO CAN STOP IT
> IS ABOUT TO SIGN ITS
> BIRTH CERTIFICATE.

The opening prologue is set in 1945 and features a scene in which children are transported ashore from a German submarine. Apart from these two cues, the massed children – the world beneath the surface – do not really feature explicitly in the narrative at all. Instead, it is the story, set in the 1970s, of Noel Holcroft, an American businessman who was the son of the deceased Nazi, Heinrich Clausen, 'the financial magician who put together the coalition of disparate economic forces that insured the supremacy of Adolf Hitler' (p. 4). As an infant, Holcroft was taken to the United States by his American mother, Althene, who renounced both her husband and Nazism in general. After marriage to Richard Holcroft, she reared her son as an American citizen.

In the opening pages of the book, Noel Holcroft is aware of his parentage when he is summoned to a meeting with a Swiss banker. The banker tells him that his real father not only renounced Nazism himself and was involved in a plot to depose Hitler – *Wolfsschanze* – but that he has arranged for a sum of money now totalling $780 million to reside in a Geneva bank. Clausen decreed that his son should be responsible for distributing this money amongst Jewish families throughout the world as a means of reparation from the German people. In order to do this he must first find two other ex-German families who are entrusted with the same task in tandem with him; having made contact, they can then proceed to release the money for charitable purposes. At this preliminary stage of the narrative, Holcroft believes he is charged with a worthy crusade on behalf of his honourable father. However, certain obstacles lie in his way.

Holcroft is continually in the dark until the late stages of the story when the narrative gradually furnishes information about the conspiracy. The acute Hitchcockian sense of unknowing on the part of the protagonist only heightens the feeling of paranoia in the novel, induced purposely by the villains. In Buenos Aires Holcroft goes to meet a man named Graff whom he believes will help him in his quest. On hearing Holcroft's purpose Graff orders his servants to eject him from the grounds, implying that Holcroft is filth. In the midst of these sundry orders to his men, the narration is conducted from a point of view close to Graff:

> One must follow the other in rapid succession until Holcroft has no judgement left. Until he can no longer distinguish between ally and enemy, knowing only that he must press forward. When finally he breaks, we'll be there and he'll be ours.
>
> (p. 91)

At this stage, the narrative has not provided any information on who Graff really is and his attempts to induce paranoia in Holcroft do not have any clear purpose. Later, the arch-villain behind the Geneva plot makes a statement in the same vein as Graff's: 'Holcroft must be convinced that Wolfsschanze is everywhere. Prodding, threatening, protecting...' (p. 281). This is the feeling that Holcroft seems to have for a great deal of the story, although by this time the narrative has provided information on the villain's intentions.

Another feature of paranoia becomes manifest in the novel when Helden (a woman with whom Holcroft falls in love) is abducted and Holcroft is attacked in a French village. He barges into a residential building to look for her and his assailants:

> Holcroft kicked the door in front of him; the lock broke, the door swung open, and he rushed inside.
>
> It was empty, had been empty a very long time. Layers of dust were everywhere...and there were no footprints. No one had been inside that room for weeks.
>
> (p. 223)

Although there is nothing unusual about this scene, it does reveal the working of paranoia. All Holcroft's deductions have led him to believe that Helden is being held behind the door and he does not hesitate to break in; yet he finds no mark of her presence. This echoes *All the President's Men* (see Chapter 2 above) when, after a meeting with Deep Throat, Woodward embarks on a process of interpreting all situations in which he finds himself. All that has happened to Holcroft (like Woodward) convinces him that the most innocuous of objects is a tool of his persecution. This is because he is no longer living in the world he has known. Repeatedly, throughout the narrative, the words from a planted note in his apartment come back to haunt him: '*Nothing is as it was . . .* ' That Holcroft has entered another, parallel, world is continually emphasized.

One of the families with which Holcroft must make contact is made up of two brothers named Kessler; Holcroft meets Erich Kessler, whom he finds to be a jolly academic. However, Kessler is in league with Johann von Tiebolt, the prime mover behind the Nazi plot. Von Tiebolt is, in fact, a member of the second family that Holcroft must meet. Holcroft is seduced in Portsmouth by the first sister of this family, Gretchen, and then falls in love with the other sister, Helden Tennyson, in Paris. However, the brother, Tennyson/Von Tiebolt, as well as being a Nazi is also a ruthless international assassin known as 'the Tinamou' who uses as his cover the fact that he is a foreign correspondent for the *Guardian*(!). Throughout the narrative there are examples of Von Tiebolt's ruthlessness: among others he kills his brother-in-law; an assassin partner; his sister, Gretchen, with whom he has enjoyed an incestuous relationship; and finally he attempts to kill Holcroft after having disposed of Althene.

If he has not already been depicted as sufficiently ruthless, sadistic and perverse, the physical description of Von Tiebolt when Holcroft meets him suggests that there is something unusual about this character (p. 309). He is a Nazi neo-classical art object, demonstrating that a perfect surface almost always implies corruption beneath. This can be counterposed to Gerhardt, the *Nachrichtendienst* stalwart, who has been silently opposing Nazism without being active until he is approached by Helden. Gerhardt is then shown to embody the ultimate deception: he is a senile old man in a French village who seems to care only for the pigeons he talks to in the square (p. 390). The contrast with Von Tiebolt is further emphasized as Gerhardt is the only man who reveals the reason why 'The coin of Wolfsschanze has two sides' (p. 407).

As with *The Scarlatti Inheritance*, *The Holcroft Covenant* climaxes with the arrival in Europe of the grand matriarch, in this case, Althene

Holcroft. What is also interesting – although one may not wish to press this point too far – is that the Kesslers and the Tennysons have lived most of their lives without fathers. Holcroft, on the other hand, has had a stepfather whom he has always loved, as the narrative reveals when Richard Holcroft is murdered (p. 191 ff.). There is room for a reading of the effects of a father's absence (although this is not to say that single-parent families necessarily enhance fascist tendencies in individuals). The main point is that the genetic evaluation of character is invalidated as soon as it arises in the narrative. Although they are all of the same family, Johann and Gretchen are both corrupt Nazis, but Helden is not, and she even collaborates in the necessary assassination of her brother in the final pages.

Possible readings of *The Holcroft Covenant* and Ludlum's work in general in the 1970s have a wealth of material to assist them beyond the roller-coaster nature of the narrative as mentioned by the critics (see, for example, the back cover of the first American paperback edition). The intrusion of a hidden, coexistent world upon another, surface world, is often couched in terms of the public sphere disrupting the domestic world. The paranoia that this entails is also very much a seventies phenomenon: surveillance is carried out less by foreign forces than by government agencies and internal security operatives. This must be borne in mind before any flip assertions about beastly Nazis are made with regard to Ludlum's work. As we have seen, *The Holcroft Covenant* is one example of a Ludlum text which features a ruthless Nazi villain with a number of distinguishing characteristics. However, the Nazi is also part of a larger conspiracy called Wolfsschanze; as Gerhardt shows in his explanation of the two sides of the coin, *Wolfsschanze* does not stop with the demonic power of Hitler but goes beyond it to a much wider, economic base.

Ludlum's own statements delineate the frame of reference for possible contemporary readings of his texts far more cogently than the critical comments of such as Mandel (1984) and Sutherland (1981). Writing in 1988 about the genesis of his novel, *Trevayne*, Ludlum states:

> It was the time of Watergate and my pencil flew across the pages in outrage. Younger – not youthful – intemperance made my head explode with such words and phrases as *Mendacity! Abuse of power! Corruption! Police State!*
>
> Here was the government, the highest of our elected and appointed officials entrusted with the guardianship of our system, not only lying to the people but collecting millions upon millions to perpetuate the

lies and thus the controls they believed were theirs alone to exercise ... [T]he lies had to continue and the coffers of ideological purity kept full so the impure were *blitzkrieged* with money and buried at the starting gates of political contests.

(Ludlum 1989b, pp. vii–viii)

The final sentences of the quote are especially illuminating for a reading of Ludlum's narratives; such words as 'purity' and '*blitzkreig*' combine with 'coffers' and American politics with consummate ease. Rather than identifying an authorial intention, this quote suggests grounds for a reading of Ludlum at the time his novels were first published.

Marathon Man

Marathon Man exists as a novel published in 1974 by the renowned screen writer, William Goldman, and as a film directed by John Schlesinger two years later from a screenplay adapted from his own novel by Goldman. The narrative is primarily concerned with the way lives of individuals in the present (the mid-1970s) are weighed down by the burden of events in their youth. Crucially, the protagonists' mother has been killed in a (suicide?) car crash while hearings were impending against her husband, their father, Columbia historian H.V. Levy. In turn, as a culmination of the ordeal that he has undergone during the anti-Communist witch-hunt, the father shoots himself soon after, in the year following Senator Joseph McCarthy's death (1954).

These kind of tragedies which take place at the interface of domestic and public life were not without their precedents in postwar American history. Ellen Schrecker opens her book on McCarthyism in academia (1986) by citing the case of Chandler Davis, a maths instructor at the University of Michigan who was sentenced to six months in prison in 1960 having refused to testify in front of a House Un-American Activities Committee (HUAC) hearing (p. 3). The most notable case which Schrecker considers, however, is that of the anthropologist Dr Gene Weltfish, who was fired from Columbia in 1953, implicitly for her leftist leanings. The point of this is not just that it took place at Columbia University, where *Marathon Man* is largely set, but that the way in which the bureaucracy clumsily disguised the reasons for her dismissal illustrates the nightmare aspect of McCarthyism, that it embodied irrational events (pp. 255–257). This is the way the McCarthy witch-hunts can be read in *Marathon Man*: as a time of tyranny which, although seemingly unreal, threatens to unleash itself again.

The main story of *Marathon Man* concerns a PhD student and amateur long-distance runner called Levy who is enrolling for a seminar with the eminent Columbia historian, Biesenthal. During the first few weeks of his period at Columbia he keeps in contact with his brother, an oil businessman whom he calls Doc and who calls him Babe. Interspersed with Babe's life and his thoughts about his childhood and youth there is a narrative about Scylla, an international assassin who is involved in transporting diamonds between various countries. It transpires that he has been doing work for Christian Szell, the Auschwitz dentist colleague of Mengele, who wishes to emerge from the South American jungle to claim diamonds from a safe deposit box in New York.

When Doc arrives in New York to stay with his brother, the latter has fallen in love with another student. Doc, Babe and his girlfriend, Elsa, have dinner at an exclusive restaurant and all goes well until Doc exposes her as an impostor seeking residence in the United States. Babe and Doc argue and separate. Meanwhile, Scylla meets Szell in New York and, during an argument, Szell unexpectedly stabs Scylla in the abdomen. Later that evening Babe receives a knock at the door of his flat only to find Doc standing there with a badly wounded stomach. So, at this point in the centre of the narrative it becomes clear that Doc is Scylla, a shock that the film version of *Marathon Man* (1976) is obviously not able to pull off.

In Babe the text invokes the figure of the outsider. His entry into the narrative is heralded with the following: ' "Here comes da creep", one of the stoop kids said' (1976, p. 15). Throughout the rest of the early part of the narrative, Babe's status as 'outsider' is played off against the established Doc.[9] Babe, at 25, is still a boy experiencing angst which is heightened by the groves of academe; Doc is successful in the oil business. Babe obsessively returns to the events of his father's death as if it was a sore tooth (like the one he has developed at the beginning of the novel); Doc seems to have put the affair behind him. Babe is clumsy and uncultured, looking for answers in his books; Doc is a wine connoisseur who taunts Babe for his lack of worldly knowledge (although Scylla is a whisky man).

Bearing in mind the plot of *Marathon Man*, it is obvious that Babe's status as an 'outsider' is far from straightforward. Doc's double life allows the narrative to draw together a number of themes of paranoia which have as their foundation a critique of the world which Doc inhabits and which he has inherited from the McCarthy era as the quintessential representative of artifice and double-dealing. Scylla/Doc is an operative of a splinter organization of government intelligence but, as becomes clear, government interests as represented by such organizations do not coincide with either the Constitution or conventional versions of the public good. Early in the narrative, just following an assassination attempt on him, Scylla has a dream in which Mengele is trying to take his skin; clearly this is a simple metaphor for robbery but at one point in the dream they are talking: '"Control is important for us", Scylla agreed' (p. 77), hinting at what is to be revealed later: that the American government is in league with Nazi war criminals.

Further grounds for fraternal difference are offered by the fact that Doc's ordinary cynicism is in direct contrast to Babe's idealistic suspicion. Yet, at the same time, the idea that Doc should come from the same family and experiences as Babe suggests in the narrative a kind of 'schizophrenic' existence of contemporary American life as a result of the McCarthy period. For Babe, there is an explicit link between McCarthyism and Nazism and a distinction between those characters in the narrative who care about the McCarthy period and have acted upon it and those who have put it behind them and continued business. Doc, of course, is the embodiment of the latter, as Babe explains later to Biesenthal (p. 191).

This lack of consensus also entails on both sides a loss of faith in the powers of authority to alleviate certain ills. Having eluded his captors, Babe goes to the house of Biesenthal who tells him to call the police: '"Police?" Babe blinked. "Police? Why should I call them, what good would that do?" He buttoned the raincoat. "I don't want justice, are you kidding, screw justice, we're way past justice, it's blood now..."' (p. 192). In thrillers, the point of such revenge as Babe's is usually social justice. In a complicated way, there are some ideals that Babe holds dear and he takes individual action, killing Szell in the name of such justice. A reading of *Marathon Man* that focussed on the integrity of local ties rather than highly organized and legislated – but ultimately corrupted – civil virtues, would be quite probable in a time when the main threat to legality, the Constitution and American political life actually came from *within* the government.

Such an argument is even more probable in relation to the film version of *Marathon Man*. When Rosenbaum picks up his car at the beginning of the film an announcement about the baker's strike is heard over the radio; when Scylla (Roy Scheider) is driven through Paris, his taxi is overtaken by a group of young people on bicycles protesting about pollution; Babe (Dustin Hoffman) refers to Doc's colleagues in the oil business as 'a bunch of polluters and thieves'; the streets of Paris are filled with unemptied bins because of a refuse workers' dispute; Janeway

(William Devane) mentions the strikes in a cafe; when Szell (Laurence Olivier) arrives in New York there is a baggage-handlers' strike at the airport. These are not features of society that would exist in the regime to which Szell formerly belonged, and a pretty explicit contrast appears to have been drawn between the state of social indecision on the streets and the obsessively organized mission of both Szell and the American government.

Another important theme of *Marathon Man* that is emphasized by the semantic features of the film is the general identity of the villains. A third of the way into the film Babe stays with Elsa in Central Park after dusk and the inevitable happens: they are mugged by two men; but the muggers are not black or Hispanics armed with knives, they are professionals – both in the way they land their blows and how they are dressed. When Doc visits Babe the latter makes a point about the attackers appearance: 'They had suits like you.' Later still, when the always impeccably attired Scylla goes to meet Szell, who is accompanied by Karl and Gerhard, they congregate loosely around a fountain in the forecourt of a building. The forecourt is spotlit and consists of various structures which appear to be made out of strips of translucent glass. The effect of modernity is coupled with industrialism and the scene ends, of course, with Scylla fatally stabbed. This event paves the way for another man in a suit to take over Babe's life when Doc is dead. This is Janeway, Doc's lover and colleague.

In the novel Babe sees Janeway first as Gatsby, then, after Babe is betrayed by him and delivered into the hands of Szell once more, Janeway becomes 'the Nixon lawyer, Dean – a pilot fish they called him. A thing that hung around the biggest shark for power' (p. 169). For Janeway there is no ideal of justice and no allegiance to nation or Constitution; there is only an arena of power where loyalties are constantly to be shifted. What Janeway represents in the film is a new ideal; in one sense he can be read as the impersonality of late capitalism that Jameson ascribes to the FBI man in *Dog Day Afternoon* (see Chapter 2 above) or a post-Foucauldian embodiment of the shifting locations of power; put another way, he is simply a representative of the vicissitudes of the market: 'Think of me as any other young executive,' he says to Szell, his feet up on the desk as William Devane's massive grin fills the face of the character. It is clear that Janeway suffuses a novel kind of mercenary streak which is associated with the corruption in government of the 1970s but also goes beyond it.

In fact the only possible effective opposition to the relentlessness of Janeway must be his other. Although it is Babe who finally despatches him in the film, Janeway's nemesis lies with the stoop kids. The Hispanic teenagers who constantly taunt Babe eventually come to the rescue; Babe persuades their ringleader, Melendez, to break into his flat with a few friends. The flat is under surveillance and Janeway is at the foot of the next flight of stairs; he hears the kids fiddling with the door and approaches them, gun in hand, with his arm extended. All but Melendez, who is breaking the lock, turn swiftly on Janeway and point various Saturday night specials at him. Then Melendez turns to him and says rather emphatically, 'Blow it out your ass, motherfucker.' Janeway is therefore effectively bested by the other side of the market, a vicious updated bunch of Dickensian urchins.

Critical reaction to *Marathon Man* as a paranoid text was largely negative (for example, Cocks 1976) although there were a few critics who recognized that the political elements in the plot were integral to readings of the film (Stoop 1976 p. 109). It is implicit in the reviews of Cocks and others that John Schlesinger, in directing a thriller, was prostituting his art; but there are also a number of other permutations in the reviews: Schlesinger is a talented director and should not be lowering himself with genre texts; or, because Schlesinger is talented, the film has greater depths than the average thriller; or, more decisively, the film is not a thriller. Such concerns contribute little to the historical reading of the film. Pauline Kael comes closer to making *Marathon Man* seem historically specific by emphasizing: 'It's "Death Wish" with a lone Jewish boy getting his own back from the Nazis. It's a Jewish revenge fantasy' (1976b).

While other critics tried to straightforwardly deny a political reading by condemning the resonances in the narrative as ham-fisted, Kael plays politics down, to an extent, by focusing on Babe's killing of Szell. It is here in the film that Babe makes Szell swallow handfuls of diamonds. When a struggle ensues, Szell is finally impaled on his own dagger and falls after the diamonds into the water: he has gone away from Babe but has landed in the city's water supply. Babe then throws his father's gun into the Central Park reservoir. Thus, traces of the killing will ultimately be found in the city's homes.

Contemporary readings of *Marathon Man* could quite easily be organized around the political implication of clandestine government activities and how they threaten to invade the realm of domesticity. Babe is caught up in the whole Szell business for a complex of reasons but most directly as a result of his brother's activities. It is also here, in the realm of the family, that the narrative provides a rationale for Babe's subsequent actions. In Kael's formulation *Marathon Man* quite clearly allows for a reading as a narrative of the point where the political concerns of the period become personal.

Capricorn One

If *Marathon Man* can be said to illustrate the revenge motif embodied in retribution for politically induced paranoia, then *Capricorn One* (1978) represents exposure as the means to combat manipulation by government agencies. An original screenplay written, and then directed, by Peter Hyams, *Capricorn One* deals with a manned space flight to Mars in the not too distant future. The film utilizes the idealistic connotations of the space programme in American life and shows that they often rest on a foundation shaped by much different interests. The idealism which fixes on space as the New Frontier is shown in *Capricorn One* to be transitory and representative of a fragmenting consensus in American social life. As there is evidence to suggest that the purpose of expensive manned space flights in times of social strife was less than clear to American citizens, there is also evidence that some Americans even saw the space programme as a literal, as well as an ideological, sham. Wise points out that, a year after the moon landing, citizens throughout the country believed that the media coverage of the moon mission was a hoax perpetrated by the government to fool the Russians and the Chinese, or to justify the cost of the space programme, or to distract the electorate from their domestic troubles (1973, p. 342).

A hoax of this kind makes up the story of *Capricorn One*. Appearing in 1978, the film, perhaps, benefits from the other paranoid texts which have gone before: various sequences in the film either consciously or unconsciously echo scenes from films such as *The Parallax View* or *All the President's Men*. When the leader of the Mars programme, Kelloway (Hal Holbrook), following the ersatz lift-off, takes the three astronauts – Brubaker (James Brolin), Walker (O.J. Simpson) and Willis (Sam Waterston) – out of a brightly lit room to another part of the building which is rigged up as a film studio, the localized lights in this room come into view at head height, the camera pulls back to an elevated rostrum shot which shows a movie set with a planet surface and a space module. The sinister tones of Jerry Goldsmith's score are heard on the soundtrack as the shot is in progress. What seems innocuous in these films is gradually made to seem portentous and charged with paranoid meaning.

Much of the film echoes the general tenor of Nixonian doublespeak and characteristic responses to it. Kelloway explains to the astronauts why the hoax must be perpetrated:

I just care so goddamn much I think it's worth it. I'm not even sure of it; I just think it...It'll keep something alive that shouldn't die... There's nothing more to believe in...Do you wanna be the ones who give everyone another reason to give up?

Brubaker counter-argues:

This is really wonderful: if we go along with you and lie our asses off then the world of truth and ideals is protected. But we don't wanna take part in some giant rip-off of yours and somehow or other we're managing to ruin the country. You're pretty good, Jim, I'll give you that....If the only way to keep something alive is to become everything I hate then I don't know that it's worth keeping it alive....I don't think this is right – all the rest is bullshit.

Brubaker is clearly responding to the kind of double-speak which characterises military discourse about events such as the destruction of Ben Tre or political discourse about the need for covert activities (see above and Mankiewicz 1973, p. 123). As he grabs Kelloway by the lapels there is a two-shot with a harsh studio light shining in the middle of them. The light illuminates Brubaker's face and leaves Kelloway's in shadow. If the audience had not recognized it before, there is a strong reminder in the narration at this point that the actor who plays Kelloway also took the role of Deep Throat in *All the President's Men*. As we have seen, Deep Throat was not the villain of that film, but he did represent shady motives and clandestine activities.

The scene which immediately follows this is set outside the house of Kay Brubaker (Brenda Vaccaro) on a bright day. The journalist Caulfield (Elliott Gould) is involved in a long discourse concerning his dislike of cynicism, lack of sincerity and of artificiality, which he illustrates in the sunlight for fellow journalist Judy Drinkwater (Karen Black), by means of the wrappers on Holiday Inn toilet seats. Conversely, whenever conspiracy is about to explicitly intrude into the lives of the protagonists there is a studied use of dark brown shades engendered by localized light sources. The control room at Houston where the most crucial part of the duplicity will be played out is very distinctively lit, with light emanating chiefly from computer consoles, an image which does not tally with authentic TV coverage of mission control which has occurred in the past. As the craft touches down the congregation in the control room stands and cheers but the camera pans from left to right, rising to a rostrum shot which surveys the triumph but which is also accompanied by very tense and sinister music. The meaning of the incongruous juxtaposition of the music and the triumphal shot is, by now, obvious. This is the centrepoint of the film in terms of narration and establishment of duplicity and it is followed by a succession of similar sequences.

Semantic cues are also employed to verify the integrity of the journalist, Caulfield, who is suspicious about the Mars mission. Apparently, he has always had a penchant for the sensational, as his editor, Loughlin (David Doyle), indicates when he chides him for not being a plodder: 'Woodward and Bernstein were good reporters, that's how they did it.' At this stage the narrative has shown that Caulfield's scent of a story is authentic; far from recasting Caulfield as a slightly unbalanced low-achiever, Loughlin's speech emphasizes that – at least at present – Caulfield is a lowly and heroic outsider. Loughlin gives him 24 hours to come up with a story and there is then a cut to Caulfield in his apartment. Again, it is a room lit like the Houston control room and, as such, is ominous. Getting up from reading his book he goes to the bathroom cabinet and opens it wide, revealing a near-empty tube of toothpaste and a bottle of mouth rinse from which he takes a mouthful. He returns to his work and then his door is suddenly broken open by federal agents who insist they have a search warrant; as they manhandle Caulfield, one of them announces he has something and there is a shot of him taking a small bottle of white powder from the bathroom cabinet which he declares to be cocaine. This is where *Capricorn One* can be said to represent somewhat of a departure from other paranoid films (for example, *The Parallax View*, 1974): the audience is in full possession of the facts from a very early stage of the narrative, partly because of semantic cues; the suspense lies in how the conspiracy is uncovered and the delays in Caulfield's quest.

One other feature of the semantic aspect of the narrative of *Capricorn One* should be mentioned. When Brubaker, Willis and Walker escape into the desert they are pursued by two black/green helicopters; contemporary readings of the film might render specific connotations to the sight and sound of these aircraft, that they embody the iconography of Vietnam (cf. Spark 1989, p. 104). The helicopters in this film also represent the faceless machinery of the conspiracy as opposed to the double-dealing of its human agents (cf. Milgram 1974, p. 163). However, there is a contrast to the helicopters which is presented in the narrative. Immediately prior to the garage scene, Caulfield has tried to hire the services of an old-fashioned populist, Albain, (Telly Savalas) and his aircraft, a crop-duster. While circling a remote disused garage in the craft, Albain and Caulfield notice that it is under attack from the helicopter pilots; they swoop down and land for a few seconds in order to allow the fleeing Brubaker to board the wing and make their escape. As the helicopters follow, one of the most breathtaking chases in the history of Hollywood cinema takes place. Albain eventually causes both of the pursuing craft to crash when he releases his fertilizer near an oncoming mountain. In terms of the cinema, it is clear that the crop-dusting aircraft is a reference to Hitchcock's *North by Northwest* (1957); however, as a result of its pilot, the crop-duster in this film serves as an emphatic human foil to the impersonality of the helicopters.

As the extra-textual cues make clear, *Capricorn One* was very readable as a parable of Watergate and Vietnam. Although Hyams had the idea for the script long before the Watergate burglary he described in the *New York Times* how he believed deception had become a feature of American life:

Didn't the long-unacknowledged part the United States played in the early days of the Vietnam war indicate that such an undertaking could easily be sanctioned and organized? 'Think of it – a country bombing another country for eight months without anyone knowing about it. Think of all the planes involved, all the barracks that had to be built, all the beds that had to be made, all the meals that had to be cooked. My idea was peanuts beside that, much smaller in scope and probability.'

(quoted in Nightingale 1978)

As a TV reporter in Vietnam in the 1960s Hyams's perspective on the power of television is transferred to the narrative of *Capricorn One*. Such readings would seem to suggest that the film fictionally resolves some of the contradictions that were left open by Watergate in American political life. However, like *All the President's Men*, the narrative can actually be said to be inconclusive (that is, the audience does not see the unfolding of the subsequent scandal); however, *history* enables a filling of what is left out of *All the President's Men* as it does with *Capricorn One*, albeit in different ways.

What *Capricorn One* can be said to represent is the pinnacle of the paranoid genre in that it incorporates aspects of other paranoid texts into the fabric of its narrative; the most pronounced of these that we have discussed is the ironic arrangement of semantic elements to encourage a paranoid reading of what seem either sincere or innocent objects, speeches and events. It is a measure of the currency of such devices by this time in the seventies that specific readings of them could now be expected without the requirement that the humorous aspects of the narrative be eliminated.

Justifiable paranoia

What we have suggested in our discussion of the paranoid thriller in the 1970s is that paranoia has to be taken seriously in the thriller, that it is the result of some historical purpose. The obvious objection to such a bald assertion has been played out by those commentators on the thriller who point to the 'ideological' nature of the structure of the thriller genre (for example, Mandel 1984; Palmer 1978). Such analyses hold that thrillers – with their fear and resolution of conspiracies against the established order, their heroism and competitive individualism, and their valorization of professionalism – are in their very structure, a vessel which shapes, contains and renders essentially conservative, any narrative 'contents' (see also Chapter 1 above). Paranoia is hence part of the thriller mindset, inaugurated at the thriller's inception in the nineteenth century, and irrespective of its directive force, has the same reactionary capitalist character as it supposedly does in the very first thrillers.

Generic structures, however, are not to be understood as omnipotent. What we have argued in this chapter is the idea that the term 'paranoia' as it is utilized in the description of many 1970s thrillers cannot be understood simply by defining it as an eternal psychological mechanism or as an immutable capitalist ideology. There can be little doubt that the paranoid thriller in film and print fiction is overwhelmingly associated with the 1970s. One needs only to think of the number of films on the theme of paranoia directed at establishment structures and individuals which have become 'classics' in spite of – in some cases – variable reviews on their first outings: *Executive Action* (1973), *The Conversation* (1974), *The Parallax View* (1974), *Three Days of the Condor* (1975), *The Boys from Brazil* (1978), and *Winter Kills* (1979). Or one might consider the print fiction of Ross Thomas, Charles McCarry, James Grady and Frederick Nolan. Paranoia need not be straightforwardly 'conservative'; it can take on a different character altogether for readers, representing a means of combatting and anticipating the offences committed by the established order. Moreover, as Kael argues, paranoia is 'justifiable' in this period, 'particularly if the natural enemies represent the whole system of authority' (1973, p. 107). If Watergate and Vietnam had not made paranoia an abundantly plausible response, then smaller agencies such as police departments could reinforce such views (and it must be remembered that Kael is referring specifically here to Frank Serpico's crusade against corruption in the NYPD – see Chapter 5).

While it could be argued, on the one hand, that the paranoid mindset in the real world achieved nothing (Salisbury 1984a, p. 6; Ungar 1989, pp. 301–2; Kolko 1974, p. 125), on the other it can be noted that the texts of Woodward and Bernstein had led directly to the removal of an incumbent president. In addition, we have already demonstrated that these texts bear a strong relation to the corpus of thrillers that we are discussing. If the discourses of news, non-fiction and the thriller can be demonstrated to overlap (see Chapter 2 above) then the investments which are brought to contemporary readings give the narrative a political character. It is here that generic innovation is to be found.

Rather than a tangible change in the formal structure of a text in putative reaction to some concomitant change in the social formation, generic innovation once more resides in the manner in which a *reading* of the text is arranged, the means by which it is socially invested, thus always already effecting a transformation of the text in flux. It is in the reading of texts – a reading that is arranged by other texts and is socially and historically located – that generic innovation lies. In this chapter we have posited the numerous ways in which the reading formation of the paranoid thrillers was characterized by the distrust of authority in various forms and the problematic location of corruption at the very heart of American life. Clearly, the protagonists of the paranoid thrillers rebel against a general *betrayal* of principles in America, after discovering that the nation is, at root, ruled by the pursuit of power and money. Violence and persecution are found to be employed in the maintenance of an ideological sham and, often, the only way to expose this sham is to blow the whistle and go to the newspapers.

Where individuals find that they cannot expose hypocrisy by resorting to the press, there is only one alternative – revenge.

Further Reading

Print

Agnew, Spiro T. 1976. *The Canfield Decision*
Anderson, Patrick 1976. *The President's Mistress*
Ardies, Tom 1975. *Russian Roulette*
Barak, Michael 1976. *The Secret List of Heinrich Roehm*
Bova, Ben 1976. *The Multiple Man*

Carroll, James 1976. *Madonna Red*

Condon, Richard 1974. *Winter Kills*

Dan, Uri with Radley, Edward 1977. *The Eichmann Syndrome*

Duncan, Robert L. 1980. *Brimstone*

Egerton-Thomas, Christopher 1978. *A Taste of Conspiracy*

Ehrlichman, John 1976. *Washington Behind Closed Doors* (a.k.a. *The Company*)

Ehrlichman, John 1979. *The Whole Truth*

Freed, Donald and Lane, Mark 1973. *Executive Action: Assassination of a Head of State*

Grady, James 1974. *Six Days of the Condor*

Grady, James 1975. *Shadow of the Condor*

Hone, Joseph 1971. *The Private Sector*

Kennedy, Adam 1975. *The Domino Principle*

Levin, Ira 1976. *The Boys from Brazil*

Ludlum, Robert 1971. *The Scarlatti Inheritance*

Ludlum, Robert 1972. *The Osterman Weekend*

Ludlum, Robert 1973. *The Matlock Paper*

Ludlum, Robert 1974. *The Rhinemann Exchange*

Ludlum, Robert 1976. *The Gemini Contenders*

Ludlum, Robert 1977. *The Chancellor Manuscript*

Ludlum, Robert 1979. *The Matarese Circle*

Mann, Patrick 1973. *The Vacancy*

Marchetti, Victor 1972. *The Rope Dancer*

McCarry, Charles 1979. *The Better Angels*

Moore, Robin and Van Doren, Ronald 1976. *The Edge of the Pond*

Nolan, Frederick 1974. *Brass Target*

Nolan, Frederick 1974. *The Ritter Double Cross*

Nolan, Frederick 1976. *The Mittenwald Syndicate*

Pronzini, Bill and Malzberg, Barry N. 1977. *Acts of Mercy*

Rostand, Robert 1973. *The Killer Elite*

Safire, William 1977. *Full Disclosure*

Salinger, Pierre 1973. *For the Eyes of the President Only*

Singer, Loren 1970. *The Parallax View*

Stewart, Edward 1973. *They've Shot the President's Daughter*

Stovall, Walter 1978. *Presidential Emergency*

Thomas, Ross 1970. *The Fools in Town Are on Our Side*

Thomas, Ross 1974. *The Porkchoppers*

Thomas, Ross 1976. *Yellow Dog Contract*

Thomas, Ross 1979. *The Eighth Dwarf*

Ziffren, Mickey 1979. *A Political Affair*

Film

Executive Action (November 1973)
McQ (January 1974)
(John Wayne contends with police corruption)
The Conversation (April 1974)
The Parallax View (June 1974)
The Stepford Wives (February 1975)
White Line Fever (July 1975)
(Corruption in freight business; Jan Michael Vincent as air force veteran)
Russian Roulette (July 1975)
(Kosygin assasination plan)
Three Days of the Condor (September 1975)
The Killer Elite (December 1975)
The Domino Principle (March 1977)
(Similar assassination theme to *The Parallax View*)
The Black Oak Conspiracy (April 1977)
(Paranoia in a small town)
The Lincoln Conspiracy (October 1977)
(Historically transposed paranoia)
The Private Files of J. Edgar Hoover (January 1978)
The Boys from Brazil (September 1978)
Last Embrace (May 1979)
Winter Kills (May 1979)

TV

Washington Behind Closed Doors (1977)

8
'Thank God for the Rain...':
Revenge From *Dirty Harry* to
The Exterminator

Since the 1980s, the reputation of the revenge subgenre has suffered, largely as a result of the formulaic sequels to films such as *Dirty Harry* and *Death Wish*. Yet, in both of these cases the originating texts were produced and consumed in a more complex way than memory, refracted by time and sequels, will allow.

In the preceding chapter we showed how the events of the Watergate/Vietnam period engendered in the public sphere and in thrillers feelings of mistrust and *betrayal*. What the revenge narratives enact, on the other hand, is *retribution*. The theme of retribution, of course, is not new and has often been highly problematized. A film such as *Act of Violence* (1949), for instance, takes as its central character a man (Van Heflin) who has betrayed his comrades in a German POW camp during the Second World War and is subsequently pursued on American soil by a limping veteran (Robert Ryan); while it is clear that the narrative allows for a great measure of sympathy for the Heflin character it is equally clear that his nemesis (Ryan) possesses a convincing measure of righteousness. Similarly, the story of Sweeney Todd in its many guises focuses on the gruesome nature of his deeds and only occasionally – the musical by Stephen Sondheim, for example – explores at length his vengeful motives. In Chapter 4 we have also seen how the depiction of a criminal milieu tends to overshadow the deep-seated determinants in the act of 'turning it around'.

It would be easy to dismiss 'revenge', then, as a mere mechanism in narrative texts. It seems to validate direct and individual action in a delimited area, eschewing the process of law and its protracted deliberations. As such, 'revenge' is often construed as a knee-jerk, right-wing reaction, especially by those assessing Hollywood films of the 1980s (for example, Kellner 1995). However, both betrayal and retribution are not straightforward themes in thrillers: as structures, they are not only ambiguous but also act as significant investment points for political readings by audiences. In reading the revenge thrillers of the seventies, then, it is important to consider the manifold nature of the impetus and the objects of revenge. All the narratives discussed in this chapter involve violent individual action, all involve antagonistic responses to contemporary liberal politics and many depict complex and sensitive social problems. But to retrospectively place a fixed political complexion on the revenge texts of the seventies would be, as we will see in the following discussion of revenge thrillers, a serious mistake.

Dirty Harry

Initially, the character of Harry Callahan (Clint Eastwood) appeared in three films: *Dirty Harry* (1971), *Magnum Force* (1973) and *The Enforcer* (1976), all of which are different in terms of possible readings of Harry's actions and motivations. *Dirty Harry* concerns the duel between a serial killer who calls himself Scorpio (Andy Robinson), and who specializes in assassinations of ordinary citizens with a long-range rifle, and a hard-bitten cop, Callahan. What seemed to infuriate contemporary reviewers when it appeared in early 1972 was that the film was found by them (and contemporary audiences) to be so entertaining despite supposed reactionary values.

While Harry can be labelled an archetypal right-wing hero, his outlook on life is, on more than one occasion in the film, dovetailed with a wry disarming humour which is stated in such a way that it convinces (at least?) the other protagonists. This is evident at the end of the first scene which follows the opening titles; at a private meeting, the Mayor (John Vernon) refers to a previous case in which Harry has used his gun to stop a man raping a woman. The Mayor is worried that Harry has apprehended someone without a felony having taken place, to which Harry says that he recognised 'intent'. Then:

> 'Intent? How did you establish that?'
> 'When a naked man is chasing a woman in an alley with a butcher knife and a hard on I figure he's not out collecting money for the Red Cross.'

In the bank heist scene which follows on directly from the interview with the mayor, Harry advances on a robber who lies injured but conscious on the steps of the bank. As the robber reaches for his rifle Harry says,

> 'I know what you're thinking: 'did he fire six shots or only five?' Well, to tell you the truth, in all this excitement I kinda lost track myself. But bein' as this is a forty four magnum, the most powerful hand-gun in the world and could blow your head clean off, you've got to ask yourself one question: 'do I feel lucky?'
> 'Well, do you, punk?'

The injured robber draws his hand from the rifle and Harry picks it up and walks away; the robber calls to him, 'I gots [*sic*] to know'. Harry nonchalantly walks back and raises the gun to the head of the now horrified robber. As Harry squeezes the trigger the gun lets off a hollow click and Harry sniggers, walking away once more after ironically punctuating a successful apprehension of a felon.

This is the kind of direct measure that is Harry's hallmark; but the robber in the sequence is an African American and, inevitably, the question of 'race' once more rears its head. It does so, however, for reasons which are not necessarily obvious to the crusader against racism, real or imagined. Lipsitz writes:

> The depiction of a black criminal cowering before white male authority in *Dirty Harry* brings to the screen an image prefigured by thousands of law and order speeches by politicians, but it also relies on our absolute faith in the rigidity of genre boundaries. (1998, p. 227)

Supposedly, then, these scenes work to 'justify' the violence of Harry, a violence which might, disturbingly, operate in the service of racist aims. It must be noted, though, that there is comic note to the scene and that Harry's dialogue in the bank robbery aftermath is reproduced in the final moments of the film to potentially different effect; where it was nonchalantly delivered in the former scene, it is delivered through gritted teeth in the latter as Harry apprehends the manic serial killer. The humour of the dialogue in the first of these scenes, then, receives a more poignant recasting in the final scene. Clearly the terms have changed: the robber is involved in a game with Harry and is cautious enough to leave his rifle alone; Scorpio is psychotic and lunges for his own gun. Like a microcosm of the film as a whole in its different reading formations, the dialogue and the violence of these scenes reveal that, even though their basic structure remains similar, their possible meanings need not.

This is not to say that we can dismiss the topic of 'race' here. In an instructive analysis of a later 'revenge' text, *Falling Down* (1993), Richard Dyer suggests that the narrative dramatizes a crisis of identity: 'whiteness, especially white masculinity, is under threat, decentred, angry, keying in to an emergent discourse of the 1990s' (1997, p. 222). We could argue that the crisis is not just applicable to the *fin de siècle*, and that Dyer, perhaps, does not go far enough with his argument. Reading Harry Callahan in terms of racial coordinates, it is clear that Clint Eastwood is a model of white manhood. Moreover, it is a manhood which is in crisis for reasons to do with another dimension of identity, the occupation to which Harry is wedded. In the wake of the extension of suspects' rights – legal decisions such as *Miranda*, which we discussed in Chapter 5 – there can be no doubt that Harry is hampered in his attempts to apprehend Scorpio.

Yet this is not to say that a white man's crisis necessary entails racist aggression; the most poignant scene in the movie, which commentators invariably overlook, features a tearful Mrs Russell, a black woman from a San Francisco project whose son has just been murdered by Scorpio. Harry's Hispanic rookie partner, sociology graduate Chico (Reno Santoni), is visibly sickened when he sees the dead boy's mutilated face and, as he moves out of the camera shot, Harry wearily utters 'Welcome to homicide'. One could argue that the indicators of poverty in the scene are as powerful as those of race (and there have even been some who have wished to invert the indicators of 'race' altogether[1]); but 'race' – not an unthinking anglocentrism – is firmly on the agenda of this film. If one wished for crystal-clear evidence of this fact, then the moment of Chico's arrival could be offered. Within earshot of Callahan in the squad room, Chico asks seasoned cop Fatso why Harry is called 'Dirty Harry'; 'Harry hates everybody. Limeys, Micks, Hebes, fat dagoes, niggers, honkies, ethnics,' says Fatso. 'How's he feel about Mexicans?' asks Chico. Winking at Fatso without being seen by Chico, Harry says to the latter, 'Especially spics'.

Harry's illiberal attitudes, then, can be demonstrated to be self-conscious and part of the same kind of revaluation of police work which we encountered in Chapter 5. Even as a fictional police operative Callahan would be expected to have an intimate knowledge of the social determinants of crime in the period. Indeed, one could argue that this occupational bearing cuts across other features of his identity. Like D-Fens in *Falling Down* he is angry and betrayed, throwing his badge away at the end of the film. Similarly, his anger stems from the fact that he is a white American seemingly endowed with all the privileges of his 'race' yet ultimately without power in a civic role which actually hinders him in preventing carnage. The complexity of the film's personal politics certainly seem to be apparent in the way that the narrative treats issues of identity, although not all the cues acting upon the film would necessarily emphasise this.

The process of politically anchoring the narrative of *Dirty Harry* began with the first reviews. Some thought it would upset liberals (Cocks 1972a); some thought it was 'sick and profoundly dangerous' (Chase 1972); some thought it a call to vigilantism (*Playboy* 1972). Pauline Kael in her review for *The New Yorker* (1972) voices nearly all the dominant criticisms of the revenge texts that we will discuss in the rest of this chapter. Her main argument is that the film is 'a right-wing fantasy of [the San Francisco] police force as a group helplessly emasculated by unrealistic liberals'. Despite the fact that numerous academic writers such as Lovell (1975) have largely agreed with Kael, it is by no means the case that *Dirty Harry* was unilaterally received by reviewers in this way. In *Rolling Stone*, Paul Nelson mentioned with some consternation that the reviews by Kael, Sarris, and Canby all 'translate minor tendencies into the wrong major premises' (1972).

Clearly, Kael's review relies on a traditional notion of politics where a consensus exists as to what political complexion an act can be said to have. Nelson's implicit argument is that certain acts are rooted in individual responses to circumstances and have a historically determined political complexion. Thus, he writes of the director of *Dirty Harry*:

> Siegel's philosophical position about the law would seem to be not dissimilar to Daniel Ellsberg's, namely, that the law itself is not sacred; in certain instances it would be immoral for an honourable man not to break it. The questions are, of course, who is honourable? and in what instances? (Nelson 1972)

The reaction of Kael to the film – as opposed to the reaction of Nelson – presupposes that the liberal consensus – the grounds upon which she assesses the film – self- evidently exists. Yet, the popularity of the film suggests, perhaps, that such a consensus was either fragile, or incorporated wider imagery within its political purview than Kael would allow. It is possible therefore that favourable contemporary readings of the text do not simply represent a residual liberal backlash; in fact, a *historical* reading of the film can be based on a *recasting* of certain liberal imperatives in terms of pressing social concerns. The key concern in revenge thrillers is invariably crime and its threat to well-ordered social relations.

Like the shark in *Jaws*, the serial killer Scorpio is definitely a menace to peaceful society; but, as we have noted (Chapter 2 above), the shark-hunter Quint also poses a menace to that society. Once again, being 'outside' of this civilization can have connotations of a pre-Constitutional America; we have seen this both in the hard-boiled stories of Robert B. Parker and in the pseudo western scenarios of Elmore Leonard (Chapters 3 and 4 above). Exploring these connections further, it becomes quite clear that a marginalized fictional character, in being 'outside' society, poses a criticism of that society. This applies directly to Harry Callahan, who, in trying to apprehend Scorpio in his own way, places himself beyond the pale. Self-evidently, Harry is a danger to society because, although he gets the job done, he flouts the law.

But what then of Scorpio?[2] Auster and Quart (1988) assess Scorpio by asserting that 'the Vietnam implications [of his character] are clear' (pp. 48–9). What this provides is a way of linking both the most severe form of political criticism – assassination – with the alienation of the Vietnam experience as they are inflected in fictional works. Both represent what is 'outside' society and both can be said, in their depiction, to constitute a certain kind of criticism of the social order. But, following Hollywood's 're-finding' of the Vietnam experience and its virtual celebration in the 1980s it would be all too easy overlook what was, for 1970s thriller readers, a recurrent and powerful motif. Moreover, even in some revenge texts of the seventies – one of which we will discuss in this chapter – the dilemma of 'outside' versus 'inside', embodied in the figure of the Vietnam veteran, is largely repressed. Before we return to this point, though, we must add a few extra dimensions to the theme of retribution that works itself out in thrillers of the seventies.

Death Wish

If one major text can be embody the theme of revenge in the seventies it is *Death Wish*. The novel by Brian Garfield was published in 1972 and was followed by the controversial film version directed by the Briton Michael Winner two years later. In short, the story of both the film and the novel is concerned with an accountant, Paul Benjamin (architect/development engineer Paul Kersey, played by Charles Bronson in the film), whose life and liberal values are shattered when his wife and daughter are brutally attacked in his apartment. Finding himself helpless when his wife dies soon after and his daughter lapses into a catatonic state, Paul takes to the streets of New York, retaliating, assaulting and then executing criminals. Both the cinematic and print narratives are far more complicated than this summary, however, and they have certain crucial differences (cf. Sutherland 1981, pp. 154ff.), most important of which is probably that the film version loses Paul's Jewish identity and substitutes it for Bronson's fledgling 1970s impassive killer persona.[3] Given that the film is now preceded by controversy – a controversy quite different from the one which attended the film for the contemporary audience – and given that the film has been followed by three sequels which have shaped readings of the first film (for example, *Death Wish* has only been shown on terrestrial TV in Britain once and, unlike the sequels, has been unavailable on video since 1983), it is worth closely examining the narrative of the novel and the movie version.

One of the most important factors in an assessment of the novel would be that Paul, rather than being a gung-ho caricature, is an avowed sharer of liberal values. Yet, if he can be said to exist within a liberal consensus at this time it is, for Paul, one which has lost sight of the paramount importance of the freedoms of the individual. It is significant that in a dialogue with himself after becoming a vigilante, Paul initially criticizes two homosexuals for being out late and acting so casually; then 'He backed up: that was wrong. They had a right to walk unmolested; everyone did' (1974, p. 156). In this way, Paul's disdain of liberalism is actually a critique of liberalism's inner contradictions, that the American doctrine of individual liberty is based on a sham. It is this which justifies his revenge in the narrative.

What is morally right for Paul stems from the fact that the body politic is not concerned with individual cases of crime. The contradiction of the narrative appears when the vigilante becomes a celebrity, demonstrating clearly that society at large *is* concerned, however, with the doing of justice. If *Death Wish* is anti-liberal in any sense it is *knowingly* anti-liberal, exploring, like *Dirty Harry*, the inner contradictions of the contemporary liberal consensus. When he meets a transparently bigoted blue collar worker in a bar, Paul starts to see his point of view, not necessarily as a bigot himself, but because he sees the basic personal requirement of protecting one's immediate environment (pp. 94–5). This would also extend to various ties, particularly family. However, it should not necessarily be assumed that Paul is suddenly going to embrace all right-wing views wholesale; instead, he occupies a reformist position in spite of his vigilantism (pp. 74–5).

Dissent from the current political system does not always entail that the dissenter wishes to replace existing structures with entirely new ones; instead, it might involve the reclaiming of enshrined virtues. After his first taste of vigilante law Paul goes on a business trip to Arizona and ponders official law enforcement down there (p. 115). This trip into 'real Western country' indicates the loss of belief in the efficacy of the existing American system which *Death Wish* shares with the paranoid narratives. But where the paranoid narratives often involve a closer adherence to certain dictates of the Constitution, particularly the First Amendment, *Death Wish* explicitly signals one man's need to reclaim and utilize a mode of law from another period in America's history – gun law. Such an identification of a set of contradictions growing out of Constitutional law represents a kind of *knowing* return to 'old' values in a way not far removed from the revivalist strategies of the New Right in the same period (see especially Peele 1984). Moreover, *Death Wish* is not the only narrative to incorporate old styles of lawmaking into the thriller at the time of the Western genre's decline (see Chapter 6 above).[4] In crime fiction at least, the lawlessness of the streets – supposedly deriving from the inability of the contemporary judicial process to deliver justice – bears the traces of the lawlessness of the Old West.

However, this is not simply a generic issue; it is also a concrete social one. In December 1984 – approximately ten years after the release of the film version of *Death Wish* – an unassuming middle-class man called Bernhard Goetz shot four alleged muggers when he was accosted on the New York City subway system. The shootings became a nationwide *cause célèbre* but, after initial widespread media and public support, Goetz was finally charged only with the illegal possession of firearms. Rubin notes that for some, Goetz 'has expressed a blow for freedom' (1987, p. 9); others, taking into account that the injured 'muggers' were all black youths and two were shot in the back, find overtones of racism in the case.

What was clear about American urban crime in the early 1970s was that it had become a suitable arena for moral panic in all the other areas of social life that it invoked. The crime boom of the 1960s, accompanied by changes in the law on suspects, meant that figures for unsolved crime went up. Only 20% of recorded crimes were cleared by the police in 1969 and 1970, for example. Although the vast majority of crime is either corporate, or in some way against businesses (Reiss 1971, p. 66), street crime, in particular, was widely publicised and feared by many. In the year that *Death Wish* was published, a major bestselling non-fiction volume was Morton Hunt's (1972) account of the long and drawn-out judicial process attendant on the street crime that led to the death of elderly Bronx citizen Alexander Helmer. In the early 1980s, Goetz was reportedly incensed at the uneven treatment he had received from police compared to that meted out to his attackers in an earlier incident of street crime in which he had been involved (Rubin 1987). Fighting back, in the light of these details, might seem a rational response to crimes against the person.

Many were concerned that Goetz's actions set a dangerous precedent or, worse, were downright criminal. Yet those who admired Goetz's stance recognized a seemingly non-politically predetermined everyday practice – retaliation. The ambivalence which is manifest in commentaries on Goetz's vigilante actions in 1984 mirror the split between condemnatory critics and enthusiastic audiences for the fictional vigilantism in the *Death Wish* film ten years earlier. Penelope Gilliatt in the *New Yorker* bluntly asserts that the film 'degrades audiences' (Gilliatt 1974b), although her main contention is that the film constitutes an assault on New York City by a Briton.[5] In addition to the depiction of New York, the key way in which the narrative of the film was offered as an arena of social investment was in the events that it was thought to have immediately 'inspired'. Before the film came to Britain and before it was shown outside New York, reports were circulating that audiences in cinemas were openly cheering Bronson's actions in the film (Rosen 1975). Amongst the details of 'copycat' antics among New Yorkers were the cases of a 60-year-old Bronx grocer who shot a mugger and a Manhattan furrier who drew his gun only to be shot first by his assailant (ibid.).

Undoubtedly, critics were concerned that the film presented an unfeasible course of social action. The 'copycat' incidents further fuelled concern that the depiction of Paul set a dangerous precedent. At the same time, however, we have suggested that the narrative of *Death Wish* is not so unsophisticated that it simply sustains a series of heroics which are to be admired. What was probably most at issue was publicity. Posters for the film carried a selection from the following captions:

JUDGE, JURY AND EXECUTIONER ALL IN ONE
HE'S THE MIDNIGHT VIGILANTE
MUGGERS BEWARE
WHAT DO YOU DO WHEN A MUGGER KILLS YOUR WIFE?
CHARLES BRONSON IS THE VIGILANTE, CITY-STYLE!
(*Death Wish* Press Book, Paramount, 1974)

The fourth of these captions is, indisputably, the odd one out, even though it is probably the most accurate shorthand representation of the film's narrative. The other captions offer a far more aggressive version of the film's events. As far as the film's reputation within the publicity goes, then, it is possible to say that such cues presented a reading of the film which played up its straightforward thriller aspects, making them explicitly indissoluble from the social content of the narrative.

Whether *Death Wish* was read predominantly by its audiences as a cartoon strip of justice or as a social document is impossible to answer. However, if one wanted to assess the narrative in its historical context it would be wrong to dismiss it as a straightforward right-wing adventure. The novel, while thrilling, is filled with dialogue – much of it far from simple – about the ethics of vigilantism and its social and political consequences (cf. the sequel to the novel, *Death Sentence*, 1977). The film, too, is not subordinate to out-and-out adventure: it has a very low-key ambience derived from 'night-for-night' shots, grainy footage, inaudibility of parts of the soundtrack and, generally, feels more like a film by Ken Loach than some of the high-budget Hollywood thrillers released in the same year (for example, *McQ*, *Earthquake*, *Thunderbolt and Lightfoot*). The crux of the matter is that, from the moment that Paul decides to take some kind of action, the texts open up an arena of overdetermined potential social investments. *Death Wish* proves itself to be far less ephemeral than it sounds by focussing on fundamental, but hitherto buried issues of the period, specifically the ideals of family and law and order which would provide so much grist to the mill of New Right politics. It is this comparative specificity – albeit one which need not be demonstrably politically pre-designated – which is manifest in *Death Wish* and which also provides a frame of reference for other revenge texts of the period.

Taxi Driver

Where the actions of the protagonists in *Death Wish* and *Dirty Harry* are easily aligned with conventional heroism, the actions of the protagonist in *Taxi Driver* (1976) are somewhat problematic. The film – from an original screenplay by Paul Schrader – concerns an insomniac ex-marine veteran of Vietnam, Travis Bickle (Robert DeNiro), who at the beginning of the narrative takes a job as a night-shift cabbie in New York. A voice-over narrative charts his disgust with the people he meets on the New York streets: 'Thank God for the rain which has helped wash the garbage and trash off the streets.... Some day a real rain will come and wash all this scum off the streets...' Travis becomes involved in a very short-lived relationship with a political campaign worker, Betsy (Cybill Shepherd), and when this fails, buys guns which it seems he intends to use in order to assassinate the Presidential candidate for whom Betsy is working. Meanwhile, he has also decided to help a prostitute called Iris (Jodie Foster) who is in her early teens and has a pimp, Matthew, also known as 'Sport' (Harvey Keitel). Travis's alienation propels the narrative to a powerful and bloody denouement.

Like Harry Callahan and Paul in *Death Wish*, Travis embodies what is outside society. But Travis is, like Paul and Harry, a human and part of society. He has represented America in an emblematic way, as a member of the elite Marine corps; but he is now, as a result of his experience, radically *at odds* with much of contemporary America and incorporates an otherness that civilians cannot assimilate to their everyday lives. The insignia of Travis's paradoxical alterity is at the very least latent throughout the whole film and can be summed up by the word 'Vietnam', the connotations of which, although complex, would not be unknown to the contemporary US consumers of media. Camacho (1980, p. 276) estimates that a criminal veteran appeared, on average, in one American TV crime series per month in the seasons from 1974 to 1976. Similarly, Figley and Leventman (1980) describe at length the way in which the Vietnam veteran is constantly stigmatized throughout the media, both in fictional and non-fictional texts. Why might the Vietnam War and its veterans – unlike previous wars and *their* veterans – prove such a troublesome force to depict without stigmatization in this period?

An approach to the answer can be initiated by considering some fundamental contradictions. The protest against the war in Vietnam in the late 1960s and early 1970s, for example, was not simply carried out by those broadly described as 'radicals'. A great proportion of the population – including both Nixon's 'silent majority' and many who actively protested – were simply citizens who wanted the boys brought home. The status of 'the boys', however, was changing: since November 1969, it had become well known that atrocities had been perpetrated by American soldiers in Vietnam, particularly at My Lai (see *Time* 5 December 1969; *Newsweek* 8 December 1969; Sheehan 1990, pp. 689–90). The protagonists of the suppression of those who were 'outside' American society therefore employed methods which placed *themselves* outside civilized life. This was compounded by the fact that the war on Vietnamese soil did not take place between two recognizable military forces; guerrilla warfare obliterated the visible distinction between peaceable citizen and paramilitary operative (see, especially, Calley and Sack 1971; *First Tuesday* 1989).

Conversely, reports from the front troops included accounts of soldiers wearing peace symbols, refusing to go into combat and 'fragging' (the use of fragmentation grenades to kill unpopular officers). American soldiers in this scenario now represented an *internalized* threat. One can imagine, therefore, that returning veterans might be viewed as disorderly peaceniks; or as brutal sadists; or as pawns in a military process; or as witnesses of unspeakable horror; or as mentally unbalanced, and so on depending on one's prior orientation. The experience that veterans represented as a group was so diverse and so divorced from the mundane exigencies of everyday life that its very complexity prevented it from being incorporated in any simple form into the social formation of America in the 1970s. And while the American public could not embrace the veteran experience, the veterans themselves often found in the 1970s that they had no place to go but down (see Polner 1971 especially, pp. 165 ff; Lifton 1973; Kovic 1990). This partly accounts for the stigmatization of the veteran in some crime fiction of the period. Yet, it must be stated in strong terms that, rather than *resolving* a range of contradictions in American life (as is often the case in narratives where veterans feature as ultimately vanquished villains), the alterity signified by 'Vietnam' is actively *emphasized* by many of the revenge texts.

Fearing accusations of stigmatization, Schrader, and the director of *Taxi Driver*, Martin Scorsese, may have played down the Vietnam angle in spite of the fact that it was so central to Travis' character. The Vietnam theme is certainly inflected in different ways in both the original screenplay and the finished film. The second time that he goes to the campaign headquarters of Presidential candidate Palantine (Leonard Harris) to say a bitter farewell to Betsy, Travis is, in the screenplay, simply ejected from the HQ; in the film, Tom (Albert Brooks) tries to escort him out of the building and Travis suddenly assumes a stance which indicates familiarity with oriental martial arts indicating that it would be ill-advised for Tom to get involved any further. Briefly, this reflects Travis's training as a marine, to which he instantly reverts. The reference to Vietnam, then, is implicit, visual, requires cultural knowledge and requires also further relevant knowledge regarding the details of marine training for it to be more fully interpreted. The most *explicit* reference to Vietnam in the screenplay is *deleted* from the finished movie. This is when Travis pays the manic arms salesman, Andy, in the original screenplay and the latter asks Travis about his past, leading to a stilted conversation about the war (Schrader 1990, p.41).

A further iconic reference illustrates the way in which the film implicitly signals the meaning of 'Vietnam'. When Travis goes on what can be assumed is his mission to assassinate the Presidential candidate, Palantine, the narrative allows various shots of the public speaking scene and its participants; Travis' exit from the taxi and his movements towards the square where the speech takes place, however, are only shown in a shot of him from the neck down. He is wearing his army combat jacket which, as previous scenes testify, allows him to hide his extensive armoury. When Travis stands still in the square and is evidently listening to the speech, the same neck-down shot is offered; the next shot of Travis in this position ascends until his head is revealed, with his hair shaved into a Mohican style. This is what the camera has avoided showing, and probably the most immediate effect that it has is to mark Travis as an outsider.

Yet the Mohican cut carries more meaning. One possible reading of it might be that it refers back to the early colonial period of pre-Constitutional gun rule proper, which is immortalised in American culture by the works of James Fenimore Cooper, particularly *The Last of the Mohicans* (1826; see also Barker and Sabin 1996). What is probably more likely, though, is that the hairstyle is another implicit iconic reference to Vietnam. Oral accounts of the war included details of crack forces who – either consciously or unconsciously – incorporated the personal iconography, as well as the savagery in battle, of their native American forebears (see Baker 1983, p. 120). In this way Travis's dramatizes the contradictions of alterity: a reading of him as forever marginalized can always carry the probability of its opposite, rooted deep in the myths of American civilization. Given that there exists this tension between Travis's status as an outsider which continually throws up the threatening vision of Travis as an archetypal 'insider' it is hardly surprising that his actions seem to be dictated by an equally inscrutable and unresolvable logic.

On numerous occasions in the narrative, including when he speaks to Presidential candidate Charles Palantine, Travis shows himself to be uninterested and even unaware of any sort of politics. However, after his break-up with Betsy, he becomes a potential political assassin. At the risk of simplifying this movement it can be referred to as 'displacement', a term used by Freud to illustrate that an idea's emphasis can be detached from its original object and pass on to associated objects (see Laplanche and Pontalis 1988, p. 121). The sexual component of such a mechanism is demonstrated in a further example: after Travis's final visit to the Palantine headquarters to see Betsy, he picks up a fare. The fare (Martin Scorsese) tells Travis to drive to an address, and when the taxi stops he insists that Travis leaves the meter on. The man stays and tells Travis that he does so because his wife is in an apartment in the building, adding 'You know who lives there? A nigger lives there.' He then tells Travis of his intention to take a .44 and fire it up his wife's pussy, presumably as punishment for her adultery. The screenplay especially makes clear that a process of displacement has taken place: Travis breaks up with Betsy, he picks up a fare who is breaking up with his wife and intends to use a .44, and then Travis buys a .44.

The chain of association will continue so that Travis is now on a combat mission, and the focus of this mission is an assassination attempt on Palantine. Not only is the presidential candidate Betsy's employer but he has also given a very weak answer in his cab when Travis has raised the issue of the filth on the streets. The assassination attempt fails before it has really got off the ground but Travis immediately has a new target. His prey is considerably smaller following the Palantine debacle: now he makes a direct attempt to rescue the child prostitute, Iris, while killing her pimp, Matthew. Although his target is now far more lowly, it is still part of a chain of displacement which includes Palantine and the characters he meets while driving his taxi every night. The displacement which Travis manifests is therefore similar to that which dictates that Harry Callahan has a personal vendetta against Scorpio and that Paul Benjamin/Kersey wipes out minor street thugs. At the same time, though, it would be absurd to assume that this is a purely psychological mechanism in any of the above named cases. There is no doubt that a socially determined chain of association is in operation here.

Far from being a study of individual psychology alone, *Taxi Driver*, like *Death Wish*, allows for a reading which ignites all manner of social questions. This is nowhere more evident than in the very last scenes of the film. Travis's final act of violence results in the delivery of Iris into the hands of her parents in Pittsburgh; this is narrated by means of a panning shot of letters from Iris's parents and newspaper clippings which depict Travis as a hero for enabling Iris to return to her father and mother, plus a voice-over which is evidently that of Iris's father giving thanks to Travis in a letter. The object onto which Travis fixes his energy, therefore, is the institution of the family, and the narrative of his catharsis operates on precisely the terrain of political struggle which was delineated as an area of interest by the broad coalition of pressure groups in the West which came to be known as the New Right. This is not to say that Travis Bickle is necessarily a New Right politician, nor that he somehow embodies the New Right position on family values. However, as the *Conservative Digest* put it in 1979, 'The New Right is looking for issues that people care about, and social issues, at least for the present, fit that bill' (quoted in Weeks 1989, p. 34).

Travis's alterity, then, entails a number of things. The first is that there is a contradiction in placing a human outside of humanity, civilization and society. Getting rid of a human will not eradicate social problems any more than killing a pimp will make prostitution disappear. The second, more palpable, feature of *Taxi Driver* is that Vietnam acts as a convenient condensation point in the film for otherness, alterity and all that which is outside American (Western) civilized society. Yet while this is largely obvious, the implicit and iconic way in which this is signalled in the film almost seems to be a means for short-circuiting inter-pretations other than those that Schrader and Scorsese claim to have intended.

Reviews of the film assisted in the task of providing grounds for read-ing *Taxi Driver* as a critique of illiberality and its embodiment, Travis Bickle. Both Kael (1976) and Canby (1976) see Travis as Everyman and as a lunatic at the same time. This mirrors the contradictions of inside/outside but one nodal point for the discussion of Travis which might have blunted the complexity which Kael nevertheless finds in the movie is the topic of assassination and especially Arthur Bremer, who made an attempt on Governor Wallace's life in 1972 (cf. Heininger 1976; Schickel 1976; see also Dempsey 1976, p. 37 and Patterson and Farber 1976, p. 27). The Warren Commission Report on the assassination of President Kennedy had devoted a significant amount of its conclusion to a discus-sion of Lee Harvey Oswald's psychological motivations, summarising them as his 'deep-rooted resentment of all authority', 'his inability to enter into meaningful relationships with people', his 'urge to try to find a place in history', his 'capacity for violence' and his 'avowed commit-ment to Marxism and communism' (in Scott et al. 1978, p. 74).[6] This provided a limited template for reviewers' assessments of Travis's psy-chology. But the exact status of Travis's alterity, as well as his revenge, was not that easy to pin down for contemporary commentators. Schra-der attempted to make clear in an interview that 'Travis is not to be tolerated. He should be killed' (quoted in Arnold 1976a, B1), indicating that numerous reviewers misinterpreted his intent (see, for instance, Rubenstein 1976, p. 35; Dempsey 1976, p. 41; Patterson and Farber 1976, p. 26) and presented readings of the film resting on the notion that the narrative celebrates, or at least supports, the actions of its central character.

Clearly, *Taxi Driver* explored psychological processes; but many of the social questions raised by Travis's actions were left unstated in commentaries on the film. The key aspect of the narrative which would provoke these troublesome questions – Vietnam – was seemingly a taboo subject. Reviewers certainly fought shy of mentioning it: Kael (1976), for instance, notes that Travis is an ex-Marine, and although his youth will suggest that he is a Vietnam veteran she does not pursue the issue; similarly, Arnold (1976a) simply considers Travis's veteran status to be incidental when he writes of him as 'a young, isolated, sexually repressed ex-GI' (Arnold 1976a). Both the reviews and the comments of the film-makers repress the Vietnam issue largely because many of the contradictions of the American social formation that the war had made manifest, could still not be stated and worked through. Travis's psychological dissonance gives him an ability, of which he is unaware, to reveal the inconsistencies that the liberal consensus has thrown up. For example, when he attempts to take Betsy on a date to a porn cinema Travis cannot understand why she is so outraged; those subtle characteristics which might distinguish porn from contemporary mainstream films are almost invisible to him despite being so definite for other citizens.

This insight into contemporary America is the key feature in terms of the revenge texts offering social investments for readers. Where the critique of the fragile liberal consensus is directly evident in *Death Wish*, it is just slightly less so in *Dirty Harry*, and considerably less so in *Taxi Driver*. Vietnam makes up the space between the critique and the narratives of the latter two texts and it is for this reason that we have, at some length, prised out this problematic theme. Clearly, the troublesome dialectic of 'inside' and 'outside' is an ongoing process in the United States. In 1995, when a lorry bomb destroyed a government building in Oklahoma City, killing 168 people, there was widespread fear that Islamic fundamentalists were responsible for the worst act of terrorism ever committed on American soil. When it was revealed that the man arrested on the bombing charge was a young American veteran of the Gulf War with firm views on the Federal government, the FBI, the right to carry arms and who called himself a 'patriot' in the mould of fighters in the war of independence, fear of enemies external to the United States was transformed into something more complex (see, for example, Kelsey 1996, p. 7).

In the 1980s, as numerous commentators have noted, the United States worked through its 'Vietnam syndrome' with the help of Hollywood (Adair 1989; Auster and Quart 1988; Walsh and Aulich 1989; Kellner 1995). A spate of films set, significantly, in South-East Asia rather than on American soil, appeared on cinema screens, the most prominent of which was the record-grossing *Rambo: First Blood II* (1985). We should not allow this fact to disguise the ongoing dilemmas of alterity which Vietnam signified for American thrillers in the 1970s. Many texts were far more explicit in this theme than *Taxi Driver*. In the series of books featuring Mack Bolan (dubbed 'The Executioner'), the narratives deal with one man's continuing war with the Mafia, started because while Sergeant Bolan has been serving in Vietnam his father has been the victim of a Mafia loansharking and intimidation operation which has resulted first in Bolan's sister becoming a prostitute, followed by his father, pushed to the edge of endurance, shooting both Bolan's sister and mother. This source for Bolan's vendetta against Mafia operations worldwide is usually signalled more or less obliquely in the prologues to each volume. However, the rest of the narrative in each case makes it quite clear that there is a strong equation between the war in South East Asia and the war on American soil.

Similarly, in the novel *First Blood* (1973) by David Morrell, the reader is introduced to Rambo, a young man who drifts into a small Kentucky town and, after persecution by the local sheriff, enacts his revenge by beginning a minor war against the local police. It is subsequently revealed that Rambo is a formidable soldier who has received special operations training while in the Marines in Vietnam. In the 1976 thriller by Noel Hynd entitled *Revenge*, Richard Silva returns from Vietnam having been mercilessly tortured when he was a prisoner of war. He knows that his vicious torturer bore the nickname 'The Imp'; but he *knows also* that 'The Imp' was a French-speaking European rather than a North Vietnamese soldier, and is now working for French intelligence forces. In both of these cases – and numerous other thrillers from the decade – that which is 'outside' relentlessly signifies the contradictions which are 'inside'. In light of the power of this theme in the period, it only remains to ask: why is the revenge thriller no longer intact in the same way as it was in the 1970s?

The Exterminator

In order to address the issue of generic innovation in the context of the revenge narrative we will very briefly comment on a film which was released in 1980, just on the edge of our broadly defined period of study. *The Exterminator*, which was written and directed by James Glickenhaus, was a revenge text whose narrative is closely related to those that we have discussed in this chapter. Two American soldiers, John Eastland (Robert Ginty) and Michael Jefferson (Steve James), are captured but escape from the Viet Cong. Some time later, Eastland and Jefferson are working for neighbouring freight depots in the Bronx when a white/ Puerto Rican gang assaults Eastland; Jefferson arrives at the right time and, at the moment the bearded gang leader calls him a 'nigger', he and Eastland are able to overcome them. Not long after this, however, Jefferson is in a nearby park and the same gang members attack him, breaking his neck. Eastland comforts Jefferson's wife and vows to avenge his friend who is now permanently paralysed in a hospital bed. This Eastland proceeds to do – violently. The rest of the film is concerned with Eastland's revenge on the gang and other, associated, villains.

Meanwhile a police inspector, James Dalton (Christopher George) is on Eastland's trail; he is worried that the city is in the grip of either a psychopathic killer or a vigilante after Eastland has sent him a letter complaining of the crime wave in New York, confessing to the murders he has committed but signing himself 'The Exterminator'. With their eyes on both Dalton and Eastland are two anonymous politicians who represent the present administration. They are both worried that the Exterminator has so much public support and that his capture will reveal a web of political corruption. They therefore enlist the CIA to assassinate Eastland.

The Exterminator incorporates virtually all the major features of the texts we have discussed in this chapter. Eastland is a Vietnam veteran who has seen a great deal of combat; his crusade is precipitated by the infestation of New York City with crime that violates the sanctity of his best friend's family; he takes revenge on those directly responsible for his friend's paralysis and eventual death, and then broadens that revenge. He is sickened when he travels through areas of New York where sex is sold; he takes pity on a young prostitute who has been burned and when he finds that the perpetrator of the burns was a customer at a 'chicken' parlour (a brothel catering for sex with minors) he visits the place. While there he frees a teenage boy who has been bound and tortured with a soldering iron by a customer whom Eastland then shoots dead (and who it is later revealed is a New Jersey senator). Then he ties up the owner of the brothel, pours petrol over him and sets the room alight. Eastland also wears a combat jacket throughout the second part of the film underneath which he keeps what looks like a .44 magnum; to the characters that he has bound and who he leaves in the warehouse in order to act on information he has gained by physical threats, he sardonically utters the words that are reproduced on the poster for the film:

If you're lying,
I'll be back...

(Publicity Brochure for *The Exterminator*, Rebel Films, 1980, p. 1)

Virtually all the syntactic and semantic elements of the revenge texts, then, are to be found in *The Exterminator*.

However, *The Exterminator* was nowhere near as commercially successful as any of the texts that we have discussed in this chapter. It did, admittedly gross enough money to generate a sequel – *The Exterminator II* (1984) – but both films were made on very low budgets (Publicity Brochure for *The Exterminator* Rebel Films 1980, p. 3). *The Exterminator* preceded the period in which Vietnam veterans became more saleable characters in fiction by a few years. It also preceded by a number of years what could be said to be a genre based on almost comic-book avengers which spawned a number of commercially successful movies.[7] All the reviews of the film were very brief and all concentrated on what was seen as excessively brutal violence, a constituent of the narrative that was considered to be what defined it and what was also believed characterize a great deal of contemporary Hollywood output, for example *Friday the 13th* (1980) and, especially, *Dressed to Kill* (1980). The marketing of the film was also predictably low-budget and low-key in comparison with other films discussed in this chapter.

More important than this, perhaps, is that *The Exterminator* appeared at a time when the subject of revenge did not have the same pristine quality that it did for the early texts. This must not be confused with the idea that the theme of revenge in the thriller had suddenly gone stale after about 1977. In fact, revenge in the thriller was not a new fad: in the American thriller alone, revenge has dominated texts as diverse in content and time as William McGivern's *The Big Heat* (1987, filmed 1953); John D. MacDonald's *The Executioners* (1967, filmed as *Cape Fear* in 1961 and 1992); Richard Stark's *Point Blank* (1962, filmed in 1967), as well as the Fred Zinnemann film, *Act of Violence* that we mentioned at the beginning of this chapter. In a mythical 'objective' reading it is probable that the same syntactic features could be generally shown to characterize say, *The Big Heat* and *Death Wish*. However, the syntactic dimension of a genre text does not really exist in isolation; instead, it is inseparable from a semantic dimension. For example, the syntactics of revenge in a film such as *Batman Returns* (1992) are incompatible with those of most thrillers because of the semantic dimension of the film's 'fantastic' verisimilitude. We can say that not only will generic expectations be activated by the semantic dimension of these texts but, because of the thriller's specific ideological verisimilitude, it will open up a series of expectations to do with the depiction of the real world.

Revenge has specific socially invested characteristics in 1970s thrillers, and it appears as a theme in narratives which are demonstrably more complex than the designation 'revenge' allows. The protagonists of revenge thrillers enact retribution for convoluted (and even sometimes unfathomable) social reasons, usually as a result of the contemporary social world's problematic conception of its own boundaries. The protagonist often treads a path and takes action which places him 'outside' contemporary American society as it is understood at that moment in time; alternatively, the protagonist is stigmatized as an 'outsider' but enacts proceedings which are popularly received as appropriate 'inside' responses to the current social world. The divergent ways in which some commentators and many audiences attempted to negotiate the tension of 'inside'/'outside' which characterized revenge texts suggests that such a tension is a focal point for the social investments which constitute generic innovation.

This generic innovation, evident for contemporary audiences in most of the texts in this chapter – and which does not seem, through the extra-textual cues, to have been evident in *The Exterminator* in the same way – is based on a convergence of two things. First, a powerful emergent concern with crime and threats to the family, personal space and well being in the real world, directly precipitated by the failure of modern law to adequately deal with these issues. And, secondly, the refiguration of these issues in the revenge thriller in terms of a localized individual violent action which can be socially invested. Extra-textual discourse about the revenge text often belied a prescriptive liberal and intellectual admonishment of them while popular response seems to have been far more favourable. The interplay of reviews and grass roots feeling, then, created a space where revenge texts were organized as texts-to-be-read, and it is here that generic innovation operates: in the realm of expectations which produce specific readings from textual material imbued with social potency.

Further Reading

Print

De Mille, Nelson 1974. *Ryker #1: The Sniper*
De Mille, Nelson 1975. *The Cannibal*
Derrick, Lionel 1977. *The Penetrator #19: Panama Power Play*
(This is just one of over 30 Penetrator novels published in the 1970s)
Hedges, Joseph 1974. *The Revenger: Rainbow Coloured Shroud*
Kelley, Lamar 1970. *That's No Way to Die*
McCurtin, Peter 1976. *Soldier of Fortune: The Deadliest Game*
McCurtin, Peter 1977. *Soldier of Fortune: Body Count*

McCurtin, Peter 1977. *Soldier of Fortune: Operation Hong Kong*
McGivern, William 1975. *The Night of the Juggler*
Morrell, David 1975. *Testament*
Osborn, David 1974. *Open Season*
Pendleton, Don 1970. *The Executioner: War Against the Mafia*
Pendleton, Don 1971. *The Executioner: Assault on Soho*
Pendleton, Don 1971. *The Executioner: Battle Mask*
Pendleton, Don 1971. *The Executioner: Chicago Wipeout*
Pendleton, Don 1971. *The Executioner: Continental Contract*
Pendleton, Don 1971. *The Executioner: Death Squad*
Pendleton, Don 1972. *The Executioner: San Diego Siege*
Pendleton, Don 1972. *The Executioner: Washington I.O.U.*
Pronzini, Bill 1972. *Panic!*
Spillane, Mickey 1973. *The Last Cop Out*
Stone, Robert 1974. *Dog Soldiers*
Thornburg, Newton 1976. *Cutter and Bone*

Film

The Night Visitor (February 1971)
Dirty Harry (December 1971)
Slaughter (August 1972)
(Jim Brown as ex-Green Beret avenges bombing murder of his parents)
Electra Glide in Blue (May 1973)
(Vietnam veteran bike cop)
White Lightning (June 1973)
The Stone Killer (August 1973)
The Outfit (October 1973)
Act of Vengeance (June 1974)
Death Wish (July 1974)
Homebodies (September 1974)
(Geriatric vigilante force)
The Human Factor (November 1975)
(George Kennedy takes revenge against terrorists in this Edward Dmy-
    tryk-directed movie; not to be confused with Otto Preminger's film of
    the Graham Greene novel which goes by the same name)
Hustle (December 1975)
Taxi Driver (February 1976)
Lipstick (April 1976)
Vigilante Force (April 1976)
(Kris Kristofferson as a Vietnam veteran)
Fighting Mad (April 1976)

Jackson County Jail (May 1976)
Massacre at Central High (November 1976)
The House by the Lake (a.k.a. *Death Weekend*) (March 1977)
Rolling Thunder (October 1977)
(William Devane as a tortured Vietnam veteran)
Who'll Stop the Rain? (a.k.a. *Dog Soldiers*) (May 1978)
Love and Bullets (March 1979)
Night of the Juggler (May 1980)
The Exterminator (September 1980)

TV

The Manhunter (1974)
(Adventures of an embittered and vengeful bounty hunter in the 1930s)

Conclusion

It would be all too easy to state in conclusion that the thriller in 1970s America was – and that it has always been – a genre about conspiracy. An even more alluring conclusion, perhaps, would be to add a historical dimension and to say that the 1970s American thriller was dominated by the secrecy and deception which accompanied the Watergate affair and successive administrations' pursuit of the war in Vietnam. What might encourage such a neat conclusion is that, firstly, there is a body of generic texts which seem to be united by key themes; secondly, there are some major historical events, happening almost contemporaneously with 1970s thrillers and sharing some parallels with them. The connection seems hard to avoid and, it must be said, such a connection has already been made on occasions in the foregoing chapters. In the contemporary history of the 1970s – that specifically hegemonic configuration of discourses that we have identified – it is true that conspiracy was prominent. The reporting of Watergate and Vietnam in the wake of a number of years of political radicalism provided fertile ground for the proliferation of conspiracy narratives which specifically located the source of conspiracies predominantly with either government operatives or agents of the political right. The reading formation of the period thus assisted in the creation of a body of texts which took a right-wing conspiracy as their theme.

Yet, as we have also seen, this is by no means the end of the story; the 1970s thriller and the relations involved in the reading of it were far more diverse than the above formulation allows. Numerous forces were at work in the reading formation of 1970s America. Even though it is somewhat arbitrary to construct a reading formation around a country, a decade and a genre, as a heuristic device the concept allows us to identify some of these forces. High on the agenda of non-fictional discourses were concerns about the difficulty of reincorporating the Vietnam experience and its physical representatives into American society; rising crime; the family; poverty; 'race'; class; and gender. These features of the history of the period, however removed they may seem from the core structural concerns of plots and heroes, did have their purchases on thrillers.

Nor can we rely on sociological influences alone to approach an understanding of generic texts within a given period: in addition to strictly non-fictional features of the historical reading formation there are further factors at work. It could not be ignored that the seventies saw a series of record-breaking fictional texts which received an unprecedented amount of publicity, some of which involved their designation as thrillers. As we have suggested, these texts had the potential to exercise quite an effect on their contemporary generic relatives. In this way, these blockbusters which, like non-fictional thrillers, were generic texts themselves, can be said to have operated alongside 'historical' and 'sociological' forces. The (omni)presence of these texts exerted its own determining power in the reading formation of the 1970s thriller.

Furthermore, a set of discourses which were not only different from 'historical' ones, but seemed to operate 'outside' texts, also worked to contribute to the determination of readings. These included 'above-the-line' devices such as the marketing and publicity which surrounded various narratives, as well as 'below-the-line' discourses of reviews and commentary. Such sources often contribute to word-of-mouth assessments of generic products whose circulation it is difficult to gauge. In any case, it is problematic to say that any of these were 'outside' texts as they might function in such a way that they were actually part and parcel of the contemporary reading of a text. As such, they might encourage specific readings of generic narratives such that those readings *'were'* the text. At other times they could appear contrary to forces which might have been instrumental in contributing to a reading – promoting a liberal critique of the perceived ideological project of a narrative, for instance – or they might even be at odds with a text's popular success.

One feature of genre represented in our study which is well-known and which poses a problem to genre analysis is the fact that those (sub)genres of the thriller that we have discussed clearly overlap with each other in various places as well as with the other discourses in the reading formation. It is worth noting this at the level of the narratives which we have discussed. *All the President's Men* and *Dog Day Afternoon* have been taken as non-fiction thrillers but might easily have fitted into an exegesis of the paranoid thriller and the crime story respectively. Texts which we discussed as 'blockbusters' might easily have been shifted into other genres altogether: *The Godfather* to the crime narrative or the family saga; *Jaws* to the horror film. Slightly more problematic, the hard-boiled in the seventies seemed to maintain some 'core' characteristics in spite of being subject to some semantic change; but, even here, the generic character of *Chinatown* was brought into question. In the case of the crime novel, Leonard's narratives of the 1970s, without too great a leap of the imagination, might have found a place in the chapter on revenge; Higgins's novels, on the other hand, have successively (and, frequently, by himself) been placed beyond the boundaries of genre.

The two main texts we discussed in relation to the police might both have been considered as non-fiction thrillers with a strong relation to the paranoid narratives of Chapter 7 and *All the President's Men*. Meanwhile, the police narrative, the hard-boiled story and the street crime narratives on which we focused in Chapter 6, might not have been included in one grouping were it not for the spectre of 'race'. The paranoid thrillers which we have analysed partook of the cynicism of the hard-boiled as well as the 'voices' of other genres, as I argued in Chapters 1 and 7 above; yet, the paranoid thrillers are strongly linked to contemporary subgenres, including the spy/espionage novel and the contemporary non-fiction exposé, as well as the texts of revenge. One of the revenge texts which we have discussed was very much part of the police genre; others descend to street level like contemporary crime narratives. The dilemma of otherness – especially 'race' – which plagued the hard-boiled also crops up in differing ways in the revenge text.

While, at a certain level, the phenomenon of generic overlap is commonplace – trivial, even – it is one contributor to the complex process of generic innovation. The fact that genres – and subgenres – are always in some kind of relation to each other, whether that be a relation of apparent isolation, peaceful co-existence, outright conflict or active poaching, entails that genre is a dynamic phenomenon no matter how static it feels. Another 'fact' of genre which contributes to an ongoing innovation is its specific verisimilitude. In the thriller, we have seen that this is the entree to the 'real' world: that is to say, readers' interactions with thrillers are governed by expectations about the enactment of certain forms of representation rather than others. These representations, by and large, concur with – or at least relate to – pre-existing beliefs about how the world is. They are the modalities which are valued by specific social groups. The potentially multiplicitous meanings in representations which, through expectations of verisimilitude, open out onto the potentially multiplicitous meanings in the real world, are embedded in the semantic/syntactic dimension of genre. These key components all have a role to play in generic innovation.

The hard-boiled story, which experienced a renaissance of sorts in the 1970s, appears to embody in some ways a quite rigid structure, allowing only a limited range of meaning based on a central, unifying 'vision' or 'voice'. The hard-boiled story in its 1970s guise, though, is usually signalled by extra-textual cues as being updated 'semantically', largely for the purposes of verisimilitude. This includes 'keeping up' with changes in beliefs about the world, as well as changes in adjacent generic texts. We have argued that change in the semantic dimension of a text – or, put another way, the potential of a new set of investments in the semantic dimension – effects a concomitant change in the syntactic dimension as it is invested by audiences. The updating of the hard-boiled story is therefore, in some sense, real; it is a generic innovation in that its designation as 'updating' will stimulate a new set of readings of the texts.

Similarly, with the crime story, the incorporation of various narrative strategies concerned with presenting certain 'views' of what is narrated does not necessarily inscribe the reader into a rigid position vis-à-vis the text. Instead, these focalization techniques allow for their own designation as a site of generic innovation and as a place where competing readings might co-exist. One reading of these texts which might enhance their potential innovation, we have suggested, would revolve around the diversity and complexity of criminal activities, a semantic issue tied also to the verisimilitudinous representation of contemporary crime. If specific focalization techniques were read as somehow 'appropriate' to the rendering of modern crime then it is very likely that the texts which incorporated these would be considered to be generically innovative.

The police genre also exhibits innovation in the 1970s. The police texts which we considered stood as a challenge to some previous narratives about policing in America; the main way that they did this was through an orchestration of certain aspects of the thriller's specific verisimilitude. Police work was shown in a way which came to be heavily noted in extra-textual discourses as inextricably tangled in social forces, forces which would hinder problem-solving in the genre and in the real world, too. One of these social forces was 'race' and, along with poverty and corruption, it might be read as a mere semantic change. Some critics even attempted to dismiss the innovations of 'black' thrillers in the 1970s in the same way, as a simple semantic content poured into a syntactic – and defining – vessel. Even if this argument can be given some credence there is mounting evidence to suggest that 'blackness' in the thriller of the 1970s so interrupts other putative generic features that it renders the genre multiplicitous once more, and open to reader investments. If this is not an innovation then it is difficult to determine what is.

Yet if the case for the understanding of generic innovation that we have laid out is at all correct, then its most significant representative is the paranoid thriller. As we have seen, there is a brand of paranoia which is thought to be specific to the thriller and is tied up with the notion of conspiracy. If one takes conspiracy to be central to the thriller, then the paranoid texts do not represent any departure whatsoever from the classic mould already established in the generic corpus. But, as we have attempted to demonstrate, the 1970s paranoid texts are, in their reading, very different from their sub-generic predecessors and descendants. They represent a specific moment rather than an evolutionary point in the thriller's history. In general, we can summarize Chapter 7 by saying that a specific configuration of forces in the reading formation of the 1970s paranoid thriller determined that the sub-genre featured conspiracies that emanated from right-wing sources. Even though one might argue that the fear of conspiracy is fundamentally a 'right-wing' mechanism itself, that it covertly entails the reader adopting right-wing attitudes, these texts were presented as texts to be read in such a way that representatives of the government and the establishment in the narratives were not to be trusted. This not only seems like an innovation but also the forging of a new genre which has spawned further texts in the post-Watergate period (Hill and Every 1998). Our eschewal of the latter formulation, however, is based on the requirement that regimes of reading must be considered before a text's status can be ascribed.

The revenge narratives also emphasize the importance of attempting to understand regimes of reading. Most salient in this respect is the status of the Vietnam veteran as he might be read in these texts in the 1970s. It is very evident that the meaning of the whole Vietnam experience in America has undergone a transformation in the last 20 years, and it is clear that the role of the Vietnam veteran would be read much differently in the 1970s as compared to the mid- to late 1980s, for example. Another area where the revenge texts might be presented as generically innovative is in their depiction of a liberal backlash: although the modes of social action that they depict are by no means new, the fictionalized social world in which they take place is. This semantic element assists in making the syntactic dimension, the resolution of the conspiratorial threat, seem all the more distinctive. Extra-textual cues in the reading formation of these texts were largely concerned with the question of the texts' depiction of the social world and the appropriateness of the social action that takes place in the narratives. This assisted in drawing attention to the importance of the semantic aspects of the narratives and the resultant investment, we have argued, acted to concomitantly transform the syntactic dimension. Revenge was by no means new in the thriller at this time; but the organization of investments in its semantic components was.

All the thrillers that we have discussed represent generic innovation in the general way that we have formulated. Moreover, there are plenty of thrillers of the period that we have not discussed that also represent generic innovation; but, as we have been at pains to point out throughout this book, the breadth of popular fiction is such that analyses of popular genres can never consider their entirety and they can never produce rigid taxonomies. So there is still work to be done on the 1970s American thriller in spite of – indeed, because of – the difficulties of generic classification. Moreover, there is work to be done beyond the 1970s in the history of the thriller. One issue which has been conspicuous by its absence in the foregoing chapters is feminism/post-feminism. Gender, of course, has been quite visible – even when marginalised or unspoken – in relation to heroism. In fact, in the hard-boiled narratives of the 1970s we also witnessed conflations of gender identity with sexuality. Yet the kind of female heroism which has been so much a feature of the post-1980s thriller, particularly in more 'masculine' sub-genres such as the hard-boiled or the police story as opposed to the 'cosy', is necessarily absent from our account.

What, then, is 'generic innovation'? Is it when the thriller mutates to allow female heroes? Is it when contemporary events are 'mirrored' in thrillers? Or is it when thrillers stay largely 'the same' but are read differently by groups of people in historical circumstances? In light of its scrutiny of the seventies and its reconceptualisation of the generic text with reference to the role of the reader this book has argued that it is all three. 'Structuralist' accounts of the thriller – and other genres – betray the belief that, to a greater or lesser degree, generic texts coerce and cajole readers into adopting political attitudes. Such a view rests on an understanding of the generic text as an 'objective' entity which has solid 'effects' on readers. In disciplines which are devoted to the study of textuality and communication, this perspective is no longer tenable: nowadays, texts are not regarded as mechanisms for the interpellation of readers but as the grounds for an interaction. In this way it can be argued that readers take an active part in the process of textuality and that texts do not have meanings as such which are intrinsic to them; rather they exist as empirical entities whose meanings may be imputed to them by readers in a variety of ways as a result of a number of complex determinants.[1]

In tandem with a due consideration of readers' roles in realising textuality, the analysis of thrillers in this book has proceeded with an understanding of texts from the past as subject to readings or presentations as 'texts-to-be-read'. This specific formulation is concerned with an area of debate which has been quite pronounced in the study of sign systems. In the investigation of distinctions between 'denotation' and 'connotation' (Barthes 1978), the conceptualising of 'interpretive communities' (Fish 1980), the social semiotic interrogation of sign acquisition and use (Kress 1993) and semiotic understandings of the function of the sign (Peirce 1955; Danesi 1999), there have been concerted attempts to address the question of whether signs or textuality can somehow precede interpretation (Cobley 1996). The idea of the 'text-to-be-read', derived from Bennett (1990; Bennett and Woollacott 1987), is an intervention in this debate which very much favours an understanding of textuality as always already undergoing the process of interpretation by readers.

The ways in which thrillers might have been read in the 1970s has, of course, been the concern of this book. We have pursued an argument in which thrillers cannot be demonstrated to actually be something 'objectively'; rather, the changing nature of generic texts can only be apprehended in an attempt to understand *readings* of them. Thus far we have made a preliminary consideration of the possible determinants of such readings as they might exist in the 1970s and it is clear that such an approach immediately problematizes previous formulations regarding the relationship between genre, history and generic innovation. Those static formulations of genre that we encountered in Chapter 1 had to be rejected in favour of a more dynamic model which analysed the flexibility and adaptability of genre through periods of social change. This meant that not only the existing corpus of the thriller genre had to be reconsidered in terms of its adaptability over time but also that the entire concept of constructing a generic corpus had to be rethought. The relation of thrillers (or any other kind of text) to history cannot simply be discerned by singling out various texts on the basis of some putative criteria of excellent craftsmanship concocted in the present. This method of constructing a corpus entails rejecting certain texts which might have had an important role to play in contemporary assessments of the genre by readers; moreover, these texts may also have provided the frame of reference within which a reading of the texts chosen for the corpus took place. It is crucial to analyse this feature of the history of a given genre in order to understand part of the frame of reference for reading generic texts.

In attempting to reconstruct the 'text-to-be-read' which constitutes the historical existence of all thrillers we have only been able to touch the tip of the iceberg of possible extra-textual cues which are at work. As a result, we have looked mainly at reviews and publicity; to even begin to do justice to the role of extra-textual cues in affecting readings of a text we would have to consider a plethora of discourses from marketing reports on the strategies and results of publicity, the results of all polls on public opinion in the period, all the way down to everyday gossip. Clearly, the task of reconstituting the historical audience ultimately faces difficulties that it cannot hope to surmount and this book has negotiated some of those difficulties by limiting the range of extra-textual cues discussed.

Yet perhaps this preliminary discussion of generic texts has demonstrated something interesting about the general status of fictional texts. From the Introduction onwards, one of the principles of genre that we have discussed is the possibility of its activity as a limiting of polysemy; that is to say, the cues which signal a work as a genre text also signal that it is to be read within certain limitations. We might therefore posit that there are cues that work upon non-genre texts which allow their polysemy free rein or even signal that the text is to be read as though it is polysemous. This would seem to have important consequences: it must be considered that the means by which texts have been constituted into corpuses – as generic texts, as non-generic texts, as part of a canon – has relied not so much on any intrinsic properties which can be objectively shown to exist, but on regimes of reading. This is not to say that these texts will necessarily be read or experienced as undifferentiated from other texts in this respect; rather, that their reading and the experience of them is governed by features 'outside' the text and 'outside' the reader, and which are at play during the text-reader interaction. The processes of reading a non-genre text with its signalled polysemy would not, in this formulation, be much different from those of reading a genre text. Such a notion would, perhaps, enable us to challenge certain conceptions of 'literariness' and what constitutes the literary canon.

Not that there is any need to argue for the literariness of the thriller or to argue the merit of a category of texts which are so popular, have survived, have experienced resurgences in the popularity of their subgenres over time, have depended upon the loyalty and expectations of readers, and which rely so heavily on a number of changing imperatives in order to exist within their generic category. Nor should there be any need to assert that the thriller is varied, multiplicitous and eminently subject to change and innovation. It may sometimes *seem* as though it is none of these just because it is generic, but the charge can be levelled equally at other structures. Take, for example, crime and the law as they are presented in the following exchange:

'Is there any end to this shit? Does anything ever change in this racket?'

'Hey Foss,' the prosecutor said, taking Clark by the arm, 'of course it changes. Don't take it so hard. Some of us die, the rest of us get older, new guys come along, old guys disappear. It changes every day.'

'It's hard to notice, though,' Clark said.

'It is,' the prosecutor said, 'it certainly is.' (Higgins 1973, p. 159)

Aptly, this comes from a narrative which deals with the very prodigality of crime and, itself, can be seen as part of a genre which, fervently embracing the diversity of life, is abundantly endowed with ideas. Genre *can*, likewise, be conceived as a limiting and changeless device; yet it, too, facilitates richness, variation and transformation. Even though it might be the kernel of a mere split-second decision by a consumer, genre is undoubtedly a slippery concept. Indeed, we might even say that genre's efficacy lies precisely in the fact that it does not exist.

Further Reading: Problematically Defined Subgenres Not Directly Represented in this Book

Capers

Print

Judson, William 1973. *Alice and Me*
Ross, Paul 1974. *Freebie and the Bean*
Thornburg, Newton 1971. *Knockover*
Westlake, Donald E. 1970. *The Hot Rock*
Westlake, Donald E. 1971. *I Gave at the Office*
Westlake, Donald E. 1972. *Bank Shot*
Westlake, Donald E. 1972. *Cops and Robbers*
Westlake, Donald E. 1974. *Help: I Am Being Held Prisoner*
Westlake, Donald E. 1980. *Castle in the Air*

Film

The Gang That Couldn't Shoot Straight (December 1971)
The Hot Rock (a.k.a. *How to Steal a Diamond*) (January 1972)
(Based on the Donald Westlake novel)
Every Little Crook and Nanny (June 1972)
Slither (March 1973)
Little Cigars (May 1973)
(Features midget bank-robber gang)
Lady Ice (August 1973)
Cops and Robbers (August 1973) (Based on Donald Westlake novel)
The Sting (December 1973)
Sugarland Express (March 1974)
Crazy Mary Dirty Larry (May 1974)
The Gravy Train (June 1974)
Bank Shot (July 1974)
(Based on Donald Westlake novel)
Freebie and the Bean (November 1974)
Eat My Dust (April 1976)
Harry and Walter Go to New York (June 1976)
(Period caper)
Special Delivery (July 1976)

TV

Sword of Justice (1978)
(Crime solving by two ex-criminals reminiscent of *The Saint*)

The Misadventures of Sheriff Lobo (1979)
(Assorted schemes of a not quite honest Georgia hick sheriff)

Espionage

Print

Collingwood, Charles 1970. *The Defector*
Coxe, George Harmon 1975. *The Inside Man*
Duncan, Robert L. 1977. *Temple Dogs*
Farris, John 1976. *The Fury*
Garfield, Brian 1973. *Kolchak's Gold*
Garfield, Brian 1975. *Hopscotch*
Hennisart, Paul 1973. *Narrow Exit*
Hunt, E. Howard 1980. *The Hargrave Deception*
Hynd, Noel 1979. *False Flags*
Hynd, Noel 1979. *The Sandler Inquiry*
Littell, Robert 1973. *The Defection of A.J. Lewinter*
McDonald, Hugh C. 1976. *Five Signs from Ruby*
McGivern, William 1972. *Caprifoil*
Moore, Robin 1976. *The Kaufman Snatch*
Moore, Robin and Dempsey, Al 1974. *Phase of Darkness*
Morre, Robin 1976. *The Terminal Connection*
Mykel, A.W. 1980. *The Windchime Legacy*
Sanders, Lawrence 1978. *The Tangent Factor*
Singer, Loren 1974. *Boca Grande*
Trevanian 1979. *Shibumi*
Wager, Walter 1975. *Telefon*

Film

The Kremlin Letter (January 1970)
(Based on a Noel Behn novel)
Scorpio (April 1973)
Day of the Dolphin (December 1973)
Rosebud (March 1975)
The Next Man (November 1976)
Telefon (December 1977)
The Fury (March 1978)
(Large dose of the supernatural in addition to espionage)
The In-Laws (June 1979)
(Hilarious espionage spoof)
Avalanche Express (July 1979)
Hopscotch (July 1980)

TV

The Silent Force (1970)
(*Mission Impossible*-style clandestine crime fighters)

'Adventure'

Print

Dickey, James 1970. *Deliverance*
Parker, Robert B. 1979. *Wilderness*

Film

Skullduggery (March 1970)
Deliverance (July 1972)
Papillon (December 1973)
The Wind and the Lion (May 1975)

Mafia Texts

Print

Lynn, Jack C. 1971. *The Professor*
McCurtin, Peter 1972. The Syndicate
Moore, Robin 1973. *The 5th Estate*
Moore, Robin with Machlin, Milt 1974. *The Family Man*
Puzo, Mario 1970. *The Godfather*
Quarry, Nick 1972. *The Don Is Dead*
Thackeray, Alex 1975. *One Way Ticket*

Film

The Godfather (March 1972)
The Don Is Dead (November 1973)
The Godfather Part II (December 1974)

Economic Thrillers

Print

Erdman, Paul 1974. *The Billion Dollar Killing*
Erdman, Paul 1975. *The Silver Bears*
Erdman, Paul 1977. *The Crash of '79*
Hailey, Arthur 1977. *The Moneychangers*
Tanous, Peter and Rubinstein, Paul 1975. *The Petro-Dollar Takeover*

Film

The Silver Bears (November 1977)
(Based on the Paul Erdman book)

DISASTER

Print

Ardies, Tom 1973. *Pandemic*

Benchley, Peter 1974. *Jaws*
Chastain, Thomas 1976. *911*
Coppel, Alfred 1974. *Thirty-four East*
DiMona, Joseph 1977. *The Benedict Arnold Connection*
Gallico, Paul 1971. *The Poseidon Adventure*
Godey, John 1973. *The Taking of Pelham 123*
Godey, John 1978. *The Snake*
Harris, Thomas 1975. *Black Sunday*
Moore, Robin 1978. *Search and Destroy*
Sayles, John 1978. *Piranha*
Scortia, Thomas N. and Robinson, Frank M. 1973. *The Glass Inferno*
Scortia, Thomas N. and Robinson, Frank M. 1976. *The Prometheus Crisis*
Stern, Richard Martin 1973. *The Tower*

Film

Airport (February 1970)
The Sky Pirate (February 1970)
Skyjacked (May 1972)
The Poseidon Adventure (December 1972)
The Taking of Pelham 123 (June 1974)
Airport 1975 (October 1974)
Earthquake (November 1974)
The Towering Inferno (December 1974)
Shark's Treasure (May 1975)
(called 'toothless *Jaws*' by *Variety*)
Jaws (June 1975)
The Hindenburg (December 1975)
The Big Bus (June 1976)
(epic disaster spoof)
Two Minute Warning (November 1976)
The Cassandra Crossing (January 1977)
Airport '77 (March 1977)
Black Sunday (April 1977)
Rollercoaster (April 1977)
Jaws 2 (June 1978)
The Swarm (July 1978)
Piranha (August 1978)
Avalanche (September 1978)
The Bees (November 1978)
The China Syndrome (February 1979)
(A liberal dose of justifiable paranoia in addition to disaster)
Beyond the Poseidon Adventure (May 1979)
Airport '79: The Concorde (August 1979)

Watergate Memoirs of the 1970s

Print

Colson, Charles 1976. *Born Again*

Dean, John 1977. *Blind Ambition: The White House Years*
Jaworski, Leon 1977. *The Right and the Power: The Prosecution of Watergate*
Safire, William 1975. *Before the Fall: An Inside View of the Pre-Watergate White House*
Sirica, John J. 1979. *To Set the Record Straight: The Break- in, the Tapes, the Conspirators, the Pardon*
White, Theodore H. 1975. *Breach of Faith: The Fall of Richard Nixon*

Film

Born Again (September 1978)
(Colson bio-pic)

Fictional Investigative Journalism as Detection

TV

Kolchak: The Night Stalker (1974)
Mobile One (1975)
The American Girls (1978)
The Andros Targets (1978)
(Often involved investigations of the supernatural)
Mrs. Columbo (1979)
(Amateur sleuthing by the famous detective's journalist wife)

Serial Killers

Print

Coe, Tucker 1970. *A Jade in Aries*
Coe, Tucker 1970. *Wax Apple*
Dunne, John Gregory 1977. *True Confessions*
Highsmith, Patricia 1970. *Ripley Underground*
Highsmith, Patricia 1974. *Ripley's Game*
Walker, Gerald 1970. *Cruising*

Film

Klute (June 1971)
The Todd Killings (August 1971)
Sweet Saviour (September 1971)
(Thinly veiled fictionalization of the Manson killings)
Play Misty for Me (September 1971)
The Mad Bomber (April 1973)
The Killing Kind (June 1973)
The Laughing Policeman (a.k.a *An Investigation of Murder*) (November 1973)
Blade (December 1973)
Have a Nice Weekend (September 1975)
Psychic Killer (November 1975)
Deadly Hero (August 1976)
The Killer Inside Me (October 1976)

The Town That Dreaded Sundown (January 1977)
Bare Knuckles (February 1978)
The Eyes of Laura Mars (August 1978)
The Toolbox Murders (November 1978)
Driller Killer (July 1979)
Windows (January 1980)
American Gigolo (January 1980)
Dressed to Kill (July 1980)

TV

S.W.A.T. (1975)
(Although ostensibly this series was about a Special Weapons and Action Team affiliated to the police, the villains were invariably psychopaths/serial killers of some kind. The SWAT team was, interestingly, made up of Vietnam veterans.)

Soft-boiled/Private Detective Fiction

Film

Who Killed Mary Whats'ername? (November 1972)

TV

The Magician (1973)
(Bill Bixby as amateur magician/sleuth)
The Snoop Sisters (1973)
(Female senior citizen sleuths)
Ellery Queen (1975)
Khan! (1975)
(Genteel Chan-like private detective)
Switch (1975)
(A pair of amateur sleuths who regularly solved cases by means of confidence tricks not unlike those to be found in the 1973 film *The Sting*)
Hardy Boys and Nancy Drew Mysteries (1977)
(Adolescent detection)
Hart to Hart (1979)
(Updated series version of *The Thin Man*)

Lawyers

Print

Hensley, Joe L. 1977. *Rivertown Risk*
Spicer, Bart 1974. *The Adversary*

Film

The Lawyer (1970)
Mr Ricco (January 1975)

TV

Storefront Lawyers (1970)
The Young Lawyers (1970)
The D.A. (1971)
Owen Marshall, Counselor at Law (1971)
Hawkins (1973)
The New Adventures of Perry Mason (1973)
Petrocelli (1974)
(Based on the 1970 film *The Lawyer*)
Kate McShane (1975)
The Law (1975)
(Much-praised courtroom-based series)
McNaughton's Daughter (1976)
The Feather and Father Gang (1977)
Rosetti and Ryan (1977)
The Eddie Capra Mysteries (1978)
Kaz (1978)

Medical Thrillers

Print

Cook, Robin 1972. *The Year of the Intern*
Cook, Robin 1976. *Coma*
Goldberg, Marshall 1972. *The Karamanov Equations*

Film

Coma (January 1978)
(Based on the Robin Cook novel with paranoid overtones)
The Carey Treatment (March 1972)
(Remarkable thriller which dramatizes issues directly connected with abortion)

TV

Quincy, M.E. (1976)

Secret Agents/Super Spies

Print

Buckley, William F., Jr. 1976. *Saving the Queen*
Buckley, William F., Jr. 1978. *Stained Glass*
Carter, Nick 1970. *The Executioners*
Carter, Nick 1973. *Butcher of Belgrade*
Kirk, Philip 1990. *Killer Satellites*
(no. 6 in the Butler series)
McDonald, Gregory 1974. *Fletch*
McDonald, Gregory 1977. *Confess, Fletch*
McDonald, Gregory 1978. *Fletch's Fortune*

Trevanian 1972. *The Eiger Sanction*
Trevanian 1973. *The Loo Sanction*

Film

The Eiger Sanction (May 1975)
(Based on the Trevanian novel)

TV

Matt Helm (1975)
(Based on the Donald Hamilton books filmed in the 1960s)

Heists

Print

Browne, Gerald A. 1978. *Green Ice*
Chastain, Thomas 1974. *Pandora's Box*
Grogan, Emmett 1978. *Final Score*

Film

The Anderson Tapes (May 1971)
(From the Lawrence Sanders novel)
Dollars (a.k.a. *The Heist)* (December 1971)
Snow Job (January 1972)
The Getaway (December 1972)
(From the Jim Thompson novel)
Thunderbolt and Lightfoot (May 1974)
Diamonds (October 1974)
Live a Little, Steal a Lot (April 1975)
Killer Force (December 1975)
Las Vegas Lady (February 1976)

Martial Arts

Film

Fist of Fury (November 1972)
Enter the Dragon (August 1973)
Black Belt Jones (February 1974)

Miscellaneous

Print

Condon, Richard 1975. *Money Is Love*
De Mille, Nelson 1978. *By the Rivers of Babylon*
Denker, Henry 1971. *The Director*
Denker, Henry 1976. *The Experiment*

Ellin, Stanley 1972. *Mirror, Mirror on the Wall*
Ellin, Stanley 1974. *Stronghold*
Ellin, Stanley 1976. *Star Light, Star Bright*
Eszterhas, Joe 1978. *F.I.S.T.*
Goldman, William 1976. *Magic*
Hardesty, John 1978. *The Killing Ground*
Kemelman, Harry 1973. *Tuesday the Rabbi Saw Red*
Levin, Ira 1970. *This Perfect Day* Littell, Robert 1974. *Sweet Reason*
Meyer, Nicholas 1974. *The Seven Per Cent Solution*
Meyer, Nicholas 1976. *The West End Horror*
Millar, Margaret 1976. *Ask for Me Tomorrow*
Mills, James 1974. *One Just Man*
(Revenge, injustice, lawyers, paranoia, police work, prison rebellion all in one novel)
Moore, Robin 1976. *Aloha*
Moore, Robin and Harper, David 1976. *The Last Superbowl*
Moore, Robin and Romain, Neville H. 1977. *Only the Hyenas Laughed*
Murphy, Warren B. 1978. *Leonardo's Law*
Roberts, Willo Davis 1976. *Expendable*
Sanders, Lawrence 1972. *Love Songs*
Schrader, Leonard 1978. *Hardcore*
Stallone, Sylvester 1977. *Paradise Alley*

Film

...Tick...Tick...Tick (January 1970)
(racial tension generates suspense)
The Forbin Project (April 1970)
What's the Matter with Helen? (June 1970)
Fools' Parade (June 1970)
Let's Scare Jessica to Death (August 1970)
The Travelling Executioner (October 1970)
The Private Life of Sherlock Holmes (October 1970)
They Might Be Giants (March 1971)
The Peace Killers (October 1971)
The Jerusalem File (March 1972)
You'll Like My Mother (October 1972)
The Mechanic (November 1972)
Sisters (March 1973)
I Escaped from Devil's Island (August 1973)
Arnold (October 1973)
The Midnight Man (March 1974)
(Psychological whodunnit)
W (June 1974)
(In which Twiggy is persecuted)
Golden Needles (July 1974)
Bring Me the Head of Alfredo Garcia (August 1974)
The Klansman (November 1974)
Shoot It: Black, Shoot It Blue (December 1974)
Race with the Devil (June 1975)

(Supernatural chase thriller)
Operation Daybreak (March 1976)
(The assassination of Heydrich)
Family Plot (March 1976)
(Hitchcock's last film)
Murder by Death (June 1976)
(Whodunit spoof)
Obsession (July 1976)
St Ives (July 1976)
The Seven Percent Solution (October 1976)
Assault on Precinct 13 (November 1976)
Twilight's Last Gleaming (January 1977)
(Anti-Vietnam tract)
The Deep (June 1977)
Sorcerer (June 1977)
(Notoriously edited remake of *The Wages of Fear*, disowned by director William Friedkin)
The Gauntlet (December 1977)
Doubles (March 1978)
F.I.S.T. (April 1978)
Five Days from Home (April 1978)
Convoy (June 1978)
Foul Play (July 1978)
Magic (November 1978)
Brass Target (December 1978)
Hardcore (February 1979)
(Possible companion to *Joe* (1970) and *Taxi Driver*)
The Onion Field (May 1979)
The Outsider (December 1979)
(IRA thriller)

TV

The Most Deadly Game (1970)
(Homicide as intellectual puzzle)
McMillan and Wife (1971)
(Light-hearted events in the life of a police commissioner (Rock Hudson); dominated by an upper-class domestic setting)
O'Hara, United States Treasury (1971)
(Adventures of a treasury agent specializing in tax evasion cases)
Sarge (1971)
(Social dramas involving ex-cop turned Catholic priest who cannot escape his instinct for solving crimes)
Hec Ramsay (1972)
(The adventures of an outdated Western deputy at the turn of the century)
Lanigan's Rabbi (1977)
(Sleuthing rabbi based on Harry Kemelman's novels)
Sam (1978)
(The adventures of a police dog)

Notes

Introduction

1 For a much fuller account of all these events see especially Ungar (1989), the *New York Times* edition of *The Pentagon Papers* (1971), and the Sunday edition of the *New York Times* for 13 June 1971.

2 Bob Haldeman was one of a number of stonewalling White House aides whom Nixon had appointed to keep the press and some governmental personnel at a distance from the President.

3 In fact, the president had apparently let slip at a White House dinner for Vietnam veterans in November 1970 that air attacks had taken place in Son Tay (Wise 1973, p. 6).

4 But these, once more, are merely the tip of the iceberg. The first head of the Senate Watergate Committee notes: 'More than 1,200 military intelligence agents in various parts of the U.S. were assigned the task of spying upon American citizens who were doing nothing whatever in most cases except exercising their rights under the First Amendment to freedom of speech and peaceably to assemble to petition government for a redress of their grievances in respect to the draft, the Vietnam war and other policies of the administration' (Ervin 1974, p. 5). At a pinch, one could argue that these were national security matters, once again necessitated by the exigencies of war. But it became clear that such measures functioned primarily to mask further secrecy (see Kissinger's speech on 23 August 1973, quoted in Kalb and Kalb 1975, pp. 505–6).

5 In 1973, for instance, Nixon's rating in a Harris poll taken before the Ervin Committee hearings gave the President 57 per cent support; immediately after the hearings, a further Harris poll found that his support rating had dropped to 32 per cent (Barber 1977, p. 64).

1. Firing the Generic Canon

1 In the twentieth century these have ranged from the work of the folklorist Vladimir Propp (1967) and the archetypal criticism of Northrop Frye (1957) to the work of film theorists trying to define the nature of the Western (for example, Kitses 1969; Buscombe 1970; Ryall 1970; Vernet 1978). Until relatively recently, the most significant theoretical advance on such an approach to genre came from those theorists, who saw in a particular genre's key moves and character functions a constant replay of the social relations which were dominant at the genre's inception. Such an approach allowed theorists to map out both the structure and the putative social determinants of, for example, thrillers (Palmer 1978), Westerns (Wright 1975) and adventure, mystery and melodrama texts (Cawelti 1976).

In addition to the studies discussed later in this chapter there have also been some useful considerations of genre in relation to reception theory: see Lindlof (1988), Gray (1992, esp. pp. 230–7), Jenkins (1992, pp. 123 ff.) and Tulloch and Jenkins (1995). Students' books, meanwhile, still tend to leave the audience out: see, for example, Tolson (1996), O'Sullivan et al. (1998) and Branston and Stafford (1999).

2 Bizarrely enough, Symons himself points out how, on perusing in the 1990s a 'Hundred Best' list of crime novels he compiled in the late 1950s, he found that it contained titles and authors unheard of now. He attributes the original selection to his 'imperceptiveness' and suggests that crime fiction is more sophisticated nowadays (1994, pp. 4–5).

3 There is, of course, no lack of sources to prevent a broader perspective on the genre; these have existed for some time (see, for example, Goulart 1965; Ruhm 1979; Ruehlmann 1974; Kittredge and Krauzer 1978). Against those who would restrict the corpus to a canon enterprising critics have stressed generic breadth (see Geherin 1985; Baker and Nietzel 1985; and the wide-ranging essays in Madden 1968).

4 The comment is taken from an interview conducted by myself in April 1992 with H. R. F. Keating. Keating is an author and critic of crime fiction and the creator of the Indian detective Inspector Ghote.

5 The genesis of this publishing venture is briefly explained in note 9 below.

6 See, *inter alia*, Q.D. Leavis (1979), Mott (1947), Watt (1972), Altick (1957), James (1973), Escarpit (1971), Laurenson and Swingewood (1972), Worpole (1984) and Hunter (1990).

7 In fact, transience is almost actively desired by the consumers of certain kitsch fictions. As Clive Bloom (1996) demonstrates, through unashamed references to cultural products forgotten by mainstream literary historians, there exists a whole history of 'pulp aesthetics' and practices of consumption which shrink from valorization by critics and wallow in their short-lived commodity fetishism.

8 A later, post-1970s 'neo-hard- boiled' is exemplified by James Ellroy's quoting of Evan Hunter (a.k.a. Ed McBain) in the rejection of the private eye tradition: 'the last time a private eye investigated a homicide was never' (see Messent 1997 p. 11). In its fixation on the police, the neo-hard-boiled is, of course, related to the police procedural subgenre and the police memoirs base. (See also Chapter 5 below.)

9 This is precisely what commentaries as different as those by Shadoian (1978), Clarens (1980) and Mandel (1984) do in relating thriller texts to some version of the 'historical context'. What invariably happens in such formulations is that the 'evolution' of a genre is outlined according to which generic texts can be argued to relate to 'history' in the way required by the analysis. This, in turn, generates a series of examples which demonstrate how the thriller has evolved from its 'origins' to a high point in the present day. Most notably absent from such accounts, of course, is a consideration of what readers have made of generic texts. In tracking a genre's 'evolution', the 'significant developments' that are registered by the commentator are the result of adopting a limited purview without asking the question 'significant to *whom*?' (Indeed, processes which canonise and processes which recognise 'significant developments', if not identical are at least mutually reinforcing as they generally agree on the corpus of 'key texts'.)

Furthermore, it is difficult to establish definitively that evolution takes place in the terms offered above. Maxim Jakubowski notes: 'There are people still writing excellent 'Cosies' as if, basically, we were still in the 1930s...And I must admit that, however much I am more in favour of the hard-boiled tradition, it can sometimes be as artificial as the country house tradition. There are not many country houses left today...'

There is therefore 'regression' as well as progression. But this is not the only feature of thriller reading that genre histories ignore: Jakubowski tells an interesting story of his running of the publishing house, Zomba, and his development of its catalogue in the late 1970s. One project which he initiated was the republishing of out-of-print detective fiction; this began with a scrutiny of the French imprint *Série Noire*, where he found 'utterly obscure American authors who were absolutely huge in France', including Cornell Woolrich, Jim Thompson, David Goodis and others. As well as expanding the corpus, the subsequent Black Box thrillers published in Britain started a trend in publishing which continues today.

These facts are indications of at least three things: the popularity of 'retro' in the 1980s (see Bromley 1988, p. 4); the unreliability of conventional thriller histories; and the commodification of fiction. (The Jakubowski comments are taken from an interview conducted by myself in April 1992. Maxim Jakubowski is a writer and critic who also owns and runs the crime fiction bookshop 'Murder One' in London.)

10 Gallagher's comments might also be applied to the way that some critics assume that genre can be read off from 'national film styles' (see Ryall 1998; Porter 1998).

2. Reading the Space of the Seventies

1 Yet there must surely be grounds for a reading of the siege as pure professionalism on the part of Sonny and Sal. For more than 12 hours, under intense pressure, in a confined space, with numerous people they did not know, on one of the hottest days of the summer, and fully armed, the would-be robbers managed to stay in control without causing any fatalities to their hostages.

2 It is worth remarking that, in the novel, the adulterous Hooper does not survive.

3. 'The Luxury to Worry about Justice': Hard-boiled Style and Heroism

1 See Parker (1971). For a contestation of the moral fidelity Spenser bears to his literary forebears see Carter (1980) and Mahan (1980).

2 A possible antidote to this and fuel for Hoffman's argument about what he finds so distasteful in the depiction of the Spenser/Silverman relationship is offered by Parker's non-Spenser thriller of the period *Wilderness* (1983b, p. 20).

3 In this context it is worth noting Byars' (1988) discussion of the TV series *Spenser For Hire*, particularly its use of voice-over narration (pp. 126–9).

4   On hard-boiled fiction's fusion of the chivalric tradition and social commen-
     tary see Parker (1977c, p. 125; 1971, p. 3).
5   Editorial comments on the invasion were mixed – the *New York Times*:
     'President Nixon's assurance in his address last night that his decision to
     send American troops against Communist sanctuaries in Cambodia will save
     lives has a familiar and wholly unconvincing ring' (p. 34). The *New York Post*:
     'Mr. Nixon has led the nation into another dead end road.' *Newsday*: 'it is all
     utterly pointless'. Detroit News: 'agrees with him'. *Chicago Today*: 'he should
     be commended'. *Cleveland Plain Dealer*: 'His maudlin appeal to patriotism was
     offensive.' *Phoenix Gazette*: 'We are grateful for a President who refuses to
     accept American defeat' (*New York Times* 2 May 1970, p. 10).
6   See especially the features in *Time 4* May 1970, p. 25; 11 May 1970, pp. 10–14;
     Washington Post 5 May 1970, p. A7
7   Construction workers, annoyed at the lowering of the flag over the mayor's
     office in New York City after the Kent State tragedy, marched, with consider-
     able support, in protest against the decision (see inter alia 'The Sudden Rising
     of the Hardhats', *Time* 25 May 1970, pp. 21–3).
8   In the 1970s: *Fadeout* (1986a); *Death Claims* (1987); *Troublemaker* (1986); *The
     Man Everybody Was Afraid Of* (1984a) and *Skinflick* (1984b).
9   When his father dies, in *Skinflick*, for a number of reasons Brandstetter
     becomes a freelance investigator.
10   In the 1979 novel *Skinflick*, Carl Brandstetter has died and Dave is almost
     immediately fired from his job at Medallion Life, ostensibly through homo-
     phobia. Perhaps it is not coincidental that this takes place right at the cusp of
     the New Right's rise to power in the West, a rise that can be seen in terms of a
     steadily fermenting backlash (see especially Weeks 1989, p. 18).
11   The discussion of motifs of vision in this film could continue for a consider-
     able time; analyses of the key role played by spectacles, the magnifying glass
     in Hollis' office, the flawed iris of Evelyn which prompts her sexual union
     with Jake, the one tail-light on Evelyn's car that Jake leaves intact so as he can
     follow her, the blacking of Curly's wife's eye, the shooting out of Evelyn's eye,
     the covering up of Catherine's eyes by Noah Cross – all of these would
     contribute to an interesting thesis.
12   Cf. screenwriter Robert Towne's comments in publicity on Jake as a 'guy who
     was sophisticated enough to be cynical about people who thought there were
     limits to how bad people could be – and that's naïve and is a nice balance'
     (CIC 1974, p. 1).

4. What Do We 'Believe' When We 'See'?
Views of Crime

1   These include Genette (1980), Chatman (1978; 1990), Mitchell (1981), Martin
     (1986), Bordwell (1988), Bordwell et al. (1988), Bordwell and Thompson (1990),
     and Rimmon-Kenan (1983). See also Branigan (1992) and Fludernik (1996).
2   His Westerns include *The Bounty Hunters* (Leonard 1979) and *Valdez Is Coming*
     (1981). His thrillers in the 1970s were *Mr Majestyk* (1986a), *52 Pick-up* (1986b),
     Swag (1984), *Unknown Man No. 89* (1986c), *The Hunted* (1985a) and *The Switch*
     (1985b).

3   Chapter 1 is focalized more or less entirely by Mitchell (p.7); Chapter 2 is focalized more or less entirely by Barbara (p. 13); Chapter 3 is focalized entirely (close to) by Mitchell (p.23); Chapter 4: Mitchell (p. 26) external/Leo Frank (pp. 26–28) Alan Raimy/external (pp. 28–29) Mitchell/external (p. 30) Alan Raimy (p. 30) Bobby Shy/external (p. 31) Doreen (p. 33) Bobby Shy (p. 34) Alan Raimy (p. 35) Bobby Shy (p. 35); Chapter 5: Mitchell (p. 36) Barbara (p. 38 – one paragraph) Mitchell (p. 38) Barbara (p. 40) Alan Raimy (p. 42) Barbara (p. 43) Leo Frank (p. 43); Chapter 6: Mitchell (p. 45) external/Mitchell (p. 51) Bobby Shy (p. 55) Leo Frank (p. 56); Chapter 7: Mitchell/external (p. 57); Chapter 8: Mitchell (p. 65) Barbara (p. 66) Mitchell (p. 68) Barbara (p. 72); Chapter 9: Leo Frank (p. 74) Alan Raimy (p. 75) Mitchell (p. 75) external/Alan Raimy (p. 80); Chapter 10: Ross/external (p. 82) Barbara (p. 86); Chapter 11: Mitchell (p. 88) Barbara (p. 91) Mitchell (p. 91) Barbara (p. 93) Mitchell (p. 93); Chapter 12: external/Mitchell (p. 96); Chapter 13: Mitchell (p. 103) Leo Frank (p. 103) Mitchell (p. 106) Leo Frank (p. 107); Mitchell (p. 108) Alan Raimy (p. 108) Leo Frank (p. 109) Mitchell (p. 109) Alan Raimy (p. 117); Chapter 14: Bobby Shy (p. 118) Alan Raimy (p. 120) Bobby Shy (p. 120) Alan Raimy (p. 121) Bobby Shy (p. 121) Alan Raimy (p. 123) Mitchell (p. 124) Alan Raimy (p. 125) Mitchell (p. 127); Chapter 15: Bobby Shy (p. 127) Alan Raimy (p. 130) Leo Frank (p. 131) Bobby Shy (p. 132) Mitchell (p. 134) Alan Raimy (p. 139) Bobby Shy/external (p. 141) Alan Raimy (p. 145) Barbara (p. 145) Alan Raimy (p. 146) Barbara (p. 148) Leo Frank (p. 149) Mitchell (p. 152) Ed Jazik (union man) (p. 156) Janet (Mitchell's secretary)(p. 157) Mitchell (p. 157) John Koliba (worker in Mitchell's plant) (p. 158) Mitchell (p. 160) Koliba (p. 161) Mitchell (p. 161) Leo Frank (p. 162) Bobby Shy (p. 165); Chapter 17: Mitchell (p. 165) Alan Raimy (p. 169) Mitchell (p.170) Alan Raimy (p.171) Mitchell (p. 172) O'Boyle (Mitchell's advisor) (p. 175) Bobby Shy (p. 178) Alan Raimy (p. 180) Barbara (p. 181) Alan Raimy (p. 181); Chapter 18: Mitchell (p. 183) Alan Raimy (p. 188) Mitchell (p. 189) Alan Raimy (p. 190) Koliba (p. 190). (Where the neutrality of the focalization is in question I have designated the focalization a combined one comprising an external focalizer and one close to a character.)

4   It is notable that, in the film version of *52 Pick-up* (1986), the motivation for Mitchell's retaliation is the need to save his wife's budding political career.

5   These are not the whole of the focalizations by any means; the following focalizations in *The Switch* are neither Mickey's nor the kidnappers':
Chapter 1: Frank/external (p. 7); Chapter 3: external? (pp. 18, 19); Chapter 4: Marshall Taylor (p. 32); Chapter 9: external (p. 62); Marshall Taylor (pp. 65, 67); Chapter 13: Frank (whole chapter); Chapter 14: Frank (pp. 105, 108); Chapter 15: external (p. 113); Chapter 16: external (whole chapter); Chapter 17: Detroit patrolman (p. 127); Chapter 20: Randy Dixon (p. 149); Frank (p. 156); Melanie (p. 157); Chapter 23: Melanie (p. 181).

6   The remarks of Senator Robert Byrd when former Presidential Appointments Secretary Alexander Butterfield revealed at the Senate Watergate hearings that Nixon had taped all his White House conversations (*Newsweek*, 30 July 1973, p. 13); see also p. 8 above.

7   Almost $200 billion according to J. William Fulbright in 1971 (Fulbright 1985, p. 300).

8 For those who wished to express the possibility of a general lack of confidence in the regulation of crime and a slackening of the sanctity of the law, similar openings existed: see Jimmy Carter's speech on the topic during the 1976 election campaign (quoted in Witcover 1977, p. 548).

9 *The Friends of Eddie Coyle* (Higgins 1973); *The Digger's Game* (1973); *Cogan's Trade* (1975); *A City on a Hill* (1985); *The Judgment of Deke Hunter* (1986).

10 Evidently the plot constitutes only a small amount of the potential enjoyment of the novels for Higgins's (and Leonard's) fans (see the interviews in *South Bank Show* 1987 and *Arena* 1990).

11 There are numerous examples of this in Higgins novels; Barthes (1993), somewhat reductively, calls it the 'reality effect'.

12 As publicity for the film suggested, 'Coyle is a hood, but he is first of all a family man' (CIC Publicity Brochure for *The Friends of Eddie Coyle* 1973, p. 2).

5. 'Keeping That Sixth Ball in the Air': The Police

1 The exception here is *The Blue Knight*, which was made into an Emmy award-winning mini-series (1973; later cut into a feature-length film), which starred William Holden as Bumper Morgan. (The character also returned in the 1975 CBS TV series of the same name, this time played by George Kennedy.)

2 And, as with *All the President's Men*, bringing such a story into the public domain provides the grounds of counter-accusations of smear tactics. Police Commissioner Leary, for example, accused the *New York Times* of 'McCarthyism all over again' (Maas 1974, p. 210), a reaction almost identical to that of Nixon aide and unofficial media subvertor-in-chief, Charles Colson, who was incensed by the *Washington Post* (see Woodward and Bernstein 1974, pp. 205, 238). Furthermore, such contentions about 'McCarthyism' became a virtual *leitmotiv* with regard to the issue of corruption and its exposure in the 1970s, as we will see in Chapter 7.

3 He adds: 'As the picture progresses, Pacino's Serpico, like Hoffman's Benjamin before him, becomes an increasingly facile figure of the counter-culture at war with the great sell-out middle-class' (Sarris 1973b).

During this period, Al Pacino (who plays Frank Serpico) was often considered to be one of a group of actors, including Dustin Hoffman, who combined youth, unconventional good looks, and a brand of method acting in star roles. In addition to these attributes, however, Hoffman's most famous film, *The Graduate* (1967), is widely considered to be a narrative of youth in conflict with the mediocrity of the middle-aged middle class. Moreover, Hoffman's off-screen persona complemented his on screen one; for instance, he displayed indifference at this time to the Oscar ceremonies where he was nominated for *The Graduate* and *Midnight Cowboy* (1969). Pacino's association with Hoffman, then, in this circuitous way, effectively lends him a similar identity to the character Hoffman plays in his first major film, and this can be said to be in place before Pacino even assumes the role of hippie policeman Serpico. If one follows this line of reasoning them both Serpico and Benjamin Braddock are characters who, in their own symbolic ways, stand against the establishment.

4   The Knapp Commission Report (1973, pp. 2–15; cf. Maas 1974, pp. 53 ff)
    demonstrated that police corruption in New York had become almost a way
    of life, barely noticeable, and into which rookies were casually inducted (cf.
    Reiss 1971, p. 171 on 'consensual' graft). The narrative of *Serpico* does touch
    on the fact that such a situation has countless determinations, none the least
    of which are to do with policemen making enough money to sustain a family.
       It must be remembered that Serpico was single and the narrative gives
    instances of those police operatives who need the extra money gained from
    graft to maintain a certain standard of living plus, in one notable case, an
    instance of someone who for the same reasons cannot afford to assist Serpico
    in exposing corruption. Delise, Serpico's soulmate in his crusade within the
    police department, responds in the following way when Serpico asks for his
    assistance in approaching the *New York Times*: 'Frank, I have twenty years or
    whatever in the department. I have a wife and two kids and I just bought a
    house and there's a mortgage on it, and if I had to leave the department I don't
    know what other field I could go into' (p. 204).
       This consideration of police work as a 'job' rather than a civic duty is in stark
    contrast to the stances taken by other heroes in thriller narratives from earlier
    periods. Eliot Ness, for example, who appears in a number of narratives about
    Al Capone, keeps secret his views on the Volstead Act but makes it very clear
    that he will do his utmost to uphold the law and to pursue the racketeers who
    violate it. Although this stance puts his family at risk it is ultimately designed
    to defend his and other families (see Ness and Fraley 1967 originally 1957; plus
    the 1960s TV series *The Untouchables* and the 1987 Brian de Palma film of the
    same title).

5   The most serious piece of information which would lend credibility to these
    brusque summaries regards the role of David Durk. Durk was a plain-clothes
    colleague of Serpico and they had known each other since training on a
    Criminal Investigation Course together. Both were about the same age, but
    Durk had joined the force four years later than Serpico having graduated from
    Amherst College. In the book, Serpico and Durk share the same concern over
    corruption and the same thirst for justice, making them confidants (see Maas
    1974, pp. 107 ff.) However, reviewers including Sarris, Hentoff and Simon feel
    that Durk gets a very rough deal in the book and especially the film, where he
    is known only as 'Bob Blair'. Writes Hentoff, 'The movie, by the way, does Durk
    a serious injustice. He figured much more importantly in the exposure of
    police corruption than the movie – focusing on Al Pacino as the star – would
    have you believe' (1974).
       More serious than this for Sarris is how the omission of Durk's role from the
    narrative fits the film's general attitude. As Durk is an articulate graduate who
    dresses smartly and utilizes aspects of the bureaucracy of police work in his
    stand against corruption, Sarris feels that this disqualifies him from the film's
    narrative: How convenient it is that Serpico's enemies should be square and
    crooked at the same time! It is nothing less than a Nixonian happenstance. In
    this context, the downgrading of Durk makes a certain amount of mythic
    sense. The spectacle of two honest men cooperating in a crooked world does
    not provide as much paranoia for the armchair reformer in the audience as
    does the spectacle of one honest man all alone against the whole world'
    (1973b).

In this way, then, the limitations imposed on the reading of the film of *Serpico* also constitute an attack on its veracity. The excision of Durk's role is, in one sense, an act of narration but it also indicates to Sarris that the text is 'false' in relation to an empirical given; whether these processes of editing and narration are indigenous to only fictional texts is not mentioned by the critic.

6 If one examines accounts of police corruption in the period, it is apparent that, in contrast to the film, the book and the TV series, *Serpico* constitutes a mere footnote to an epic story involving many individuals (see, for example, Sherman 1978; cf. Cohen 1970; Beigel 1974; Richardson 1974; Fogelson 1977).

7 This is how the name of the detective, originally envisaged as a Pole, was spelt in the pilot.

8 One of the reasons that pressure was put on the police in the real life case was that the uncle of one of the victims was the author Philip Wylie, who pulled as many strings as possible to make sure that the horror of the case was publicised.

9 Reiss notes: 'The only offenses for which detectives accounted for at least two in every ten arrests were arson and fugitives from justice' (1971, p. 108).

10 A comparable case of a police show dedicated to exploring intricate social issues but renowned for its violence in the period was *The Streets of San Francisco* (September 1972). The standard of violence here, though, is one set informally by American television. Neither of these could compare with the likes of *Special Branch* (1973) or *The Sweeney* (1974) on British television.

6. Sambos or Superspades?

1 Romm (1986, p. 29).

2 In fact, one of the most interesting thrillers of the 1970s, Blake Edwards's film *The Carey Treatment* (1972), is directly and thoroughly about the issue of abortion.

3 Reid, for example, (somewhat bizarrely) suggests that the semi-clad bodies of Tamara Dobson and Pam Grier (*Coffy* 1973; *Foxy Brown* 1974; and *Friday Foster* 1977) de-emphasize their ability to ward of physical violence. As a result, the female characters are actually in subservient roles amenable to a male ego (1993, pp. 87-8).

4 A brief summary of Hayes's recording career with Stax and his acting career prior to his role as the voice of Chef in the TV series *South Park* is given in Cashmore (1997, pp. 74-9).

5 It is well known, for instance, that Richard Roundtree received just $12,500 for his role in the first film.

6 Moreover, it is not unrelated to the treatment of otherness in many blaxploitation texts. *Cleopatra Jones*, for instance, has three main figures of otherness in its narrative: a profoundly unnattractive white henchman, Tony (uncredited), who is English; a melodramatic white lesbian villainess, Momma (Shelley Winters); and the mincing chauffeur/valet of Doodlebug (Antonio Fargas), a character called Madingley (uncredited), who hits the jackpot by being white, homosexual *and* English.

7   Following Ice T's *Baadasssss TV* season on Channel 4 (1995), Tarantino's nod to blaxploitation in *Jackie Brown* (1997), his support of it in print (1998) and at a season run by the National Film Theatre in Britain (1996), as well as the emergence of specialist video reissue companies such as Super Fly, there are now plans to remake the original film of *Shaft* and to film the works of Iceberg Slim. There are also a number of places on the Internet where one can gain information of varying qualities on black genres and 'blaxploitation' (including the Truck Turner homepage: http://www.zenweb.com/century/truck). Critical material in other media, however, has been surprisingly sparse.

8   A position rehearsed in a convincingly detailed way most recently by Cashmore (1997).

9   There is a rich literature exploring the history of misrepresentation, caricature, stereotyping (Gilman 1985) and denigration of blacks in film and elsewhere (see, for example, Bogle 1994, Cripps 1978, Gross and Hardy 1966, as well as Leab 1975) above and beyond the blaxploitation of the seventies. In tandem with arguments about the 'black culture industry', historians have identified the proliferation of a myth of the primitive: the use of black people as a spectacle for white audiences (for example, minstrelsy, and even in the 'high' cultural sphere of the Harlem Renaissance where one commentator identifies 'blaxploitation' (Dorsey 1997)). Other critics have pointed to the work of some black artists as constituting 'conservative' tendencies (see hooks 1996, p. 7 on film-makers).

10   Such arguments are not new, a fact which adds to their substance. The postwar foundations of more contemporary assessments of an African-American tradition can be found in diverse disciplines and figures: history (Melville Herskovits, Herbert Gutman), literary historians, (Arna Bontemps, Robert Hemenway), popular narrative (Alex Haley), folklore studies (Lawrence Levine), music commentary (Ben Sidran), and others.

11   See Gilstrap (1998); Stone (1977, pp. 141 ff.). In Britain, any of Goines's novels can be readily purchased from the 'black writing' section of the avowedly non-specialist high street newsagent W. H. Smith.

7. Just Because You're Paranoid It Doesn't Mean They're Not Out to Get You

1   Berke et al. argue that the word 'paranoid', in light of its Greek root, tends to suggest a state of being outside or *beside* one's mind in conjunction with a fear of persecution (1998, p. 1).

2   The launch of Sputnik I against the backdrop of the Cold War in October 1957 had a profound impact on the American public; a famous discussion of this occurs in Wolfe (1980, pp. 56 ff.), but see also King (1982, pp. 22 ff.) and Kovic (1990, pp. 44–8).

3   For a much fuller account of all these events, see especially, Ungar (1989), the *New York Times* edited volume of *The Pentagon Papers* (1971) and the Sunday edition of the *New York Times* for 13 June 1971. See also Introduction, above.

4 Interestingly, the last of these journalists said in 1983: 'I do not think the press is very relevant at all.' He was referring to the Pentagon Papers, the Vietnam War and the fact that 'all the horrors of the Nixon administration' were only learnt after the 1972 election (see Hersh 1984).

5 Undoubtedly, heroic acts by journalists took place; but this is by no means the whole or even the dominant truth of the matter. Hentoff supplies us with a more mundane example of the hazards of investigative journalism: 'In March 1973, with the Boston *Globe* engaged in an investigative series that could put a number of people on its staff in jail if the grand jury decides to subpoena them, two reporters refused to work on that series' (1973, p. 221).

6 One of these which is specifically important as the site of conspiracy and paranoia is the spate of assassinations of political figures in the 1960s (see Scott et al. 1978; Roffman 1975; Noyes 1973; Meagher 1967; on Governor Wallace and Arthur Bremer see also Woodward and Bernstein 1974, p. 326). The ramifications of this can be seen in such paranoid texts as *The Parallax View* (1974) and *Executive Action* (1973) (see also Chapter 8).

7 In fact, Hill and Every (1998, p. 102) suggest that the paranoid films' delivery of audiences to 'safe ground', only replays the sense of the (Freudian) uncanny to be found in the familiar. See also the relentlessness of the uncanny in paranoid fictions of the period from other genres – for example *The Illuminatus Trilogy* (1975) of Robert Shea and Robert Anton Wilson; Robert Coover's *The Public Burning* (1977); and, of course, Thomas Pynchon's *Gravity's Rainbow* (1973). See also Cobley (forthcoming, ch. 7).

8 This was followed in the 1970s by *The Osterman Weekend* (1972b), *The Matlock Paper* (1973), *Trevayne* (1989a; originally 1974, under the name 'Jonathan Ryder'), *The Rhinemann Exchange* (1976, [1974]), *The Road to Gandolfo* (1982; originally 1975, under the name 'Michael Shepherd'), *The Gemini Contenders* (1977a, [1976]), *The Chancellor Manuscript* (1977b), *The Holcroft Covenant* (1979a, [1978]) and *The Matarese Circle* (1979b).

9 This is also articulated with the theme of Olympic 'outsiders': see references in the text to Gary Wottle (p. 15) and Abebe Bikila (pp. 181 ff.) and compare with the mythical status of Jesse Owens in the 1936 Berlin Olympics.

8. 'Thank God for the Rain . . . ': Revenge from *Dirty Harry* to *The Exterminator*

1 Like a sixth-form Eng. Lit. student drunk on the potential of textual analysis, Lovell (1975, p. 42), for example, goes to absurd lengths to prove the film's racism. He also makes mistakes about the detail of the narrative.

2 One way of reading his character is to make reference to his presumed real-life counterpart. A serial killer calling himself 'Zodiac' has been thought to have been operating in the San Francisco area since at least 1968 (see Graysmith 1992). Moreover, *Dirty Harry* can be said to have prefigured some of Zodiac's activities: in October 1969, Zodiac sent a letter to the SFPD threatening to hijack a school bus. This is exactly what happens at the climax of *Dirty Harry* over two years later. However, the Zodiac letter containing the threat was only made public in 1992 (Graysmith 1992, pp. 102–3). This is one more example of life imitating art or, more accurately, fact being reinvested in terms of a work of

fiction. What the Zodiac connection makes apparent, though, is that Scorpio can perhaps be read in these terms: whether the character was read as such by a number of non-San Franciscans in the contemporary period is open to question.

3 See, for example, *The Mechanic* (1972), *The Stone Killer* (1973) and the Elmore Leonard scripted *Mr. Majestyk* (1973)). Sutherland points out (1981, p. 156) that Bronson himself believed that Dustin Hoffman should have been given the Paul Benjamin/Kersey role, a fact which has links with the remarks that Kael makes about *Marathon Man* (see Chapter 7 above). This reminds us that even if it is possible to identify a strand of revenge thrillers in the 1970s their existence is by no means isolated from other texts and is not available to be read as such.

4 As Sutherland (1981, p. 158), points out, Brian Garfield – like Elmore Leonard – had been a noted Western writer for about ten years before writing his vigilante novel.

5 See also the comments of the mayor's press office and Michael Winner's riposte quoted in Robinson (1975).

6 That this kind of portrait of the assassin was almost a standard became clearer in the early 1980s when John Hinckley, the assassin who attempted to kill President Reagan, was placed under extensive psychiatric evaluation and revealed that *Taxi Driver* had directly inspired his plans (see Shaw 1981 and 'Jury Goes to the Pictures', *The Guardian* 24 May 1982).

7 The most famous of the last of these would be *The Terminator* (1984) which, although the Schwarzenegger character is that of a villainous android, was popular enough to warrant his return as a hero in *Terminator 2: Judgment Day* (1991). (Also, cf. *The Terminator*: 'I'll be back'; and *The Exterminator*: 'If you're lying, I'll be back').

Conclusion

1 There are also strong arguments to suggest that the political complexion of the American thriller cannot be pinned down unproblematically. Pepper (2000) argues that the American crime novel has always simultaneously embraced 'left' and 'right' political ideologies in a way which both undermines and reasserts capitalist social relations.

References

Adair, G. (1989) *Hollywood's Vietnam* Rev. edn. London: Heinemann

Alex, N. (1969) *Black in Blue: A Study of the Negro Policeman* New York: Appleton Century Crofts

Alexander, E. (1996) '"We're gonna reconstruct your life!" The making and unmaking of the black bourgeois patriarch in *Ricochet'* in M. Blount and G. Cunningham eds. *Representing Black Men* London: Routledge

Altick, R. D. (1957) *The English Common Reader: A Social History of the Mass Reading Public 1800–1900* Chicago and London: Universiy of Chicago Press

Altman, R. (1986) 'A semantic/syntactic approach to film genre' in B. K. Grant ed. *Film Genre Reader* Austin: University of Texas Press

Altman, R. (1987) *The American Film Musical* Bloomington: Indiana University Press

Altman, R. (1998) 'Re-usable packaging: generic products and the recycling process' in N. Browne ed. *Refiguring American Film Genres: Theory and History* London and Berkeley: University of California Press

Altman, R. (1999) *Film/Genre* London: BFI

Anderson, J. with Clifford, G. (1974) *The Anderson Papers* London: Millington

Ang, I. (1984) *Watching Dallas: Soap Opera and the Melodramatic Imagination.* London: Routledge

Ang, I. (1991) *Desperately Seeking the Audience* London: Routledge

Ang, I. (1996) *Living Room Wars: Rethinking Media Audiences for a Postmodern World* London: Routledge

Arena (1990) 'Elmore Leonard's Criminal Records' BBC Television

Arendt, H. (1983) *Eichmann in Jerusalem: A Report on the Banality of Evil* Harmondsworth: Penguin

Armes, J. J. and Nolan, F. (1978) *Jay J. Armes Investigator* London: Futura (originally 1976)

Arnold, G. (1976a) 'Scorsese's "Taxi Driver" igniting the slow fuse of repression' *Washington Post* 10 February, B1, B7

Arnold, G. (1976b) 'Review of *All the President's Men' Washington Post* 4 April

Athey, S. (1999) 'Poisonous Roots and the new World blues: rereading seventies narration and nation in Alex Haley and Gayl Jones' *Narrative* 7(2), 169–93

Auster, A. and Quart, L. (1988) *How the War Was Remembered: Hollywood and Vietnam* New York and London: Praeger

Austin, B. and Gordon, T. (1988) 'Movie genres: toward a conceptualised and standardized definition' *Current Research in Film* 3, 12–33

Babuscio, J. (1976) 'Gay terrorists: a critique of *Dog Day Afternoon' Gay News* 86

Bailey, F. Y. (1991) *Out of the Woodpile: Black Characters in Crime and Detective Fiction* Westport: Greenwood Press

Baker, H. A., Jr. (1984) *Blues, Ideology and Afro-American Literature: A Vernacular Theory* Chicago: University of Chicago Press

Baker, M. (1983) *Nam: The Vietnam War in the Words of the Men and Women Who Fought There* London: Abacus

Baker, R. A. and Nietzel, M. T. eds. (1985) *101 Knights: A Survey of American Detective Fiction 1922–1984* Bowling Green: Bowling Green State University Popular Press

Bakhtin, M. M. (1981) *The Dialogic Imagination: Four Essays* ed. M. Holquist, trans. C. Emerson and M. Holquist, Austin: University of Texas Press

Bakhtin, M. M. (1984) *Problems of Dostoevsky's Poetics* ed. and trans. Caryl Emerson, London and Minneapolis: University of Minnesota Press

Barber, J. D. (1977) *The Presidential Character: Predicting Performance in the White House* 2nd edn. Englewood Cliffs: Prentice-Hall

Barker, M. and Sabin, R. (1996) *The Lasting of the Mohicans* New York: University of Mississippi Press

Barley, T. (1986) *Taking Sides: The Fiction of John Le Carré* Milton Keynes: Open University Press

Barthes, R. (1974) *S/Z* New York: Hill & Wang

Barthes, R. (1993) 'The reality effect' in L. Furst ed. *Realism* Harlow: Longman

Beigel, H. (1974) 'The investigation and prosecution of police corruption' *Journal of Law and Criminology* 65(2), 135–56. Reprinted in Potholm and Morgan (1976)

Bell, D. ed. (1964) *The Radical Right* Doubleday: New York

Bennett, T. (1987) 'Texts, readers, reading formations' in D. Attridge et al. eds. *Post-structuralism and the Question of History* Cambridge: Cambridge University Press

Bennett, T. (1990) *Outside Literature* London: Routledge

Bennett, T. and Woollacott, J. (1987) *Bond and Beyond: The Political Career of a Popular Hero.* London: Macmillan

Bennington, G. (1987) 'Demanding history' in D. Attridge et al. eds. *Post-structuralism and the Question of History* Cambridge: Cambridge University Press

Berke, J. et al. (1998) 'General introduction' in Berke ed. *Even Paranoids Have Enemies: New Perspectives on Paranoia and Persecution* London: Routledge

Binyon, T. J. (1989) *Murder Will Out: The Detective in Fiction* London: Oxford University Press

Biskind, P. (1975) 'Between the teeth' *Jump Cut* 9 (Oct./Dec.)

Biskind, P. (1990) *The Godfather Companion: Everything You Ever Wanted to Know about All Three Godfather Films* New York: Harper Perennial

Bleiler, E. F. (1978) 'Introduction' in *Three Victorian Detective Novels* ed. Bleiler New York: Dover

Bloom, C. (1996) *Cult Fiction: Popular Reading and Pulp Theory* London: Macmillan

Bogle, D. (1994) *Toms, Coons, Mulattoes, Mammies and Bucks: An Interpretive History of Blacks in American Films* 3rd edn. Oxford: Roundhouse

Boller, P. F., Jr. (1985) *Presidential Campaigns* New York: Oxford University Press

Booth, W. C. (1961) *The Rhetoric of Fiction* Chicago and London: University of Chicago Press

Boyer, J. C. (1996) 'Race and the American city: The Kerner Commission report in retrospect' in J. C. Boyer and J. W. Wegner eds. *Race, Poverty and American Cities* Chapel Hill and London: University of Northern Carolina Press

Boyers, R. (1973) 'The woman question and the death of the family' *Dissent* 20, 57–66

Braestrup, P. (1983) *Big Story: How the American Press and Television Reported and Interpreted the Crisis of Tet 1968 in Vietnam and Washington* Abridged edn. New Haven and London: Yale University Press

Braestrup, P. (1984) 'The Tet Offensive: another press controversy: II' in H. E. Salisbury ed. *Vietnam Reconsidered: Lessons from a War* New York: Harper & Row

Branigan, E. (1992) *Narrative Comprehension and Film* London: Routledge

Branston, G. and Stafford, D. (1999) *The Media Student's Book* 2nd edn. London: Routledge

British Film Institute (n.d.) 'Production notes on *All the President's Men* ' London: BFI

Bromley, R. (1988) *Lost Narratives: Popular Fictions, Politics and Recent History* London: Routledge

Brooks, J. (1974) 'Rampant corruption' in Schnapper (1974)

Brooks, P. (1984) *Reading for the Plot: Design and Intention in Narrative* Cambridge, MA: Harvard University Press

Browne, N. (1979) 'Introduction', *Film Reader* 4, 105–7

Browne, N. (1996) 'The spectator-in-the-text: the rhetoric of *Stagecoach*' in Cobley (1996) (originally 1975)

Byars, J. (1988) 'Gazes/voices/power: expanding psychoanalysis for feminist film and television theory' in E. D. Pribram ed. *Female Spectators: Looking at Film and Television* London: Verso

Calley, W. and Sack, J. (1971) *Body Count: Lieutenant Calley's Story as Told to John Sack* London: Hutchinson

Camacho, P. (1980) 'From war hero to criminal: the negative privilege of the Vietnam veteran' in C. R. Figley and S. Leventman eds. *Strangers at Home: Vietnam Veterans since the War* New York: Praeger

Canby, V. (1971) '*Shaft* – At last, a good Saturday night movie' *New York Times*, 11 July, B1

Canby, V. (1975) Review of *Dog Day Afternoon, New York Times* 28 September

Canby, V. (1976) Review of *Taxi Driver, New York Times* 15 February

Carmichael, S. and Hamilton, C. V. (1968) *Black Power: The Politics of Liberation in America* Harmondsworth: Penguin

Carpini, M. X. D. (1990) 'US media coverage of the Vietnam conflict in 1968' in M. Klein ed. *The Vietnam Era: Media and Popular Culture in the US and Vietnam* London: Pluto

Carter, S. R. (1980) 'Spenserian ethics: the unconventional morality of Robert B. Parker's traditional American hero' *Clues* 1(2), 109–18

Cashin, F. (1975) 'All you need to know about the shark that scared a nation half to death and founded a £76m industry' *The Sun* 27 October, 12–13

Cashmore, E. (1997) *The Black Culture Industry* London: Routledge

Cawelti, J. G. (1976) *Adventure, Mystery, and Romance: Formula Stories as Art and Popular Culture* Chicago and London: University of Chicago Press

Cawelti, J. G. (1985) '*Chinatown* and generic transformation in recent American films' in G. Mast and M. Cohen eds. *Film Theory and Criticism: Introductory Readings* 3rd edn. New York and London: Oxford University Press (originally 1979)

Chandler, R. (1984) 'Letter to Frederick Lewis Allen, May 7, 1948' in D. Gardiner and K. Sorley Walker eds. *Raymond Chandler Speaking* London: Allison & Busby

Chase, A. (1972) 'The strange romance of "Dirty Harry" Callahan and Ann Mary Deacon' *Velvet Light Trap* 17, 13–18

Chatman, S. (1990) *Coming to Terms: The Rhetoric of Narrative in Fiction and Film* Ithaca and London: Cornell University Press

Clarens, C. (1980) *Crime Movies: An Illustrated History from Griffith to* The Godfather *and Beyond* London: Secker & Warburg

CIC (1973) Publicity brochure for *The Friends of Eddie Coyle*

CIC (1974) Publicity brochure for *Chinatown*

Cobley, P. (1986). '*Roots* as an American Cultural Paradigm' MA thesis, University of Sussex

Cobley, P. ed. (1996) *The Communication Theory Reader* London: Routledge

Cobley, P. (1997) 'The specific regime of verisimilitude in the thriller' in I. Rauch ed. *Synthesis in Diversity: Proceedings of the 5th Congress of the IASS* Berlin: Mouton

Cobley, P. (forthcoming) *Narrative* London: Routledge

Cocks, J. (1972a) 'Outside society' *Time* 3 January

Cocks, J. (1972b) 'The Godsons' *Time* 3 April, 37–9

Cocks, J. (1972c) Review of *The New Centurions*, *Time* 4 September

Cocks, J. (1974) 'Los Angelenos' *Time* 1 July

Cocks, J. (1976) Review of *Marathon Man*, *Time* 18 October

Cohen, B. (1970) *The Police Internal Administration of Justice in New York City* New York: Rand Institute

Cohn, D. (1966) 'Narrated monologue: definition of a fictional style' *Comparative Literature* 18(2), 97–112

Coles, R. (1971) 'Policeman complaints' *New York Times Magazine* 11 June. Reprinted in Potholm and Morgan (1976)

'Color Adjustment' (1992) BBC2 (broadcast September)

Cooper, D. (1971) *The Death of the Family* Harmondsworth: Penguin

Cranny-Francis, A. (1988) 'Gender and genre: feminist rewritings of detective fiction' *Women's Studies International Forum* 11, 69–84

Cripps, T. (1978) *Black Film as Genre* Bloomington and London: Indiana University Press

Daly, M. (1975) *Telly Savalas* London: Sphere

Dan, U. with Radley, E. (1977) *The Eichmann Syndrome* New York: Leisure Books

Danesi, M. (1999) *Of Cigarettes, High Heels and Other Interesting Things: An Introduction to Semiotics* London and New York: Macmillan

Daniels, C. (1996) 'Blaxploitation or liberation?' *Black Film Bulletin* 4(3), 13–15

Davis, B. (1973) *The Thriller: The Suspense Film from 1946* London: Studio Vista

Davis, D.B. ed. (1971) *The Fear of Conspiracy: Images of Un-American Subversion from the Revolution to the Present* Ithaca, NY, and London: Cornell University Press

Day, B. (1975) 'How promoters are biting into Jaws' *Campaign* 12 December

Degler, C. N. (1980) *At Odds: Women and the Family in America from the Revolution to the Present* New York and Oxford: Oxford University Press

Dempsey, M. (1976) 'Review of *Taxi Driver*' *Film Quarterly* 29(4), 37–41

Denning, M. (1987) *Cover Stories: Narrative and Ideology in the British Spy Thriller* London: Routledge

Denning, M. (1998) *Mechanic Accents: Dime Novels and Working-Class Culture in America* 2nd edn. London: Verso

Denzin, N. and Lincoln, Y. S. eds. (1998) *The Landscape of Qualitative Research: Theories and Issues* Thousand Oaks and London: Sage

DeWaard, E. J. and DeWaard, N. (1984) *History of NASA: America's Voyage to the Stars* New York: Exeter Books

Divine, R. A. ed. (1987) *The Johnson Years I: Foreign Policy, the Great Society and the White House* Lawrence: University of Kansas Press

Dobrovir, W. A. et al. eds. (1974) *The Offenses of Richard M. Nixon: A Guide to His Impeachable Crimes* 3rd edn. New York: Manor Books

Dorsey, B. (1997) *Who Stole the Soul? Blaxploitation Echoed in the Harlem Renaissance* Salzburg: Institut für Anglistik und Amerikanistik

Drinan, R. F. (1974) 'Abuse of war powers' in Schnapper (1974)

Dyer, R. (1997) *White* London: Routledge

Ehrlichman, J. (1982) *Witness to Power: The Nixon Years* New York: Simon & Schuster

Ellroy, J. (1994) 'Without Walls: The American Cop' Channel 4 (broadcast 29 November)

Ellsberg, D. (1974) 'Secrecy and security' in Harward (1974)

Erdstein, E. with Bean, B. (1979) *Inside the Fourth Reich* London: Sphere (originally 1977)

Ervin, S. J. (1974) 'Historical and political perspectives' in Harward (1974)

Escarpit, R. (1971) *Sociology of Literature* London: Frank Cass

Evans, T. J. (1980) 'Robert B. Parker and the hardboiled tradition of American detective fiction' *Clues* 1(2), 100–8

Evening Standard (1973) 'BBC and ITV battle for Telly the US cop' 10 December

Farber, D. (1994) *The Age of Great Dreams: America in the 1960s* New York: Hill & Wang

Farson, R. C. et al. (1969) *The Future of the Family* New York: Family Service Association of America

Fiedler, L. A. (1984) *Love and Death in the American Novel* 3rd Rev. edn. Harmondsworth: Penguin (originally 1960)

Figley, C. R. and Leventman, S. (1980a) *Strangers at Home: Vietnam Veterans since the War* New York: Praeger

Figley, C. R. and Leventman, S. (1980b) 'Introduction: estrangement and victimization' in Figley and Leventman (1980a)

Finler, J. W. (1992) *The Hollywood Story* London: Mandarin

First Tuesday (1989) *Four Hours at My Lai* Yorkshire Television (broadcast February)

Fish, S. E. (1981) 'Why no one's afraid of Wolfgang Iser' *diacritics* 11 (March) reprinted in Cobley (1996)

Fletcher, R. (1988) *The Abolitionists: The Family and Marriage under Attack* London: Routledge

Fludernik, M. (1996) *Towards a 'Natural' Narratology* London: Routledge

Fogelson, R. N. (1977) *Big-City Police* Cambridge, MA, and London: Harvard University Press

Forsyth, F. (1973) *The Odessa File* London: Corgi (originally 1972)

Foucault, M. (1986) 'What is an author?' in P. Rabinow ed. *The Foucault Reader* Harmondsworth: Penguin

Freese, P. (1992) *The Ethnic Detectives: Chester Himes, Harry Kemelman, Tony Hillerman* Essen: Verlag die Blaue

Friedan, B. (1977) *It Changed My Life: Writings on the Women's Movement* New York: Random House

Friedman, N. (1955) 'Point of view in fiction: the development of a critical concept' *PMLA* 70, 1160–1184

Fulbright, J. W. (1985) 'Impact of the Vietnam war' in W. A. Williams et al. eds. *America in Vietnam: A Documentary History* Garden City: Anchor

Gallagher, T. (1986) 'Shoot-out at the genre corral: patterns in the evolution of the western' in B. K. Grant ed. *Film Genre Reader* Austin: University of Texas Press

Garfield, B. (1974) *Death Wish* London: Coronet (originally 1972)

Garfield, B. (1977) *Death Sentence* London: Pan (originally 1976)

Gartner, A. et al. (1973) *What Nixon Is Doing to Us* New York: Harper & Row

Gates, H. L., Jr. (1986) 'Talkin' that talk' in Gates ed. *'Race', Writing and Difference* Chicago and London: University of Chicago Press

Gates, H. L., Jr. (1988) *The Signifying Monkey: A Theory of African-American Literary Criticism* New York: Oxford University Press

Geherin, D. (1985) *The American Private Eye: The Image in Fiction* New York: Frederick Ungar

Geherin, D. (1989) *Elmore Leonard* New York: Continuum

Gelfand, M. I. (1987) 'The War on Poverty' in Divine (1987)

Genette, G. (1982) *Narrative Discourse* Oxford: Basil Blackwell

Gibbins, J. (1974) 'When fame brings fear' *Daily Mail* 27 May

Gillespie, M. (1995) *Television, Ethnicity and Cultural Change* London: Routledge

Gilliatt, P. (1971) Review of *Shaft*, *New Yorker* 7 August, 19

Gilliatt, P. (1972) Review of *The New Centurions*, *New Yorker* 12 August

Gilliatt, P. (1974a) 'Private nose' *New Yorker* 1 July

Gilliatt, P. (1974b) Review of *Death Wish*, *New Yorker* 26 August

Gilliatt, P. (1975) Review of *Dog Day Afternoon*, *New Yorker* 22 September

Gilliatt, P. (1976) Review of *All the President's Men*, *New Yorker* 12 April

Gilman, S. L. (1985) *Difference and Pathology: Stereotypes of Sexuality, Race and Madness* Ithaca and London: Cornell University Press

Gilstrap, P. (1998) 'The house that blacks built' *New Times Los Angeles* (15–21 October) www.newtimesla.com/1998/101598/feature1–1.html

Gittlin, T. (1980) *The Whole World Is Watching: Mass Media in the Making and Unmaking of the New Left* Berkeley and London: University of California Press

Gittlin, T. (1984) 'Home front resistance to the Vietnam war' in H. E. Salisbury ed. *Vietnam Reconsidered: Lessons from a War* New York: Harper & Row

Goines, D. (1971) *Dopefiend* Los Angeles: Holloway House

Goines, D. (1973) *White Man's Justice, Black Man's Grief* Los Angeles: Holloway House

Goines, D. (1974) *Kenyatta's Escape* Los Angeles: Holloway House

Goines, D. (1977) *Black Gangster* Los Angeles: Holloway House (originally 1971)

Goines, D. (1978) *Crime Partners* Los Angeles: Holloway House (originally 1974)

Gold, R. (1971) Review of *Shaft*, *Variety* 30 January, 27

Goldman, W. (1976) *Marathon Man* London: Pan (originally 1974)

Gottlieb, C. (1975) *The Jaws Log* London: Tandem

Goulart, R. ed. (1965) *The Hardboiled Dicks: An Anthology and Study of Pulp Detective Fiction* New York: Pocket Books

Granberg, D. (1978) 'Pro-life or reflection of conservative ideology' *Sociology and Social Research* 62 (April)

Gray, A. (1992) *Video Playtime: The Gendering of a Leisure Technology* London: Routledge

Graysmith, R. (1992) *Zodiac: The Shocking True Story of America's Most Bizarre Mass Murderer* London: Mondo

Green, A. (1972a) 'All Time Champ Plots Way Ahead' *Variety* 6 September

Green, A. (1972b) '"Everyone a Millionaire Already"' *Variety* 6 September

Green, C. (1986) 'The role of the media in shaping public policy: the myth of power and the power of myth' in Kaplan and Cuciti (1986)

Greenberg, D. (1977) *The Super Cops Play It to a Bust* London: Futura (originally 1975)

Greene, H. ed. (1970) *The Rivals of Sherlock* Holmes Harmondsworth: Penguin

Greiner, D. J. (1984) 'Robert B. Parker and the Jock of the Main Streets' *Critique* 26, 36–44

Grella, G. (1980) 'The hard-boiled detective novel' in R. Winks ed. *Detective Fiction: A Collection of Critical Essays* Englewood Cliffs: Prentice-Hall

Gross, S. L. and Hardy, J. E. eds. (1966) *Images of the Negro in American Literature* Chicago and London: University of Chicago Press

Haldeman, H. R. with diMona, J. (1978) *The Ends of Power* London: Sidgwick & Jackson

Hall, S. (1992) 'What is this "black" in black popular culture?' in G. Dent ed. *Black Popular Culture: A Project* Seattle: Bay Press

Hall, S. (1997) 'The work of representation' in Hall ed. *Representation: Cultural Representations and Signifying Practices* London: Sage

Hamilton, C. (1987) *Western and Hard-boiled Detective Fiction in America* London: Macmillan

Hamilton, P. (1996) *Historicism* London: Routledge

Handler, J. F. and Hasenfeld, Y. (1991) *The Moral Construction of Poverty: Welfare Reform in America* Newbury Park and London: Sage

Hansen, J. (1984a) *The Man Everybody Was Afraid Of* London: Panther (originally 1978)

Hansen, J. (1984b) *Skinflick* London: Panther (originally 1979)

Hansen, J. (1986a) *Fadeout* London: Grafton (originally 1970)

Hansen, J. (1986b) *Troublemaker* London: Grafton (originally 1975)

Hansen, J. (1987) *Death Claims* London: Grafton (originally 1973)

Harper, R. (1969) *The World of the Thriller* Cleveland: The Press of Case Western Reserve University

Harvey, J. (1997) 'The last good place: James Crumley, the West and the detective novel' in P. Messent ed. *Criminal Proceedings: The Contemporary American Crime Novel* London: Pluto

Harward, D. W. ed. (1974) *Crisis in Confidence: The Impact of Watergate* Boston and Toronto: Little, Brown

Harwood, J. (1975) 'Anticipated success mutes squawks on costs, rental terms' *Variety* 4 June

Haut, W. (1995) *Pulp Culture: Hardboiled Fiction and the Cold War* London: Serpent's Tail

Haut, W. (1999) *Neon Noir: Contemporary American Crime Fiction* London: Serpent's Tail

Haycraft, H. ed. (1974). *The Art of the Mystery Story* New York: Carroll & Graf

Haycraft, H. (1979) *Murder for Pleasure: The Life and Times of the Detective Story* New York: Carroll & Graf

Heath, S. (1981) *Questions of Cinema* London: Macmillan

Heilbrun, C. (1988) 'Gender and detective fiction' in B. A. Rader and H. G. Zetler eds. *The Sleuth and the Scholar: Origins, Evolution and Current Trends in Detective Fiction* New York: Greenwood Press

Heininger, D. (1976) Review of *Taxi Driver, National Observer* 20 March

Hellman, J. (1986) *American Myth and the Legacy of Vietnam* New York: Columbia University Press

Hentoff, Nat (1973) 'Subverting the First Amendment: Nixon and the media' in A. Gartner et al. *What Nixon Is Doing to Us* New York: Harper & Row

Hentoff, N. (1974) 'You're not all right, Jack' *Village Voice* 7 February

Hermes, J. (1996) *Reading Women's Magazines: An Analysis of Everyday Media Use* Oxford: Polity

Herr, M. (1978) *Dispatches* London: Pan

Herrnstein Smith, B. (1981) 'Afterthoughts on narrative III: narrative versions, narrative theories' in W. J. T. Mitchell ed. *On Narrative* Chicago and London: University of Chicago Press

Hersh, S. (1984) 'The press and the government: II' in H. E. Salisbury ed. *Vietnam Reconsidered: Lessons from a War* New York: Harper & Row

Hess Wright, J. (1986) 'Genre films and the status quo' in B. K. Grant ed. *Film Genre Reader* Austin: University of Texas Press (originally 1978)

Higgins, G. V. (1972) 'The private eye as illegal hero' *Esquire* (December), 348–51

Higgins, G. V. (1973) *The Friends of Eddie Coyle* London: Pan (originally 1971)

Higgins, G. V. (1975a) *Cogan's Trade* London: Coronet (originally 1974)

Higgins, G. V. (1975b) *The Friends of Richard Nixon* New York: Alfred Knopf

Higgins, G. V. (1985) *A City on a Hill* New York: Critic's Choice (originally 1975)

Higgins, G. V. (1988) *The Digger's Game* New York: Penguin (originally 1973)

Higgins, G. V. (1991) *On Writing* London: Bloomsbury

Hildyard, N. (1983) *Cover Up: The Facts They Don't Want You to Know* Rev. edn. London: New English Library

Hilfer, T. (1990) *The Crime Novel: A Deviant Genre* Austin: University of Texas Press

Hill, R. B. (1972). *The Strengths of Black Families* New York: National Urban League

Hill, V. and Every, P. (1998) 'Postmodernism and the cinema' in S. Sim ed. *The Icon Critical Dictionary of Postmodern Thought* Cambridge: Icon

Hoffman, C. (1983) 'Spenser: the illusion of knighthood' *Armchair Detective* 16, 131–43

Hofstadter, R. (1964) '*The Paranoid Style in American Politics' and Other Essays* London: Jonathan Cape

Hohimer, F. (1975) *The Home Invaders* London: Star

Holm, E. (1976) 'Dog Day Aftertaste' *Jump Cut* 10/11, 3–4

hooks, b. (1996) *Reel to Real: Race, Sex and Class at the Movies* London: Routledge

Hughes, D. B. et al. (1982) 'Writers and their books: a consumer's guide' in H. R. F. Keating ed. *Whodunit? A Guide to Crime, Suspense and Spy Fiction* London: Windward

Hunt, E. H. (1975) *Undercover: Memoirs of a Secret Agent* London: W. H. Allen

Hunter, J. P. (1990). *Before Novels: The Cultural Contexts of Eighteenth Century English Fiction* New York: Norton

Hynd, N. (1976) *Revenge* London: New English Library

Iser, W. (1974) *The Implied Reader: Patterns of Communication in Prose Fiction from Bunyan to Beckett* Baltimore and London: Johns Hopkins University Press

Iser, W. (1978) *The Act of Reading: A Theory of Aesthetic Response* Baltimore and London: Johns Hopkins University Press

Iser, W. (1981) 'Talk Like Whales' *diacritics* 11 (September); reprinted in Cobley (1996)

Iser, W. (1989) *Prospecting: From Reader Response to Literary Anthropology* Baltimore and London: Johns Hopkins University Press

Jacobs, P. and Landau, S. (1967) *The New Radicals* Harmondsworth: Penguin

James, L. (1973) *Fiction for the Working Man* Harmondsworth: Penguin (originally 1963)

Jameson, F. (1979) 'Class and allegory in contemporary mass culture: *Dog Day Afternoon* as a political film' *Screen Education* 30, 75–94

Jauss, H. R. (1982) *Toward an Aesthetic of Reception* Minneapolis: University of Minnesota Press

Jaworski, L. (1977) *The Right and the Power: The Prosecution of Watergate* New York: Pocket Books

Jenkins, H. (1992) *Textual Poachers: Television Fans and Pariticipatory Culture* London: Routledge

Jenkins, H. and Tulloch, J. (1995) *Science Fiction Audiences: Watching* Doctor Who *and* Star Trek. London: Routledge

Jenkins, K. ed. (1997) *The Postmodern History Reader* London: Routledge

Jensen, K. B. (1993) 'The past in the future: problems and potentials of historical reception studies' *Journal of Communication* 43(4), 20–8

Johnson, B. B. (1970) *Black Is Beautiful: Superspade #2* New York: Paperback Library

Jost, F. (1998) 'The promise of genres' *Réseaux* 6(1), 99–121

Kael, P. (1972) Review of *Dirty Harry, New Yorker* 15 January

Kael, P. (1973) 'The hero as freak' *New Yorker* 17 December, 107–8

Kael, P. (1976a) 'Underground man' *New Yorker* 9 February

Kael, P. (1976b) 'Running into trouble' *New Yorker* 11 November

Kael, P. (1980) *When the Lights Go Down* New York: Holt, Rinehart & Winston

Kalb, M. and Kalb, B. (1975) *Kissinger* New York: Dell

Kaplan, M. and Cuciti, P. L. eds. (1986) *The Great Society and Its Legacy: Twenty Years of U.S. Social Policy* Durham: Duke University Press

Kay, K. (1976) 'Lumpen Lumet' *Jump Cut* 10/11, 3

Keitel, E. (1994) 'The woman's private eye view' *Amerikastudien: Eine Viertel-Jahresschrift* 39, 161–82

Kellner, D. (1995) *Media Culture: Cultural Studies, Identity and Politics between the Modern and the Postmodern* London: Routledge

Kelsey, T. (1996) 'The Oklahoma suspect awaits day of reckoning' *Sunday Times News Review* 20 April, 7

Kennedy, L. (1997) 'Black *noir*: race and urban space in Walter Mosley's detective fiction' in P. Messent ed. *Criminal Proceedings: The Contemporary American Crime Novel* London: Pluto

King, S. (1982) *Danse Macabre* London: Futura

Kissinger, H. (1982) *Years of Upheaval* London: Weidenfeld & Nicolson and Michael Joseph

Kittredge, W. and Krauzer, S. M. eds. (1978) *The Great American Detective* New York: Mentor

Kluge, P. F. and Moore, T. (1972) 'The boys in the bank' *Life* 13(12), 66–70, 72, 74

Knapp, W. (1973) *Report by the Commission to Investigate Allegations of Police Corruption in New York* City New York: George Braziller

Knight, S. (1980) *Form and Ideology in Crime Fiction* London: Macmillan

Knightley, P. (1975) *The First Casualty: The War Correspondent as Hero, Propagandist and Myth Maker from the Crimea to Vietnam* London: André Deutsch

Knox, R. (1974) 'Detective story decalogue' in Haycraft (1974)

Kolko, G. (1974) 'Secrecy and security' in Harward (1974)

Kovic, R. (1990) *Born on the Fourth of July* London: Corgi (originally 1976)

Kozloff, S. R. (1989) 'Narrative theory and television' in R. C. Allen ed. *Channels of Discourse: Television and Contemporary Criticism* London: Routledge

Kress, G. R. (1993) 'Against arbitrariness: the social production of the sign as a foundational issue in critical discourse analysis' *Discourse and Society* 4(2), 169–191

Kress, G. R. and van Leeuwen, T. (1996) *Reading Images: The Grammar of Visual Design* London: Routledge

Lang, G. E. and Lang, K. (1983) *The Battle for Public Opinion: The President, the Press, and the Polls during Watergate* New York: Columbia University Press

Laplanche, J. and Pontalis, J.-B. (1988) *The Language of Psychoanalysis* London: Karnac

Lasch, C. (1975a) 'The family and history' *New York Review of Books* 22, 33–6

Lasch, C. (1975b) 'The emotions of family life' *New York Review of Books* 22, 37–42

Lasch, C. (1975c) 'What the doctor ordered' *New York Review of Books* 22

Lasch, C. (1977) *Haven in a Heartless World: The Family Besieged* New York: Basic Books

Laurenson, D. and Swingewood, A. (1972) *The Sociology of Literature* London: Paladin

Lawrence, D. H. (1971) *Studies in Classic American Literature* Harmondsworth: Penguin (originally 1923)

Leab, D. J. (1975) *From Sambo to Superspade: The Black Experience in Motion Pictures* London: Secker & Warburg

Leavis, Q. D. (1979) *Fiction and the Reading Public* Harmondsworth: Penguin (originally 1932)

Leonard, E. (1984) *Swag* Harmondsworth: Penguin (originally 1976)

Leonard, E. (1985a) *The Hunted* Harmondsworth: Penguin (originally 1977)

Leonard, E. (1985b) *The Switch* Harmondsworth: Penguin (originally 1978)

Leonard, E. (1986a) *Mr. Majestyk* Harmondsworth: Penguin (originally 1974)

Leonard, E. (1986b) *52 Pick-up* Harmondsworth: Penguin (originally 1974)

Leonard, E. (1986c) *Unknown Man No. 89* Harmondsworth: Penguin (originally 1977)

Leuchtenberg, W. (1995) '*All the President's Men*' in T. Mico et al. eds. *Past Imperfect: History According to the Movies* London: Cassell

Levin, I. (1977) *The Boys from Brazil* London: Pan (originally 1976)

Levine, L. W. (1974) *Black Culture and Black Consciousness: Afro-American Folk Thought from Slavery to Freedom* New York and Oxford: Oxford University Press

Liebes, T. and Katz, E. (1993) *The Export of Meaning: Cross-Cultural Readings of Dallas.* 2nd edn. Oxford: Polity

Lifton, R. J. (1973) *Home from the War, Vietnam Veterans: Neither Victims Nor Executioners* London: Wildwood House

Light, A. (1991) *Forever England: Femininity, Literature and Conservativism Between the Wars* London: Routledge

Lindlof, T. R. 1988. 'Media audiences as interpretive communities' *Communication Yearbook* 11 (ed. J. Anderson) Newbury Park and London: Sage, 81–107

Lipsitz, G. (1998) 'Genre anxiety and racial representation in 1970s cinema' in N. Browne ed. *Refiguring American Film Genres: Theory and History* London and Berkeley: University of California Press

Livermore, J. (1980) 'Policing' in Lundman (1980)

Lodge, D. (1981) '*Middlemarch* and the idea of the classic realist text' in A. Kettle ed. *The Nineteenth Century Novel: Critical Essays and Documents* 2nd edn. London: Heinemann

Logsdon, J. M. (1970) *The Decision to Go to the Moon: Project Apollo and the National Interest* Cambridge, MA, and London: MIT Press

Lovell, A. (1975) *Don Siegel: American Cinema* London: British Film Institute

Lubbock, P. (1926) *The Craft of Fiction* London: Jonathan Cape (originally 1921)

Ludlum, R. (1972a) *The Osterman Weekend* London: Panther

Ludlum, R. (1972b) *The Scarlatti Inheritance* London: Grafton (originally 1971)

Ludlum, R. (1973) *The Matlock Paper* New York: Dell

Ludlum, R. (1976) *The Rhinemann Exchange* London: Panther (originally 1974)

Ludlum, R. (1977a) *The Gemini Contenders* London: Panther (originally 1976)

Ludlum, R. (1977b) *The Chancellor Manuscript* London: Grafton

Ludlum, R. (1979a) *The Holcroft Covenant* New York: Bantam (originally 1978)

Ludlum, R. (1979b) *The Matarese Circle* New York: Bantam

Ludlum, R. (1982a) *The Road to Gandolfo* London: Grafton (originally 1975)

Ludlum, R. (1989a) *Trevayne* London: Grafton (originally 1974)

Ludlum, R. (1989b) 'Introduction' in Ludlum (1989a)

Luke, T. W. (1986) 'The modern service state: public power in America from the New Deal to the New Beginning' in A. Reed ed. *Race, Politics and Culture: Critical Essays on the Radicalisms of the 1960s* Westport: Greenwood Press

Luker, K. (1984) *Abortion and the Politics of Motherhood* Berkeley: University of California Press

Lull, J. (1990) *Inside Family Viewing: Ethnographic Research on Television's Audience.* London: Routledge

Lundman, R. J. ed. (1980) *Police Behavior: A Sociological Perspective* New York and Oxford: Oxford University Press

Maas, P. (1970) *The Valachi Papers* London: Panther

Maas, P. (1974) *Serpico* Glasgow: Fontana (originally 1973)

MacCabe, C. (1974) 'Realism and the cinema: notes on some Brechtian theses' *Screen* 15(2), 7–32

MacCabe, C. (1977) 'Principles of realism and pleasure' *Screen* 17(3), 46–61

MacCabe, C. (1978) *James Joyce and the Revolution of the Word* London: Macmillan

MacDonald, J. D. (1967) *The Executioners* London: Coronet (originally 1957)

Madden, D. ed. (1968) *Tough Guy Writers of the Thirties* London and Amsterdam: Southern Illinois University Press

Mahan, J. H. (1980) 'The hardboiled detective in the fallen world' *Clues* 1(2), 90–9

Mandel, E. (1984) *Delightful Murder: A Social History of the Crime Story* London: Pluto

Mankiewicz, F. (1973) *Nixon's Road to Watergate* London: Hutchinson

Mann, P. (1975) *Dog Day Afternoon* London: Mayflower

Marchetti, V. (1974) *The Rope Dancer* London: Sphere (originally 1972)

Marchetti, V. and Marks, J. (1975) *The CIA and the Cult of Intelligence* New York: Dell (originally 1974)

Marcus, S. (1975) 'Introduction' in D. Hammett, *The Continental Op and Other Stories* London: Pan

Martindale, D. (1991) *Television Detective Shows of the 1970s: Credits, Storylines and Episode Guides for 109 Series* Jefferson, NC and London: McFarland

Mayne, J. (1993) *Cinema and Spectatorship* London: Routledge

McCracken, A. (1998) *Pulp: Reading Popular Fiction* Manchester: Manchester University Press

McGivern, W. (1987) *The Big Heat* London: Blue Murder (originally 1953)

McQuaid, K. (1989) *The Anxious Years: America in the Vietnam–Watergate Era* New York: Basic Books

Mead, L. (1986) *Beyond Entitlement: The Social Obligation of Citizenship* New York: Free Press

Meagher, S. (1967) *Accessories After the Fact* New York and Indianapolis: Bobbs-Merrill

Menzies, I. (1986) 'Random observations on the role of the media in covering the War on Poverty' in Kaplan and Cuciti (1986)

Mercer, K. (1994) *Welcome to the Jungle: New Positions in Black Cultural Studies* London: Routledge

Merry, B. (1977) *Anatomy of the Spy Thriller* Dublin: Gill & Macmillan

Messent, P. (1997) 'Introduction: from private eye to police procedural – the logic of contemporary crime fiction' in Messent ed. *Criminal Proceedings: The Contemporary American Crime Novel* London: Pluto

Milgram, S. (1974) *Obedience to Authority* London: Tavistock

Moretti, F. (1988) *Signs Taken for Wonders: Essays in the Sociology of Literary Forms* Rev. edn. London: Verso

Morley, D. (1980) *The Nationwide Audience* London: British Film Insitute

Morley, D. (1992) *Television, Audiences and Cultural Studies* London: Routledge

Morrell, D. (1973) *First Blood* London: Pan (originally 1972)

Mott, F. L. (1947) *Golden Multitudes* New York: Macmillan

Moynihan, D. P. (1965) *The Negro Family: The Case for National Action* reprinted in its original format in L. Rainwater and W. Yancey (1967) *The Moynihan Report and the Politics of Controversy* Cambridge, MA: Harvard University Press

Mulvey, L. (1975) 'Visual pleasure and narrative cinema' *Screen* 16(3), 6–18

Munt, S. R. (1994) *Murder by the Book: Feminism and the Crime Novel* London: Routledge

Murray, C. (1984) *Losing Ground: American Social Policy, 1950–80* New York: Basic Books

Murray, C. and Cox, C. B. (1989) *Apollo: The Race to the Moon* London: Secker & Warburg

Neale, S. (1990) 'Questions of genre' *Screen* 31(1), 45–66

Nelson, P. (1972) Review of *Dirty Harry*, *Rolling Stone* 2 March

Ness, E. with Fraley, O. (1967) *The Untouchables* London: Hodder and Stoughton (originally 1957)

New York Times ed. (1971) *The Pentagon Papers* New York: Bantam

Nightingale, B. (1978) 'What if a Mars landing were faked? asks Peter Hyams' *New York Times* 28 May

Nightingale, V. (1996) *Studying Audiences: The Shock of the Real* London: Routledge

Nolan, F. (1976) *The Ritter Double Cross* London: Futura (originally 1974)

Novak, M. (1971) *The Rise of the Unmeltable Ethnics* New York: Oxford University Press

Noyes, P. (1973) *Legacy of Doubt* New York: Pinnacle

Oberbeck, S. K. (1971) 'Black eye' *Newsweek* 19 July, 80

O'Brien, G. (1981) *Hardboiled America: The Lurid Years of Paperbacks* London: Van Nostrand Reinhold

Ogdon, B. (1992) 'Hard-boiled ideology' *Critical Quarterly* 34(1), 71–87

O'Reilly, K. (1995) *Nixon's Piano: Presidents and Racial Politics from Washington to Clinton* New York and London: Free Press

O'Sullivan, T. ed. (1998) *Studying the Media* 2nd edn. London: Arnold

Owano, N. (1971) 'Nothing less than a man' *Village Voice* 8 July

Palmer, J. (1978) *Thrillers: Genesis and Structure of a Popular Genre* London: Edward Arnold

Panek, L. L. (1987) *An Introduction to the Detective Story* Bowling Green: Bowling Green State University Popular Press

Panek, L. L. (1990) *Probable Cause: Crime Fiction in America* Bowling Green: Bowling Green State University Popular Press

Parker, R. B. (1971) 'The Violent Hero, Wilderness Heritage and Urban Reality: A Study of the Private Eye in the Novels of Dashiell Hammett, Raymond Chandler and Ross Macdonald' PhD thesis, Boston University Graduate School

Parker, R. B. (1976) *The Godwulf Manuscript* Harmondsworth: Penguin (originally 1973)

Parker, R. B. (1977a) *God Save the Child* Harmondsworth: Penguin (originally 1974)

Parker, R. B. (1977b) *Mortal Stakes* Harmondsworth: Penguin (originally 1975)

Parker, R. B. (1977c) 'Marxism and the mystery' in D. Winn ed. *Murder Ink: The Mystery Reader's Companion* Newton Abbot: Westbridge Books

Parker, R. B. (1978) *Promised Land* Harmondsworth: Penguin (originally 1977)

Parker, R. B. (1980) *Looking for Rachel Wallace* New York: Dell

Parker, R. B. (1983a) *The Judas Goat* Harmondsworth: Penguin (originally 1978)

Parker, R. B. (1983b) *Wilderness* Harmondsworth: Penguin (originally 1979)

Parker, R. B. (1992) *Pastime* New York: Berkley (originally 1991)

Parker, R. B. (1997) *Small Vices* New York: Berkley

Patterson, P. and Farber, M. (1976) 'The power and the gory' *Film Comment* 12(3), 26–30

Peele, G. (1984) *Revival and Reaction: The Right in Contemporary America* Oxford: Oxford University Press

Peirce, C. S. (1955) 'Logic as semiotic: the theory of signs' in *Philosophical Writings of Peirce* ed. J. Buchler, New York: Dover

Pepper, A. (1996) 'United States of Detection: Race, ethnicity and the contemporary American crime novel', PhD dissertation, University of Sussex

Pepper, A. (1999) 'Review of Haut (1999)' *European Journal of American Culture* 19(1), 62–3

Pepper, A. (2000) *The Contemporary American Crime Novel* Edinburgh: Edinburgh University Press

Pileggi, N. (1976) *Blye, Private Eye* Chicago: Playboy Press

Piven, F. and Cloward, R. (1971) *Regulating the Poor: The Functions of Public Welfare* New York: Pantheon

Polner, M. (1971) *No Victory Parades: The Return of the Vietnam Veteran* London: Orbach & Chambers

Porter, C. (1990) 'Are we being historical yet?' in D. Carroll ed. *The States of Theory: History, Art and Critical Discourse* New York: Columbia University Press

Porter, V. (1998) 'Between structure and history: genre in popular British cinema' *Journal of Popular British Cinema* 1(1), 25–36

Potholm, C. P. and Morgan, R. E. eds. (1976) *Focus on Police: Police in American Society* New York and London: John Wiley

President's Commission on Law Enforcement and the Administration of Justice (1967) *The Challenge of Crime in a Free State* Washington: US Government Printing Office

Puzo, M. (1970) *The Godfather* London: Pan

Puzo, M. (1972) *The Godfather Papers and Other Confessions* London: Pan

Pye, M. (1975) 'Enter the shark' *Sunday Times* 3 August

Pykett, L. (1994) *The Sensation Novel: From* The Woman in White *to* The Moonstone. Plymouth: Northcote House

Quarry, N. (1972) *The Don Is Dead* London: Coronet

Radway, J. A. (1984) *Reading the Romance: Women, Patriarchy and Popular Culture* Chapel Hill and London: University of North Carolina Press

Radway, J. A. (1988) 'Reception study: ethnography and the problems of dispersed audiences and nomadic subjects' *Cultural Studies* 2(3), 359–76

Rainwater, L. and Yancey, W. (1967) *The Moynihan Report and the Politics of Controversy* Cambridge, MA: Harvard University Press

Rance, N. (1991) *Wilkie Collins and Other Sensational Novelists* London: Macmillan

Rapp, R. (1982) 'Family and class in contemporary America: notes toward an understanding of ideology' in B. Thorne and M. Yalom eds. *Rethinking the Family: Some Feminist Questions* New York and London: Longman

Reid, M. A. (1993) *Redefining Black Film* Berkeley and Oxford: University of California Press

Reiss, A. J. (1971) *The Police and the Public* New Haven and London: Yale University Press

Rhea, J. T. (1997) *Race Pride and American Identity* Cambridge, MA: Harvard University Press

Richardson, J. F. (1974) *Urban Police in the United States* Port Washington and London: Kennikit Press

Riley, C. (1971) 'A black movie for white audiences?' *New York Times* 15 July, B13

Rimmon-Kenan, S. (1983) *Narrative Fiction: Contemporary Poetics* London: Methuen

Robinson, D. (1975) Review of *Death Wish, The Times* 7 February

Roffman, H. (1975) *Presumed Guilty* Rutherford: Fairleigh Dickinson University Press

Romm, T. (1986) 'Role conflict in the portrayal of female heroes of television crime dramas: a theoretical conceptualization' *Interchange* 17(1), 23–32

Rosen, J. (1974) 'Film sets off new vigilantism' *Guardian* 21 September

Roth, M. (1995) *Foul and Fair Play: Reading Genre in Classic Detective Fiction* Athens, GA, and London: University of Georgia Press

Rubenstein, L. (1976) 'Review of *Taxi Driver*' *Cineaste* 7(3), 34–5

Rubin, L. B. (1987) *Quiet Rage: Bernie Goetz and the New York Subway Shootings* London: Faber & Faber

Rubinstein, J. (1980) 'Cop's rules' in Lundman (1980)

Ruehlmann, W. (1974) *Saint with a Gun: The Unlawful American Private Eye* New York: New York University Press

Ruhm, H. ed. (1979) *The Hard-boiled Detective: Stories from* Black Mask *Magazine 1920–1951* London: Coronet

Ryall, T. (1998) 'British cinema and genre' *Journal of Popular British Cinema* 1(1), 18–24

Sanders, E. (1989) *The Family: The Manson Group and Its Aftermath* Rev. edn. New York: Signet

Sarris, A. (1973b) 'Straight-arming crooked cops' *Village Voice* 13 December

Sauerberg, L. O. (1983) 'Literature in figures: an essay on the popularity of thrillers' *Orbis Litterarum* 38, 93–107

Schickel, R. (1975) 'Lost Connection' *Time* 6 October

Schickel, R. (1976) 'Potholes' *Time* 16 February

Schlesinger A. M., Jr. (1968) *The Crisis of Confidence: Ideas, Power and Violence in America* London: André Deutsch

Schnapper, M. B. ed. (1974) *Conscience of the Nation: The People Versus Richard M. Nixon* Washington, DC: Public Affairs Press

Schorr, D. (1974) 'Secrecy and security' in Harward (1974)

Schrade, P. (1984) 'Workers resist overt resistance' in H. E. Salisbury ed. *Vietnam Reconsidered: Lessons from a War* New York: Harper & Row

Schrader, P. (1990) *Taxi Driver* (screenplay) London: Faber & Faber

Schrecker, E. W. (1986) *No Ivory Tower: McCarthyism and the Universities* New York and Oxford: Oxford University Press

Scott P. D. et al (1978) *The Assassinations: Dallas and Beyond – A Guide to Cover-ups and Investigations* Abridged edn. Harmondsworth: Penguin

Seale, B. (1970) *Seize the Time: The Story of the Black Panther Party* London: Arrow

Seiter, E. et al (1989) *Remote Control: Television, Audiences and Cultural Power* London: Routledge

Setlowe, R. (1971) 'On *The Godfather*' *Variety* 17 February

Shadoian, J. (1977) *Dreams and Dead Ends: The American Gangster/Crime Film* Cambridge , MA, and London: MIT Press

Shaw, G. (1981) 'Film inspired Hinckley's murder plan' *The Guardian* 2 April

Sheehan, N. (1990) *A Bright Shining Lie: John Paul Vann and America in Vietnam* London: Picador

Sherman, L. W. (1978) *Scandal and Reform: Controlling Police Corruption* Berkeley and London: University of California Press

Silber, I. (1976) '*Serpico*' in B. Nichols ed. *Movies and Methods I* Berkeley and London: University of California Press

Simon, J. (1974a) Review of *Serpico, Esquire* (March)

Simon, J. (1974b) Review of *Chinatown, Esquire* (October)

Slung, M. B. (1988) 'Let's hear it for Agatha Christie: a feminist appreciation' in B. A. Rader and H. G. Zetler eds. *The Sleuth and the Scholar: Origins, Evolution and Current Trends in Detective Fiction* New York: Greenwood Press

Smith, H. N. (1950) *Virgin Land: The American West as Symbol and Myth* Cambridge, MA: Harvard University Press

Soitos, S. F. (1996) *The Blues Detective: A Study of African American Detective Fiction* Amherst: University of Massachusetts Press

South Bank Show (1980) 'Roman Polanski' Thames Television

South Bank Show (1987) 'George V. Higgins' Thames Television

Spark, A. (1989) 'Flight controls: the social history of the helicopter as a symbol of Vietnam' in Walsh and Aulich (1989)

Spear, J. C. (1989) *The Presidents and the Press: The Nixon Legacy* London and Cambridge, MA: MIT Press

Staiger, J. (1997) 'Hybrid or inbred: the purity hypothesis and Hollywood genre history' *Film Criticism* 22(1), 5–20

Stark, R. (1962) *Point Blank* New York: Fawcett

Steinfels, P. (1979) *The Neoconservatives* New York: Simon & Schuster

Stevenson, W. and Dan, U. (1976) *90 Minutes at Entebbe* New York: Bantam

Stewart, R. F. (1980) . . . *And Always a Detective: Chapters on the History of Detective Fiction* Newton Abbot: David & Charles

Stone, E. (1977) *Donald Writes No More: A Biography of Donald Goines* Los Angeles: Holloway House

Stoop, N. M. (1976) Review of *Marathon Man, After Dark* December

Sutherland, J. (1978) *Fiction and the Fiction Industry* London: Athlone Press

Sutherland, J. (1981) *Bestsellers: Popular Fiction of the 1970s* London: Routledge and Kegan Paul

Symons, J. (1974) *Bloody Murder: From the Detective Story to the Crime Novel: A History* Harmondsworth: Penguin (originally 1972)

Symons, J. (1992) *Bloody Murder: From the Detective Story to the Crime Novel: A History* 3rd edn. London: Macmillan

Symons, J. (1994) *Criminal Practices: Symons on Crime Writing 60s to 90s* London: Macmillan

Tagg, J. (1988) 'The burden of representation: photography and the growth of the state' *Ten-8*, 10–12

Talese, G. (1971) *Honor Thy Father* London: Panther

Tarantino, Q. (1998) 'The boy from the blax stuff' *Neon* (December), 82–8

Taylor, B. (1987) Interview with Robert B. Parker, *City Limits* 30 April, 93–4

Taylor, B. (1997) 'Criminal suits: style and surveillance, strategy and tactics in Elmore Leonard' in P. Messent ed. *Criminal Proceedings: The Contemporary American Crime Novel* London: Pluto

Teresa, V. with Rennen, T. C. (1973) *My Life in the Mafia* London: Panther

Thernstrom, S. and Thernstrom, A. (1997) *America in Black and White: One Nation Divisible* New York: Simon & Schuster

Thornton, R. (1974) 'Accountability to the people' in Schnapper (1974)

Todorov, T. (1977) *The Poetics of Prose* Ithaca: Cornell University Press

Tolson, A. 1996. *Mediations: Text and Discourse in Media Studies* London: Arnold

Tudor, A. (1976) 'Genre and critical methodology' in B. Nichols ed. *Movies and Methods I* Berkeley and London: University of California Press

Uhnak, D. (1978) *Policewoman* London: Star (originally 1964)

Uhnak, D. (1988) *The Ledger* London: Mysterious Press (originally 1971)

Ungar, S. J. (1989) *The Papers and the Papers: An Account of the Legal and Political Battle over the Pentagon Papers* Rev. edn. New York: Columbia University Press

Van Dine, S. S. (1974) 'Twenty rules for writing detective stories' in Haycraft (1974)

Vanacker, S. (1997) 'V. I. Warshawski, Kinsey Millhone and Kay Scarpetta: creating a feminist detective hero' in P. Messent ed. *Criminal Proceedings: The Contemporary American Crime Novel* London: Pluto

Variety (1971) 'Black-owned ad agency on *Shaft* credited for B.O. boom, 80% black' July, p. 5

Veeser, H. A. ed. (1989) *The New Historicism* London: Routledge

Vološinov, V. N. (1973) *Marxism and the Philosophy of Language* New York: Seminar Press

Voorhis, J. (1973) *The Strange Case of Richard Milhous Nixon* New York: Popular Library

Walsh, J. and Aulich, J. (1989) *Vietnam Images: War and Representation* London: Macmillan

'Watergate on Film' (1976) *Time* 29 Mar., 40–5

Watt, I. (1972) *The Rise of The Novel: Studies in Defoe, Richardson and Fielding* Harmondsworth: Penguin (originally 1957)

Watts, W. and Free, L. A. (1974) *The State of the Nation 1974* Washington, DC: Potomac Associates

Weeks, J. (1989) *Sexuality and Its Discontents: Meanings, Myths and Modern Sexualities* London: Routledge

Weitzman, L. J. (1985) *The Divorce Revolution: The Unexpected Social and Economic Consequences for Women and Children in America* London and New York: Free Press

Welsch, T. (1997) 'At work in the genre laboratory: Brian De Palma's *Scarface*' *Journal of Film and Video* 49(1/2), 34–51

Westin, A. F. (1967) *Privacy and Freedom* New York: Atheneum

Wexman, V. W. (1985) *Roman Polanski* London: Columbus Books

White, H. (1973) *Metahistory: The Historical Imagination in Nineteenth-Century Europe* Baltimore and London: Johns Hopkins University Press

White, H. (1987) *Tropics of Discourse: Essays in Cultural Criticism* Baltimore and London: Johns Hopkins University Press

White, T. H. (1975) *Breach of Faith: The Fall of Richard Nixon* New York: Dell

Whittlemore, L. H. (1974) *The Super Cops: The True Story of the Cops Known as Batman and Robin* London: Futura (originally 1973)

Wiley, M. G. and Hudik, T. L. (1980) 'Police–citizen encounters: a field test of exchange theory' in Lundman (1980)

Willett, R. (1992) *Hard-boiled Detective Fiction* Keele: British Association of American Studies

Willett, R. (1996) *The Naked City: Urban Crime Fiction in the USA* Manchester: Manchester University Press

Williams, J. (1993) *Into the Badlands: Travels through Urban America* London: Flamingo

Williams, L. (1991) *Hard Core: Power, Pleasure and the Frenzy of the Visible* London: HarperCollins

Williams, N. (1999) 'The Great Detectives: Hercule Poirot' BBC2 (broadcast 23 May)

Wilson, J. (1975) *Police Report* Boston and Toronto: Little, Brown

Winks, R. ed. (1980) *Detective Fiction: A Collection of Critical Essays* Englewood Cliffs: Prentice-Hall

Wise, D. (1973) *The Politics of Lying: Government Deception, Secrecy and Power* New York: Random House

Witcover, J. (1977) *Marathon: The Pursuit of the Presidency 1972–1976* New York: Viking Press

Wolfe, R. (1971) 'American imperialism and the peace movement' in K. T. Fann and D. C. Hodges eds. *Readings in U.S. Imperialism* Boston: Porter Sargent

Wolfe, T. (1980) *The Right Stuff* New York: Bantam

Wood, R. (1976) 'American cinema in the 1970s: *Dog Day Afternoon*' *Movie* 23, 33–6

Woods, P. ed. (1996) *Spooks, Spies and Private Eyes: An Anthology of Black Mystery, Crime and Suspense Fiction of the 20th Century* London: Payback Press

Woodward, B. and Bernstein, C. (1974) *All the President's Men* London: Quartet

Woodward, B. and Bernstein, C. (1977) *The Final Days* London: Coronet (originally 1976)

Worpole, K. (1983) *Dockers and Detectives* London: Commedia

Worpole, K. (1984) *Reading by Numbers: Contemporary Publishing and Popular Fiction* London: Comedia

Wright, W. (1975) *Sixguns and Society: A Structural Study of the Western.* Berkeley and London: University of California Press

Zarefsky, D. (1996) *President Johnson's War on Poverty: Rhetoric and History* Birmingham: University of Alabama Press

Zimmerman, P. D. (1972) 'Boy scouts in blue' *Newsweek* 7 August

Index